A retired high school teacher, Darrel McGovern lives with his wife, Helen, in a modest home in the Newcastle suburb of Fletcher. Their family have left the roost, and they are proud grandparents. Until retirement, Darrel hadn't found the time to pursue his passion for Australian history, research or writing. As well as writing, Darrel is a keen fisherman, lawn bowler and golfer. He loves being surrounded by family and friends, and along with Helen visits Adelaide and Darwin to see his grandchildren as often as possible.

I would like to dedicate this book to my wife, Helen, and my children: Kelli-Ann, Scott Fenton and Amanda Jane. They have all been very patient with me and my writing over several years.

Darrel William McGovern

THE PRICE OF A GIFT

AUSTIN MACAULEY PUBLISHERS™

LONDON • CAMBRIDGE • NEW YORK • SHARJAH

A CIP catalogue record for this title is available from the British Library.

ISBN 9781788485784 (Paperback)
ISBN 9781788485791 (Hardback)
ISBN 9781788485807 (E-Book)

www.austinmacauley.com

First Published (2018)
Austin Macauley Publishers Ltd
25 Canada Square
Canary Wharf
London
E14 5LQ

Synopsis

A four-part story of forbidden love. An entwined vendetta takes the reader from the horrors of the First World War in Europe to the pampered lives of the aristocracy in London and a race across the vastness of Australia to secure aspirations for one man, domination for another, and reparation for yet another.

The narrative follows the destiny of Jack Carter, an American who settles in Australia after the Great War determined to make his fortune, and forces Katrina, the love of Jack's life, and the daughter of Lord Anthony, a corrupt and scheming aristocrat determined to steal the young man's dream, into an arranged marriage by her mother when she steadfastly refuses to abort her pregnancy.

A card to Katrina from Jack, advising his pending arrival from France, is intercepted by Lady Elizabeth Anthony who conspires with her husband to have certain letters written, for a gift, which is meant to quash any thought of marriage between their daughter and Jack Carter.

In Katrina's absence, having been conveniently sent to the family cottage on the pretext of planning her wedding, Jack arrives in London to a hostile reception from Lord and Lady Anthony when he reveals plans for his and Katrina's future. During the ensuing argument, his lordship concludes Jack Carter is a very dangerous man who would use his influence and inheritance to alienate the young colony, Australia, from Great Britain. Lord Anthony threatens Jack, stating he will do all in his power to destroy him while informing the young man he is an unacceptable suitor for their daughter. As well, Australia is out of the question, Anthony's have a skeleton in the closet and the last thing they want is for their daughter inadvertently discovering a secret which she could use to ruin their family name.

Prologue

Aristocrats spoke, politicians listened, generals obeyed and minions died. A third assault against the high country would go ahead at any cost. General Charteris, Haig's propaganda machine exponent had fed the gullible war media with misconceptions of the real situation at the front. Field Marshal Haig found seventy-percent casualties acceptable; he wasn't to be disappointed for the rains turned Flanders fields into a quagmire. Mud! Craters of mud and slime made it impossible to bring up badly needed heavy artillery to shell the highly fortified German blockhouses. Batteries were uselessly firing into the mud several feet thick, doing little or no damage to the enemy and compounding the problem for any infantry assault.

The trolley was an innovation of man's ingenuity to a situation, a light timber base with a motorcycle engine attached. The frame stood above the mud-splattered base some sixteen inches, constructed from any readily available timber. As well as horse drawn ambulance, the trolley was used by the Allies to withdraw wounded considered able to travel from the field hospital near the front, back to a base hospital well behind allied lines.

With scarcely enough room two men lay side by side on bloodied stretchers in the crude field ambulance. They had never met, were expendable, yet through their individual gallantry they initiated the destruction of a strategic German blockhouse on the western end of the Hindenburg Line in a covert operation, which would allow the allies to initiate their planned thrust against the high country and ultimately bring a cessation to hostilities in 1918. One an Australian, lay supine, facing the heavens, he took a Mauser bullet to the lower side of his abdomen at close quarters in their final charge against the bunkers' well-fortified pillboxes. Although badly wounded, adrenalin coursed madly through his system. Sergeant Smith had charged the bunker with hand bombs and finally the bayonet. The American, the second man, also in German uniform, necks craned to see his surroundings through a hole where a bolt had worked loose, led the demolition team. He was blown up when the compressed forces from the blast hurled him from the cleverly concealed, concrete munitions bunkers built into the side of the fortress, and flung his body into a crater of mud covered in early snow. He suffered a broken leg and severe burns. As it had been necessary to use a short fuse and hand detonate the explosives, his was considered a suicide mission with little visualised escape, for which he volunteered, 0600 hours 29 September 1917.

The trolley lurched and swayed along the narrow gauge line. At times the two corpsmen would alight the vehicle, pushing the rig up the gentle slopes before climbing aboard as the engine picked up revs for the brief ride down slight inclines.

A hand, soiled with dried mud, twisted the shoulder strap tight, pulling the weight of the Mauser hard against his shoulder. Two eyes, bloodshot from lack of sleep and pitted with mud splatter, sighted along the barrel picking up the khaki uniform through the cross hair of the telescopic lens, the uniform which bears the corpsman's emblem, it mattered little, he was the enemy, no longer would a code of ethics apply, they would be ruthless now until the end. The sniper waited, hunched over the weapon, lovingly fondling the stock against his cheek. The hours of waiting lying on the cold ground saw the Nimrod shivering under his greatcoat. Now, anxiously watching the approach of the conveyance, a vehicle until recently used to convey soldiers of the once mighty German army, beads of water ran down his jowls to mingle with the dirty stubble of growth that passed as a beard. He waited with a patience of a man who had fought a long hard war and who had learnt the art of killing, not wasting his shot, but concentrating so his enemy would die quickly. He sighed, loosing off the shot, at the same time allowing for the recoil of the heavy rifle. The distance was two hundred yards and the German sniper watched from his concealment as the 7.92mm projectile struck the medic, hurling him from the lurching trolley to lay between the tracks, his body kicking convulsively in death. The Nimrod moved the rifle gently, bringing it to bare on the second target.

Sergeant Michael Smith heard the crack of the Mauser rifle. He tried to prop himself to see above the sides of the wooden conveyance when a hand with surprising strength steadied his movement. Lieutenant Jack Carter also heard the shot above the din of the cycle motor, he strained to hold himself so he could see through the bolt hole. He sensed rather than felt the other man's movement and placed a restraining hand on his leg. The rifle cracked again, this time closer and Carter made out the puff of smoke from below a clump of shattered stumps which overlooked the track and within easy rifle range. The torso of the second corpsman pitched forward as another round hit his prostrate form, pinning the sergeant beneath. The dead medic's hand locked to the throttle. Both could feel the pitch and sway increase, could hear the wheels pass over the joints at more frequent intervals, the Douglas motor peek revving,

Smith clawed the fingers of the corpsman free from the throttle and heaved with all his might. The body slid back. Smith heaved again and the face was gone, only the memory of the moment remained, imprinted in the young Australian's mind. The smell of death overwhelmed him as it had many times before, water formed in his mouth, he swallowed continuously, the twitching stomach muscles giving off bubbles of gas. He lay dry retching, shaking. A lump coming and going to his throat until finally he succumbed to the overpowering desire and was sick. He heaved all over himself, stomach muscles tightening in contraction until only bitter brownish yellow bile came away from his lips. Drained and pale Smith lay his head back on the stretcher, softly moaning, listening to his pounding head keep time to the joins in the line.

Numbly he felt something cold and wet under the uniform, his exertions had opened the wound; he was bleeding.

On the left side of the trolley, a bank was forming; it appeared to the American to be the commencement of a cutting. It was then, easing up on his elbows, back bent to stay positioned longer, he made a startling discovery. The rails disappeared into a mound of earth some distance ahead. The high side of the cutting had slumped, a consequence of the rains.

On impact with the soft mound of slumped earth, the wheels nearest the bank rode up causing the trolley to tilt precariously for what seemed an eternity to the men before it flipped over flinging them down the side of a slope studded with long grass and shrubbery where bracken and stunted shrubs stilled their progress.

Smith squinted against the glare of brittle sunlight filtering through the canopy above him. For a while, he lay staring at the trees, smelling their fragrance, exalting in their beauty, and a splash of blue through green foliage. Green, yellow, blue and gold filled his spectrum instead of white mist, rancid grey-brown mud, barren cratered earth, blackened stumps and wire brambles, the garbage of war.

In their weakened condition it would be impossible to climb the steep embankment to the railway line. Instead, they decided to crawl down the valley heading generally east. The air was fresh, uncontaminated by the rancid smell of gunpowder and stench of decaying bodies' both animal and human left to rot in the fetid mud; it gave them strength.

They plodded north-east, away from the coast leaving the low country. The wind swept its icy path from the north where snow covered the country for several months of the year. It would be some time before the sun's appearance through the blanket of mist. No longer could they hear the guns. The brambles of war were far away. Now they must survive to see the peace.

Part 1

Chapter 1

France, October, 1917

Timber cracked and splintered at their first attempt. Smith used his shoulder against the water barrel, while Carter pulled from the other side until the barrel tilted then overbalanced, its contents spilling against the lieutenant's bare splinted leg. Smith rolled the empty cask under the window. With Carter supporting him, standing atop the barrel, he proceeded to enlarge the opening, using the American's crutch, which they had constructed from the sides of the trolley to good effect, prying the boards away from the framework of the old window sill.

After what seemed an age, both men stood on the earthen floor of the former dwelling, a shaft of light showing dust particles suspended by their forced entry. Carter reached out and closed what remained of the shutters. They could smell the potatoes, stacked high on the cart. The laden cart indicated persons unknown could return presently. Eyes accustomed to the dimly lit interior peered into the darker corners of the dwelling. In a corner, eyes spied a plough; freshly tilled soil had attached itself to the blade.

Their surroundings held little interest for Carter. He could hardly keep his eyes open. He spread some stale hay piled in a chute, presumably to feed the horses that were used to plough and cart the produce. Dead tired, bone weary, using his crutch, he spread their army field-grey blanket out over the straw and was soon snoring, oblivious to his wounds, the rank smell of mice, and their droppings.

The young Australian settled down to the first watch but shortly sleep overcame him so he did not hear the chain being removed from the heavy timber door.

When the shaft of light spread to fill the doorway, it spilt across the earthen floor and up the far wall revealing the shape of two men slumbering. The girl stopped in her tracks, a look of shock registered on her young face. She clutched the woollen shawl tighter about her shoulders, a habit adopted to keep the icy north wind at bay. It wasn't the wind which caused her to grasp the shawl now. Rather, fear for what confronted her. They smelt like pigs in a sty to her child's nose, the strong rancid smell of men who needed to bathe.

A new excitement, quickened heartbeat, a face, pleasantly rounded, cheeks coloured and flushed, lips full and naturally red, trembled. At the corners of brown eyes faint creases of white skin told of years spent on the land squinting against the sun's glare. Slowly, she backed away from the doors absently dropping chain and padlock in her trepidation. Then she was running, burgundy strands, shining in the sunlight, fell about her face shimmying around her shoulders. A small sound escaped her lips; she fought to control her anxiety until sure she was out of hearing of the dwelling. With heart pumping she ran, towards the man and women approaching on the dray across the fields.

The man strained against the leather reins, jumping from the dray to stand by the lead Clydesdale while stroking its ears and listening to its snorting. He had longed for sons to work the soil, instead he was graced with daughters and now, watching the youngest darting across the field, pride crept up through his body fit to choke him.

'Papa! There are men… in the barn… asleep.' She blurted.

'Easy girl, you are puffing fit to bust.' Her heavy breathing formed pale wisps of steam in the still crisp air. Her expression betrayed alarm, fear, evident for the others to see. The man climbed up onto the hub of the wheel. He leaned over the high side of the dray. His weight caused the empty wagon to list markedly. Huge hands fastened about the stock of the gun, covered by an old chequered rug. Gripping the steel rim of the wooden-spoked-wheel, he lowered himself to the field letting the rug slip away from the ugly weapon to fall in the grass.

The weapon gleamed in the sunlight. He broke open the breechblock feeling in his woollen jacket for cartridges with his other hand, pushing the two 16 gauge shells with their cardboard casings into the chambers while listening to the thump, as the heavy loads forced air down the barrels. Closing the breech, he cocked the heavy weapon, the smell of gun oil cutting the air; its fragrance lingering in his nostrils.

'German's Papa?' asked Henrietta the eldest, hoping he would allay her mounting anxiety.

'I don't think so girl, they haven't been near since the beginning of the war,' he consoled her in a soothing voice.

'I am aware, but according to Karl Emerson, the French and their allies are pushing the Germans back, maybe… '

'Just stay with the team until I get back.' He patted her hand, which was resting on his arm, the pressure of her fingers relaxing with his reassurance. Like her sister the hand on his arm was that of a field worker, the fingers were long and tapered, stained with the soil and juices from the crops.

Cautiously, he approached their former home hefting the shotgun, his finger resting lightly on one of the double triggers. Looking over his shoulder, he saw his daughters huddled together, the horses grazing nonchalantly in the hock deep grass dividing the crops. He realised he was sweating freely. Every fibre of his body was tense, ready to fling himself to the ground at the first discharge of a rifle. Still nothing stirred, he timed his approach, only twenty paces from the aperture lay the padlock and chain and the thought of fear that these strangers evoked in the child brought the first stirring of anger. Hunched over, he went in bisecting the opening. If someone were waiting in the deep shadow, he could strike with the barrel or butt of the heavy gun. His advantage was familiarity with his surroundings. In four bounds he was on top of the laden dray, the potatoes moving, like living creatures beneath his feet. Another pair of eyes, the barrels of the shotgun swept the dim interior, the walnut stock pressing against his hip to smother the weapon's recoil. Nothing stirred. Slowly, amongst the smell of raised dust, hay, and potatoes, came the man smell and with it, to his sensitive hearing, the heavy breathing of men sleeping.

Lieutenant Carter came awake with a start to the thrust of a boot rocking him, like a dog shaking a bone. The harsh shard of light allowed him to focus on a large black bearded man holding a shotgun with both deadly barrels pointed directly at the bridge of his nose and not two feet away.

The man motioned with the weapon, satisfied when the bald one managed to drag himself to the rim of the dray, the muzzle following him across the intervening space, before turning his attention to the other sleeping figure. Unlike Carter, the young Australian resented being wakened, he pushed the foot away and rolled onto his other side, the weight of his body plus the Belgian's heavy soiled work boot rocking his left shoulder soon brought him awake, the pain in his chest a throbbing reality.

'What the hell… ' got out Smith before the muzzle of the shotgun pressed against his lips, forcing his silence. He needed no second urging, slowly, painfully, he backed away following the direction of the flickering barrel as the man indicated for him to join his mate against the rim.

Corneilius Le Brun stood facing the pair. He cradled the shotgun under one beefy arm, using the other to extract his pipe and makings from a pocket of the woven jacket. It was impossible to get good pipe tobacco he reflected, looking to the overhead beams with their spiders webs and rocking on the balls of his feet in disgust at a war which embargoed one of the few luxuries he indulged upon himself. Their uniforms were German indeed thought Corneilius. However, the insignia belied the fact they were officers. He could never recall any German officer being dishevelled. The bald one only had one boot. After all, they were gentlemen were they not?

They were pigs, swine, he was not mistaken and the officers were the worst, raping, plundering and succumbing all, who could work into her factories and industries, to produce guns and steel for the Kaiser. Suddenly, he felt an overwhelming desire to kill, to hit back at the uniform he despised. The shotgun was raised to his shoulder, the butt pulled tight into his armpit; his cheek pressed against the plate as he stood looking along the twin barrels at the bald headed man slumped against the wheel before him.

The barrels of death never wavered, holding steady between his eyes. Jack looked from the twin spouts of the shotgun to the man holding the deadly weapon. Their eyes locked and held as each tried to read the others thoughts. Jack saw the fight going on within the big man. The struggle of his will so intense, unnoticed the pipe fell from his mouth. He was no killer thought Jack, but he was full of hate.

Smith also saw the struggle and shouted, 'Don't shoot American, Australian!'

The sergeant's shouted cry seemed to have little effect on either man. The bearded man stood, like a marble statue, sweat glistening on his brow, tears streamed down his cheeks and a growl which commenced deep in his diaphragm emitted a cry of anguish and hate from his throat, like lava gushing from a volcano before the gun was finally lowered. While the American knew he was not going to die, least ways not at the hands of this gentle giant of a man. He felt clammy; even now the second of death had passed because he knew that the venom within the big man would have to be spent. He saw the blow coming, heard the shouted cry, and tried to go with it until his head made contact with the hub of the wheel. He felt his jaw snap like a twig as the stock of the gun took him full on the side of the face. Everything was out of focus, sounds… dim… fading… until blackness descended upon him.

When their father had not returned after a reasonable period, impatient as ever, the young women edged towards the barn. Within hearing they discerned the high-pitched words of anger. Together they burst into the barn.

'I thought I told you to stay with the animals until I called for you,' he shouted at them, his face a mask of anger, the shotgun poised above Mike Smith's head.

The girls were stunned. They gaped at the bleeding face of the unconscious figure slumped before them. Blood gushed from a deep open wound, the flap of skin dropped away revealing bone, the nose did not look as though it belonged to a face, and the head without hair looked forever like a skull.

Sergeant Smith looked from the man to the girls, his expression one of bitterness. 'English!' He pointed to himself. 'Allies,' pointing to the American. 'No Boche!' He got out spitting into the straw to show his disgust. 'American, Australian, allies of France, General Foch, King George,' he blurted.

'Papa, English!' Cried out the youngest. Those were the only words in the conversation which followed he understood.

Smith comforted the American by holding his hand against the wound to stifle the flow of blood. Shortly they made their decision, and one of their number left the barn to return leading a team and cart. Mike's hands were securely bound by the girl with the auburn hair. She was an expert, being used to tying the sacks. He was unceremoniously prodded until

15

seated on the floor of the dray, the walls of which were tapered, wider at the top and so high he was unable to see over them. He heard the ripping of an undergarment and presently, his face swathed in petticoat, Carter joined him in the dray. Smith observed they were strong yet gentle, he watched, unamused, as they folded the field blanket over his legs and torso.

The girl turned from the sprung seat and smiled briefly at the despondent Australian before gigging the team into action. He could only stare at and through her. He was bitter. More bitter than he could ever remember. Not even the death of his elder brother, or his mate Bluey Cameron, affected him the way this did. The American understood, until now Smith had not understood. But now the penny dropped, the man's action, release of pent up hatred, not against the Yank or himself, against the uniform they were wearing. Mike felt his unkempt nails bite into his palms.

Smith's mind wandered, thoughts came and went, his body swaying with the motion of the cart feeling the bandaging, cold across his torso. The grit and grime on his body made him long for home, a bath, one of his mum's baked dinners, with home-made pudding for desert covered in golden syrup. He wondered about the quiet American. He felt drawn to the man. In many ways they were alike he decided, both essentially quiet, raised as part of the land, the cities a necessary evil. He stared realising he couldn't be of much help to him now, the paled face was turning yellow and blue, mottled with dark dried blood, bruising and swelling hidden to a certain extent by the crude bandaging. Smith judged him to be in his mid-twenties, of fifteen stone and taller than himself by a good two inches, solid not flabby, hard muscle, tanned deep brown by the sun through many years of outdoor living. It was hard to judge because of his present condition whether the Lieutenant would be attractive to women, he was certainly rugged, big boned, and the growth of stubble on his chin suggested his hair would be fair. However, it was the eyes he remembered so vividly, they were blue as the sky, seemingly laughing, even in the face of death. Smith also admired the man's control. There was an air of self-reliance, an inner strength which he had not encountered lately, and after three years of bitter fighting in the trenches, Smith considered he was a fair judge of men. To behold men crippled, gassed and with bodies nearly cut in two by Maxim machine gun fire who still fought, only to observe others turn and run, cowards! Yes, he was sure of the American. They would survive to see the peace. Smith's mood mellowed; maybe the American would join him, in good old Aussie, at the end of the war. Together, they could make a good team.

An overhead sun replaced the cloud and soaked his dry skin, he licked his lips still tasting the corpsman's blood; a thought process would not let him forget. His mind wandered on, him and the American, the plateau country, headwaters of the mighty Margaret River, the old Hopkin's place, mustering, driving their cattle to the coast for shipment. It never occurred to him that the American might die of his horrific wounds.

Chapter 2

Paris, Early November 1917

Lady Katrina Anthony, Princess Mary's companion and only daughter of Lord and Lady Anthony of Bedfordshire resolved she must stay in France.

Katrina had made her decision after inspecting the English-based hospitals with the princess. While not determined to uphold family tradition like her brother, who never came home from the Boer War campaign, Katrina saw France as an opportunity to escape the clutches of her domineering mother. Her mother's matchmaking embarrassed Katrina. Her suitors were clumsy and awkward, Katrina always polite but aloof. The tall handsome men she observed from their family box at Ascot, the theatre, or opera, seemed beyond her reach. That which interested her mother—bloodline, breeding and station—held no interest for Katrina. She wanted a husband. An intelligent and virile man who would love her for herself, not her title, wealth, or standing in society.

Before his Royal Highness accompanied by Princess Mary returned to England, he requested a personal favour of Sir Arthur Sloggett Director General Army Medical Services; that he take Lady Katrina Anthony under his guidance.

So it came to pass on a bleak autumn day in October 1917, Katrina Anthony signed the hospital's registrar admitting two wounded soldiers from Amiens.

They had been heavily sedated with laudanum to relax them during their journey in the ambulance to the Paris-based hospital. The roads being better suited to horse and cart travel rather than the hard sprung 'T' Model Ford, which lurched and swayed over the rutted surface.

Katrina was summoned to assist with pyjamas and robes for the new arrivals. What happened next was most irregular. Instead of the pair being placed in her charge to be wheeled through the ward for a good body wash and change, they were removed to an unused room marked 'private' which was always kept locked. Katrina gave a gasp, under the char grey field blankets they were wearing German uniforms. A Major attending, explained the uniforms to be part of a covert operation during which the two men had been wounded. He further stressed Sir Arthur would look in on the pair to see they got the best possible medical treatment afforded by the hospital. Major Evans gathered in the uniforms and instructed that they should be incinerated immediately, he further issued an order; not a word of what transpired was to go beyond the four walls of the stuffy little room. He glanced from matron to nurse Anthony. Katrina looked away.

Katrina had learnt, she learnt through bitter experience. Nothing surprised her anymore. The smell of decomposed flesh, urine discharge, gangrenous limbs, excrement and gastric bouts, bilious yellow viscid bile, ulcers, poisons and bed sores were now part of her daily life. Liniments, starch, ammonia, laudanum tincture, bandaging, blood, sutures were common familiar names, as were the doctor's tools of his profession, the saw, the scalpel… as was the suffering. Men who had lost limbs, had been victims of mustard gas in the trenches, men who had been shot, bombed, blown up by shrapnel, shelled and nearly drowned in the stinking fetid mud; she had nursed them all.

< >

For some time the racking cough accompanied by a cry for water came issuing from the bed on the other side of the ward. It seemed nobody cared, nor had the man's croaky plea for water roused the other patients from their slumber. However Jack Carter was awake, it seemed that all he presently did was sleep. He cast a look downwards easing himself to a sitting position in the bed. Even in the semi dark he could see the bridge of his nose with the right eye without closing the left to squint.

They broke his nose again and reset the bone. However, it would always hook to one side giving him the appearance of a street fighter. Surgeons had since wired his jaw, and put the broken leg in a plaster cast. The burns a result of the blast, were healing, which was as well for his badly bruised ribs had to be strapped, consequence of the accident with the trolley and his landing on part of the frame. His sandy coloured hair was growing back, apart from a small circular spot at the back of his skull, for some reason the growth would not cover, however it was of small consequence and caused him no qualms. He was sporting a fashionable moustache neatly trimmed and the healthy colour was returning to his skin.

It was Broady, a sergeant from Jack's home town, he had been gassed and not expected to live, yet still he fought and he was crying out for a drink of water. Jack fumbled in the darkness and found his crutch. The linoleum floor covering was cold to the touch as was the air trundling through the building, damp, and rank with the smell of a phalanx of bodies, the odour of liniments and bandaging, of plaster and the foul smell of starch used to clean the ward. Jack advanced on Broady's drawer and poured the man a small drink of water from his bedside pitcher. He was in the act of holding the glass to the man's lips when a voice startled him.

'What do you think you are doing? Get back to bed!' The voice quietly admonished him. Katrina peered about the ward to be sure she hadn't woken the others.

Jack gave an exasperated sigh. He turned to face her, about to say something he may have regretted, but found he was unable to utter a word. Even in the dim light of the ward she was beautiful. Jack imagined her in a motorised carriage being escorted to the opera, or taking the final bow after the curtain was drawn on a stage play with her as the star, a thousand eyes drinking in her beauty. But not here. Not amongst death. Not in this morbid place. She pointed and meekly he handed her the glass. It was like a static kick from an electrical current and both stared at the other before Jack got the crutch moving. That one brief touch would not be easily forgotten.

Katrina reminded herself to chastise the tall man with the close-cropped hair and moustache further when the opportunity presented itself. When she was again seated at her desk, she realised it was more than that; he had touched something, something deep within her that made her tremble. Presently she promised herself to view his file. She wanted to know all there was to know about the American admitted to her care wearing a German uniform on that autumn day in October.

Chapter 3

Paris, November 1917

> *On 22 November, in the year of our Lord, Nineteen Hundred*
> *And Seventeen, Sergeant Michael Smith, Australian Infantry*
> *Forces, General Sir Herbert Plummer Commanding, is to*
> *Be in attendance at Windsor Castle for drinks and then to*
> *Hyde Park for investiture of the Victoria Cross.*
> *By command of his Royal Highness King George V.'*
> *Given this day 12 November 1917*
> *Under the hand of Lord Derby,*
> *Secretary to the King.*

Jack read the citation returning the letter to its embossed envelope.

'Congratulations Mike! Well deserved,' he offered his hand.

The two men were rugged up against winter's chill, seated in the deserted rotunda, used in better times to conduct open-air concerts in the hospital grounds. Today, much to Mike's surprise, Jack produced a bottle of Bells Scotch Whisky and two tumblers.

'A present from Nurse Collins,' he mumbled, breaking the seal with his teeth and pouring two generous slugs into the tumblers.

'That explains why we are out here freezing,' replied Mike, looking around him and thinking he must be mad for leaving the warmth of the ward for his present surroundings.

Jack handed him the glass, 'Happy birthday,' Jack could see Mike was pleased he had remembered. 'Twenty-one today… ' Jack broke into verse saluting the younger man with raised glass.

'Knock it off. I was only one of a twenty-man squad, and seven of them died during the siege against the bunkers. I don't deserve any medal. I was only doing my job.'

The lieutenant sat quietly, listening to the wind whistling through the stand, a whispered version of *Soldiers of the King*, or that's how it sounded to Jack, while the man beside him, a mere boy when he went to war, sat despondently, his hand swirling the scotch in the tumbler, his face, a stained mask of remembrance. He understood what, as yet, Mike could not put into words.

He waited, he knew what was coming and silently he contemplated the answer he would give. He must make Mike realise that courage has many faces. It took courage just to face the enemy, with legs that felt leaden and a heart pumping at the rate of knots as one left the safety of the trench to run blindly across no-man's land, with machine gun bullets zipping round you and men falling like nine pins, crying out and wondering if you would be next, to capture a thousand yards of ground, only to retreat and see it retaken in a retaliatory surge by the enemy shortly thereafter.

'I can't accept the citation Jack. How can they possibly single out one man when a whole bloody squad was involved? We had the element of surprise, and were successful because the Germans thought we were their troops returning from a sortie. We were among them before they could alter the trajectory of their machine guns,' Mike bowed his head.

Jack reflected how lean he was, the skin taut over his features, the broad shoulders so much skin and bone under the flannelette pyjamas. He had fought and won his fight against infection and pneumonia, which almost killed him a month back. He lay fighting for breath determined not to give in and when the chaplain visited to give him the last rights, he fought harder. Recovery was slow, but recover he did.

'You owe it to the squad, if you don't want it for yourself then accept it for them. That way the action gets recognition in the War Annals, and when talk turns to the high country and the taking of the concrete fortress on Hill 60 which gave the Allies the Wytschaete, Messines and Passchendaele ridges, they can reflect with pride that they played their part in the true tradition of soldiers.'

They sat in comparative silence drinking the fiery scotch, languishing in their own thoughts. Already Mike was contemplating being reunited with his family, this senseless war forgotten as he rode his pony around the property mustering the cattle. For Jack it was a time of reflection and a realisation of the hate he felt for the aristocracy whom he blamed for the war, which profiteered big business and sent thousands of men like himself and Mike to do their fighting, while they dictated policy and made fortunes.

Smith topped up their glasses again, 'I'll probably be discharged and sent home after the investiture.'

'You've done your bit,' responded Jack. 'What will you do when you get home?'

'Don't really know, I thought you might like to join me? Don't know whether I could settle down now.' Was the frank reply.

'Australia?' Jack was amused.

'Yes Australia!' Mike turned on him.

Jack smiled, a disarming smile, more to humour him than anything else. 'What would I do in Australia, Mike?'

'There's this place, up in the high country, Tempi Station. Jack you should see it, it could be one of the finest properties in the Territory. Wild cattle everywhere, just waiting to be branded.'

'Wild cattle?' Jack was curious.

'Lloyd Hopkins abandoned Tempi well before I left to come to the war,' Mike was honest with him.

'Why isn't it a working ranch?'

'Old Lloyd wasn't a cattleman I guess, he let the place run down to search for gold.'

'I'm not a cattleman Mike.'

'I see.' Mike couldn't hide his disappointment.

Jack shook his head, 'You don't understand.'

'What's to understand?'

Jack sighed; he put the tumbler on the cement floor between his legs linking his fingers together and brooded for some time before looking up and addressing his friend. 'My father and mother died when I was very young. I was raised by my gramps. I never had possessions, a family. A home. We wandered about in his search for gold until I was about ten and old enough to attend school. I wore hand-me-downs, had no shoes to wear to school, boarded with a family and walked five miles to school each day. When I was lying out there in the mud waiting to die, I promised myself if I lived, I would amass wealth, position and influence. If the War has taught me anything, it is that we are all dispensable. Now I have a second chance, I want to amount to something Mike,' he finished, his eyes averting those of the young Australian.

'I see… '

'No, you bloody-well don't! I'm not cut out to be a rancher, I want more from my life than to push some cows around a paddock.' Jack's voice was harsh and full of feeling.

A poignant silence settled between them finally broken by Jack as he further explained. 'Mike don't ask me to give up my dream. You're my buddy and I owe you, but I want more than a ranch. My interests are in minerals and the new industry the world will now demand. Steel, therein lies the future, my future. I'm sorry. It was not my intention to hurt you. Primary industry will still have a major role to play. You should buy that property, I'm sure you will make a good rancher.'

Mike sat for some time before lifting the glass to his lips and finishing the raw spirit in one last gulp. 'Well, old Ike McKenzie found haematite on the property, a bloody mountain of the stuff if that means anything.'

'Iron ore? You're joshing me.'

'Saw the samples he had in his poke. Dad's no geologist but he reckons it's very rich. He and old Ike talked about a venture once, during the cattle market collapse of 1911 but then things got better and dad forgot about the scheme. Apparently Ike told dad there was plenty of limestone, he was pretty keen to have a go. What did they need limestone for?'

'Smelting,' Jack told him, a smile playing at the corners of his mouth.

Mike nodded, 'Dad said limestone was essential, I wasn't particularly interested, but I know they poured over maps old Ike put together, sometimes for hours on end.'

'A mountain of iron? Didn't this Hopkins fella know the value of such a find?'

Mike shrugged, 'Old Lloyd left well before Ike told my dad of his find.'

'Where is this property?'

'Oh, about two-hundred miles north-east of Margaret River Downs. It's in the Northern Territory, not Western Australia. Why?'

'Transport?' Jack was vague, not on purpose, an idea was forming. *Iron to make steel,* he mused, the geologist in him suddenly aroused. The world was ready for change, wars brought about change, developing technology, new industry, nobody wanted to go back; the way was forward. And Jack saw himself as part of that future.

'Is there any coking coal on the property Mike?' He asked before Mike could answer.

'Hell I don't know? Why?'

'To smelt the iron. Iron on its own is of no value. But the world will be crying out for steel as soon as this war finishes.'

'Steel to build ships and bridges and factories; I see what you mean. I know they ship coal back to the old dart from the eastern seaboard.' Mike, informed him.

'You are certain?'

'Sure, ships call in at Edge Rock to take baled wool and supplies of beef.' Mike informed him.

'Railway lines, locomotives, automobiles,' Jack was becoming enthusiastic with their discussion.

'The only transport from Tempi to the coast is the Margaret River which becomes Queens Channel, and the old stock route,' Mike appended.

'Is it a large deep river?'

'Navigable if that's what you mean, but a region of very large tides at the coast and prone to flooding during the wet up north.'

Jack pondered this statement for a while, 'Suitable for shallow draught barges?'

'I reckon it is,' Mike responded after some thought, the scotch languishing his thinking.

'We would need to ship the ore, or, bring coking coal up the river to a site we could clear for the purpose of making a smelting works to produce the steel.'

'Bloody hell! A mining venture would cost thousands and thousands of pounds. Jack I haven't got that sort of capital… ' Mike was stunned by the man's daring.

'I have a property Gramps left to me, back in the States, for some time there has been talk of oil. If, as I suspect, it is oil bearing ground, I will be able to finance the deal.'

'But it would take years to develop such an industry as you propose.'

'Then we will just have to round up a few of them beeves you are talking about and sell them off to keep things going in the interim.' Jack was smiling.

'You're joshing me… ' Mike shook his head in resignation.

'I'm deadly serious Mike! If you want me to join you in Australia, those would be my terms, my ambitions, and motive for doing so.'

Mike was witnessing his first glimmer to the other side of Jack's character and it perturbed him to a degree. Also he had a disturbing thought, what if old Lloyd had taken the property off the market? Or worse, already sold it, after all, six years had lapsed since Mike first heard the property was for sale.

Chapter 4

Paris, November 1917

Katrina Anthony and a colleague were summoned by matron to discover the whereabouts of two patients believed to be missing for several hours. All the obvious places having been checked, Katrina decided to look over the grounds. Katrina drew the cape tighter around her, the stiff starch uniform creaking in protest against the rustle of the wind's advance. Tentatively, she stood head turned with the breeze, listening, her eyes probing the shrubbery close at hand. The sound of laughter came on the wind. It was light and carefree, devoid of the tensions of men at war. She picked her way through the shrubs to the grassy veld beyond. She remembered helping patients to their chairs, the brass band tuning up on the rostrum for the afternoon's concert, the sun reflecting on the player's instruments. Now the lawn was wind-swept and covered with branches twigs and leaves of various description, their multi colours making a patchwork quilt of the green. They are mad, she thought to herself. The day was bleak with dark ominous clouds blotting out the sun, threatening to snow. No one in their right mind would be out of doors today unless they had to be, she told herself. Boldly she approached the rotunda to a point where she could clearly overhear their conversation.

'What do you mean it's not our war, Australia is part of the Commonwealth?'

'Sail is being replaced by steam. Timber by steel. Big business. The war moguls... '

It was as far as the conversation dwelt before Katrina confronted them with scalding tongue. 'I might have known,' she accused, pointing a shapely finger at Jack. 'It is not enough that I have to chastise you for leaving your bed the other night; what are you trying to do, catch pneumonia? Back to the ward with you both, straight away!' Her voice had a ring of impatience to it, which was not lost on her charges.

Hands on shapely hips, she confronted them. 'Sir Arthur Sloggett will hear about this incident. You mark my words! Now off with you both.'

'Sir Arthur Sloggett. That name rings a bell.'

'The letter, the letter in your pocket,' Jack reminded him.

'Oh that Sir Arthur.' Mocked Mike.

Katrina's features flushed with anger, not trusting herself to say another word she turned and fled the rotunda.

<>

Sir Arthur Sloggett's secretary was at her desk busily catching up on some unfinished correspondence when she acknowledged the quiet knock at the outer office door.

'Come,' she called, not bothering looking up until the shadow of Katrina Anthony fell across her desk. Cassy was piqued. She wondered what possible connection this slip of a girl could have with Sir Arthur. This was her second visit in the past week and on each occasion, he patronised her to the point where Cassy felt a tinge of jealousy. To make matters worse, he was very tight lipped about the nature of the young woman's visits.

Generally Cassy was his confidant, his right arm. Their relationship spanned twenty years. A spinster, with very few interests outside her work, Miss Cassy Ableson lived for her memories, books and cats, and Sir Arthur upon whom she doted her undivided attention.

'Just a moment, I will see if he will receive you.' She eased herself from behind the mahogany desk, pausing to smooth the minute creases from the tight ankle length skirt before disappearing through the frosted glass panelled door. Katrina stood facing the door reading again the gold painted lettering.

SIR ARTHUR SLOGGETT
DIRECTOR GENERAL ARMY MEDICAL SERVICES.

It was very impressive, she thought to herself, reminded of her father's office block, which occupied an entire floor in the heart of London's Fleet Street and from where he controlled his shipping empire. Her thoughts returned to the present, barely had Miss Ableson left her before the handle turned, the door opened to behold a beaming, drooling, Sir Arthur.

Cassy also saw the look and clouds of anger built up on her countenance; unknowingly she broke the pencil clutched in her hand as though it were a twig. Katrina brushed passed her into Sir Arthur's office, watching Cassy who bent to retrieve the broken section of the pencil from the new carpet pile and understanding clearly the surreptitious relationship which existed between the pair.

Katrina was conducted to a plush leather upholstered chair. They talked of generalities, with Sir Arthur occasionally glancing at his time piece; they were late. Not that Sir Arthur was concerned; he was enjoying the moment. Every time Nurse Anthony crossed her long shapely legs, her uniform revealed a most fascinating sight to delight his whimsical fantasies. The knock at the door saw his manner change in the twinkling of an eye to one of serious expectancy.

'Come!' He uttered the word with a crispness that could not be ignored. His voice was deep and articulate, his walrus moustache twitched with the movement of lined facial muscles silvery grey, like his hair. His appearance reminded Katrina of her uncle, James Loxton, only her uncle wasn't a womaniser.

They stood at attention waiting for Sir Arthur who had risen at the sound of the door rapping, to stand facing where the sun bridged the single pane window with glowing warmth. Not a cloud graced the turquoise sky, nor a breath of wind disturbed the large oak trees across the courtyard. Lazily, he lingered, letting the sun soak through the uniform's fabric. Slowly, hands clasped behind his back, he turned to face them, still at attention and awaiting his salute.

'At ease,' he instructed while returning to his desk. Silently, he looked to the charge sheet laid out before him. 'You have been very irresponsible, rude, insolent and jolly inconsiderate towards my staff, in particular to this young lady for whom I have the greatest admiration. Therefore, I have no alternative but to place you both on a charge.'

'Your name and rank soldier?' He addressed the question to Jack, pen poised to take down the information.

'Carter sir, Lieutenant Jack Bryson Carter,' Jack turned towards Katrina as he spoke. 'And if you will permit me the opportunity sir, I would very much like to apologise to the lady, what Sergeant Smith and I did was unforgivable and we are truly sorry sir and ready to accept your judgement regarding internment.' Jack's eyes locked to those of Katrina, it was as though they had the room to themselves.

Mike watched fascinated by this turn of events, he saw Katrina smile at the big bloke, saw their eyes lock, two people suddenly discovered another. More importantly, Jack

24

was attacking the situation; he had this old boy at sixes and sevens. The charge was serious. When sober, both agreed they could be court-martialled and jailed.

Suddenly Sir Arthur's features went ashen. Carter and Smith, could this be the Carter and Smith mentioned in dispatches from Sir Herbert Plummer and whom he had promised to look in on as a matter of courtesy and report back on their progress?

'Smith?' Sir Arthur pointed a bony finger at Mike.

'That's right sir… ' Mike was puzzled.

'By jove. Sir Herbert sent a dispatch concerning himself with your welfare gentlemen. Something to do with that skirmish on the high country. Commendable it was too. As I recall, you sir, are to be the recipient of the Victoria Cross,' he looked expectantly at Mike. 'And you sir to be awarded the Croix de Guerre to go with your Distinguished Conduct Medal,' nodding at Jack. 'Well, this throws a different light on the charges I was about to inflict on your personage. Excuse me while I arrange for chairs. I would very much like to hear your account of the assault which brought you under scrutiny. Can I offer you a brandy? A cigar perhaps?'

'A brandy would be fine thank you sir.' They chorused.

'I'd give pounds to be your age again, gave the Huns heaps what! It reminds me of the Boer War, bloody good show that, mind you I was in my prime then, a field surgeon.'

A caustic Katrina asked. 'Sir Arthur! Have you forgotten why these men are here?'

'Lady Anthony. Yes of course, frightfully sorry my dear. Apparently you do not know who these men are.' The look persisted, Sir Arthur cleared his throat, 'and apparently you don't care.' He turned to address Mike and Jack again when there came the forceful closing of his office door, Katrina was gone.

'My goodness. Well take a seat gentlemen,' He indicated the chairs Cassy had made available. He commenced to fill their glasses.

'Sir Arthur would you forgive me, I have a bout of dysentery,' lamented Jack, adding, 'Sergeant Smith knows all the details we are cleared to divulge, I'm sure he would only be too happy to oblige.'

'I'm sorry to hear that my boy, perhaps you had better not indulge.'

'That's OK sir, it may help bind me up.'

'Perhaps some other time when you are feeling more like a chat then,' encouraged Sir Arthur handing him the goblet.

'Yes sir, it will be a pleasure sir,' responded Carter, accepting the brandy and swallowing it down in a gulp before returning the goblet to an astounded administrator. Saluting he made for the door, Smith giving him a quizzical glance.

Jack closed the outer office door, not before assuring Miss Ableson that everything was under control and no, he didn't think Sir Arthur needed the military police. Once outside, he pushed the crutch to the limit. He hurried down the marble corridor, which linked the administration building with the hospital proper. He nearly missed her, it was instinct that made him look through the window into the hospital's kitchen block, part of which served as a cafeteria selling razors, soap, bar chocolate, hot tea, coffee and the like. Katrina sat at one of many empty tables brooding into a white china cup. He closed on her warily, not wanting her to escape before he had the chance to clear the air between them.

'May I join you?' He asked, addressing her with a naturalness that surprised him.

Katrina looked up at him, her eyes were streaked with red and tears streamed down her cheeks to form blots on the white paper tablecloth. He felt in the pocket of his battle jacket and removed a clean handkerchief, handing it to her. He watched as, timidly, she took the folded cloth without a word and dabbed her tear stained face.

'Thank you,' she murmured into the folds of the handkerchief, her eyes, large and glassy from crying, locking on his and Jack fell hopelessly in love.

It was the face which most attracted him, he couldn't take his eyes from her, like some marble goddess in a museum that he had promised to study in every detail, his eyes, like magnets, were drawn back to her face. Her eyes, brown in colouring, surrounded by a sea of white tinted as they were with red streaks, the lashes, long, dark and curved, her eyebrows were barely thicker than a crayon line. It would be the laughter in those lovely eyes he imagined that would turn men away, but they were not tantalising, not flirtatious nor cruel, they sparkled with life he decided. High cheekbones typified her Anglo-Saxon forebears, giving a slight stretched appearance to delicate milky white skin. Her nose was fine in structure and slightly rounded at the tip, her lips full and pouting over even white teeth, a gold-capping evidence of care for appearance. A slight dimple graced her chin above the curved jaw-line, the chin being slightly rounded. Her throat was smooth and delicately white under the high cut of her uniform, the ears daintily pushed close to the sides of her head, the lobes hidden by a single pearl earring, the only ornamentation apart from the small gold watch and chain pinned to her bosom. As he watched, she removed the white bonnet and one by one, the whalebone pins until finally with a shake of her beautiful head, the golden strands fell to her shoulders; it completed the picture as far as Jack was concerned.

Katrina was conscious of his gaze yet somehow she didn't mind, it wasn't like Sir Arthur's seductive stare, more like one of admiration and she felt the colour rise in her cheeks. Jack also saw it.

'I'm sorry for staring. May I… ' He indicated the unoccupied chair. She nodded meekly.

Jack drew the chair out from under the table; he placed the crutch beside the chair and positioned himself slightly to one side, allowing his leg more room. He would be glad when the medical staff said the plaster cast could be removed. It weighed a ton.

'I will wash and iron your handkerchief.'

'That won't be necessary, besides it's my fault,' he placed his hand over hers.

'Oh, so now you are going to take an advantage,' Katrina withdrew her hand and commenced to rise from her chair.

'No! Hey, I'm sorry, it was my fault and I'm trying to apologise.'

Katrina felt that same tingle at his touch and she knew she did not want to leave the table. 'Where I come from, a lady must be formally introduced to a gentleman before conversing so freely with him, and then a chaperone is always present.' She heard herself say to overcome her self-consciousness.

'Fine,' Jack threw his hands in the air. 'I don't wish to take advantage of you, excuse me.' Jack palmed the table, pushing to his feet.

For one horrible sinking moment Katrina thought he was preparing to leave. Before she could find tongue to stay his movement he had hobbled to the cafeteria counter and addressed the young lass in attendance, intentionally loud enough for Katrina to hear.

'Excuse me, do you speak English?' She nodded. 'Good! Do you know the young lady over at the table?' Again the girl nodded, a smile creasing the corners of her mouth.

'Wonderful! Would you introduce us? My name is Jack Bryson Carter and the young lady is refusing to speak with me because we have not been formally introduced.' Again she smiled to wave a lock of hair from her forehead.

Jack took her by the hand. He led her around the end of the counter and with her supporting him they closed on the table where Katrina was close to tears with laughter and relief. The slip of a girl took her charge seriously and formally made the introductions. Katrina covered her mouth to prevent from laughing. Jack thanked the lass over and over, she thinking he was shell shocked, glad to get away. They talked of generalities, of the war, the hospital, of Nurse Collins, until Katrina felt it was time to change the subject.

26

'Will you return to America?'

Jack reflected for a second, his head raised, looking at the ceiling. 'Initially. I intend to settle my affairs and join Mike Smith in Australia.'

'Australia! What would you do in Australia?' Katrina was bemused.

'Make my fortune. Australia is one of the last frontiers, just waiting to be developed; iron and steel, engineering, prospecting, gold, diamonds.' He shrugged, his fingers absently turning the lid of the stainless steel sugar bowl.

'I see,' did he detect her anxiety? 'You do not see yourself behind a desk running... oh, a shipping company? For example,' she was quick to add. Katrina looked away, holding her breath with anticipation.

'No. If this war has taught me one thing, it is that the fighting man is only the means to accomplish the aims of aristocrats and politicians; he is expendable. I was a fool. I believed the posters, God and country and all that rubbish. Besides, I enlisted because I was tied to a desk. There's more to being an engineer than working in the field apparently,' he emphasised with a sigh.

'You don't believe in capitalism?' Katrina was shocked by his revelation and the cadence in his voice.

'I don't believe the common man should be asked to fight and die while tyrannical capitalists feather their nest.'

'And yet you profess that you would become one of them by seeking wealth and power.' She reminded him.

'And I would use my influence to denounce all war. This should be the war to end all wars.' Was the candid reply.

'Are we having our first argument?' Katrina laughed.

They had conversed for what seemed minutes however when Katrina glanced at her watch two hours had lapsed. 'Oh, I must go,' she began to rise.

'Can we meet tomorrow? Shall I ask if our chaperone is on duty?'

Katrina laughed, 'I do not think that will be necessary, and yes I would like very much to meet here tomorrow,' she rose to leave tingling all over from his touch. Already surreptitious thoughts stirred within her, Katrina had met the man she wanted to marry. However, she knew full well her mother and father would never sanction such a marriage.

Chapter 5

14 November, 1917

Lieutenant Carter, Katrina and Sergeant Michael Smith stood waiting on the wind swept platform for the train which would take the young Australian to Calais and from there across the English Channel for his investiture on the 26th, before he boarded a troopship bound for Australia. Mike casually glanced at Jack and Katrina; huddled together, they made a handsome couple. He felt the odd one out and was thankful when the train shunted into the station.

'Well, I guess this is goodbye,' began Mike, fiddling with his kit.

'I'll see you soon,' encouraged Jack.

'Katie look after him, and if you decide to tie the knot, we'll make you welcome over home.'

'Thank you Michael, take care.' Katrina leaned forward standing close before kissing him gently on the cheek. She marvelled at the change a few weeks had made, the hollow cheeks were filling out and some of his natural colouring was returned, he was lean by nature but tall with broad shoulders and a pleasant smile, an attractive man, an athlete she decided moving back to let them embrace one last time and was reminded of the day they were admitted wearing German uniforms. The porter beckoned for the last time, anxious that the train depart as scheduled.

Katrina had met the man she wanted for a husband, to love her and father her children. For an ordinary girl like Irma, her Parisian room-mate, this would not have presented a problem. However, for the sole heiress of the Anthony Shipping Millions, one of the most influential families in Great Britain, it presented formidable obstacles. Time was running out, Jack was to be presented to Poincare, the French President, at a special ceremony on the twentieth of December and then possibly sent home and lost to her forever, unless she took the initiative and made a decision. They met in the tearoom as they had every day since that first meeting. On this occasion, Katrina broached the subject of marriage again. Jack was hesitant, would she be willing to accompany him to Australia? Then there were her parents to consider.

'Katrina I love you and I want to marry you. There is no hurry. The war must soon be over.'

'I won't wait.' Katrina stubbornly replied, not meeting his fixed gaze.

'Well I won't marry you until I meet with your folks and get their approval. It wouldn't be proper.'

'Jack I have tried to explain. You do not know my family, they would move heaven and earth before they would let us marry. Our time is now my darling. Trust me.'

'Surely you want me to talk with your father and ask for your hand in marriage,' he responded.

'He would refuse Jack. Please try and understand. My parents want me to marry… a person of their choice,' she added at length not wanting to hurt his feelings any more than was necessary, while having no intention of revealing the exact reason her parents would look with disapproval at Jack as a suitable suitor.

'You mean to say you cannot choose your husband?' His voice carried an incredulous tone.

'That is correct.'

'I find that hard to believe Katrina.'

'Please trust me my darling; when the time is right, I will introduce you to Mother and Father, please,' she waved those big brown eyes at him and Jack went weak.

'What about where we live Katrina, and what I do? I may be away a lot of the time, explorations for minerals can be time consuming, I may be away for months at a time, how would you cope?'

'I've coped with this situation,' said Katrina. 'What makes you think I could not cope with isolation?'

'I would like to settle in Australia?'

'So you have said. Several times.' She smiled taking his hand in hers reassuringly. *There is a mountain of iron ore, Mount Hopkins, I'm going to make my fortune.* She remembered their first conversation in the tea-room.

'You would be my husband; I would follow you to the end of the earth,' she added her eyes locking to his troubled pools of blue before he lowered his gaze. He sat silently letting her hold his hand, brooding into the dregs of his cup of tea as though he were reading the leaves and not enjoying the account they were offering.

'You know you remind me of Harrison, so tall so... charismatic,' she blushed at her own frankness.

'Your brother?'

Katrina nodded, 'I was only five when he went away, yet I still think of him. Father had every memory of him removed when we received the news of his death. I cried for him then Jack, please, I don't want to cry for you now, just love me and let me worry about our life together; it will be wonderful darling. Please do not spoil the time we have together,' she was pleading with him and unselfishly Jack relented.

'Tonight then,' Katrina gripped his hand forcing a positive reply. He nodded; she leaned over the table and kissed him boldly on the lips before rising quickly and excusing herself.

To contact her mother on the question of marriage, Katrina knew, would be out of the question. Jack had no title, no wealth that she knew about, and no position having resigned before joining the forces. He planned to settle in Australia, a colony to her parent's way of thinking. This would be frowned upon by her father in particular. He thought of Australia as the Antipodes, both opposite culturally and in diversity. Katrina had come to realise Jack was his own man. He would not accept a position on her father's board even if offered and listening to him talk, evidently he detested all that her father represented. Her mother's reaction would be that he was a commoner. Then there was the man himself; Mother would take one distasteful look, miss the gentleness, the charisma, the intelligence, and see only the countenance of a bare knuckle street fighter. Her father, reflected Katrina, would shudder on hearing the American drawl, considering correct English can only be spoken by the English, and then only if acquired at Cambridge, Eton or Oxford. However he was a war hero, and that would count for something. Katrina was ready to risk all for the one she loved, her virginity, her inheritance, the love of her parents and the thought she may never see them again once she and Jack settled in Australia.

The only way she could have this man is if she were pregnant with his child. She realised her mother would not let her have a baby out of wedlock. Katrina prayed their lovemaking would see her pregnant; she had chosen the time carefully, around her ovulation. She could do no more than wait, that and correspond with her family advising them she would be home for Christmas and that she had met the man she wished to marry, Lieutenant Jack Bryson Carter, an engineer and hero attached to the American contingent.

That night they made love for the first time. Katrina could feel his manhood resting against the soft furry of hair below her navel. The wetness of him was warm against her skin. Then gently, ever so gently while she arched, he was over, searching, and finding her inner depths, feeling the slight parting of her maidenhood with his penetration, his lips fondling the nipples of her breasts, throat, ears and eyes, as their breathing came in gasps, and a sudden shudder individually seconds apart in time climaxed their lovemaking. Katrina clawed at his shoulders, murmuring and crying quietly into his hairy chest, silently and with delight, as mentally she planned their engagement and future.

Chapter 6

London, January 1918

There is a man, a Cambridge scholar, who, for a gift, will purge himself on your behalf. Lady Elizabeth Anthony stared at the card reading it again before tucking it into the folds of her blouse and hurrying to her room. The name, what was his confounded name? Libby searched her memory. She had no desire to contact Lady Parker Brown-Stope again. This would be her secret, she would confide in Sedgwick and nobody else. No matter the cost they must rid themselves of this American, and Elizabeth did not care if he had decorations for bravery plastered all over him; he was her enemy, a threat to her femininity, her precious belief in her Anglo-Saxon heritage. Katrina would marry a peer of the realm, not some unknown with no breeding, heritage, or position. She shuddered as she imagined that American drawl, the pronunciation, the procrastination and belligerence of his race. Dobson, Robson, Hobson! That was it, Ashford Hobson, Professor of Language. A hero to the few who could afford the price of a gift. Not that a figure was ever mentioned she was reminded, that was left to the party he represented. If the gift were not substantial then no further favours were fore-coming, even if requested.

Elizabeth took a pen to paper, sealed the brief message in an embossed envelope with the family crest, melted red wax across the seal and summoned Benson. Soon she and Sedgwick were in serious discussion in the library.

'Katrina will go to our cottage in Swanage,' she said while her husband, the Lord of Bedfordshire read the card posted from France a week earlier.

My Dearest Katrina,
It would appear I will be able to join you earlier than expected. Your mentor Sir Arthur Sloggett approached the authorities on our behalf and my discharge is now imminent. I look forward to meeting your folks; should arrive Thursday next, about three in the afternoon, if that is OK? Trusting this brief note finds you well I remain;
Yours always,
Jack Carter.

'Folks. What kind of word is that for a young gentleman to use?' Lord Anthony shook his head, folding the correspondence and returning it to Elizabeth.

'An American. An orphan? Only the good Lord knows what his parents were like,' Libby retorted. 'He may be a bastard for all we know.'

'Yes, then there is Katrina's continual mention of Australia,' his Lordship chided.

'Sedgwick Australia is definitely out of the question. If Katrina ever found out about… you know,' she told him with a passion.

Sedgwick pondered over the name they never mentioned before replying. 'What would our daughter see in such a man Libby?' Sedgwick shook his head. 'For once I agree with you, this man is not a suitable person to marry into our family; the relationship must be quashed.'

'You agree then, we send Katrina away and organise for Professor Hobson to write some letters?' Little did he know, Libby had already written to Hobson requesting an attendance at their London residence for two-thirty the following day.

'It seems to be the only way my dearest. I'll not have any daughter of mine going off to live in Australia.'

'Besides, he may be gold bricking,' she pointed out.

'Do you think so dear?' Sedgwick was only half listening. He had other things on his mind.

'Why you are an aristocrat Sedgwick, there is always mention of our several business enterprises, shipping tea here, or lumber from there and so on. If he has ever read the Financial Review or studied the stock market, he would know who you are, mark my words!'

'Very well then, can I leave the details to you?'

'Certainly dear.'

'Good! Because I have a ten o'clock appointment,' Sedgwick glanced at his gold fob watch. Closing the case, sure he had made his point.

'The gift?' She encouraged.

'At your discretion my dear, really, I must be going.'

< >

Professor Hobson was punctual, or Benson who had been in the family's employ for some time, was punctual in having the learned man brought to her ladyship. And Libby wasted no time making the man feel right at home. She conducted him personally to the drawing room where the afternoon sun glittered through the fragmented cloud and splashed across the Axminster carpet pile. Outside it had stopped snowing giving lies to the sun breaking through the wind swept mass from the North Sea. Professor Hobson closed on the open fireplace while Benson, Sedgwick's gentleman butler, prepared him a brandy and a Wintermann cigar. At a nod from Elizabeth, Benson left them alone, closing the door discreetly behind his tall groomed frame.

'Professor, so good of you to accept my invitation at such hasty notice,' Lady Elizabeth extended her hand.

'The pleasure was all mine my lady.' Hobson bowed at the waist briefly brushing his lips over her hand while noting the clustered diamond rings adorning her shapely manicured fingers.

He was a slim well-groomed man with the noticeable paunch of middle age, his hair long and flowing. Speckled grey through brown. He wore thick brown horn rim spectacles, with bearded jowls and long sideburns, which blended into his goatee beard that flowed silvery grey towards his chest. The high rich Oxford voice was diminutive but deliberate. A scholarly appearance thought Libby conducting him to a high back ornately carved chair, before removing her hand from his grip.

'Brandy Professor Hobson?' Libby indicated the sideboard where Benson had filled a crystal goblet moments earlier and left it beside an almost full decanter on a sterling silver plate.

'That would be splendid,' Hobson rubbed his hands together in anticipation.

'Napoleon, I hope it is to your satisfaction. Can I get you something else?' Libby handed him the glass, her attention for the cigar Benson had prepared.

With a wave of hand, Hobson declined. 'You fuss too much my lady. Please, how can I be of service?' He sipped on the brandy, his face a bland mask.

32

'I would like a favour Professor, we trust to your discretion naturally.' Libby busied herself with the short note they had intercepted from the American, and a letter written to her and Sedgwick from Katrina when she was in France. She placed them on the surface of the mirrored mahogany writing desk and Hobson's gaze was drawn again to the many exquisite pieces of jewellery, which adorned her finely manicured fingers.

Hobson rose and joined Libby at the desk. 'Dear Lady, you can rest assured of my confidentiality.' Libby remained silent while he studied the flowery scrawl of Carter and then the refined calligraphy, the public school writing of Katrina.

'Neither hand present a problem my lady,' he quipped at last, looking at her over the rim of his spectacles.

'Excellent Professor. Would you, using their separate hands copy the drafts I have made?' She patronised him, placing both hand written notes on the writing bureau besides the letters he had been studying.

'There is one question my lady. Have the young couple been corresponding with one another?'

'No why?' Libby asked, a frown of worry crossing her comely features.

'Authenticity my lady, I can only copy what I see,' he replied.

'There has been no correspondence, of that I am certain Professor Hobson.'

'Good, very good! Then when did you want the material made available Lady Elizabeth?'

'Would the weekend be suitable for you Professor?' Libby hung on his answer.

He chortled. 'Seeing the young man will be here on the thirteenth, next Thursday, I will have to give this favour my priority.'

'Money is no object Professor,' Libby hastened to inform him.

'The gift will be at your discretion. My ladyship,' he bowed his head slightly at her across the desk.

'Shall we say the tenth then?' He asked, smiling.

'That would be perfect Professor Hobson,' Libby beamed and it was noticeable to the learned gentleman that she visibly relaxed. Hobson finished his drink and an elated Libby escorted him to their front door personally. She watched as Benson helped him into his overcoat.

'Do be so kind as to join us in our private box at Ascot on Saturday week Professor Hobson, I feel sure you will enjoy your afternoon.'

'I would be delighted. My Lady.' Hobson tipped the brim of his hat in her direction, before exiting the house and being escorted to the chauffeur driven, limousine.

Chapter 7

London, January 1918

A tall thin man with an intelligent face, dark hair brushed straight back, and in black formal attire complete with tails answered the chimes. Hesitantly, Jack Carter inquired whether he had the correct address. He was assured that he was expected and asked to wait in the parlour. The gentleman in tails excused himself.

'Lord and Lady Anthony will receive you in the library sir, please follow me,' he informed Jack in a cultured and deep voice on his return, indicating with a gesture for him to fall in behind.

The American gazed in awe at his surroundings, noting the marble staircase spiralling upwards towards another vastness of excellence in baroque architecture. He followed the long-coated figure who patiently stopped every so often, conscious he could no longer hear Jack's squeaky footsteps, and to allow him to admire his surroundings. Jack paid laudatory glances at the several paintings that adorned the coachwood panelling which made up the interior walls of the lower floor. He quickly gawked at Picasso abstracts, a Bruegal's Village Marketplace Scene, the Vandyke portrait of Charles the First, a tapestry by Sheldon depicting the Harvest, and a Madonna in stone sculptured by Henry Moore. He bestowed admiring glances at the many and varied pieces of period furniture that graced his lavish surroundings.

Following the gentlemen's gentleman, his new shoes squeaked and echoed hollowly on the mosaic flooring, the only sound to be heard apart from the ticking of the large Grandfather Clock, which was encased in a polished cabinet of Beechwood. Benson stopped before the library doors, he could feel the tall man's breath on the nape of his neck as he knocked against the heavy, ornately panelled timbers and waited for permission to enter.

'Mister Carter Sir, your Ladyship,' he announced, at the same time moving aside and encouraging a hesitant Jack to enter the room.

They stood together, near the large open fireplace, whether for strength in the nearness of one another's presence, or, to display a united front for Carter's benefit. One glance was all he needed to see who Katrina resembled. It was like looking at a picture of her thirty years from now, or so he imagined. If anything, he thought Katrina would be slightly taller, favouring her father in that respect.

'That will be all for the moment Benson,' said the same husky voice.

'Very good my Lady,' Benson replied, bowing and closing the door behind his retreating person.

They stood facing Jack for what seemed an age before Lord Anthony broke the silence. 'I am Katrina's father, Lord Anthony of Bedfordshire and this is her mother, Lady Anthony,' he began, walking forward distastefully to shake Jack's hand. Jack nodded, the man had introduced his title, his position, he was immediately wary.

'Won't you be seated young man?' Lady Anthony invited, indicating the ornate hand carved Sheraton lounge piece.

It seemed to the American she was being courteous rather than kind. He felt uncomfortable. For the first time in his life he wanted to turn and run. When the carriage had stopped in front of the large Mid-Georgian House with the sash windows, leadlight stained glass, and the elegant doorway, he queried the coachman, feeling he had made a mistake.

'No mistake Guv,' was the rejoinder. 'They're loaded that lot, tis only the Town 'Ouse, got mansions and castles all over the bleedin' country. Four pence sir,' he added, holding a gnarled hand to collect the money. 'Thank you Guv.'

He was gone, leaving Jack standing on the cobblestone gazing at the coat of arms that graced the entry between two pillars of marble. He turned away once, then plucking up courage, he returned. After all, he was engaged to Katrina, he wasn't marrying her parents, nor did their influence interest him. He accepted that she was a lady at their first meeting. However, in his wildest dreams he never imagined… and then the door had opened cutting across his thoughts.

'Would you care for a brandy my boy? You look as though you could use one.' His lordship pressed the button by his side which would summon Benson again.

'That would be fine sir, if you are having one; I don't wish to impose upon your hospitality.' Jack eased his trousers to avoid knee marks in the new tweed, he realised he was sitting stiff backed in the floral-covered chair and slowly he let himself ease back and adjust to the luxury which surrounded him.

Benson appeared as if by magic, 'you rang my Lord?'

'Yes Benson, be a good chap and fix our guest a drink.'

'You're usual sir?'

'Thank you Benson, and Benson,' he added as an afterthought, 'cigars, Wintermann I should think.'

'Your smoking jacket my Lord?'

'That will not be necessary, I will change for dinner.'

'Very good sir, just as you wish. Dinner sir, will Mister Carter be staying, may I ask?'

'But of course Benson,' Lady Anthony admonished him. However Jack couldn't quite make out why she glared at the man.

'Thank you my Lady I shall inform cook,' Benson bowed then moved away to an ornately carved Sheraton cocktail cabinet.

A short while later, during which time there was no conversation, Benson placed a side table within easy reach of where Jack sat nervously in the chair. Upon the parquetry top he rested the goblet of brandy and a cigar case made from hand carved ivory, buffed to lustre, it glistened under the chandelier of light from above. He stood expectantly, patiently, waiting for Jack to open the box and select his cigar, finally, with a shrug for his employer and guessing correctly that their guest was unaccustomed to the refinements of a gentleman's lifestyle, he patiently coughed into a white gloved hand stooping and accompanying his action with quiet words of encouragement. 'Would you care to select your cigar sir?'

Self-consciously, Jack lifted the box and Benson indicated where he should apply a little pressure with his fingers. Suddenly, the lid sprang open startling Jack and some six cigars fell onto his lap. Jack, his cheeks colouring with embarrassment, apologised profusely for his awkwardness.

Benson, quick to assist, replaced the cigars and expertly prepared the end of one on the edge of the box where a hidden blade of Sheffield steel severed the tip. Next, he removed the gold crest, which bore the famous Henry Wintermann trademark, the lion, sword and crown. He flicked the tortoise shell lighter cupping the flame, watching Jack's expression as he puffed the cigar to life. The American coughed once and Benson disclosed a smile, secretly admiring him and having guessed correctly the young gentleman had never smoked a cigar before.

'That will be all Benson,' Lord Anthony addressed the man after he had similarly prepared his cigar.

'Very good my Lord.'

The brandy was smooth, undoubtedly Napoleon Jack decided, not knowing nor really caring. It gave him something to concentrate on as silently he wondered why Katrina wasn't present to greet him. He felt certain she would have been here once she had read of his pending arrival from France.

Lord Anthony cleared his throat, 'Captain,' he began.

'Excuse me sir, I'm a civilian; my discharge was effective from the end of December and I held the rank of Lieutenant,' corrected Jack.

'H'm, yes of course, forgive me,' replied Lord Anthony, however his tone indicated to Jack that his Lordship did not like to be corrected.

'Katrina speaks highly of you, naturally, and your war record speaks for itself,' he continued. 'Yet we know so little about you and she is our only daughter, our only living child. Our son gave his life fighting against the Boer under Kitchener.'

'I'm sorry to hear that sir; Katrina had spoken of him. Naturally, I'll do my best to answer any question you may wish to ask.' Jack's eyes rested on the individual family portraits, one was missing, he could only assume it was their son, strange, he thought to himself, perhaps the reminder was too great a burden to bear. He held his silence, believing that if it were his son, he would want to remember him in any way possible.

'Very well, what is your station young man?'

Jack took his time. He looked long and hard at the crystal goblet in his hands before letting his eyes rest on Lord Anthony. He was a lean tall figure of a man, the silver hair combed forward and sharply across the forehead to cover pending baldness, a vain man. His sideburns reached his jowls, not bushy as was fashionable, but trimmed to suit the straight hair. He sported a military moustache and carried himself with the bearing of an officer. Even while seated, Jack observed, his back was as straight as a ramrod, or was that partly tension, Jack didn't think so, his knees jutted away from his body in a direct line with the way he was facing, even to the points of his highly spit polished shoes. It is said of such men Jack remembered, that to all intent they are never relaxed, yet years of discipline, and practice allow them to give this impression, while inwardly they are perfectly comfortable. Jack suspected it was intentional. Lord Anthony wished him to know he was dealing with a man of strong character, although why this charade was necessary, Jack did not understand.

'Well sir, I'm an engineer, having graduated from the University of California,' he began tactfully. 'Before my involvement in the hostilities, I was employed by an American Mineral Research Company.'

'Yes, yes,' cut in Lord Anthony irritably, dismissing this area of discussion as unnecessary having had his broker in New York check the activities of United Mineral Consultants.

Seeing the frustration in the wave of the hand and on the countenance of his Lordship, Jack's careful thought out presentation fizzled; he squirmed awkwardly in the chair. He would much rather talk to this man alone. Some men are gifted speakers, never lost for a word; Jack was not such a man.

'Mister Carter, how do you intend to support our daughter? As we are given to understand you resigned your commission, you have no present station. Is that a correct assumption?' Lord Anthony was brusque with his charge.

Jack felt like telling him to refrain from interrupting, he was beginning to appreciate this was not going to be easy. During his drive across London in the carriage, he vividly envisaged this meeting and had tried while he had the time to put his thoughts into perspective. Alas, he had not allowed for this reception, nor the circumstances surrounding their meeting. Katrina had tried to warn him, had told him in no uncertain terms, he had ignored her...

'I intend to settle my affairs and join a very good friend of mine in Australia.' Jack was determined to tell it his way.

'To what purpose?' The moustache twitched.

Lady Anthony crossed shapely legs, folding her arms over her ample bosom in the one movement, her glass of sherry forgotten. It took all Jack's self-control to hide his feelings behind a jovial grin, never could he remember feeling so uncomfortable.

'Australia is a very young country, and some say, a very rich country; a place of unending opportunity if one is prepared to work.'

'My boy, be reasonable, Australia is thousands of miles away. Compared to Europe and the Americas it represents the antipodes to all that I feel sure you are accustomed. And speaking quite frankly, Katrina, being English and of noble birth, would never fit into the vast wilderness of Australia. Why sir it is a mere colony, a dumping ground for devious whites of questionable breeding and character, not to mention marauding blacks!'

'Sir!' Jack made to reply.

'Hear me out young man,' Lord Anthony paused until he was certain of Jack's attention, 'as you can see, Katrina is used to a certain lifestyle; she has to live up to our expectations. Why even in France we insisted Sir Arthur Sloggett, Director of Army-based Hospitals in France... surely you would have heard of him?' His lordship leaned forward expectantly to no response. 'He was to keep us acquainted with regular correspondence,' this name-dropping to suitably impress Jack of his Lordship's influence.

'If we had only known what was going on behind our backs... ' Lady Anthony cried.

'Hush Libby! I'll do the talking thank you.' A look passed between them.

Jack sat stone-faced; he felt a sudden animosity and was doing his best to control it.

'What employment would you acquire in Sydney?'

'I wasn't going to Sydney... sir,' he added.

'Not going to Sydney,' murmured Lord Anthony, loud enough for Jack to hear his sarcasm.... 'Well Melbourne then?' He sighed, drawing on the cigar.

Jack deliberately sipped the brandy before replying. 'Sir, I intend to join my friend in Western Australia, the nearest town Edge Rock is one hundred and fifty miles away as the crow flies, Mike Smith lives on a ranch, Margaret River Downs he... '

'Oh no! No, never! I would never allow it, never!' Lady Anthony cut him short, one hand catching at her throat.

'What!' Shouted Lord Anthony, his voice ringing like the crack of a stockwhip.

'Well I understand the territory where Mt Hopkins is situated is untapped. However, it could develop into the largest state of Australia.' They were ignoring him. Jack felt the blood rush to his cheeks; enough was enough.

They were not listening, Lord Anthony having moved from his chair to comfort his wife who was close to tears. He pointed an accusing finger at Jack. 'You mean to sit there and tell us you intend to take our little girl to the far corners of the earth on a... a whim! Sir, I forbid any talk of marriage. Have you considered what this would do to her mother? Look at her man. She is upset at the mere mention of your future plans.'

'With all due respect sir, I planned to marry Katrina, not her mother!'

'That sir, is the height of impertinence,' Lord Anthony rose to face Jack, his hands were shaking, his countenance contorted in deep simmering anger. Instantly he regretted the display of temper, it was a sign of weakness a shrewd antagonist could exploit, and in his dealings with men Lord Anthony had learnt long ago to be strict and disciplined.

Now it was Jack who was calm, the situation more to his liking. 'I apologise if you and your good Lady were hurt by my remarks. However, I feel Katrina has her own life to fulfil. She is an adult, and if she sees fit to share her life with me, I would make the decisions regarding where we live and how we would live, she would want for nothing. Besides,' he continued, their eyes welded to his, 'with advances in shipping and the advent of aircraft, Australia will soon be much closer in terms of travel than is presently the case. Sir, I propose to purchase Tempi Station, a proportion of which Mount Hopkins is a highly concentrated iron ore deposit from which I plan to mine, smelt, and eventually produce steel. Australia will need industry, and technology to advance her cause for independence from your king,' he paused, certain his outspoken tirade cut to the quick. 'I plan to develop a corporation that will realise international trade within ten years.' Jack's lowered voice was a brusque icy whisper.

'And Sir while I am about it, as far as Australia and Australians are concerned, they volunteered to fight for your King, and they were among the most gallant soldiers in the fighting. Without them it is my considered opinion that Great Britain and France could not win your war, and, with respect, you can take that any way you like.' He turned to face Lady Anthony. 'Now, if you do not have any objection, I would like to see Katrina.'

'A republic indeed! Great Britain is the sovereignty of Australia.' Lord Anthony bristled, ignoring the request.

'America won its war of independence from Great Britain,' Jack reminded.

'I warn you sir, I will crush any attempt by you or any covert clandestine organisation who would try and detach Australia.'

Jack smiled taking up the gauntlet… 'You can try! Besides, I thought you aristocrats only saw Australia as a dumping ground for your criminal element.'

Lord Anthony rocked on the soles of his feet as though struck a silent blow. 'Sir I do not like your politics! Nor your cocksure attitude,' he shook a pointed finger at Jack. 'You are a dangerous man and I will see fit to crush you if you persist in your blasphemous ways,' his lordship did not try and hide his sudden repugnance for the American.

This followed a poignant silence, which settled over the room. Their eyes locked, the gauntlet thrown, before Jack lowered his gaze and stubbed out his cigar in the marble ashtray, the aroma of the fine-blend tobacco cutting the air, lingering around him, filling his nostrils. He commenced to finish his brandy, fully expecting at any moment to be asked to leave.

In the short time allotted him, Lord Anthony studied this brash young man anew from behind his wife's chair. The diatribe was so unexpected. The blighter was a trouble-maker, a bounder, reference to his encouraging Australia to become a republic indeed. Although he had to admit Carter radiated a certain confidence, an assuredness. Qualities not generally associated in one so young, and certainly not evident in any of the other bounders who had come to ask for Katrina's hand. But then they were not war heroes either. He did not wear his Legion of Honour Medallion, like a crutch, flaunting his valour for all and sundry to observe, nor had he mentioned turning down the field promotion to Major; Lord Anthony knew, he made it his business to know everything there was to know about this young upstart as soon as it was known he was held in favour by their daughter. Damn him! Maybe if he had said America, Libby may have begrudgingly consented, but Australia was out of the question, of that they were both adamant. And now he had made a sworn enemy, another to be crushed before he could do uncountable mischief against the realm and his king.

Jack placed the goblet on the table. He could feel Lord Anthony's eyes following his every movement, choosing to ignore the close scrutiny he repeated his earlier request, while rising to his feet. 'May I see Katrina please?'

Not surprisingly it was Lady Anthony who answered him. 'I am afraid that is impossible Mister Carter, she is not here, nor has she read your last correspondence announcing your arrival from France.'

'What? You had the audacity to read my letter?' Jack exploded.

'That will be all young man!' Lord Anthony sprang to his wife's defence.

Undaunted by the show of temper, Libby replied, 'It was a card as I recall, stating you arrived earlier than expected and that you would call at three this afternoon,' explained Libby, her matronly breasts rising and falling with anxiety. Like a lioness fending for her cub, Libby took up the challenge written in the steel blue eyes of Jack Bryson Carter.

'We sent our daughter to our country estate, not before putting some sense into her young head,' snarled Lord Anthony.

'Oh, which one?' Mocked Jack, instantly sorry for the taunt.

Libby saw the change come over the man, the frustration, the insolence, now it was her turn to press her advantage, and she was quite familiar with this situation. She ignored the gibe; her voice was soft, controlled, 'Mister Carter, before she left Katrina, wrote this letter.' She took the embossed envelope from folds of her clothing and held it out for Jack, who moved quickly to possess it.

Jack stood facing her. He was overcome with a sudden fear, that of losing Katrina. He could feel perspiration breaking out under his armpits and down his back, its clamminess at his groin; the envelope was not sealed. It had been opened, read. Jack looked down at her accusingly.

'Yes we have read the letter Mister Carter, do sit down, you too Sedgwick,' nodding at her husband knowingly.

Hesitantly, Jack backed towards his chair and commenced to read, and it was noticeable to the pair that his hands shook. Opposite him Lord Anthony saw his wife's look, their prearranged signal for him to summon Benson with yet another guest.

Shortly, the door opened and Benson emerged followed by a well-dressed gentleman, slightly overweight, in his mid-thirties with a leonine mass of hair covering insipid features and sporting an enormous handle bar moustache. Jack tore his eyes away from his reading long enough to observe his entry.

'Ah, Chester my boy. How good to see you, how is your dear father? Let me fix you a drink. Sit down my boy. Sit down. Benson, get Lord Chester a cigar.' His Lordship was blatantly patronising the man. After the new arrival was seated and Benson had prepared his cigar and was subsequently dismissed, the young man, brandy in one hand, cigar in the other, his portly carcase filling the chair was wont to thank them for the invitation.

'I received your invitation yesterday, jolly decent of you my lord.' Chester gave the room's other occupant a sideways glance. 'Jolly nice to see you again Lady Elizabeth, Mother sends her fondest regards.'

'Thank you Lord Chester, it is refreshing to have the pleasure of your company. Sedgwick! Are you going to introduce Mister Carter to Lord Chester?'

The name came staring at Jack from the page in front of him.

--- *so I am going to honour the wish of Mother and Father and marry one, Lord Chester Thornton. I might have mentioned him to you before. I have come to realise they are right, a marriage between us would be folly ---*,

39

Jack was stunned; he sat there, his heart breaking. Groggily he rose to his feet, perspiration breaking out on his brow. The outstretched hand focusing after what could only have been part of a second. He stood like that, dimly aware of a smirking Lord Anthony making the introduction and his taking the weak grip in his own, that and the grin on sallow chubby jowls.

'Jolly pleased to meet you. Been to war have you? Wish I could have gone. Gave Gerry a hiding what?' So the rapport went on, it was lost on Jack.

Jack broke the man's weak grip, 'Excuse me, I must leave,' and the steel blue eyes were misted with emotion. Not trusting himself to say another word, he shoved the letter into the envelope, crossed the room without a backward glance and let himself out.

'I say, what an extraordinary fellow,' remarked Lord Chester, standing with his hand still extended.

'Yes,' replied Lord Anthony giving the fire a savage poke with an iron and not paying Chester much attention. 'Rather sad really, shell shocked, casual acquaintance of Katrina's, met at that beastly hospital over in France, going home, called to say goodbye; poor fellow.'

'Oh... I see, what a shame,' Chester exposed two rows of large white teeth in what passed for a knowing grin.

'Thank heavens you didn't have to go to war Chester,' Lady Anthony dropped the formality now the American was gone and unable to contain her relief.

'Yes... thank heavens,' reiterated Lord Anthony, meaning something entirely different.

'If you will excuse me Chester, I have a dreadful headache,' Libby excused herself, one hand placed on her forehead, 'I really must go and lie down.'

<>

Jack Bryson Carter burst from the house into the English twilight, neither looking right nor left as he moved aimlessly away from the House of Anthony. He pulled the collar of his coat high and tugged at the brim of his felt hat to keep the chill of the wind, blown in from the North Sea bringing with it light flakes of sleet, at bay. He slid the envelope into his suit coat pocket, his face a mask of fury, his mind going over the letter's contents; it didn't ring true, how could she do this to him after all they meant to each other?

<>

20 January 1918, Jack Bryson Carter stepped aboard the *Dresden Star* a German freighter bound for New York. The freighter was impounded by the Americans after the fateful sinking of the *Lusitania* by a German submarine. Although not carrying passengers, he secured working passage as fourth engineer, the captain being disposed towards him once convinced his papers were in order and that he could perform a valuable service on the already undermanned vessel as it voyaged the icy wind-blown Atlantic.

Chapter 8

London, January 1918

Katrina's return home was the excuse for great excitement. She had changed, like all people who leave home and family to return a short while later, fads of speech, dress, hair style and generally a new found confidence, this, and in Katrina's case, a radiant glow of true love. After the usual rounds of the theatre, lawn parties, dinners and Christmas carolling, Katrina soon settled back into the ways her family's life style demanded. She would never forget France, torn upside down, nor the hospital and the horrors she had witnessed, nor would she ever talk about them. They were sacred, she could never forget the fine young men who were dispensable, who gave their lives, sacrificed their future, she knew, and that was enough. All talk of her activities in France centred round the light and amusing, and of a certain American Lieutenant who swept her off her feet. She only had to concentrate to imagine him holding her within the confines of his arms, she felt safe and secure, like never before.

It had been at her mother's insistence that Katrina should visit the family's country house near the little hamlet of Buxton in Derbyshire, there to spend a week planning her wedding and relaxing before Jack's arrival from France. Her mother seemed to take the pending marriage very well, once she got over the initial shock that there would be no traditional engagement period.

Back in London, sitting in the drawing room, the open-hearth fire admitting a warm glow to match her spirits, Katrina opened Jack's letter...

< >

Lord Anthony would never understand women; first, Katrina confined herself to her room, then Libby. The difference being, Katrina would see no one, whereas, Libby requested her physician, barrister, and finally Lord Chester Thornton, in that order, not necessarily on the same day. When he tried to see his wife, he was politely told by Agatha, her lady in waiting:

Lady Elizabeth is resting comfortably your Lordship. A contagious virus, she does not want you exposed to its influence.

With that, Agatha had closed the door to his wife's suite leaving him standing there like a schoolboy outside the Headmaster's Office.

When Lord Chester Thornton finally caught up with his Lordship at his club, he was well on the way to forgetting Libby, Katrina and everything else. The past three days saw him frequenting his club instead of attending business, consuming several measures of brandy, smoking cigars and reading the Financial Review, particularly those pages which made glowing reference to his business interests. Through the haze of cigar smoke he welcomed Chester.

'Chester my boy, how is your dear father? Come, join me in a brandy, or maybe a gin, two fingers or one?' He inquired, his hand on the pull cord which would summon James.

'Ah James, please bring Lord Chester a double gin and tonic, and I'll have another brandy.'

'Very good sir.' James bowed his way clear of the pair.

'Fellow mixes a better drink than Benson, been trying to entice him into my employ for the past two days,' he confided to Chester after James had retired.

Chester nodded his understanding, and realising he would not get his Lordship in a more amiable mood, 'Sir,' he began nervously, 'as you know… '

'Yes I know,' Lord Anthony began, waving his arm through the air, 'young blighter, she'll see you but not me.'

Chester had no idea what his Lordship was on about. 'Sir Katrina and I…,'

'Katrina is another who won't see me, my own daughter,' Lord Anthony mumbled into his brandy balloon.

'Excuse me sir. Should you be drinking so heavily?'

'Do not presume to tell me how much I should drink Chester! Besides, why aren't you confined to your bed if the virus is contagious?'

Thornton looked blandly at Lord Anthony. 'Sir?'

'It doesn't matter Chester, you were saying.'

'Sir, I'd like permission to marry your daughter!' Chester blurted the words.

Lord Anthony sat pondering the statement in his brandy filled mind. After what seemed an age to Chester, he rose unsteadily to his feet and slowly extended his hand. 'Congratulations my boy, you are not contemplating leaving Great Britain for Australia are you?'

'Australia sir?' replied Chester, dumbfounded by mere mention of the country.

'Never mind,' muttered Lord Anthony, pushing the bemused man towards his chair. 'This calls for a celebration. Where is that confounded waiter?' He reached for the cord giving it a couple of lively tugs.

'Sir we plan to get married next month… if that meets with your approval,' Chester was quick to add, seeing the changed expression on his Lordship's features.

'You do not waste any time, do you young man?'

'Sir, your good Lady explained that Katrina intends going back to France; she is anxious to prevent this happening at any cost.'

'What?' burst out Lord Anthony, and seeing his future son-in-law was about to repeat himself, waved him to silence.

'She wants to go back to that beastly hospital.'

'Lady Elizabeth feels that if we get married right away, Katrina will settle down, you know sir, children, a home, responsibilities of her own, that sort of thing,' he smirked.

'I see, it is becoming clearer.' Suddenly Lord Anthony's thoughts were not so muddled; he sat sipping the fresh brandy while waiting for the waiter to return with the champagne, absently listening to Chester's rapport, his own thoughts far away. Charter… Carter, yes, that was it, Carter. The bloody hide of the man, a tyrant, a republic indeed, if he rose to prominence he could ruin free trade and influence the Workers Party with his nonsense. He must be stopped at all cost. Nor had he forgotten what Carter had said about a certain mountain of iron ore, after all, he was first and foremost a business magnate and such as was described by that young philanderer should be investigated. If Libby had made up her mind Katrina was to marry this pompous ass, then there was nothing he could do, or would do, as Thornton was steel and already he was contemplating a merger.

<>

42

26 February, 1918. The motorcade of limousines moved sedately up Ludgate Hill, passed the statuette of St. Ann and on to the Christopher Wren designed, St. Pauls Cathedral. There under the dome amidst the massive arches, paintings of the Holy Crusades, the stained glass windows, kneeling and rising from golden threaded cushions on the black and white mosaic floor, surrounded by their five hundred guests, Katrina and Lord Chester Thornton were married. After the ceremony, the wedding party moved through the south arch to sign the registrar while their guests were entertained by the St. Pauls Choristers, dressed in their black and white regalia, and accompanied by the rich notes of the pipe organ, the acoustics, throwing the rich sounds to all parts of the cathedral.

Part 2

Chapter 9

Great Britain, 1919

Majestic Roxburgh House cast long black shadows across the snow-covered courtyard. The manor was situated on a 250-hectare estate near the little hamlet of Henley on The Thames in the county of Berkshire, England. Normally its lush green sprawling grounds, lawn and gardens fringed with a hedge, mazed with woods and bisected with streams, were a very picturesque setting for the twenty-bedroom-mansion of white stone thought to be designed by Christopher Wren. However, winter changed its demeanour and snow camouflaged much of its charisma. Many of the walls were covered with creeper vines, ghostly white, in places extending to the guttering but never darkening the many and various lower windows and trimmed away from the upper small cape windows with their domed coverings.

Behind the manor in the lee of the house, away from the direction of bad weather stood the stables where his lordship catered to the needs of several brood mares of Arabian stock, two stallions, many racehorses and several ponies.

Roxburgh House was home for Katrina, this was her wedding gift from Chester—her own mansion complete with thirty staff, if one included the gardeners and gamekeeper. The surrounding countryside was hers for as far as the eye could see. Yet for all that Katrina was a lonely woman, married to a man she endured, rejected by the only man she could love. It was a marriage of convenience. The plans she had so carefully contrived to have Jack accepted, even if reluctantly, had all come to nothing as begrudgingly she succumbed to the wishes of her mother. She had no choice. She wanted Jack's baby more than anything else in the world. To have the pregnancy aborted was unthinkable as far as Katrina was concerned. Lady Elizabeth was inflexible; to have the bastard was contrary to what the Anthony name stood for and therefore not an option. Libby believed it to be Harrison coming back to haunt her all over again, a scandal with the potential to destroy their status and standing among the ruling class. Compromise was essential. Katrina got to keep her baby, Sedgwick expanded his business interests, and Libby got to see her daughter marry a peer of the realm, a family as noble as their own with ancestry and bloodline dating from the fifteenth century when flourishing trade gave rise to an aristocratic class.

From the beginning, the marriage was electrically charged. This was mainly because of Katrina's decision, no, her obsession with caring for the child. No governess for David and although a nanny was employed at Libby's insistence, Katrina would cater to his every need until he was old enough to attend school. To say Katrina doted on the infant would be an understatement, for she worshipped him, and Chester could not begin to understand.

Slowly Chester registered change, Katrina eventually being unable to hide her repugnance. He was a weak man and soon turned to his club and other women. There were occasions when he would force his way into her bedroom, usually too drunk to perform the act of the one-sided affair and Katrina was compelled to change the lock on her suite. There reached a stage when he didn't come home at all, discretion a thing of the past as he realised Katrina's indifference. Openly he would parade his women around the night spots frequented by London's socialites. When confronted by newspaper apocryphal and her mother's lashing tongue over the telephone, Katrina and Chester would openly argue and fight, with the whimpering of their son bringing hostilities to a cessation as Katrina would leave the room to attend his needs.

Not that Lord Chester had much time to reflect on his wife's obsession, it was necessary for him since the merger to engulf himself in company business. Because of the distance from Roxburgh House to the company's offices in Fleet Street and his frequent sojourns overseas, it was more practical for him to stay at one of the many company properties in London only coming home during the weekends and then only if there was not some pressing business to attend. Katrina knew she had to thank her uncle, Sir James Loxton in no small way for his organising for Chester to be heavily involved in the company.

Formerly a corporate lawyer, with his own flourishing practice, Sir James Loxton was attracted by a challenge, a challenge to merger Anthony and Thornton business interests to form one company. This approach came shortly after the fairy-tale marriage of Lord Chester Thornton to Lady Katrina Anthony. The draught took all of six months before he felt reasonably confident to approach the Tribunal for approval and registration under the Company's act. Both parties were so impressed for his handling of their affairs, he was invited to join the board as a director and company secretary, a position which strengthened almost immediately until he was forced to sell his law firm. He loved to travel which was as well, for he spent several months of the year expanding his knowledge, purchasing companies and updating technology in the company's less advanced steel plants throughout Europe.

Sir James was made aware Chester was assaulting his niece shortly after Chester returned from a two-week business trip to Scotland. What sparked the fight, he did not know. However, he suspected it was because Katrina found her husband's advances to be repugnant, particularly after he had considerable brandies and was sufficiently inebriated to strike her. He understood Katrina, was her confident, had been since she was a little girl. She had disclosed to him her love for the American before revealing her intentions to Libby, seeking advice, on how she should approach his sister with the news of her engagement. And James insisted he should be present when she spoke to her parents. Both Libby and Sedgwick were calm, James wondered at the time if Katrina's fears were but a storm in a teacup, as both had gladly accepted their only daughter had found someone to share the rest of her life, to have his children and to grow as one over their life span. Not that his sister or Sedgwick ever mentioned the American, or Katrina's pending marriage in his presence, apart from a brief conversation about the man's ambitions where Australia was concerned. And James was aware Katrina was heart-broken when shortly her engagement was annulled, indeed, never officially announced. Her marriage to Lord Chester Thornton had been arranged. Even before Katrina turned to him for support, Sir James smelt a conspiracy, certain in his own mind Chester was not the father of Katrina's baby. He was powerless to do anything but give Katrina a shoulder to cry on. Then one morning, before the staff had assembled for the day, Sir James had opened his office to find Katrina curled up on his leather couch nursing baby David. He studied her features, saw the welts concealed by her make-up; tears ran down her cheeks as she tried brokenly to explain their fight. The thought of that pompous idiot striking Katrina saw James' bile rise in anger and he promised to keep the oaf so busy he wouldn't have time to think about women and sex let alone perform the act. After a hasty cup of tea and several assurances their conversation would be kept in the strictest confidence, Katrina had opened her heart. She had finished by telling him of the dreams the American had for their future in

Australia, of the mountain of ore he hoped to mine and from which he would make his fortune.

The conciliatory ever, James Loxton mediated over a surreptitious meeting, which took place at his small but modest country home at Kettering in Northamptonshire. Sir James promised to reveal Chester's true character to his father if it ever happened again. He had Lord Chester's word that he would never strike Katrina again, and Katrina for her part would try to make the marriage work for the sake of their son.

Now, four months later, given the agenda for a pressing board meeting Sir James realised Sedgwick Anthony intended to strike Jack Bryson Carter a cruel blow. In a clandestine coup d'état with Sir Bruce Thornton, Sedgwick planned to buy the Mount Hopkins range.

Chapter 10

Edge Rock, Western Australia, 1919

Jack Carter debarked the coastal lugger at the new Edge Rock shipping terminal recently completed by a consortium of businessmen. He stood in the shade initially, out of the oppressive heat, waiting for what seemed an eternity for Doctor Clayton Andrews to appear; he never did. Jack watched huge nets sucked into the air by the jib crane unload cargo from the ship's hold. He took pleasure in seeing small native children diving into the harbour after silver coins thrown into the water by the sailors. That is, until an old tar sidled up to him and explained there were sharks and crocodiles in these waters. Jack gave an involuntary shudder and immediately lost interest in the spectacle moving back into the shadows of the terminal building, out of the direct heat. His trunk now safely ashore, he would wait no longer. The clerk in the terminal office was obliging and Jack left his valise into that man's custody with the promise he would collect it later.

In the main street he asked for directions to the good Doctor's surgery much to the amusement of the local and Jack was soon to discover why. The town was small and the surgery quickly located. A note was pinned to the front door telling anyone who required his services that Doctor Andrews was away delivering misses Cotter's baby. Jack turned on the balls of his feet and went down the side of the building. Out the back he discovered many stalls, kennels, and holding pens. In some of the pens were a variety of animals from goats to pigs and even a camel. Jack smiled; he felt Andrews must be a veterinarian.

He left the shade of the old wooden building and made his way back to Main Street. Glancing about in the heat of the midday sun, he observed no movement. The street was deserted. A hush hung over the dusty rutted road, while in the distance, the only sound to break the stifling silence was that of the surf beating against granite outcrops at the entrance to the harbour. His shirt, sweat stained, stuck irritably to his back. He used his coat to brush at the horde of flies plastering themselves to his person to no avail. He made his way to the nearest intersection where he observed a fine two-storied sandstock building with surrounding balconies in the distance. Jack made for it surprised, as he approached, to find it was a club. Before entering the establishment he donned his coat, the matching tweed suit out of place here in the heat and dust. However, the impressive establishment he felt, warranted the action. Jack pushed against the large glass door and it gave under his touch. He moved into the aperture, letting the heavy timber frame, which supported the glass, close behind him.

Jack approached the bar surprised to see he was the only occupant apart from the man behind the mahogany timbered planking. The room was large and airy with a huge raked ceiling and a stairwell leading up to another floor overhead. Paintings of ships, horses, bare knuckle fighters and pearling divers graced the walls, that and a large mirror which ran the length of the bar. The floor of polished timber was spotlessly clean. Evenly positioned at intervals were heavily ornate spittoons.

Harry Street looked up from his reading of the London Financial Review, slightly irritated. He was loathed to serve the customer believing that to be below his station, while at the same time not wishing to appear rude. Just then from below the floor, came the sound of bottles being moved about.

'My bar manager.' Harry explained, and although the dour expression was supposed to convey a friendly greeting it didn't quite come off and Jack stood mystified removing his coat and hat, placing them on the barstool next to the one he would occupy.

'Take your time, I'm in no hurry,' he replied. 'Can you accommodate me for a couple of days?' He asked when seated on the stool.

'Clarence will attend your domestic needs as soon as he has finished down in the cellar,' Harry informed him and already had turned his attention back to the paper.

Jack shrugged, the thought persisting that the man wasn't very cordial. 'So this is your place then?'

Harry nodded above the paper, not bothering himself with the American. He detested the sound of the twang, rolling the words out of the mouth instead of speaking them in a clear and concise manner.

'You're to be congratulated,' Jack tried again to make conversation with the man.

Harry sighed, an irritating sound which matched his mood where the stranger was concerned. He let the paper drop to the polished surface of the bar top. 'Shan't be long. I'll see what is holding up Clarence, probably dozing the lazy blighter!'

And with that he was gone leaving Jack sitting there. Cautiously, Jack craned his head and turned the paper towards him so he could read the small print. His eyes registered surprise. An article featured Lord Anthony. With Harry forgotten, Jack grabbed the paper and started to read the article. *Anthony Shipping Company successfully completed a merger with Thornton steel and by so doing were set to create the greatest heavy industry monopoly ever seen in Great Britain,* exposed the writer. And below that article another feature concerning itself with dwindling iron ore deposits in Great Britain and Central Europe which Jack did not have the time to peruse before the Englishman's return.

'Do you always take it upon yourself to read another person's private material?' Jack had not seen Harry's re-entry. His quizzical frown of worry for what he was reading, and his absorption for the material, was greater than his fear of being caught out.

'I'm sorry. Could I purchase your paper Mister,,' the frown deepened?

'Street, Harry Street and no you cannot.' Harry held out a hand for the paper and Jack reluctantly surrendered the material.

'Could you tell me where I might purchase a copy of that paper?'

Harry laughed. 'It was forwarded to me from the old country. The only copy unfortunately.' Harry folded the Financial Review with a contemptuous stare for Jack before moving away. Jack's eyes were stilled by the movement; a simple thing like long tapered fingers folding a newspaper. He saw the ring on Harry's index finger for the first time, and it registered with frightening clarity. Suddenly he was carried away with his thoughts to another room, much larger, with high ceilings, beautiful hand carved furniture and crystal glass cabinets encased in leadlight which concealed volumes of precious literary works, paintings and portraits of kings, queens, nobles and family and above the majestic fireplace the family banner, their coat of arms rich and splendid in colouring. He stared at the mirrored glass behind the bar while not seeing it, the resemblance was there he told himself, eyes large and brown, high cheekbones and the lips, he had a cruel lip-line Jack reflected. Minutely, he visualised the coat of arms. It was most impressive. And the ring Harry was wearing was a cartouche' of the Anthony crest. A red gemstone set into a pure gold band, nearly the size of a halfpenny piece, thin carved lines showed two swords, their tips pointing towards the sky, not crossing, beneath the swords a gauntlet and below that again, in Latin, the word's *Death with Honour.*

'Their crest!' Jack muttered to himself.

'You talkin' to me mate?'

Jack shook himself free of his trance to behold a portly balding man dressed in a white shirt with bow tie commanding his attention. 'Huh? No.' Jack was visibly shaken.

'Christ ya looks like you've seen a ghost mate.' Clarrie stood with hands on the bar staring up into the white face of the stranger.

'Give me a beer please.'

'Sure, won't be too cold, the ice chest,' Clarrie explained with a wave of his thumb towards the cumbersome piece of machinery responsible for keeping the beer cool. 'On the blink. Been trying to fix it for the last hour.'

Jack nodded, 'As it comes.'

Clarrie looked towards the stairs, Harry could be heard walking along the upstairs corridor. 'You're boss?' Jack regained his composure, while looking towards the stairwell.

'Yeah, Pommy Harry,' Clarrie pulled the top off the long neck bottle pushing it towards Jack.

'Pommy Harry?'

'Came out 'ere a few years ago.' Jack hung on Clarrie's every word. Just then the door swung inwards and a local sidled up to the bar.

'Mornin' Rafe, what'll it be?' The bar manager moved away to serve the new arrival.

Jack digested the information barely tasting the beer. There was much here to occupy his mind. He was glad of the intervention. Jack did not doubt his memory; the crest was just like Harry's ring only the swords were heavily jewelled full size duelling foils, their blades of the finest tempered steel, glistening at him from where he sat facing Lord Anthony and his Lady. Suddenly Jack remembered, instinctively he removed his wallet. Inside its leather pocket was a letter, the folds permanently creased from much handling. He didn't read the letter. Rather, studied the embossed letterhead, their crest, before nodding his head slowly and putting the letter away. As the beer soothed the worried plains from his features, he remembered a conversation with Katrina, insignificant at the time, now it struck home like a thunderbolt.

I had a brother. He was killed fighting the Boer under Kitchener. A sudden pang of pain tugged at Jack's innards, a hurt cut deep, as though they had parted just yesterday, without explanation. Katrina had been right the thought nagged at him. Her parents didn't see him as suitable to marry her. But had they influenced her decision?

'Crikey ya haven't finished ya beer yet mate. Drink up.'

Jack gave the barman a frosty glare for the suppressed memories. The barman quickly lifted the bottle, mopped the ring of water on the bar and moved away. Jack drowned his sorrows in the cool amber fluid. He made no further mention of accommodation deciding he wanted to be alone, removed from Harry Street and company, he would doss down in Doc's surgery if he had to, and he needed time to think. The Boer war was over several years ago. He vaguely remembered the conflict. *So what was Harrison Anthony doing here?* He pondered. In his own mind he was certain even if he had never met the man, had not seen a photograph. He prided himself on his memory, he would have recognised Katrina's mother anywhere and he saw the family resemblance in Pommy Harry as he was widely known, if not before he recognised the crest. But why? If Harrison were dead, then who was the man wearing the ring? A cousin? And the paper and the man reading those sections which bore reference to the Anthony shipping empire? It was a dilemma and he determined to solve the mystery. All in time, first he needed to get his hands on that bloody paper.

Chapter 11

Anthony Thornton Building, London

The boardroom of Anthony Thornton Enterprises was filled with an air of expectancy on this particular winter's morning. Would the senior directors announce their decision on the chosen candidate for the position of senior vice-chairman? Lord Bruce Thornton, well-groomed in a dark three-piece suit from Harrows, balding, tall, stocky, in his late fifties with a walrus moustache and a lazy eye struck the small gavel lightly onto the polished timber surface to bring the meeting to order. Once the muttering of conversation had expired, Sir James Loxton handed out the brief agenda for this special meeting, to the disappointment of Thornton's sons.

'Gentlemen, ladies,' Lord Bruce nodded to where his cousins, both widowed, Mrs Parker Brown-Stope and Mrs Bellamy-Jones sat talking in quiet undertones. 'The reason this special meeting of the board was called is to convey a concern brought to our attention a short time ago by the management of our Birmingham Steel Plant. Sedgwick and I have met privately to discuss this concern, namely a shortage of quality iron ore deposits in Europe. We are in agreement the consortium will have to look further afield to eradicate this emerging dilemma.'

'I don't understand Father, we have stockpiled enough raw materials to generate steel for the next five years.' Lord Chester looked along the table past his two brothers to where the glare his father gave him indicated he disapproved of being interrupted while speaking. Chester, being the eldest son, had been inducted into the House of Lords as decreed by his birthright. Although the least talented of Thornton's three sons, and therefore kept under a tight rein by his father, his duties were vague and tedious at times as far as Chester was concerned. In the main they consisted of visiting their several plants and factories, mostly accompanied by Merrick his younger brother, where a lot of hand-shaking took place and not much else. His expense account was open and he was encouraged to take staff management to dinner and report back on morale, which seemed to Chester a mundane chore, an opinion he expressed to his father once, whereupon he had been informed he was being groomed to take a vice-chairman's role and what he considered to be trivial pursuits were essential grooming for his future with the company. Further, Lord Bruce told the young man, if Sir James Loxton considered he should clean the toilet block then he would!

'However,' continued Thornton senior, certain of his eldest son's undivided attention, 'this would mean Anthony Thornton Company Limited committing to an overseas operation. Indeed it will require reorganisation therefore, of necessity, to be managed by members of this executive.' He paused to look at each member of the board in turn before resuming. 'James has compiled some reading material for your close perusal. The documents convey our limited iron-ore deposits, illustrated by the graph on page three and the mines which supply us and our competitors with ore. James, be so kind as to distribute the material.' Thornton senior paused again to watch as each of the executives got their copy of the information.

'Page three ladies,' encouraged Thornton, his patience tested by their ephemeral indifference for the document's importance and their wanting to continue their former conversation.

'Sedgwick would you like to put your proposal?' Thornton invited his counterpart to address the board some minutes later, a knowing look passing between them.

Sedgwick Anthony rose slowly to his feet holding aloft the document while giving his audience time to focus on his person. 'Thank you Bruce, yes, a shortage of quality iron ore deposits throughout Central Europe will mean our competitors addressing the same problem if not now, then in the very near future. It should be the intention of our board of directors to act with expediency in this matter. Meanwhile in the interim, so succinctly pointed out by Lord Chester, we have sufficient stocks to maintain our present production while controlling the price of steel throughout Europe. Profits are and will remain high, due to increasing demand, which should make our share-holders happy,' Sedgwick beamed a smile upon them before resuming his oration. 'Nevertheless we cannot and will not dither. We must secure stockpiles of raw materials now before increased demand results in soaring prices for raw materials, which may see declining markets for our products as more developing countries encourage the establishment of steel-making to compete on the world market, of which as you would be aware our consortium presently enjoys a monopoly. Indeed I am given to understand Australia is attempting to establish an ultra-modern steel plant. Now is the time to secure the future. Shipping and steel making is our industry. The world is our market. We,' Sedgwick paused to look along the table at Lord Bruce for support, 'do not intend to let developing countries usurp our monopoly.' His piercing gaze took in Chester fiddling with a pencil, doodling a design onto the corner of a blotter, however his son-in-law never looked up to see the condemnation in those eyes. 'To this end Australia can provide a solution. It has come to my attention that large iron ore deposits have been found inland from the colony's western coast. Hopkins Mountain is a range of iron ore which takes in hundreds of square miles, the size of Great Britain, and enough iron ore to take us into the next century.' Lord Anthony paused listening to their gasps of amazement. He thrust his reading glasses in place, opening the report ready to draw their attention to the carefully constructed bar graphs which illustrated their iron-ore reserves along with those of the German-based Krupp Steel, their major competitors. About to address them again, he was interrupted.

'And how did you come by this information Sedgwick?' Mrs Bellamy-Jones asked, for the sake of something to say.

'Dear lady such information is irrelevant,' a reticent Sedgwick drummed his fingers on the surface of the table while looking around the room. However, it was apparent from the inexorable looks they wished to know how he came by the information and seeing Chester was about to voice his dissension, he decided to reveal his source.

'An American chap, Carter, called to say good-bye to Katrina before he was dissociated with the war, Chester met him,' he added, as an afterthought.

'Sir I thought you implied he was mentally... you know,' Chester looked at him twirling a finger around his cranium, 'unstable.'

'Nothing of the sort, just shell shocked, completely dependable information if that's what you are implying Chester. Besides, I have had the information confirmed by an independent source.' He lied to silence further comment from Chester.

'Australia?' Clayton was a spit out of his father's mouth apart from the lazy eye and the middle Thornton son, interjected. His patriarch believed Clayton should become the next chairman when he retired. Clayton had a certain animal cunning, was the brains of the family and displayed the initiative so necessary to lead. His war was over and a bitter and restless young man would carry a cane and limp for the rest of his life. The maxim machine-gun bullet opened his thigh like an exploding ripe melon and although in a lot of pain and with copious amounts of blood seeping down the leg of his flying suit, Wing Commander Clayton Thornton managed to land the biplane before lapsing into unconsciousness. Recovery was slow, his discharge, imminent, however he was alive. Reports indicated the average life expectancy for pilots' dog fighting over Flanders in 1917 to be three weeks.

'We ship coal, timber, beef, and wool from Australia in return they buy our steel, what's the problem?' Bruce willed his son to silence with a frosty glare.

'Do continue please Sedgwick or we will be here all morning at this rate.' Sir Bruce intervened.

'Yes of course, we are wasting valuable time. Having read the material in front of you, you would be aware the eastern seaboard of the colony has unsurpassed deposits of coking coal so necessary to produce steel,' Lord Anthony's close scrutiny was meant to silence further remarks, before he resumed his seat.

'It has been well documented that Australia has vast mineral wealth… ' Lord Bruce added his support to his counterpart.

During a previous surreptitious meeting Sedgwick had revealed to Lord Bruce that the American had closed his affairs and at this moment was on his way to Australia. Sedgwick had further explained to Lord Bruce they must act to secure the Mount Hopkins mineral rights before their competitors one of whom was the American, and whose politics were dubious at most, secured the mineral lease. Sedgwick explained that he had met with this American, Jack Carter, and that the fellow wanted to see the new nation become a republic, removed from Great Britain and the Empire. That was enough reason as far as Thornton was concerned and he agreed Clayton should be sent to Australia to report on and establish their business interests. For his part Lord Anthony saw the influence the young man had over his father, saw the threat posed by this influence, and savoured the prospect of having the young pup twelve thousand miles away, assured by his father Clayton knew the steel business backwards.

Lord Bruce cleared his throat. 'If after reports are confirmed and the Mount Hopkins Range is proved to be a substantially rich range of iron-ore, we will purchase the mineral rights and establish a subsidiary company to produce steel in Australia, much cheaper than shipping the ore back here for processing. Clayton, you along with Merrick will oversee our investment, initially.' He added seeing the frosty glare Clayton thrust his way.

Lord Anthony drummed on the mahogany table's surface to encourage the other board members, they followed suit. Mrs Parker Brown-Stope lent across and patted Clayton on his thigh reluctant to release her hold; a flirtatious smile crossed her features coupled with a silent invitation. Clayton ignored her advance.

Clayton Thornton was a metallurgist, late of the Royal Flying Corps, while Lord Bruce's youngest son, Merrick: a young man with a shock of red hair, being wiry and ungainly like his mother Constance, and whose sole interest was photography, was an official photographer attached to the War Department. His role had been to capture the war on celluloid for the war chronicles. At the cessation of hostilities, he succumbed under pressure and was given public relations as his portfolio and the responsibility that went with such a position. Together they would report on the validity of Lord Anthony's information.

Lord Bruce informed his sons of the immense responsibility the consortium was placing in them to complete this covert operation to beat their competitors, and of the confidence the firm had in their ability to get the job done. The meeting adjourned some two hours later after Sir James Loxton outlined a modus operandi for the venture. The minutes of this special meeting were compiled in Sir James's hand and filed away under lock and key.

<>

Clayton made his travel arrangements for Australia in the same professional way he led his squadron into battle. Along with Merrick he pondered for several days how they could find Hopkins Mountain Range in the shortest possible time given so little information. The Northern Territory was shown on this latest map of Australia, first chartered and drawn by the English navigator Matthew Flinders in 1814. However, not much else in the way of cities or towns, nor was the Margaret River and certainly no mention was made of the huge cattle stations. They too were non-existent. Yet they were expected to find these places and secure holdings for the Consortium. Finally, he decided upon using an aeroplane. Merrick was excited when his brother explained he would be responsible for taking aerial photographs of the terrain so Mount Hopkins could be identified and maps made for future reference.

Clayton, after consultation and approval from a specially convened lunch attended by himself, Merrick, their father, and Lord Anthony, finally gained approval to crate an aeroplane and have it shipped to Fremantle on the West Australian coast. Lord Anthony felt it to be extravagant. However, he was prepared to endorse the attempt, *anything to stop that Carter chap from gaining influence which could see the colony Australia alienated from Great Britain,* he informed them. It was emphasised by his Lordship however, they must evaluate the worth of the venture. Hopkin's Mountain must be all it purported to be. Afterwards, a cable must immediately be sent to the home office advising of their success whereupon funds would be forwarded to purchase immediately. Both men nodded their understanding for the undertaking, Clayton for the responsibility of his role and Merrick for the pending adventure.

Sir Bruce would consult with the ministry, re-purchase of one of their recently acquired Fokker DVII biplane, after Clayton insisted on this particular aircraft. German in design, the Fokker was the only plane to be turned over to the victorious allies on the cessation of hostilities as part of the Armistice Agreement. Powered by the ubiquitous 160 horsepower Mercedes engines, the Fokker had a top speed of 120 miles per hour, not quite as fast as some of the allied aircrafts, but a very forgiving aircraft with good manoeuvrability, Clayton had argued, and ideal for aerial photography as far as Merrick Thornton was concerned. Clayton explained by dismantling the wings from their struts, he would be able to ship the aircraft in two large wooden crates. He proposed to use one of the company's ships en-route to Australia to ship baled wool for the purpose. The remaining cargo would more than pay for the time and cost Clayton had informed an anxious Lord Anthony. He envisaged one slight delay to his plans and paused to be sure the others fully understood.

Enjoying his sumptuous lunch, a fork full of medium rare fillet steak about to enter his cavernous mouth, Lord Bruce was want to ask. 'A slight delay?'

'I have never flown a Fokker Father.'

'You have not flown the damn thing!' Lord Anthony leaned forward across the table, the gold watch concealed in his fob pocket making contact with the edge of the table in a soft clang, his features set in a mask of contempt.

'I'm certain Clayton could fly the biplane with a few practice sessions,' Merrick supported his brother nervously.

'Yes, rather, I selected the plane because of its ease of flying. What I meant was, the signage is German and where we are going, I shouldn't imagine there would be any landing strips, open paddocks I should think. So I need to put in a few landings on some of our rougher fields.'

'If you're lucky,' grinned Merrick referring to the open paddocks, which made his freckles more pronounced.

'I would like to spend some time familiarising myself with the Fokker and that's that!' Clayton paused to look about the table to a general nod of agreement if begrudgingly from Lord Anthony.

'Also I want Merrick to accompany me once I get the knack of it so he can take some photographs from the air and work out the best technique.'

'How long?' His Lordship was brusque.

'Oh, say two weeks at the most. Does that suit you Merrick?'

'Rather.'

'One more thing gentlemen, I'd like to request two personnel to join the group.'

'Go on Clayton,' Lord Bruce got out before Lord Anthony could interject again.

'My squadron engineer Freddy Moylan, first class chap, can strip a motor and put it back together again in the dark. He also knows how to tune carbies.'

'Carbies?'

'Carburettors Father.' Merrick, chastised him.

'And?' Encouraged Lord Anthony, wiping a crust from the sleeve of his suit.

'Reginald Bundy my former physical training sergeant, just in case there is a bit of rough stuff, jolly good at settling arguments is Reggie, if you get my meaning.'

'You have until the fifteenth of next month young man. Assuming your father can persuade the ministry to sell the company... A... what was it again?'

'A Fokker,' reiterated Merrick.

'Yes, the fifteenth! Time is of the essence.' Lord Anthony resumed eating his smoked salmon with a certain relish now his plans were in place.

'And should you meet with any opposition, you are to crush it!' Lord Anthony was thinking of the American Jack Carter. His lunch finished, he rose to leave. He didn't particularly like hare-brained schemes however, he had to admit Clayton's idea had some merit. There were some things he liked about the young man, mores the pity Chester wasn't off fighting the war and Libby organised for Katrina to marry Clayton. But then Clayton held no title not being the eldest.

Chapter 12

Edge Rock, Western Australia

When a dishevelled and dusty Doctor Clayton Andrews returned to Edge Rock three days after delivering the Cotter's baby, it was to discover he had a visitor. Jack had made himself at home opening the windows to air the place through and to let some light into the dim interior of the old slab dwelling with its galvanised iron roof. He had found a millet broom and dusted the place, washed the windows, which were covered in cobwebs and wind-blown dust, deciding Andrews, wasn't exactly house-proud.

Andrews, lean and spry for his fifty-five years, wasn't entirely surprised and gave the young man a toothy grin while extending his hand. In a short while they were talking like old friends, and Jack could only respect the old man and appreciate his hospitality.

'So you'll be off as soon as young Mike arrives I gather?' Doc commenced to set the table offering Jack another long neck.

'I want to look the property over before making a commitment Doc.' Jack replied truthfully, accepting the beer.

'And if the iron is as rich as the samples suggest?' Doc left the way clear for the younger man to reveal his thoughts.

'Then I'll sink my last dollar into the formation of a company. Australia is large enough to support heavy industry. Wouldn't you agree?'

'Never gave it much thought but yes, I do agree.'

'Doc I've been wanting to ask you a question… '

'Fire away.'

'The Englishman who owns the club up the street… '

'Pommy Harry,' Doc cut in brushing a hand across his groomed moustache.

'What do you know about him?' Jack rested his hand around the bottle, his thumb wiping the droplets of water down its long neck to the table-top where a ring of water was forming.

'Millicent Taylor runs the post office, she handles all the mail in and out of the district when she's not down at the school teaching. She has been getting mail for Pommy Harry now for about eighteen years. Initially she returned the first letters to the sender… ' he paused.

'Nobody had ever heard of Harry Street. Shortly they were back again with a cover letter explaining that when the party was ready, he would make an appearance to collect his mail. Millicent has been keeping them safe for Harry ever since.'

'How often did the letters arrive?'

'Oh about every six months. Must have been money because shortly after Harry arrived, he was approaching the town's council for permission to build that whorehouse.' Doc indicated with his thumb over his shoulder in the general direction of the club.

'Anyway, why the interest in Pommy Harry?' Doc was curious. He broke an egg, then another into the cast iron pan. They hissed in the hot fat. With a skillet handy he moved their steaks to one side, making room for the runny eggs.

Jack explained while turning the bottle around on its base.

'You divulged to this Lord Anthony your plans for the future.' Doc said knowingly, expertly turning the eggs with the skillet.

'Yes. Doc I have to get my hands on that blasted paper!'

'You asked Harry could you read the paper after he'd finished with it?'

'Yes and he refused, much to my surprise. I was willing to compensate him for it?'

'Sounds about right for Pommy Harry.' Doc shook his head. 'But Australia is twelve thousand miles away from the old dart, I don't know what you are so upset about Jack.'

Jack sighed deciding he would have to reveal more than he intended, 'Lord Anthony is an aristocrat, a shipping magnate and a war-monger. I understand from what I read that he has completed a merger with another company who specialise in making steel. That was as much of the article as I was able to read before Harry returned and admonished me. Now if his lordship remembered my revelation, he would know exactly where to get enough raw materials to monopolise the industry, possibly commence his own steel producing plant here in Australia, a subsidiary of the mother company. Correct me if I am wrong, but isn't the east Australian coast a continuous coal seam?'

Doc nodded, his attention for serving their plates with hot food. 'So you're worried, he will take it into his head to investigate your story and establish his own company here in Australia.'

Jack shrugged, 'the war is over Doc, the world is crying out for the new technology it generated: automobiles, locomotives, ships, boiler plate, farming machinery, and so on.'

'Well I guess your right Jack. I suppose if reading a six-month-old newspaper will put your mind at rest then you should burgle his bloody whorehouse and be done with it! Let's eat before the flies beat us to it.'

< >

Clarrie Ferguson bar manager of the Ocean View Club left the crowded bar and bounded up the stairs two at a time. He wrapped his knuckles against Harry Street's door urgently once, then again with more vigour, as he realised no response.

'Enter!' Came a deep articulate voice from the other side of the solid timber door.

Clarrie let himself in. He advanced on the desk where Harry was seated counting the weekly taking. The rosewood pedestal desk was littered with notes and silver of various denominations. It was the only furniture in the room of two building squares apart from three matching floral-covered chairs, Harry's leather high back chair, a portrait of some decadent, sporting a monocle and a gold tooth, a half corner dresser upon which was a large glass pitcher always full of water, and an enamel hand basin and towel. Clarrie knew as soon as Harry had finished counting, he would rinse and wipe his hands, as though he despised handling the currency and Clarrie felt the man's actions defied logic, money was money as far as Clarrie was concerned.

'Boss!' Began a nervous Clarrie, nervous because he well-remembered his first encounter with Harry. Clarrie had introduced himself and Harry had immediately insisted on calling him Clarence and Clarrie resented it whereupon Harry struck him flush on the jaw and Clarrie agreed when he regained consciousness, this one man could call him Clarence, but God help any of the others in Harry's employ who might get smart, and that included Lenny, a known local bar-room brawler and employee.

'Clarence, you really must learn to leave me in peace when I am totalling the weekly taking. Now get out of here and let me finish my counting. While you are about it, you may light the lantern,' he requested, flipping through a pile of notes a second time before

59

recording the figure in a leather bound ledger with a thin red ribbon that allowed correct page selection.

'But boss,' Clarrie tried again. 'We've got a live one down stairs, a pigeon,' he protested, adjusting the lighted wick and setting the coal oil lamp on the desk, careful to place the chequered cloth under its polished base so it would not mark or burn the desk top. Harry was very particular about such things.

The vernacular was lost on Harry. 'What in blazes are you mumbling about?' Harry paused, his pen poised long enough to glare up at his bar manager.

The look of exasperation would have been enough to convince Clarrie at any other time. However, he remembered an earlier experience he shared with Harry which convinced him Harry wanted wealth, so did Clarrie, but Harry had the finance so necessary to support such ventures or so Clarrie believed. Harry had become really excited when he thought an acquaintance of Clarrie's had struck it rich south of Kununurra. Harry offered to finance the venture, it turned out the diamonds was only industrial quality and Harry could not hide his disappointment. Now as then Clarrie saw an opportunity but he would need Harry to finance the deal, they would both be rich. However, how did one convince the well-groomed Englishman?

'Please boss, listen to me... ' He pleaded.

'Oh what is the use?' An irritated Harry shrugged. He swivelled in his chair reaching into a drawer producing a revolver. 'If you are not out of here in the time it takes me to cock this firearm… whatever it is you are raving about, must wait! Is that understood?' He brandished the ugly weapon in Clarrie's direction.

'Gold boss, gold!' Clarrie got out, stumbling over the Axminster rug in his haste to reach the door.

'Just a minute, what was that you said… gold?' Clarrie could only nod, he was looking into the loosely held gaping rounded bore of a .455 calibre colt as Harry rounded the desk in one swift movement.

Clarrie palmed the nugget before placing it on Harry's desk.

'Gold.' Harry absently turned and placed the revolver on the desk before picking up the nugget and weighing it in his palm, Clarence momentarily forgotten.

'Yes boss,' wailed Clarrie.

'Go on.' Soothed Harry, returning to his chair. Absently, he removed a tightly rolled piece of paper from the barrel of the weapon. Harry always kept the round under the hammer empty. He used the space to hide the written combination to the wall safe, hidden behind the grinning features of the moustached gentleman sporting a monocle and a solid gold tooth.

Clarrie gaped, wiped the sweat from his brow before explaining how he gave the stranger fifty English Pounds from the till in exchange for the gold nugget and how he was now, downstairs playing cards with Flash Bill, Toad, and Lenny McPherson. All locals who did odd jobs for Harry from time to time.

'Fifty Pounds! You gave him fifty Pounds of my money!' Harry's voice rose in pitch to suit his wrath for Clarrie's indulgence.

'Well boss I figured the nugget to be worth more than that.'

'And what makes you such an astute judge of the price of gold Clarence?' Was Harry's snide re-joinder.

'Hell I figured... ' Harry stopped him with a raised hand.

'All right, enough!' Harry exclaimed.

'He has a poke full of gold boss.'

'Hmm… go downstairs, keep him playing,' instructed Harry, and after some deliberation, 'get the locals out a little early this evening, oh, and no visitors upstairs, have the girls retired early, you do understand?'

Clarrie reached across the desk for the nugget.

'Leave the gold Clarence.'

'Yes boss,' scowled Clarrie, scurrying from the room to do Harry's bidding.

With trembling fingers Harry opened the safe. He was unable to contain his rising excitement, at last, this may be the opportunity he had been waiting for and he would make the most of the occasion. He stuffed the currency along with the ledger into the gaping hole and turned the handle listening to the chambers locking into place. Hurriedly, he wrote the new combination and slid the cylinder of paper into the barrel of the revolver. He returned the weapon to the drawer, taking the time to lock it.

Shortly, catching Clarrie's attention, Harry indicated for him to clear the bar, the locals by this time having had a skinful anyway. The card game was still in progress, and it looked like the stranger was doing the plucking if one could gauge the look on Johnny Stool's features.

'Time gentlemen please,' Clarrie called.

'Gentlemen, it looks as though we are being evicted,' quipped Homer B. Jones grinning at *Toad,* (Johnny Stool) and Flash, so called because of his fancy clothing. The prospector commenced to gather in his winnings.

'Not you sir,' Harry addressed him. 'That was only for the drunks, please, finish your game.'

When they had the bar area to themselves, it only took Harry minutes to extract the information he required from the now luckless miner. Begrudgingly, not wanting to be struck again by Clarence, he handed the poke to Harry, but not before concealing a nugget for himself in a diversionary ploy during a fit of coughing blood over the barroom floor. At the Englishman's insistence, he drew a fabricated map of the gold's location. Armed with this information Harry ordered Lenny McPherson, accompanied by a caste who hung about the place, and the miner, to a place called the Red Mountain part of the Hopkins Range, to verify the information.

61

Chapter 13

Roxburgh House

It wasn't unusual for Lord Chester Thornton to come home on those weekends he knew he would be playing host. He was affectionate and flirted incessantly with Katrina, very conscious that he had married one of the most desirable women in all of England, never missing the opportunity to show others that he Chester Thornton won the hand of Katrina Anthony where many other suitors had failed, and Chester knew that Derek for one, envied him. This particular weekend he seemed very excited about something and couldn't wait to share his news with Katrina and their guests. Two of his cousins with their husbands were down for the weekend, Chester having promised Sam and Derek some excellent fishing on the Saturday and then a fox hunt after church on Sunday.

'You are looking at the next vice-chairman,' he blurted with a mouthful of quail.

Katrina let her spoon slide back into the turtle soup and looked inquisitively at Chester.

'Oh, that is good news darling,' she played her dutiful part.

'Yes, rather sudden really,' Chester continued when he had their undivided attention.

'Clayton and Merrick have been sent to Australia of all places,' he shook his leonine head, a smirk implanted on his features.

'I say old boy, why are they sending them to the antipodes?' Derek asked in all innocence although he could hardly contain his curiosity.

'Why they robbed a bank of course,' Sam replied in a gravelly voice, consequence of a recent mouth operation to remove a decayed molar, unable to stop a chortle escaping his diaphragm.

'Did they get life Chester?' Derek laughed, wiping a curly lock of hair aside.

'Why are they being sent to Australia Chester?' Katrina cut across their ebullient banter to focus a worried look on her husband.

'To establish a steelworks apparently.' Chester fixed his attention on her.

'A steelworks! Daddy detests Australia, why would he contemplate, indeed, sanction such action?' Katrina was bemused.

'Because he likes to make money,' suggested Derek, looking about the table with a smirk. Derek was a chartered accountant, middle aged, small and portly in statue but with a sharp and calculating mind.

Chester ignored the mocking remark, his mind was focused, maybe now he could get Katrina to admit her knowing the American to be more than just a hospital flirtation. 'You would remember that chap you nursed over in France during the beastly war? Carter?' Katrina felt something tug at her innards; she tried to remain calm, outwardly indifferent. However, the mere mention of the name sent goose bumps up and down her spine. She nodded giving the soup her undivided attention, silently willing him to go on while unable to hide a tell-tale rash that suddenly appeared down the side of her neck.

Chester smiled, he had touched a nerve. 'Well, it appears as though he found a mountain of iron-ore and your father is determined to take it from him,' Chester's voice tried to hide any sarcasm, while his eyes gave Katrina close scrutiny, she never looked up. Often, Chester believed Katrina's relationship with the American to be more than nurse and patient. Several times he had asked himself since their meeting why the man was at the house particularly if Katrina were away, it didn't make sense. And why was Sedgwick so intent on crushing him, a man he had described as sick in the mind?

Katrina wanted to excuse herself, her first reaction to pick up the telephone and plead with her father not to sanction buying the mountain; then she realised she would be playing into Chester's hand. She knew he felt there had been a relationship between her and the American, and she may have let slip a word or sentence which may have aroused his suspicions, particularly when they were fighting and she was trying to hurt him as much as he was hurting her with his verbal abuse. Instead, she would attack the situation.

'Father, revealed to you he was going to buy the Hopkins Range?'

'So you are familiar with the American's ambitions?' Chester glared at her from the other end of the long rectangular table, his guests forgotten as his jealousy surfaced.

Katrina gathered herself, 'why yes he was joining an Australian, Michael Smith, in a joint venture as I was given to understand.' Katrina sipped on the soup even though she nearly choked.

'Vice chairman, does that mean you won't be traipsing all over the kingdom from now on?' Sam, tall and slim with long jawline fashionable sideburns, smiled at Katrina as he spoke, it was common knowledge the pair did not enjoy a good marital relationship and many were the discussions between Sam and Derek that Lady Katrina and Lord Chester Thornton would annul their marriage.

'Well it's not certain just yet, actually you are the first to be told and I would appreciate your confidentiality until it becomes official.'

'Who else could they give it to with both Clayton and Merrick in Australia?' Supported Derek.

'Yes I suppose you are right,' Chester was sorry now he had spoken out, maybe the position would remain unfilled in which case he had just made a right fool of himself.

For Katrina the weekend was the longest of her life, she made her decision while folding her dinner napkin after Chester's revelation. She would speak with Sir James Loxton as soon as possible. Father, would only fob her off. The Hopkins Mountain Range was Jack's dream; she would not let her father take that away from him.

Chapter 14

Edge Rock, Western Australia

Receiving word of Jack's arrival, Mike Smith quickly made his way to Edge Rock only to find Jack, accompanied by a guide had gone exploring along the coast. Doc Andrews wasn't perturbed, even if it meant Mike may have to wait a few days before renewing his friendship with the American. The truth of the matter was Doc wanted to have a quiet word with young Smith, alone, so he welcomed the timely arrival of his former boarder and Jack's sojourn up the coast. When Mike was settled in his old room where he boarded during his school days and Doc had opened a couple of long necks, Doc broached his concerns.

'Jack seems in a hurry to look over the old Hopkins place.' He began.

'That reminds me, I brought the ore samples with me. I knew he'd want to see them.' Mike was looking about the small dwelling. 'Doc is Katrina with Jack?'

'Katrina? No,' Doc shook his head. 'He's alone.'

'Something must have gone wrong, I felt certain Katie would be here.'

'I'm worried about Jack's ambitions; I want a word with you while he's not about.'

'As you like,' but it was obvious Mike was pondering what had happened. He felt certain they would have married, he had hoped to be best man but realised under the circumstances that was out of the question.

'Jack is a very ambitious young man Mike,' began Doc, pausing to swill on his beer while it was still cold.

'What has he been saying?'

'He intends to build an empire, not cattle, steel.'

'Yeah, I told him about the Hopkins place. I thought we could run it as a property.' Mike sat forlornly on the chair his attention to removing his riding boots.

'Clem isn't getting any younger.'

'Yeah. I opened my trap. Now I'm committed Doc. Besides, Clem's got a good crew working for him.' Mike did not elaborate that the property was to be run by Gavin, his elder brother. Not that the pair did not get along just that they had different ideas on how the property should be managed. It was one of the reasons Mike sought the adventure of war. Gavin being ten years older felt his loyalty was to his father and so stayed to work the property even if it were very patriotic to enlist and fight for the cause.

'You sure as hell are committed. Do you know what you are getting yourself into young man?'

'Not exactly, just that Jack and I are mates.' Mike shrugged.

'Well he's sinking his inheritance into this venture boy and then some if I'm any judge. He is an angry young man, mark my words.'

'Must be something to do with Katrina Doc, they were sweethearts I fully expected her to be here?'

'Who's this Lord Anthony he's dirty on?'

'I don't know, unless he is some relation of Katie.'

'Well he's hell bent on getting his hands on a newspaper Harry Street has in his possession. Whatever he read sure has him worried.'

'I don't know what you are talkin' about Doc,' Mike shook his head.

'Hmm, very well but you be careful Mike, there's a lot of hate in that young man and I don't want to see you get hurt.'

'Hell Doc he's my mate. If he's got a fight with Street or some Lord then so have I.' Mike stared at the practitioner anew.

'I'm not saying he's not a good bloke, I'm simply saying he's very ambitious and this determination might lead to trouble. Hell boy, what do you know about making steel?'

'Nothing sir, but I'm sure Jack will know enough for both of us.'

'Anyway, I thought old Lloyd was going to hold that property for his step son, young McTaggart.'

'It was for sale Doc; you know that.'

'Yes but a man can change his mind. And old Lloyd is a good field man. If he knew there was a range of iron on the property, he may not wish to sell the place.'

'A risk we have to take Doc,' replied a worried young Smith.

'So you are going to go along with Jack on this venture. Live another man's dream, support his ambition?'

'Hell Doc it isn't like that at all. I'll develop the place. A working cattle station; it may take years before we are equipped to produce iron.'

'And iron isn't any good on its own, steel is what the world will be crying out for.' Doc quipped.

Two days later, the front door swung in and a sunburnt Jack Carter entered the room more than pleased with his sojourn to the mouth of Queens Channel. Their greeting for one another was genuine and warm, like lovers they clasped each other dancing about the room in their joy. Jack was the bigger by a good two inches, strong and muscular, while Mike was the more graceful on his feet. Shortly they stood apart looking at one another exchanging jibes in good fun until Doc got their attention by opening three cold long necks and they sat with him around the kitchen table. Finally it got the better of Mike and he asked after Katrina and was told she would not be joining them, Jack was not disposed to talk about Katrina. Mike, feeling he may not want to speak in front of Doc, nodded in understanding, even if he didn't comprehend. Talk turned to why Jack was here and shortly Mike handed him the samples whereupon he nearly fell out of his chair with excitement. Katrina buried for the moment in that abyss of his creation. He explained his intention of rummaging through Harry Street's office and that he wanted to know if Mike would support him whereupon the young Australian declared his proclivity much to Jack's relief. Jack told how he had revealed to Lord Anthony his plans for the future.

'Lord Anthony?'

'Katrina's father,' Jack expanded.

'You're joking.' Jack shook his head but did not expand on his statement, which worried Doc Andrews as he felt Mike was entitled to an explanation.

It was further evidence as far as Doc was concerned that Jack Carter was self-centred and Mike was being manoeuvred to suit his aspirations. Was he truly concerned about Mike or was ambition overriding? Only time would tell whether he was right and whether Mike would become his own man.

< >

Jack and Mike stood inside the entry letting their eyes accustom to the darkness before making their way stealthily up the stairs to the top floor. Once outside Harry's office, Jack tried the lock but the door would not give under his touch. He gave Mike a cursory glare as if to say Harry didn't trust the locals and Smith grinned in the darkness. He thrust Jack out of the way, producing his pouch knife and shortly fitted the blade into the narrow opening pushing down on the lock with all his might. There came a sound, which seemed deafening within the confines of the building and both men froze, sure they would be discovered. A minute passed. They waited flattened against the wall tense, sweating profusely anticipating the sound of a door opening and the flicker of a candle spilling a glow along the blackened corridor. With the passage of time and no evidence that they were discovered, Mike turned the handle and the door gave under his touch. A musty paper smell greeted them as they filed through the aperture, closing the door quietly behind them. Mike discovered the lantern and while he lit the lamp, Jack pushed the towel from the dresser under the door to prevent light being seen from the corridor, after which the search began in earnest. The desk drawers were also locked and Jack requested Mike's knife. He held the top drawer down with all his weight, placing the blade into the cavity and over the top of the moveable brass plate forcing downwards as he did. The clasp gave under pressure. Jack silently slid the drawer open to reveal several letters, a thick ledger, but no Financial Review newspaper. During the repeat process to open the side drawers, the steel blade broke with a sudden piercing sound which both men swore would be heard down on the docks. Jack froze. Mike extinguished the lamp throwing the room into darkness.

It wasn't uncommon for Harry to be woken by noises during the night, the creak of timbers, the iron roof cooling, customers with the girls, or a drunk singing in the alleyway. Now, fully awake, Harry removed the eye patches. He pulled his frame to a sitting position and the four-poster bed minutely creaked its protest. Harry listened intently for some moments for the sound to repeat itself. It was several minutes before he heard another noise not unlike the ring of steel. Not that Harry could distinguish what made the noise only that it came from his office. Swiftly for a big man, Harry thrust the mosquito netting aside and danced to his feet. Silently, he let himself into the corridor. He stood outside his office certain someone was inside; he could smell the fumes from the coal oil lamp. Harry shouldered the door while turning the knob just in case someone was leaning against the other side and using his weight to advantage. The door swung inwards, Harry briskly closed it behind him standing with his back against its timbers to survey the room bathed in the beams of moonlight from the double doors.

'Light the lamp please so that I might see the face of thieves and first class scoundrels.'

'Do as he says Mike,' sighed Jack.

With the lamp lit Harry squinted against the sudden glare. 'You,' he said at length addressing Jack.

'Good evening Mister Street,' Jack replied using all the composure he could muster.

'And to what do I owe this unexpected visit. A thief in the night, and his accomplice,' he turned to look at Mike Smith.

'Mister Street it's not what it seems... '

'Oh, it isn't, well constable Mountier will be very interested to hear your account.' Harry rocked back and forth on the balls of his feet.

'Sir, I needed to see the contents of the paper you were reading the other day.'

'The same day you were an honest customer, willing to pay for your drink?' Smirked Harry, enjoying himself.

'The same.' Was the candid reply.

'And what was so important about my private mail, if a piece of news copy?'

'It made mention of Lord Anthony, of the merger between himself and some steel company.' Jack decided the truth may be the best option under the circumstances and did he detect a slight tightening of facial muscles in the otherwise deadpan expression.

'Oh that article,' Harry nodded. 'Pray tell what possible interest a scoundrel like yourself could have in such concerns?'

'That is my business. Look, all I want is to read your paper. I'll willingly pay you for the privilege.' Harry shook his head and Jack could feel his anger rising.

'I think it is a reasonable request under the circumstances... ' Mike supported Jack. Harry turned on him, 'Who asked you?'

But Mike was not flustered by the man's petulance. 'You look vaguely familiar.'

'I was thinking the same thing,' supported Jack before Harry could frame a reply.

'Nonsense, I've never laid eyes on either of you before the other day when this brazen fellow stole my news copy.' Harry pointed an accusing finger at Jack. 'Now he is at it again.' Harry moved away from the door and strode purposefully around his desk elbowing Mike out of his way and well satisfied when he could see the side drawer where he kept copies of the financial review was still intact.

'I need to see that paper, my whole future may depend upon it,' Jack thumped a closed fist against the desk-top.

'Yours and mine both old boy.' Harry didn't elaborate. 'However, your immediate future depends on you leaving my room now and we will forget this incident ever happened.' Harry locked his eyes to the tall American.

'Mike I'll meet you back at Doc's place.' Jack addressed Smith while his eyes never left those of Harry.

Not our... my, Mike tucked this knowledge away, maybe Doc understood the American better than he ever would. 'Are you sure you know what you are doing?' Mike gave him a sullen glare.

'Yes, Mister Street and I have to settle this.' Impatiently they waited until Smith closed the door behind him.

The American had given the first indication he knew more than he was presently revealing and this worried Harry; there were questions he wanted to ask, it was written in his eyes. 'Queensberry rules suit you, old boy?'

Jack nodded. If he had to fight this man to get the paper and answers to some puzzling questions, then so be it. It was Mike who confirmed what Jack now believed. The man before him was Harrison Anthony, Katrina's brother, not dead after all. Jack watched while Harry felt under the desk and produced a key. He unlocked the drawer feeling inside before producing the copy of the Financial Review Jack remembered from the other day. The broken knife blade he distastefully deposited in a cane paper basket, which was located under the pedestal of the desk. Looking Jack directly in the eye and with some semblance of a smirk, a loosening of flesh at the corners of his mouth, Harry placed the review on the top of the desk and stepped away.

'To the winner the spoils.' Harry's actions were goaded by instinct; he realised if he could knock the American senseless he would not have to answer questions he felt sure the young man wished to ask.

Jack was wary. He had to assume Street was a clever adversary. He estimated the man would weigh around two hundred pounds, maybe a shade heavier. The night-dress pronounced a little midriff bulge, he appeared flabby around the jowls, but his breathing was even and he moved on the balls of his feet, like a cat, smooth and deadly. He proceeded to circle Jack in a manner which suggested he had been taught to box. They were both big men, evenly matched if one forgot that Harry was Jack's senior by sixteen years. His stance was that of a bare-knuckle fighter, his right foot well forward, as was his right hand, fists bunched, his left hand protecting his face.

Carter was quick; he jabbed with the right hand and learnt his first lesson. Harry was no gentleman. Leaning back from the jab, he lashed out with his foot catching the younger man with a cruel blow to the groin, his eyes never leaving those of Jack. His features were chiselled from stone, a dead pan, only the brown eyes came alive as he concentrated, waiting for Carter's next move, content to let the younger man bring the fight to him. He watched the American fight for breath. He saw tears of hurt in his eyes and witnessed beads of sweat suddenly appear on his brow as the tan left his features.

Beneath his clothing Carter felt hot and clammy from the shock of the blow, pain was secondary to the feeling of dizziness. His throat was dry, his eyes misted. Slowly, almost doubled over, he backed away fighting the giddiness, his brain telling him to keep moving, regardless of how wobbly his legs may feel. Cautiously, Street followed him and Jack waited. Then without warning he dived at him, deciding attack may be his best form of defence, besides, Street wasn't going anywhere.

As expected Harry stepped back, his heels catching the chair Mike had moved to one side of the desk. Unbalanced, he fell backwards. Harry met the carpeted rug with Jack's two hundred pounds of brawn and muscle on top of him and it was the Englishman's turn to realise the power behind that body. Here the speed and strength of Jack asserted themselves and all Harry could do was try and ward off as many blows as possible.

'Let me on my feet so we can fight like men instead of dogs grovelling on the ground,' Harry tried to push him away.

'Still Queensberry rules? Old boy!' Jack mocked, before obliging.

Both men stood toe to toe slugging one another, their breathing coming in gasps, chests heaving, each trying to punch the other harder, most of their blows glancing off arms or elbows as they covered up. Sweat glistened on every part of exposed flesh. Their legs were leaden. They were unable to avoid the other's punches. Several times they sank to the carpet, one or the other offering a snide remark, which willed them back to their feet, neither escaping the blood-letting. It was Harry who finally sagged to his knees unable to rise. Jack stood over him swaying on his feet.

'Come on, you pommy bastard, you aren't finished yet are you?' He began to pull Harry to his feet using his nightshirt as leverage.

Realising the Englishman was wavering on the point of unconsciousness, he released him letting him sag back against the wall. He grabbed for a water pitcher on the corner dresser and poured its contents over him before retiring to a chair and lowering himself into it, every part of his body tingling with his exertions, until Harry stirred and began to take an active interest in his surroundings. Jack beckoned him to get to his feet.

'Come on, we are not finished by a long shot.'

Harry said nothing, slowly he moved away from the wall and again they exchanged blows. There was no power in Harry's punches whereas Jack had found a new strength with his determination to have Harry, answer his questions. His blows jarred Harry. He was hurt, gasping to breathe. Still Jack hit him with powerful blows, driven by hate for the man he believed sired Harry and all he purported to be. Harry was propped by the wall, slowly he sank to the floor, hands limp by his sides, and Jack hit him again and again, until something made him stop. He stood panting over the Englishman, hands shaking, heart pumping, thumping beneath his breast-bone. Slowly, he carried his heavy body back to the chair, afraid that if he didn't sit down he would fall down, his legs were leaden. He looked at his skinned knuckles when he was able and rubbed his sleeve across his face only to see the fabric stained with blood, lots of blood; his blood. There was an enamel bowl on the dresser, it contained some water, slowly Jack moved to it sluicing his face several times before dabbing the tender skin on the towel he recovered from near the door. He heard Harry stir. Grabbing the bowl, tottery legs carried him to the prone form where he threw the bloodied water over Harry. Harry didn't move. Carter sank to his knees studying Harry for a long time. Certain in his own mind he was Harrison Anthony.

Impatiently, Jack rose and moved away. Harry gave a grunt, then another, Jack turned from the window where he had been watching lightning flickering across the night sky somewhere over the Indian Ocean, preluding a storm at sea. Harry raised himself on one elbow, then the other, grimacing with pain for the effort.

Jack went to him, 'have you got anything to drink up here?'

'Brandy, bottom drawers of the desk,' was the faint reply.

Jack also found glasses and filled two of them to the brim. Harry pulled himself to a sitting position, his back resting against the white painted plaster, one hand absently feeling for the six-inch skirting board, which bore against the base of his spine. Painfully, he eased away until his shoulders made full contact with the wall, it taking his weight. He watched disinterestedly Jack's approach with the brandy.

Jack handed Harry the glass of brandy. 'Where did you get the ring?' He tried not to show any special interest, but the question was not lost on Harry. Harry detected the interest in the man's voice.

'Why?'

Jack hesitated, fully realising that any line of questioning would be useless unless Harry wished to cooperate, and then he could be telling a pack of lies. Jack decided he would reveal what he knew; hopefully it would be enough to invite the truth. He hesitated for a long swallow, the brandy caught his breath, stung his cut and swollen mouth, tore at his gullet and caused a fire in his chest before finally warming his stomach.

'Whew!' He got out. 'I believe I am familiar with the crest on your ring.' Glimpsing a flicker of expression cross the dead-pan features he pressed on. 'I met a family in England, during the war, the crest on your ring is their banner. Anthony is their name. Lord Anthony of Bedfordshire is his title. They have a daughter, a very beautiful woman.'

'Katrina... ' Jack caught the hoarse whisper. The Englishman stared into space, his mind cast back to that morning on the lawns of their stately Bedfordshire mansion.

At age twenty-four, the ring fitted perfectly the index finger for which it had been designed. It had been especially crafted for Harry prior to his departure for Africa, where he was to follow in the tradition of his ancestors and uphold the family name and honour. That morning with their ghosts beaming down on him from above, Harry was immensely proud. He remembered little Katie, just five year's old holding onto his hand, only breaking the grip when her governess ushered her away so the Royal's photographer might focus on his subject. The uniform was hand tailored from the finest cloth money could buy. The hand spun golden thread that formed the braid on his shoulders, cap and waist sash, glistened in the crisp autumn sunshine. He remembered Katie crying, reaching out for him and his promise to bring her home something special from South Africa. If only he had known what the future held for him, Harry thought to himself. In that instant his life flashed before his eyes. Now there was another digging up the past.

'Yes,' continued Jack, 'she believes her brother is dead, but we know differently. Don't we Harrison?' Jack looked intently at Harry. He was not disappointed. Like an electric shock the look passed across Harry's features. Another might have missed it, but Jack was alert to the slight twitching at the corners of the mouth, besides he saw Harry's lips form Katrina's name, too much of a coincidence.

'I really do not know why you are telling me all this old boy, it has nothing to do with me,' said Harry, impassive features, his cold expressionless eyes holding those of Jack.

'Care for another?' Harry asked, pushing the empty tumbler towards him.

Jack grabbed the glass not saying a word. There was a new stirring of anger, evident in the way he took Harry's empty glass. Jack realised if he could get to the truth, this man may be able to explain so many things to him concerning Katrina that he found puzzling.

There were many questions to which he sought answers, had, over and over since that strange meeting with her parents.

With Harry swirling his recharged drink around in the tumbler Jack continued his story, outlining events in detail, from the time he first met Katrina until their parting in France, the card explaining his early arrival in England, his meeting with her parents and the letter addressed to him and left in the custody of her mother.

Harry sat brooding into yet another empty glass, as if it were a crystal ball. *First me, now Katie,* he told himself and it was that more than anything else which made him break his silence, for he owed this man nothing. 'You were a victim of Mother's scheming,' he said at last, his eyes not leaving the glass.

'What!' Uttered Jack, not really believing his good fortune.

'I said—'

'I heard what you said. Then you do not deny that you are that son, Harrison Anthony, supposedly buried somewhere in South Africa?'

Harry shrugged his shoulders and released a long breath. 'What does it matter?' He said at last. 'There are no witnesses, just you and myself. Naturally I would deny this conversation ever took place.'

'Why?' Jack was puzzled.

'You ask me why Mister… ' began Harry looking intently at Jack.

'Carter, Jack Carter.'

'I cannot say I am pleased to make your acquaintance Mister Carter.'

'Nor I yours now get on with it,' Jack's voice dropped in pitch to suit his wrath.

Harry ignored the curt reply, 'Because of the disgrace it would bring to my family.' He said at length while giving Carter a long silent stare, as if he were committing his features to memory for some later occasion more to his choosing.

'I don't understand.'

Harry grunted, he looked steadily at Jack for what seemed an eternity, pondering whether he could reveal the truth, and trust in this person's integrity.

'You love Katrina do you not?'

'Yes I do, but what has that got to do with anything?'

'Can I trust to your confidentiality?' Jack nodded moving to rest himself in the padded chair behind the desk.

'I live here not by choice. I was exiled, banished for all time, never to set a foot in my beloved England again, never to correspond with my family again, never to see my father, mother, or Katrina, ever again.' His voice lost some of its volume. 'Mister Carter. I am the perfect example of the dead living. If you would care to refill my goblet again, I will acquaint you with my story,' sighed Harry.

Chapter 15

Edge Rock, Western Australia

Harry smirked into his tumbler, 'I graduated from Sandhurst Military Academy. I was following in the footsteps of my grandfather; an officer and a gentleman,' His voice a mere whisper as he recalled the past, a past he had hoped to decimate from his memory. 'When war broke out in British South Africa, 11 October 1899, I held the rank of Lieutenant Colonel, attached to Lord Kitchener's personal staff.' Harry paused, reflecting.

'A small force of Australians and Rhodesians were posted to secure a crossing and supply depot on the Eland's River at Brakfontein in the Western Transvaal. They numbered five-hundred men, were equipped with a seven-pound muzzle-loading screw-gun, which was useless, and two Maxim machine guns. Opposed to them under General De La Rey was a Boer commando, an artillery force numbering upwards of three-thousand men with heavy Howitzer field guns, three Pom Poms (Vickers Nordenfelt), and a Maxim machine gun, not forgetting their bolt action Mauser carbines.' Harry hesitated to sup on his brandy.

'The colonials had barely settled into their defensive position to fortify the depot when the Boers took up position on the high bank on the opposite side of the river crossing. The Boers commanded a natural fortress atop the levee bank, which rose to approximately two-hundred feet above sea level. On the other hand, the site for the depot had been poorly chosen as the ground was virtually level and afforded little natural cover, apart from scattered kopje and some trees. The river was nearly half a mile away and all water had to be carried. That was the position on the fourth of August.' Harry paused again.

'Between then, and when I arrived with a column of cavalry four days later, more than fifteen-hundred shells had exploded in the colonial's laager. All the horses and transport animals had been killed by shell or rifle fire. There were many casualties. Many died. So I arrived to find a chaotic situation. A Colonel Hore, one arm shot away, his mind decayed with pain, stubbornly refused to surrender their position. In my better judgement, I called a cessation to the hostilities, ordering the immediate withdrawal of the colonials to a point out of range of the Boer's awesome fire power. The Australians point blank refused, telling me to go to buggery... they were an undisciplined lot!'

Jack waited for Harry to continue, watching the beads of his sweat run down his jowls over a dried, bloodied moustache, into the hairs of his chest, seeing him reliving this affront to his authority as senior officer commanding. *They may be undisciplined those Australians*, mused Jack, *but the men I encountered in France were the best fighters I have ever known.*

'Again I ordered their withdrawal,' said Harry, his voice a little above a whisper. 'Again they refused. Our arrival was the signal for renewed shelling and many of my direct command had their animals shot from under them. The looks on their faces told me they thought this disorderly rabble could go to buggery. Again, I ordered them away, threatening Colonel God damn Hore with my service revolver. I would have shot him too, only my horse was shot from under me and I fell from the saddle amidst their cheers, losing my revolver in doing so. Calmly, the bastard handed it to me, wiping the dust from

71

its workings on his breeches, I was furious and swore I would have him court-martialled. However, they would not budge. They had sworn to hold the position for Buller at all costs. You can see can you not. They gave me no choice. I was following orders. The situation was useless, eventually we rode away and left them,' finished Harry, eyes downcast, not able to look at the American. With unsteady hand he gulped at the brandy.

'Eight days later Lord Kitchener secured the river with a large force by attacking from behind the Boer lines. Hore was still at his post. Still commanding, oh God how I hated that man's guts,' cried Harry clenching the glass so hard that it exploded in his hand. But he was oblivious to the shards of glass, blood or any pain; nothing it seemed was going to stop the flow of his story.

'When Kitchener appraised the situation, I was called to give just cause for my actions. I explained that I was only following his orders. I thought that would be the end of it. It was not to be. I was served with a summons and confined to quarters until further notice. To my astonishment, I was asked to submit a full written report and shortly afterwards committed to trial, subsequently court-martialled and sentenced to be executed before a firing squad. The charge, cowardice in the face of the enemy! Through my father and his influence I was granted a pardon. The sentence, at Fathers' request, committed to a life in exile.'

'Do you know what the mongrels did to extradite me from the situation? They took some poor bastard from the cells, dressed him in my uniform, draped a hood over his head and shot him. The night before it happened they came and took my uniform, I wondered about that. The only conclusion I could reach was they considered me unworthy to die in the uniform of an officer and a gentleman. At daybreak the following morning I heard the firing squad and reasoned that that would be my fate the following day. I was dead! However unexpectedly, in the middle of the night I was whisked away and transported to the docks where a Dutch freighter impounded during the hostilities took me aboard. When I returned to England, I was confronted by my uncle, Sir James Loxton. I was not allowed to see my family, my passage already being arranged for Australia. A cable followed explaining that every six months I would receive an adequate sum deposited to a post office in a frightfully remote little coastal town, called Edge Rock.'

'Wait a minute, one minute, did you say Edge Rock?'

'Yes why?'

'So, that explains why they would be against me bringing Katrina to Australia. I told them Mike lived on a ranch, the nearest town being Edge Rock. They were frightened Katrina may have run into you. They couldn't afford that to happen at any cost, you are the skeleton in their closet, a well-kept secret which had to remain that way.' Jack was smiling with his summation; now he understood.

Harry looked up at Carter, 'Are you finished?' Jack nodded. 'I understand a headstone bearing my name can be found in the Durban military cemetery; so officially, I am dead Mister Carter. Cut off without a penny, no name, no title, never to sit in the House of Lords as my birthright decreed. Never to take my rightful place at a board meeting, never to be accorded the respect as head of one of Britain's oldest and distinguished families… I've been dead for years,' mumbled Harry at length, tears streaming down his face, the alcohol breaking through the hard rocklike exterior to reveal the man beneath.

Jack eased to a more comfortable position on the padded chair, not saying anything. He felt sudden remorse for the man, while not understanding why he gave in so easily. If the account Harry had given him was the truth, then why didn't he fight for justice?

'You still love your family?' He asked at length.

'I didn't think so, until now that is,' he sighed, a gut wrenching sigh.

'I've never spoken to anyone but Jonathon, a colleague,' Harry added for Jack's benefit. 'Not even Sir James,' he wiped his face and only then conscious that he was bleeding from the cut glass, allowed Jack to hand him the towel from the dresser.

'Don't you think that was rather stupid? Not telling your uncle your side of the happening?'

'My side of the happening! Oh my God that is laughable. I was made to be the scapegoat in an understanding between General Buller and Lord Kitchener!'

'How could that be?' Jack's curiosity was aroused again.

'My orders were from Kitchener direct, he specifically stated I was to report on the situation at Eland's River, at the Brakfontein crossing. We had received reports from a scouting party that there was heavy fire coming from that sector,' Harry further explained for Jack's benefit. 'It was routine. We were confirming information all the time of the Boer's actions. They were very hard to pin down, fighting running engagements, picking the place and time of their own choosing. Alas, Kitchener did not confer with Buller and Buller had ordered the mixed brigade to hold the supply depot at all cost, and to the last man. The mistake I made was placing my trust in Kitchener's hands. As, until sometime later he was still unaware that Buller had given the order to hold. When he did find out proceedings against me, had begun, it was too late for me and too late for him. He sided with Buller to save face; after all, what is a colonel in comparison to the Chief of Staff?'

Jack, rose slowly from his chair and moved to open the French doors, where could be heard the first rumblings of thunder like some distant cannon, followed by more flashes of lightning and more thunder. 'Wasn't there anything you could do?'

'You forget, I was an officer, and a gentleman, my first loyalty was to my commanding officer; I did not enter a defence. I honestly could not believe such a mountainous case was pending against me. I believed in Kitchener,' said Harry, a slur in his voice.

'You have never written your version of what transpired? Not even a note to your folks?' Jack was amazed to think the man had succumbed to this life of exile so diminutively.

'It would have appeared as sour grapes. My father would not have been suitably impressed. Besides, he bought the official transcript of the trial.'

'How did he manage that?' Again Jack was stupefied by yet this new turn of events.

'He donated a ship to the British Navy.'

'He did what? He's that rich?' Jack stood as though in a trance.

'Afraid so old boy.'

'The price of a gift, just to have a mistake squashed, quelled for all time,' Jack shook his head in disbelief.

Absently Harry nodded, his eyes cast to the floor, his mind wandering over their conversation. Jack was thinking, if they would do that to their only son then they would stoop to anything to be rid of him.

'All these years,' Harry said finally, 'all these years I have lived with a burning hate, coupled with hopelessness, a frustration that has led me to do many things I am ashamed of, not quite knowing why I did them, unless it was to hurt like I have been hurt. Above all I have lived with a dream, a dream so strong that it has become an obsession, replacing reality.' Harry unwrapped the towel; the hand had stopped bleeding.

'I'm beginning to get the general idea.' Jack told him, his voice neutral, like his position.

In the twinkling of an eye Harry's mood changed. Jack filled his own glass and handed it to the man. Harry was quiet for a long time and Jack wondered what was going on behind the mask. His eyes were glued to a spot on the Axminster rug. He gulped the

73

brandy down in three swallows handing Jack the empty glass. 'Oh my God,' he whimpered. 'Oh God… I never did want to go to war.'

Suddenly both hands covered his beaten face, his head lowered and the storm bottled up inside him for so long matched that which was falling on the Indian Ocean. Finally he spoke, slowly at first, deliberating each word. 'I have lived with a burning desire, to attain wealth and power, enough to match that which was rightfully mine. And now I have the foundation for that wealth and power. I find my father is interested in Australia. He intends to establish a steel industry here. Damn him. Damn him to hell!' Harry shouted.

Jack was desperately trying to understand. A knot of trepidation was forming in his belly for Harry's words. 'He hates Australia!' He began, silently willing Harry to agree.

Harry sighed shaking his head his normally well-groomed hair falling about his tear streaked face, 'You do not know father; he loves making money. Where it comes from would hardly concern him. At this very moment representatives from Anthony Thornton are on their way to Australia to secure leases of iron ore.'

'What?' Jack's gravest fears were realised.

'It says so right there.' Harry pointed to the paper.

Jack snatched the paper from the table, Harry forgotten as he sat down again to read by the light of the lamp. Harry watched the change of expression come over the American, his ghostly white appearance coupled with copious beads of perspiration, which formed on his brow as he digested the words, which came darting at him from the transcript like so many bullets he could not avoid. He saw the effect the passages had on the younger man and silently wondered why Jack Carter was so interested in his father's affairs. Finally, the American screwed the paper and flung it across the room.

A painful utterance escaped Jack's diaphragm and tears of frustration flowed down his cheeks to mingle with the blood. His bloodied fist struck the surface of the desk several times until he seemingly remembered Harry. Dispirited he closed his eyes fighting to control his rage for some time before Harry's voice cut across his thoughts.

'Is something wrong old boy?' For Harry the position was now more to his liking he was in control again.

A long time passed before Jack eased himself from the chair. Ignoring Harry, he opened the French doors connecting the veranda even wider and stood leaning against the railing looking at the twin peaks of granite in the break of day. The smell of the ocean filled his nose, it was refreshing after the repugnance of congealed blood which he coughed up and disposed to the courtyard below.

Although there was no mention of where in Australia the British company would be looking for ore extract, Jack knew with a certainty that started his innards rumbling with anxiety. He wanted to take his leave, there was an urgency now. He must cable Hopkins not to sell the property until he had a chance to speak with him. More importantly, he must see for himself the range of iron ore, not however before questioning Harry further about Katrina.

Australia was taboo. Katrina must never know the truth? What a family! Jack returned to Harry's office conscious of the smell of stale air and of their sweat and blood. 'You stated before that I was a victim of your mother's scheming,' Jack prodded. 'What did you mean by that statement?'

Harry's face was a mess. The water now dried saw streaks of blood on every square inch of skin. 'Mother used subterfuge to be rid of you,' was the reply, Harry wiping his face on the soiled towel. 'I doubt, very much whether Katrina wrote the letter you spoke of. You seemed very sure of her affections for you. However, because you held no station, were not well educated by English standards and because your family were an unknown quantity, Mother would move heaven and earth to be rid of you.'

'And just how would she go about that?'

'Oh there are ways,' was the candid reply. 'By your own admission Mother had your card; she could quite simply contact an acquaintance who, for a gift would duplicate another note or letter in your handwriting.'

'What!'

'Goes on all the time old boy.' Harry told him.

Jack's upbringing would never allow him to believe such things went on. However, Harry had planted the seed of doubt. *'Christ, I'm as silly as he is,'* the thought suddenly occurred to him.

'Surely you must have thought it strange Katrina was not present to greet you. Naturally they did not want a scene in her presence. She would have been conveniently away on your arrival,' he informed Jack, watching as the hurt spread across the American's features.

'You were duped old boy!' Harry cut across his thoughts. 'She married his Lordship, Chester Thornton; they have a son,' again the look, the hurt, the frustration, when told this news. 'Yes, an heir to the Anthony millions and the article would indicate my uncle is presently completing a merger of interests.' Harry was becoming loquacious now.

'I say old Chap, you didn't know?' Harry leaned away from the wall, a look of mock astonishment on his features. He pushed the empty tumbler forward again.

'No... ' Jack spat at him. 'I was unaware she had married so soon. I was under the assumption that you aristocrats believed in long engagements.' Jack was suddenly fearful, the merger would be complete the news copy must be all of six months old, he shuddered uncontrollably.

'So they do old boy, Mother must have her reasons.'

'How do you know all this?' Jack could not conceal his vexation.

'My uncle, Sir James Loxton, he sends me information from time to time. There are some newspaper clippings of their wedding in the top right-hand drawer of the table, if you would care to look,' he added, smiling for the first time.

Jack knew he was goading him, but he was unable to control himself. 'No!' His reply was raucous. 'No thanks,' he said again, his voice, soft, even, controlled.

Jack paced the room with the empty glass in his hand. The thought of that pompous bore Chester, touching Katrina set the lines of his face in a mask of fury.

'So Chester Thornton's being there was no accident,' he said, standing with his back to Harry, not wanting the man to see the anger in his expression. Deliberately he sought another glass, pouring himself a stiff drink, and refilling the clean glass for Harry, gently corked the nearly empty bottle and returned to where he was propped against the wall.

Harry raised the offered glass, 'Cheers!' Then, 'Certainly not old boy, Thornton is Iron and Steel, very big, an amalgamation between families uniting shipping to steel would constitute a perfect marriage, wouldn't you agree?'

Jack rose to leave, was it too late? Had Katrina made her decision? Her, or her conniving mother? If only he could turn back time armed with the knowledge he now possessed. More than this, his mere inheritance a paltry sum compared to the many millions at Lord Anthony's disposal was all he had to fight the large monopoly to secure the mineral rights of Tempi Station. If Mount Hopkins was a range of iron ore and two representatives were on their way to secure a purchase or lease on the mineral rights, then he had a race on his hands, a race he may not be able to win, and if he did win, could he outbid his Lordship? Harry's voice cut across his thoughts.

'Your interest in Father's activities centres around Australia does it not?'

'Yes,' came the circumspect response.

Harry nodded, 'The reference to expand their interests... Australia and the possible development of a steel industry here? You both want the same thing... ?' Harry was guessing, his voice dropped to a mere whisper as he suddenly realised Carter being in Edge Rock was no coincidence. But Carter couldn't possibly raise the money necessary to establish heavy mining? He must want the property for grazing. Harry had heard there was a lucrative market for Australian beef in Asia. Yes, that had to be the reason for Carter's interest.

'A very perspicacious summation,' Jack shrugged.

'A damn accurate appraisal I should say,' Harry responded regaining his composure for his considered revelation and hoping to learn more.

'I made the mistake of telling your father of my intentions once I reached Australia; I have no intention of revealing my plans to his son, a castaway or not you are his blood.' Jack looked Harry squarely in the eye; Harry read the message in those clear blue eyes.

Jack moved towards the door ignoring Harry, his mind too full of his thoughts and a plan which was forming to consider the Englishman any further. 'Katrina's address? I want her address!' He turned, back towards the desk.

'Help yourself old boy. No mention of me you understand.'

'If I write to your sister, you would be the furthest thing from my mind Harrison.' Jack scrawled the information onto a piece of paper before throwing the pencil onto the desk. He turned to take his leave once more.

'You are up against a financial empire Carter, he will destroy you like he has others in the past,' Harry's voice carried to Jack as he closed the door.

Chapter 16

London

After her husband left on the Monday morning, Katrina telephoned her uncle requesting to meet with him as a matter of urgency. When pressed by her uncle she revealed briefly the events of the weekend. She knew Chester was motoring up to Scotland the same morning on company business so felt confident they would not encounter each other in the Anthony Thornton Building.

Sir James Loxton opened the gold case of his Rolex fob watch and glanced at the dials for the second time in a space of ten minutes. Possibly it was because he was a little agitated this morning. Absently he rose from his desk and with a report still in his hand strode to the window. He drew the curtains fully open and stood looking to where the tower of London would have been if not for the heavy fog. His mind cast back to another morning long ago. He had been summoned to his brother-in-law's office and asked if he would meet with Harrison on his return to England. At first his face lit up with pleasure for he hadn't seen the boy since his departure to serve under Lord Kitchener. Then something made him wary, he wasn't aware the boy was due home…

Sedgwick had been near tears, his face was blotched and red from heavy drinking and the mere mention of the boy started him off anew. James remembered how he was told to make the necessary arrangements for Harrison to spend the rest of his life in Australia, exiled, never to set a foot in Great Britain again as long as he lived. *He is to be sent to the colony Australia.* For although Sedgwick recognised there was such a place, he could only imagine it as a colony, a convict colony at that, if part of the British Empire.

Sir James had sat stunned for nearly a minute at the command. *Harrison is your* son. He found his voice at last.

We never want to lay eyes on the boy again. He no longer exists. Libby and I would appreciate you handling this matter personally James, Sedgwick's voice dropped to a whisper.

A new identity? A substantial allowance? A residential address? James stood before his brother-in-law's desk his brow knit, sombre countenance, hands raised in submission.

Whatever has to be done, just do it James and stop badgering me with questions!

Now Australia had emerged again, this time it was Katrina. She had found out about the Mount Hopkins arrangement? He realised Chester must have told her of the board's decision.

'Lady Anthony to see you Sir James, shall I show her in?'

'H'm yes, by all means, and I do wish you would knock Mildred.' Sir James was caustic with his secretary for her breach of courtesy. Mildred was with him when he had his law practice and James insisted she come and work with him in his new role with Anthony Thornton, a substantial increase in salary and status as far as Mildred was concerned. He moved from the window towards the door placing the report he was perusing back on his desk in passing.

'I'm terribly sorry sir. I'm almost certain I did knock. Sir, Mister Gilstone phoned, he cannot promise the new cloth before next week and trusts this will not cause any inconvenience.'

'Damn the fellow, doesn't he know I'm off to France again next week. It will have to wait until my return Mildred, see to it please.'

Katrina smiled to herself from the doorway. How like Mother her uncle was when it came to dress, always immaculate, not like Father she thought, one suit a year. By contrast, Sir James would have his tailor measure him for suits every three months, selecting cloths which, while being conservative, displayed the in trend as far as cut and style were concerned.

'Katrina, you look radiant this morning,' he welcomed, moving to embrace his niece.

'Thank you uncle,' Katrina beamed, turning her head slightly to allow him to brush her cheek with his lips while placing her arms around him in a fond embrace and letting him seat her opposite where his desk was situated in the lavishly furnished office. She watched idly as her uncle eased himself behind his desk, shafts of light engulfed him, capturing minute particles of dust like the light from a projector during the screening of a film.

'So, what is so important that you would leave young David and come down to the city especially to see me?' he smiled paternally at her.

Katrina clasped her kid-gloved hands together, 'Is it true Daddy is going to purchase some valuable property in Australia? Mount Hopkins... ' She added leaning forward anxiously in the well-padded chair.

James looked towards the office door as though fearing they could be overheard. Absently he drummed his fingers on the surface of his desk contemplating momentarily before replying. 'Do you really want to know Katrina?'

'Yes!' Her voice rose in pitch. 'Chester came home for the weekend boasting he was going to become vice-chairman and that Clayton and Merrick were being sent to Australia to establish a steelworks,' she blurted waving her arms and close to tears. 'He said Father was bent on crushing... Jack,' she got out. James smiled and shook his head, as far as he knew the directors had no intention of giving that pompous ass a position of such importance. He realised there was no point trying to explain why the expansion was necessary. This wasn't what Katrina wanted to hear. 'My dear, I'm afraid the board is contemplating purchasing some property in Australia for the purpose of attaining iron-ore.'

'He is trying to ruin Jack isn't he?' She sobbed.

James sighed shaking his head in sympathy. 'You are still carrying the torch aren't you my dear?' Katrina nodded.

'I cannot accept that he doesn't love me Uncle. I can't!' She shook her head sobbing quietly into a scented handkerchief.

'It is beyond my power to reverse the decision of the board Katrina. Clayton and Merrick are sailing to Australia, arrangements have been completed.' James left his desk to comfort his niece.

He had stood by and let Sedgwick banish Harrison, not this time, even if it meant his resigning from the firm, if he could help Katrina then he would. Maybe it would cleanse his soul. He still had sour memories for that past incident. He had gone to his sister Libby and pleaded with her. However, Libby stoutly defended Sedgwick's position, stating only that any revelation purporting to Harrison's behaviour, would ruin the Anthony name.

'I must warn Jack. I must!' She sobbed, hands clasped together.

'I can arrange for you to send a cablegram Katrina, do you have an address... ?'

Katrina nodded, 'Edge Rock, it is a small village.' She hesitated.

'Edge Rock would most certainly have a post office.' James spoke with authority, suddenly realising why Sedgwick and Libby didn't want a bar of the American's ambition. 'Very well, then I shall have Mildred bring you some paper, you compose what you want to say and I will see to it that she sends it today. It must remain our little secret.' He added smiling.

'Thank you uncle; I thought of asking Daddy.'

'Quite so my dear.' James realised that would have been a very interesting meeting.

James eased himself out of his chair and moved towards Katrina. After some serious deliberation he had reached a decision. 'Katrina, I feel you were part of a clandestine plot by my sister to discredit your war hero and to end the… relationship.' He soothed, placing an arm protectively about her shoulders.

Katrina shook her head in contrition not wanting to believe her mother capable of hurting her, 'Mother would never stoop to something so sinister,' she blurted.

'You do not know your mother,' sighed Sir James, patting her softly as though comforting a child.

'What do you mean I don't know Mother?' She challenged him.

He smiled locking his fingers together. 'Libby can be a very protective and decidedly self-conceited person when the occasion warrants. She would move heaven and earth to prevent you making a… mistake.'

'A mistake?' The words nearly choked in her mouth.

'Your American suitor. He held no station, he wanted to settle in what your mother believes to be a penal colony, he wasn't educated at Oxford, Eton, or Cambridge,' Sir James expounded.

'If I discover one shred of evidence that mother somehow conspired to prevent my marrying Jack, I will never speak to her again.'

'She is your mother Katrina and I am sure she would have been acting in your best interests.'

'In her best interests you mean; I was given no choice!' The defiance in her voice registered painfully on James, he knew Libby was capable of crushing anything or anyone who opposed her will.

'Can I get you a cup of tea before you leave my dear?'

'No I am anxious to get home to David. He hasn't been well since our return from Ireland.' James nodded his understanding.

James walked to the door. He requested Mildred join them with her notepad. After deliberating and some prodding from James, Katrina watched as Mildred jotted down the essence of the cablegram. James explained to his secretary that he would like the cable sent immediately and discreetly. With a smile of understanding Mildred left them to follow his instructions.

Chapter 17

Hopkins Range, Northern Territory

Their stopover at Margaret River Downs had been brief. Mike introduced Jack to his family and told of their venture to the Red mountain. Old Clem, Mike's dad, insisted Barney accompany them. Five days later on the plateau above the falls which heralded the commencement of the Margaret River, Jack and Mike were waiting for Barney to return from scouting the track. Shortly, Barney reappeared as silently as when he left. He was big framed for a black, broad face, high forehead and a broad flat nose, the beard, tinted with streaks of grey, flowed to his barrel chest.

'Any luck Barney?' Mike addressed the man.

Barney didn't waste a breath, he waited until he stood by the two men before replying. 'Dem Black fella been 'ere boss. Myall, alonga track we gonna follow 'em,' he told them, pointing towards the commencement of the narrow track along the scarp.

'Which way Barney?' Mike was understandably nervous and it carried to Jack who placed the binoculars aside to face the pair. He had been using them to admire the view.

'Plenny sign.' The tracker waved his arms.

'Blacks?' Jack asked the tracker.

'Dem fella wild black fella's boss,' Barney nodded.

Mike explained, 'Tempi was first established as a property in 1883 by Lloyd Hopkins, its boundaries are approximately 500 square miles. It's mostly hilly country with splendid waters, some located at the base of the northern ranges, some in gorges fed by tributaries of the Margaret River debauching upon well-grassed flats, the whole, forms what should have been an ideal combination for the raising of cattle.'

'Should have?' Jack was curious.

Mike was removing burrs from his socks, he gave Jack a cursory stare from under the rim of his Bushman's hat. He could imagine the man's torment and further explained. 'There has been trouble between blacks and whites up here since the Station came into being. It started because this range is a favourite gathering ground for the western tribes. Their spearing of cattle became a favourite pastime. They would spear the cattle, dismember the slain beasts and bring them up here for cooking where they are safe from pursuit. The number of cattle speared was considerable, but more important as far as Hopkins was concerned was that after several ambushes the cattle would no longer graze on the flats, preferring instead the rugged hilly country. Mustering became increasingly difficult, time consuming, and bloody dangerous. Finally, the cattle became scrubbers, almost impossible to brand and tally.'

'There must be at least five hundred head still running wild up here, the makings of a good mob wouldn't you agree?'

Jack nodded, 'they wouldn't be easy to get out of the terrain.'

Mike nodded his agreement. 'The last straw as far as old Lloyd was concerned was a retaliatory ambushing of his foreman and two aboriginal stockmen by the blacks.' Jack shook his head in sympathy for the senseless slaughter.

'To this day they never caught those responsible. Two constables were sent down from Darwin, they engaged a tracker and set out to apprehend the blacks thought to be responsible, all three disappeared without trace. In the same year, old Ike McKenzie, who found the samples of iron ore, was discovered by a boundary rider; his body was wrapped around a tree in the valley, a skeleton, every bone in his body had been broken. All of this only took place five years ago, just before I left for the war. Do you still want to have a look at the Red Mountain?'

'I've come this far.' The certainty in his voice told Mike he would not be fazed.

Mike turned his thoughts back to Belgium, to the day Corneilius La Brun took them to his home and treated their wounds, and a memory that one-day he and the American would muster cattle up in the high country. He smiled to himself, it had come true, Jack was with him now and the bush was sweet and fresh and the scrubbers were here waiting to be branded, just like he knew they would be and silently he wished Jack would forget about the range of iron-ore. They were rich beyond their wildest dreams, why did Jack need the mountain? They could stock and run their own brand, who could ask for more? But Jack wasn't interested. And Katie still plagued Mike's thoughts, what had happened? Mike would never ask, yet if Jack were his mate, why hadn't he told him?

Chapter 18

Anthony Thornton Building, London

The cables were marked confidential, and addressed to: *Sir James Loxton C/o the Anthony Thornton Building 214-218 Fleet Street London.* Sir James read the contents of the first cable anxiously twice, astounded by the audacity of Jack Carter, before folding the correspondence placing it in a company envelope with its prominent business crest and hurriedly making arrangements through Mildred to consult with Lord Anthony. Before leaving his office he read the second cable from Harrison requesting covert information about his father's interest in Australia. Mildred was sent to arrange an immediate audience with Sedgwick. Sir James wanted privacy, not the telephone, not this time; he wanted her out of the office. Silently he wondered why Harrison wanted to know where the company's Australian interests were centred. He pondered his brief reply before composing the return cable which he addressed: *Harry Street C/o Edge Rock Post office,* and marked confidential, before allowing his mind to wander to the contents of the first cable, the frown of worry etched deep into his tanned features. If Sir Bruce Thornton were in the building, he would whisk Sedgwick away somewhere private so the two of them could talk; it was not necessary.

Ten minutes later, he was seated in Sedgwick's office waiting anxiously for him to finish reading the cable. His lordship looked over his reading glasses at James, 'Have you read this?' He waved the cable about.

'Naturally! It was addressed to me.'

'This Carter fellow knows the whereabouts of… Harrison. We were so careful, how could he possibly know?' He lent forward, his voice barely audible still waving the cable in front of him.

'Alas, I do not have an answer to your question Sedgwick; however, he most definitely has met and opened the skeleton from your closet.'

'You said we would never have to worry about Harrison again.' accused Lord Anthony, venom in his voice for James.

'We agreed Harrison would be directed to a village where he couldn't possibly be known. We avoided the cities, coincidence,' Sir James shrugged for he knew Harrison resided in both Sydney and Melbourne for several years before moving to Edge Rock. The only reason James selected Edge Rock was he happened to read somewhere about a gold strike and the coastal village was mentioned. He had no idea where Edge Rock was because it did not appear on any map he had of Australia at his perusal, he needed the town to have a Post Office.

'Coincidence my eye! That bounder Carter must have found out somehow.'

'I am at a loss to understand what could have happened. Harrison was sworn to secrecy. To jeopardise our trust was to see him cut off without an allowance, Harrison understood the conditions of the agreement, of that I am certain.' Not that it mattered, James would wave the rules; Harrison would get his allowance no matter the situation.

Too, if chance or fate brought Carter and his nephew together then so be it, there was nothing he or anyone else could do under the circumstances.

'Carter could not possibly have recognised him. We had everything which reminded us of Harrison sealed in a vault. Nor Libby or I talk of the boy and we certainly do not speak of him in front of Katrina. As far as she is concerned, he died fighting the Boer and that is the way it will remain!'

A poignant silence settled between them, each with his thoughts. For James it was concern for his nephew, a man he would never see again, and thoughts of resentment surfaced for his brother-in-law. As for Sedgwick: apprehension lest he loses his fortune and position in the power struggle of life's ambition.

'How could the American possibly know of our intention to establish heavy industry in Australia?' Sedgwick asked, raising his hands as if appealing to God for an explanation.

James felt a spasm of guilt for suggesting, nay letting Katrina warn Carter with a cablegram sent from his office before remembering the Financial Review News he sent every so often. However it was done, besides he believed there would be more than one rich large iron-ore deposit in Australia.

'Harrison is sent mail regularly, the Financial Review, so he can keep abreast of your augmentation.' He shrugged.

'What!'

'It was an agreement reached between Harrison and myself; nothing for you to be concerned about Sedgwick.'

'An agreement! Nothing for me to be concerned about! You realise you have jeopardised my family name and standing with your foolish arrangement!' Sedgwick was seething with anger for his brother-in-law's stupidity—an anger he was just managing to control.

James remained calm folding his arms he replied, 'I imagine the Financial Review would be widely circulated, why not Australia? After all, many pastoralists would be keen observers of foreign markets for their precious wool.' This seemed to allay Sedgwick's fears.

'Carter has threatened to reveal Harrison's identity if I so much as contemplate investment in Australia. I hate being threatened!' Sedgwick glared accusingly at James.

'Don't look at me old boy; I'm not the one threatening you.'

'If you hadn't been so damn soft in the head, sending Harrison correspondence, none of this would have happened!' Sedgwick was nearly shouting now.

'And if you had stood up to Libby and allowed Katrina to marry the love of her heart, we would not be in this precarious position.' James would not be intimidated by his brother-in-law.

'Don't you take that tone with me, on that issue I sided with Libby, the fellow was a bounder, not good enough for Katrina, had no station, no inheritance to speak of... you keep your place sir.'

So my sister did connive to have the relationship quashed, James mused, coughing into his hand. It was further evidence that a conspiracy had taken place and in the heat of the moment, Sedgwick had supported his theory, which he hoped to substantiate through Rigby's report.

'Suit yourself Sedgwick, you have no idea how unhappy Katrina is, you rarely see her or your grandson!' James sat back in the plush leather chair folding his arms, with a bland look for his lordship.

'What do you mean unhappy? She has everything she could possibly want, wealth, position, title,' Sedgwick threw his hands in the air.

'Love? With that pompous bore for a husband?'

83

'No such thing! And you can leave Chester out of this… A lot of nonsense.' Sedgwick was brusque with James.

James was sorely tempted to reveal to Sedgwick the truth regarding Chester, just managing to keep his silence; instead, 'Don't you think you owe your daughter the truth Sedgwick? Shouldn't you explain to her Harrison's banishment? I am sure she will understand your position.'

'We will do nothing of the sort!' Sedgwick bellowed, partially rising from his chair in a display of temper. Slowly, he recovered his composure sitting again and letting his fingers drum on the surface of his desk, his face a mask of concentration for the problem at hand.

'We could buy this Carter fellow off I imagine.' James suggested at length, knowing full well Sedgwick would not part with currency to solve their dilemma, he may be rich but Sedgwick was a frugal man at heart. James had to fight tooth and nail to come to a sound financial arrangement for Harrison when he was exiled.

'I intend to crush him. The audacity of the bounder, to think he can bribe me. Send a cable to young Thornton. Instruct him to buy at any price! Meanwhile, I intend to compile a return cable to Mister Carter. I will not bow to his gutter snipe tactics.'

'Do you think that wise?'

'The fellow will be told James, I intend to purchase that deposit now at any cost.'

'As you will Sedgwick, but how long do you think you can keep up the charade? Carter's next cable may be to your daughter what then?'

'You leave Katrina to Libby and me James.'

'Certainly old boy, however I think you are treading on thin ice, in more ways than one.' James rose from the chair; suddenly he needed some fresh air.

'Explain yourself sir.'

James lent over the desk his hands supporting his weight. 'The company,' Sir James looked towards the door before continuing. 'Young Clayton is being groomed by his father to become its managing director. If you do not act shortly and take sound advice, you may end up being disposed as chairman of the board.' James spoke softly yet with authority.

'Oh?' Sedgwick hooked his thumbs into his waistcoat pockets and settled back into the padding of his chair. 'And what would you suggest?' Sedgwick was also concerned for his standing; he knew the elder Thornton was grooming his son to take a more active interest in the management of the organisation.

'Have Katrina join the board of directors.'

'Katrina?'

'Katrina is your blood. Besides you may just need her vote in the near future to maintain your control of the company. She is bright,' appealed James, seeing the indifferent even aberrant look for his hypothesis. 'And she could assist me initially while I teach her the business. She would make a fine company secretary.' James pushed himself upright to take his leave.

Sedgwick lent forward over the desk his hands locking together supporting his chin as he deliberated his brother-in-law's advice. 'I'll give it my consideration. More to the point, you are to have no further correspondence with Harrison; he is dead we have a death certificate and a cemetery plot in Durban to prove it.' Sedgwick glared at the retreating slim figure of his brother-in-law before the door closed behind him.

Chapter 19

London

Once again, Sir James Loxton found himself visiting the premises of Thomas Rigby rather than the other way around. James could not afford to have their conversation compromised by innuendo, which may filter back to Sedgwick or Lord Bruce Thornton. Therefore, it was easier for him to change his busy schedule and meet with the investigator in his offices.

A portly figure with close set eyes partially hidden behind steel rimmed reading spectacles, Thomas was a clean shaven man of middle-age, a white faced Londoner with sparse brown hair. He indicated a chair to Sir James Loxton, a slim, debonair man of gentle demeanour with flecks of white through mousey grey hair and sporting a trimmed beard.

When they were comfortably seated in Rigby's office with the door closed, separated by an occasional table upon which a silver tray with tea and biscuits were served, did Thomas enlighten Sir James. Their discussion was brief, if fruitful, and at times frustrating for James when informed by Thomas, that the man in question, a Cambridge scholar, had passed away recently. 'Pneumonia as I am given to understand,' Thomas elaborated for James.

'Do go on,' James encouraged.

'When my investigator, reported back to me, initially I thought this was the end of it. However, it appears he has a brother living in Salisbury. We traced him...'

'Just a minute Thomas,' James cut across the running discourse. 'Who is it that we are discussing here?' Thomas apologised for his tirade.

'Oh, frightfully sorry old Chap. Professor Ashford Hobson, the man in the newspaper clipping, apparently he was a genius at reproducing the written word, if you get my meaning.' Thomas looked up at James over his reading glasses and smiled a knowing smile. James waved a hand irritably for him to continue.

'Initially, his brother Charles was reluctant to disclose or be privy to any information regarding his late kin. However when arbitrating, with some people, the English Pound spoke volumes.' Whereupon Thomas pushed a Fry's metal chocolate container across the desk towards James, with instructions for him to peruse the contents.

Sir James opened the brightly coloured tin in this game of seek the prize and you shall find your reward, while Thomas did his best to hide his piquant pleasure for the discovery. James rifled through several thick envelopes, some accompanied with short jotted notes, reminders of the favour not being returned in kind by substantial remuneration and therefore no future favour would be accepted for that party, before coming across the envelope he was seeking. The name Anthony was boldly written across the front of the slightly creased envelope. Carefully as though his life depended on it, he placed the other envelopes back in the metal container. On opening the envelope of concern, he discovered two letters. The first, addressed to Jack Bryson Carter, consisted of four pages. The second, a single page addressed to Katrina from Jack Carter.

'These are the original letters of the duplicated forgeries?' He waved them aloft towards Thomas whose smug smile told all.

Sir James smiled looking up from his reading, 'Definitely Libby's handwriting!'

Thomas chortled, 'I feel you have your proof Sir James and if you like to open other envelopes you will find Lady Bellamy-Jones has had more than one discreet use of our late friend's skills.'

'That won't be necessary,' James smiled, he waved the envelope of interest at Thomas to a nod, before placing it inside his overcoat pocket.

< >

Katrina sat demurely, her gloved hands clasped in front of her waiting impatiently for Mildred to leave her alone and close the office door. Five weeks had passed since she had approved of her uncle's undertaking on her behalf. The chimes from the hand crafted Chippendale grandfather clock in the corner of the ornately furnished room told Katrina she had been waiting for several minutes for her uncle to return. Katrina rose from the high back chair and absently moved towards the fireplace when she heard the door open and close behind her.

'Sorry to keep you waiting my dear.' Sir James rounded his desk, advancing on the fireplace to join her.

Katrina saw he wasn't smiling. He handed her the wax-sealed envelope. 'I'm not sure you want to see the contents Katrina; however after much deliberation, I felt I had no choice but to conduct the enquiry on your behalf. The originals, a keepsake, or should I say Professor Ashford Hobson's insurance.'

With shaking hand Katrina opened the seal revealing the envelope inside turning away from Sir James as she did so and walking back to her chair opposite his desk. Katrina let herself sink into the padded leather chair, yet she was not conscious of sitting, as the hurt of Jack's letter sprang at her from the page. Large tears welled in her eyes with the memory of his indelible words and slowly the truth etched itself into her brain as she recognised her mother's handwriting. Slowly, she folded the letter and commenced to read that which she supposedly composed to Jack. Suddenly Katrina felt weak, dizzy, she tried to steady herself before fainting and falling off the chair to lay sprawled on the floral patterned Axminster carpet.

Alarmed, Sir James rushed to her aid feeling her brow before throwing wide the office door and shouting for Mildred. On entering the office the first thing Mildred saw was the crumpled form of Lady Anthony, then the pieces of paper clutched in her hands. Instinctively, her hands went to her throat with disbelief. Although it was none of her business rationally, she was certain the contents of the pieces of paper were responsible for the young woman's collapse, Katrina's lovely features etched with shock told all.

'The couch?'

'No. Do not move her,' anguished James.

'Shall I fetch Doctor Symonds, he is with Lord Anthony as we speak.' Mildred eased the buttons at the throat of Katrina's blouse before turning her supine and pulling her rumpled skirt to its full ankle length.

'Find something to use as a pillow woman!' Sir James could not hide his exasperation.

Mildred was shortly back with some folded towels which she placed under Katrina's head, 'The doctor?'

'Yes, yes, straight away,' James stooped, removing the pages of writing from Katrina's clenched grasp before Mildred was out of the room. He rounded his desk with the discarded envelope, placed the letters inside, then thrust the correspondence in a side drawer of his pedestal desk being sure to lock it and then depositing the key into the fob pocket of his waistcoat.

86

When Mildred returned, closely followed by Doctor Symonds and Lord Anthony, Sir James was kneeling beside Katrina softly patting her cheeks. Symonds took one look at Katrina before opening his bag and reaching for a bottle of smelling salts. Indicating for Sir James to move aside, he knelt beside Katrina removing the lid from the bottle and placing it against her delicate nose. The pungent crystals of ammonium carbonates soon had the desired effect and Katrina was seen to stir then blink.

Lord Anthony looked down on his daughter, a prosaic look on his features. 'What happened?' He turned to James for an answer.

James was reticent, 'you had best ask Katrina, Sedgwick.'

'I'm asking you James!'

'Very well, Katrina has come into possession of some disturbing information which I can only assume distressed her, to the point where she fainted.' If asked James would tell the truth, he didn't imagine Sedgwick would wish to pursue the matter in front of witnesses.

'She doesn't know about… Libby?' Sedgwick's lips formed his wife's name, his gaze locked to James.

'Not yet, I'll tell her, all in good time Sedgwick,' James shook his head. It was just something else left to him; something Sedgwick was only just now coming to terms with. James fully expected Sedgwick to continue probing for answers. However, it appeared as though he were preoccupied, his expression was vague, James surmised.

With Doctor Symonds and Mildred supporting her, Katrina was assisted to the chair. 'What happened?' She asked at length.

'You fainted my dear girl.' Her father placed a hand on her shoulder.

'Oh, yes, how silly of me, the fire,' she explained, looking towards the fireplace.

'It is rather warm in here, I feel that is all it was; however I would like you to make an appointment with my secretary young lady, just to be sure,' doctor Symonds chided, although he was smiling at his charge.

'Well you being here saves me telephoning you Katrina,' Sedgwick gave her another perfunctory pat. 'James and I believe it is time you joined the board. I've arranged with my broker to have some stock transferred to you. I'll talk with you later, my dear.' Said Sedgwick, in a matter of fact tone. Not given to displays of affection in public it was as much as Katrina had come to expect from her father.

Before Katrina could respond, James stepped forward and kissed her on the cheek, 'Congratulation's Katrina, not before time if you ask me,' he smiled.

'Charles you will have to excuse me, can I contact you tomorrow?' Began Lord Anthony addressing his physician. 'I have an appointment with Lord Bruce,' Sedgwick glanced at his time-piece.

'As soon as there is further change, I will contact you Lord Anthony.' Charles closed his bag.

'Very good! Mildred would you show Doctor Symonds out please.' Sedgwick indicated the door with a nod while shaking the good Doctor by the hand.

Katrina waited until the others were gone, only then did she address her uncle. 'It is my intention to confront Mother with the evidence after which, I will never speak to her again,' she sobbed into a handkerchief.

'For the moment I wouldn't do that Katrina.'

'Why she has ruined my life!' Katrina sobbed again.

'Doctor Symonds wasn't here to examine your father.' Katrina gave James a sardonic glare through red-rimmed eyes.

'After what she has done! I should hold my tongue?' Katrina was brusque with her uncle.

'Libby isn't well Katrina. The meeting between Symonds and your father this morning was to discuss her ailing health. Her headaches… a growth inside her brain,' his voice was barely a whisper.

'A tumour?' Katrina had heard the medical term to describe an abnormal growth although she did not fully understand the complications and she guessed, correctly, nor did her uncle.

'She is dying Katrina,' sighed James holding her elbow while shakily she seated herself.

'I saw her just the other week and we spoke on the telephone yesterday; she had one of her headaches she explained when I depicted the change in her voice. Now you mention it she sounded emotionally drained, but then I was only half listening, David had woken and was crying to be picked up.' Katrina, covered her mouth; her frown of worry crossing the boundary of bitterness she felt only moments earlier.

Chapter 20

Edge Rock, Western Australia

Back in Harry Street's office Lenny told how the prospector found the nugget, indeed was caught trying to conceal it in his shirt pocket, Lenny explained, depositing the nugget on the stinkwood desk. Harry could barely contain his elation. The bruising from his fight with Jack Carter was disappearing and although he was stiff and sore, he allowed himself a thin smile; the pain was secondary to his relief at the good news. He scooped up the nugget as Lenny produced the map passing it to him. Harry briefly examined the map while Lenny looked with curiosity at his battered and bruised sallow countenance. Shortly Harry looked up from the map, and Lenny diverted his gaze. 'The prospector Lennard?'

'Fed him a cock and bull story about bad blacks out that way Harry, told him to clear off and never come back, gave him the gunny sack of food and all the spare water,' Lenny smirked.

Harry gave him a frosty look, 'I was prepared to return his poke and cut a deal with the man.'

Lenny gave a disinterested shrug.

'Oh well, I suppose one man's misfortune,' said Harry not completing the proverb before issuing an order to Lennard. 'I want two men sent up there to discourage any prospectors. Oh and by the way,' Harry paused to rub his moustache between his fingers, a habit he had when excited, 'should any strangers come to town, I want them discouraged, particularly if they show the slightest interest in the Red Mountain. I will warn Mister Myre to keep his mouth shut.'

'Sure boss. Where are you going?' Lenny asked, observing Harry hastily grabbing for his hat and coat.

Harry turned on the man, 'Down to Myre's store to register a claim Lennard, where else?'

It was one of the rare occasions Lenny could ever remember seeing Harry smile, twice in less than a minute. Lenny watched amused as Harry doffed his hat to passers-by, a practice which was very out of character for Harry. Grinning to himself and betting the locals thought Harry was going around the twist with the heat, Lenny quickened his stride to keep pace with the tall Englishman.

'Boss. A boat could get up the river quicker than a man on horseback!' A nervous Lenny informed him, anxious that nobody should use the old stock route to get to the mountain.

'Good, very good Lennard! See to it! There's a good chap.'

Harry's mood changed in the time it took him to enter and emerge from the Lands Registry Office. Meanwhile, Lenny settled himself on the veranda in the shade to await the Englishman's return.

'South Australia! Where about in South Australia? But surely you are authorised to sell the property on his behalf, you useless bounder.' Lenny overheard him shouting at Bill

Myre. Soon he stormed from the building and Lenny could never remember him being so upset.

'Oh Mister Street there is a cable for you... ' Millicent ran into the street waving aloft the communication.

Without turning Harry waved for Lenny to fetch his mail. Lenny grabbed the cablegram from Millicent and wisely fell in behind Harry as he strode, eyes straight ahead ignoring the doffed hats of people he had spoken to not ten minutes before. It was like following a black cloud back up the street, a Jekyll and Hyde, which gave the locals something to gossip about in the days to come.

When he entered the club, Lenny handed him the cable. Without a word, Harry ascended the stairs summoning Clarrie to his room as he went with a swipe of his arm and a finger indicating his office. Harry thrust the door open and stormed across the room knocking the coal oil lamp to the floor in a display of temper. He crossed to his desk and unfolded the correspondence. While Clarrie commenced to clean up the mess created by slurps of oil and shards of glass, Harry read the cable before omitting a howl and several blasphemous words before crumbling the cable into a ball and flinging it at the waste paper bin under the desk. Shortly, Harry commanded Clarrie leave the mess to another and bid him book passage on the first ship leaving for the eastern coast.

'Charter the ship if you must,' he shrieked. 'Now get out of here.' And Clarrie down on his knees his hands full of broken glass were forgotten as Harry stormed out of the office for his bedroom where he commenced to throw shirts and his personal belongings onto the bed. In his mind, Harry was reading the cable again and again.

Anthony Thornton is interested in a range of iron ore known as Red Mountain, a part of Hopkins Range on Tempi Station, believed to be north east of the town Edge Rock....Stop.

Party should arrive Fremantle May.... Stop.

Kindest regards, Uncle James.... End.

Should his father purchase the property, along with mineral rights, both he and Carter stand to lose everything. Whereas, he may just be in a position to make Carter a deal; grazing rights as opposed to mineral rights, they both win, *and I get back at my father*, mused Harry. Harry was instantly thinking of the future, his company would need beef to feed his employees, yes, this could work to the advantage of both parties; *all I have to do is prevent the property falling into the hands of my father.*

<>

Mike Smith heard the discharge of the rifle and cringed before the round splattered rock fragments into his face. Instinctively, he closed his eyes and clawed at the rock-face trying to disappear beneath its surface. It was Belgium all over again, the sniper carefully hidden, ready to release death to the first careless soldier to show any part of his body above the rampart.

A second bullet struck the outcrop just above them whistling away in a whirr of sound, while dislodging conglomerate from the rock face to fall upon them. They jumped, turning, twisting away from the face and falling free, like large jungle cats, plummeting towards the alluvial fan thirty feet below. They hit the soft base of material etched away over countless years and it moved with them as they rolled and careered to the base of the rock-face. Crouched, they ran to where Barney attended the horses some five-hundred yards away.

Barney was standing with their string gently stroking the brow of his horse when they materialised from the scrub. 'I heard shots boss!'

'Some bastard tried to bushwhack us.' Mike was shaking with anger and fatigue for their mad dash through the scrub.

'Someone is trying to scare us. Someone doesn't want us near the mountain.' Jack wheezed through tortured lungs. His ribs ached from his fight with Harry Street the other night. The fall, and running fit to bust didn't help any.

'Have you seen enough Jack?' Mike took the offered reins of his horse from Barney.

'Hematite. A bloody mountain of it.' Grinned Jack.

Mike nodded. 'Let's get out of here.'

They walked the horses for nearly a mile before Barney considered it safe enough to ride. He led them past the old Hopkins station house, sadly in need of major repair due to termites and white ants having riddled the timber framing. Window shutters hung uselessly and creeper vines shrouded the timber slabs of the walls. The spangled-iron water tank had fallen from its termite-riddled base to lie on the ground. The outhouse was collapsed rubble and the stockyard overgrown with grass and vine.

They didn't stop. Barney led them on to the Margaret River and an unexpected surprise. Here the river was braided due to a portion of the bank slumping during a flood. The main channel was flowing steadily. This secondary channel was a mere pond. Tied to an overhanging tree trunk was a boat, almost certainly the property of the bushwhacker. It was a sleek vessel, a clinker hull approximately twenty-four feet in length. On further inspection the boiler proved to be a Derr, water tube design and the engine a single-cylinder Shipman, capable of cruising at ten-knots per hour.

It was agreed, Barney would cross the river with their string and proceed to Edge Rock along the old stock route, while Mike and Jack confiscated the vessel and made their way to the coast. Two horses were left tied to the tree along with some supplies. Bushwhackers or not, no man should be left in the outback without a horse.

Four days later, with favourable winds and current, they pulled the boat into a pylon at the jetty where the town's kids used to fish from. Their haste motivated their decision. The harbour wharf was still another twenty minutes down river.

Barney was there waiting for them, having barely stopped after discovering the decomposed corpse. He told Mike of his grim discovery whereupon Mike left Jack to report Barney finding the prospector. Constable Mountier was the soul officer attached to the district and Mike knew he had to convince Mountier that the prospector had been murdered before the policeman would leave the comfort of the sandstock building to face the oppressive heat experienced away from the coastal fringe. Those who knew Mountier said he was the laziest officer ever appointed to the district. Long and lean, thin faced with close set eyes, pale skin and a hooked nose, Mountier wasn't exactly the physical type, much preferring to stay indoors and let trouble sort itself out; unless of course he was summoned by Harry Street. Those who should know said he was Street's flunky.

Mountier was making himself a cup of tea when Mike entered the police station and explained why he was there.

'Hell Mike, I'll need a couple of days just to get ready,' Mountier moaned.

'Three men left town and only two returned. Barney read the sign, he said one was a black fella the other bow-legged; that should narrow it down don't you think?'

'Never saw him leave town but I was told Lenny McPherson and a caste accompanied a bloke to the Hopkin's range.' Mountier informed him.

'My tracker Barney, believed the dead prospector could have been Homer Jones, a mate of old Ike McKenzie; they used to fossick about up on Hopkins range and over at

Kalgoorlie and Boulder. They killed his mule and scattered all his equipment, the mongrels.' Mountier nodded his thanks for the information.

'Anyway, now it's your problem; I've told you where the body is. I've done my duty now you do yours. Mike left the cool shelter of the gaol and headed back up Main Street to Myre's store and more bad news.'

Chapter 21

Edge Rock, Western Australia

It was noticeably cooler at the back of the shop where a dusty open window faced the harbour. Bill Myre sat on a high back cane chair eating a sandwich and reading a month old copy of the Gazette newspaper. Bill, middle aged and bald, was habited in a Jacky Howe singlet covered by bib overalls and work boots. He wore reading glasses attached by a chain around his neck.

'G-day Mike. How are ya boy?' He greeted Mike Smith, spying the tall frame of the young man in the doorway.

Mike peered into the gloom of the emporium; it took a while before he clearly saw Bill. 'Good thanks Bill, yourself?' He asked politely, moving down the long room with its smells of packaging, cheeses, hardware, oil and paints, over creaky, worn floor boards, towards the back of the store.

'Oh, never seen the world brighter boy!'

'Glad to hear it. Bill. I'd like you to meet a good mate of mine. Jack Carter... Bill Myre.'

Bill clambered out of the sunken chair with the patched cushion and took Jack's extended hand in a sound grip. 'Pleased ta meetcha. 'Scuse me dirty 'ands, been moving a bit of stock about,' he added.

'That's OK Bill.'

'Carter, of course, Millicent Taylor who runs the post office next door has mail for you. Well, and what can I do for you boys?' Myre moved to lean on the counter, using the cheesecloth to wipe clean its dusty surface. Bill was studying Carter's battered face, he was curious but managed to constrain himself.

'We want to know about the Hopkins place, Tempi Station,' explained Mike.

Bill was surprised, 'You and that bleedin' Englishman both.' Bill ignored Harry's advice to keep his trap closed; young Mike was a friend.

'Where is Hopkins now Bill?' asked Mike.

'Got himself a copper mine near the little town of Marree on the north western spur of the Flinders ranges.' Bill supplied the information.

'Would you know if he owns the mineral rights to Tempi as well as land rights?' Jack was apprehensive.

'Sure, says so right 'ere,' Bill bent below the counter and produced a thick ledger. Bill wet his thumb, blowing dust from the cover he commenced to flip through the pages until he found what he was looking for. After a brief glance at the document he turned the ledger towards them, his grubby finger pointing to Hopkins signature.

'It states here that it was a company property!' Jack turned to Mike accusingly.

'Yeah Lloyd purchased it when the New Zealand, Australia Land Company walked away from the investment around 1890.' Bill delighted in passing on his knowledge and seeing the information register on young Smith.

'Are you empowered to sell the property?' Jack was anxious.

'Nah. Unofficially it's been taken off the market. Besides, the mineral rights are registered with the Department of Lands and Mineral Resources. Thought you would 'ave knew that Mike. The Territory is administered by the Commonwealth Government Jack, even if old Lloyd wanted to sell it would have to be cleared by them first.'

'No, I didn't realise.' Mike was chagrined by this piece of news.

'I thought you said the property was for sale?' Jack glared at Mike.

'I've no doubt he would sell to Mike if approached, but he took it off the market all the same. Overheard he had a bit of an argument with young Jimmy over the property being for sale. The young bloke wanted to stay and work the place but old Lloyd was adamant, wasn't he?'

'Hell you're telling the story Bill, dad didn't say anything about a rift between them.' Mike responded in the only way he could.

'Who is Jimmy?' Jack could not hide his irritation for this unexpected turn of events.

'Lloyd's adopted son, surly young bugger if you ask me,' Old Bill told him. 'Mike's dad would be able to tell you the story.'

'Huh?' This was the first time Mike had heard that statement.

'Sure, they came across from Queensland, together with Harry Clifford, Clem would know.' Bill was adamant.

Jack turned to face Mike. 'Your dad and Hopkins are buddies?'

'Been good mates for years.' Mike replied, looking at Bill quizzically.

'Is there gold out there boys? Rumours have been floating around town for a couple of weeks now,' Bill's face shone with expectancy.

'Gold? No!' Mike shook his head.

While disappointed Bill wasn't easily fobbed off. 'Pommy Harry is very interested in the old Hopkins place. Could only be gold, Harry's no cattleman.'

'Only a rumour Bill.'

'Is that so? Well two of Harry's boys were in here to purchase supplies and ammunition. Said something about a boat an' goin' up river for a while.' Jack looked at Mike who nodded. It explained the ambush.

'So you are certain he would sell the ranch?' Jack looked directly at old Bill for an answer, ignoring Mike, believing the young man was not charged with all the facts surrounding the property.

Bill nodded, 'Certain he would.'

'Looks like we have a sea voyage ahead of us if that's the case,' Jack regained some of his enthusiasm for the answer.

'I wouldn't bank on it.'

'Why not?' Jack was suddenly defensive.

Bill explained, 'Both Reutenbachen's ships are at sea, that's why! The Englishman took passage on *Scagway*, it's on its way to Melbourne with Otto himself, and the *Scrooge* won't return from Darwin for weeks.'

'Melbourne?' Jack didn't understand.

'Via Adelaide,' Mike informed him. 'It would appear Harry Street is going in person to purchase the Hopkins place.'

'That's right. He had me compose a couple of cables, one to Hopkins; I gave them on to Millicent, slipped me a fiver for me silence he did.' grinned Bill.

'Damn him! There must be another way. There has to be!' Jack thumped the counter top with a closed fist.

'Sorry to be the bearer of bad news boys,' Bill got out, seeing the look of despair on Jack's features.

'Not necessarily, are you certain about this venture Jack?'

Jack gave him a stony glare, 'I'm more confident now that Bill has confirmed Hopkins will sell. I won't let his lordship have it Mike! I'll fight him every step of the way.'

'His lordship?' Old Bill picked up on what the American had said, now his curiosity was aroused.

'What about Harry Street?' Momentarily Mike ignored old Bill.

Jack's shake of the head was with certainty, 'There's no gold on Tempi.'

'Lord Anthony leads a consortium from Great Britain, they are interested in the property,' Mike explained to the storekeeper. Jack silenced further explanation with a look of acrimony for the younger man. 'OK, take it easy Jack. Bill, have you got any maps of the Territory and South Australia?' Mike had a gleam in his eye and determination written all over his features.

'Should 'ave somewhere, 'scuse me while I take a look.'

While Bill searched out the maps, Jack brushed flies from his bacon sandwiches. Presently the men were pouring over maps and thumbing through old documents and accounts. Mike proposed in mid-summer to cross some of the most rugged, desolate, uninhabited country imaginable anywhere in the world. After haggling and arguing points for quarter of an hour, Jack felt he should bring this madness to an end.

'Just answer one question, Mike. Can you guarantee water for every day of the crossing?'

Mike shook his head, 'Nobody could make that kind of guarantee.'

'Then how in blazes do you expect to keep horses and mules alive? It's sheer madness. Your own common sense should have told you that. Even if you were lucky enough to get water for a string every second day it would not be enough to sustain them, nor us, we would all be dead in no time at all.' Jack didn't try and hide his belligerence for Mike's preposterous proposal, nor for the way things were turning out.

Mike grinned; he dropped his bombshell, 'camels!'

'Camels.' Jack could not believe his ears.

'Now that's not as silly as it sounds. I read somewhere about the early Afghan camel trains. Why not?' Bill reasoned. 'You can't go by sea, so, use the ship of the desert!'

'Yes camels, come on let's go and see Doc. We'll be back for supplies later. And Bill, will you have Millicent cable Hopkins? Explain that Mike Smith from Margaret River Downs is interested in purchasing Tempi Station. He is making his way overland. He will match any reasonable offer,' Mike looked at Jack as he spoke for approval, dictating to Bill who subsequently found a pencil and scribbled down the message.

'Sure thing Mike; I'll have Millicent send it today. Oh, don't forget to pick up your mail next door Mister Carter.' Jack nodded; already they were heading towards the front of the store.

Impatiently, Jack pulled some change from his pockets and placed it on the counter as Mike made the introductions. Pleasantries complete, a matronly Millicent reached under the single kauri pine counter and produced the cablegrams. It was left to Mike to thank her as Jack, trance-like, headed for the door tearing at a folded and sealed paper as he went.

Mister Jack Bryson Carter.... Stop.

I will not tolerate bribery. Your slanderous innuendo will see you served with a writ for defamation and libellous action should you persist with such scurrilous tripe.... Stop.

My son Harrison Anthony died while discharging his duty for God and country during the Boer conflict.... Stop.

Evidence of this can be found in the annals of war records (British War Museum). Further, his grave is well attended by the family in the military cemetery at Durban.... Stop.

My associates will purchase the property Tempi Station now, at any cost! Should you try to oppose my interest in this endeavour you will be unmercifully crushed…. Stop.
Signed:
His Lordship Sedgwick Anthony Esq.
Managing Director;
Anthony Thornton Corporation London.

Absently, he handed the cable to Mike before walking out into the sunshine to stand leaning against a veranda post for support and opening the second cablegram. 'It's from Katrina,' and Jack's heart missed a beat. 'She has gone against her father to warn me of his intention to purchase Hopkins Mountain.' Jack looked at Mike; a smile creased his features, the first cablegram already forgotten.

< >

A bachelor whose true love was medicine, Doc Andrew's needs were simple. His kitchen also served as his living room, the office fronting onto Main Street was where he spent most of his time, there and down at Stoddart's pub, some said Dot thought more of Doc than her husband, but Doc had never raised the subject with Mike. He poured them both a beer from a long neck bottle joining them at the table and waving Jack back to his seat when the younger man saw him reach for the box with the words "T.N.T. DANGER" written down the side in bold print, refusing to swap for the more conventional chair with the leather padded back.

'Now then! You want me to select a string of camels? What's this all about?' He asked, looking from one to the other.

'The Hopkins spread,' Mike disclosed with a grin for their confident.

'Have you pair confirmed there is gold on Tempi?' Like the rest, Doc had heard the rumours.

'No Doc, just a range of iron-ore.' Mike told him.

'The type of red gold necessary to build a nation,' Doc nodded harking back to a previous conversation with Jack.

'So the sample's old Ike discovered were genuine eh? And you can't wait for Reutenbachen to return, you are going overland, is that it?' Doc was aware both ships were at sea.

'Can it be done Doc?' Jack folded the correspondence carefully placing it in one of the pouches of the money belt he always wore under his shirt, his expression willed the practitioner to say yes, the older man saw the expectancy.

'Well yes it can be done,' Doc paused, 'have you any idea how far it is to South Australia? A more desolate and barren country doesn't exist. Daily temperatures can reach 120 degrees.'

'We calculated roughly, from maps put together by Forrest, Gosse, Warburton and Giles that it would be within the vicinity of eleven hundred miles.' Mike gave him a cursory look.

'Anyhow, don't you think it would be a damn sight easier to cable the Lands Registry Office in Adelaide to represent you?'

'We sent a cable, but according to Bill Myre, Hopkins has taken the property off the market, we need to approach him personally,' Mike told him.

'I need to know why Hopkins never worked the place. According to Mike, he was a good field man, surely he would have known about the mountain.' Said Jack.

< >

Mike Smith was taking an inventory while sorting equipment into a systematic order at their camp just out of town near the new cattle holding pens. Mike poked about the camp securing the several loads into canvas, ready to tie them off to the camels, his thoughts for their daring. A lot of capital would have to be invested in the enterprise and Mike was not really interested in mining; all he knew were cattle, all he wanted to do was settle down, court Molly Barker, get married have a tribe of kids, and work a property.

Mike saw Molly for the first time in five years on his return to Edge Rock from the war. He had been having a welcome home drink with Doc Andrews and a few of the locals when he spied the petite, auburn haired Molly passing the front door of the pub; she was wearing a tight fitting blue blouse tucked into jeans which showed off her shapely figure. He determined then and there to court and marry her. He was beginning to understand that Jack and he had different goals; Jack was driven by anger, and something that as yet Mike did not understand, but he felt it, and it played on his mind. He tried to shrug off his instinct and Doc's cynicism, he believed in Jack; he was the only real friend he had ever known. But not even he knew what went on behind that jovial mask. And there was a mystery surrounding Katrina. Had Jack been jilted? Mike felt they were suited for one another. He was very surprised when Jack arrived alone. Would Jack tell him in time? Sometimes some things were best left unsaid. However, it did not help him to understand the deep fathomless pit which characterised Jack Carter.

Chapter 22

Southern Indian Ocean

Harry Street was standing at the bow of the ship leaning over the railing watching the brilliant red ball appear above the horizon. Never could he remember such a sight, but then Harry rarely ventured out of doors. Behind him seamen were placing heavy tarpaulin in preparation for painting the forward jib crane. Below and just in front of the ship, playing their own form of Russian roulette, porpoises dived to surface some distance away, only to repeat the manoeuvres, it seemed, for Harry's benefit. Not a breath of wind, only the passage of the hull cutting through ocean, salt-filled air touched tantalisingly against the Englishman's freshly shaved jowls. Ahead and to port seagulls and terns darted from the sky, folding their wings and dropping like bombs into the water to feed on a school of surface fish which would periodically break the crest of the bow wave in a spangle of colour. Turning away and moving towards mid-ships, Harry could barely feel the swell lift the nose of the hull. The deep blue of the ocean contrasted to the lighter blue of the sky and Harry marvelled at the tranquillity of it all. He was in a good frame of mind as, under these conditions, they were making good yardage. All that changed in the time it took him to read the cable handed him by the steward.

Harry.... Stop.
Smith and Carter know about your interest in the Hopkins Range ---. Stop. --- They left early yesterday overland --- Stop.
Clarrie. End.

Carter couldn't possibly know about the gold. However if he secured the mineral rights as well as a grazing lease, it would amount to the same thing, he mused. 'Damn! I say, steward, would the captain be in his day cabin?' Harry had no idea how long it would take two men to travel overland but the thought of Carter racing across the wastes to beat him caused an anguished look to cross his features.

'I believe he is sir.' Came the polite reply.

'Good! I must speak with him at once.' Harry hurried off leaving the bemused steward to contemplate the meeting between Harry and the Skipper.

If he had finances none of this would have been necessary, Harry scowled to himself. He could have cabled a land buyer. As it was, his money was tied up in the club. It was the single reason he had cabled ahead to an old acquaintance, Jonathon Fischer. Even the pouch of gold strapped around his midriff was useless. He daren't go flashing it about. Reutenbachen acknowledged his urgent knocking and Harry burst into his cabin.

'Come in Harry,' he called, expecting the Englishman. He had seen the cable as part of standing instructions, insisting on complete co-operation and loyalty from the ship's company.

Reutenbachen was a handsome man, in his early forties with grey flecks through his wavy hair and the slightest indication of a paunch around his belly. While Harry stood patiently, for he had refused the invitation to sit, with the cable like an extension of his hand, Otto cupped his hands and sluiced again to remove the last remaining lather from his shaving. Water ran down his hairy chest to the towel tucked into the top of his trousers. A stocky man, the muscles rippled as he towelled himself down.

'Now then Harry, what can I do for you?'

'Something has developed, rather unexpected really. How is our running? Can we increase the speed of this tub?'

Moving behind the table shackled to the floor to prevent it moving in wild seas Otto replied, 'We are at full speed Harry. Is there something else I can help you with?' Otto saw the big man hesitate.

'Would you have any idea how long it will take to complete the voyage?' Harry patronised, which for Harry was unusual; however he had little control over this situation.

'Not really Harry, there are too many things that can happen, unforeseen intervening variables which could alter our schedule,' Reutenbachen deliberated.

'I see, well could you take into account obvious things and give me an estimate?'

Otto noted the slight agitation in the Englishman's voice. He was thoughtful for a while, 'Possibly forty days,' he replied at length.

'What! You mean to say I will be aboard this tub for forty days?' There was a flicker of anger and frustration on the deadpan features. Harry believed this would give Carter enough time to cross the continent and back.

'Maybe more, maybe less.' Otto shrugged. 'Does this sudden urgency have anything to do with the cable you received?'

'You read my cable!' Harry took a deliberate step towards the table.

'Only as a matter of course; nothing personal Harry. There are pirates operating this coast, they could take over the ship if they had a plant aboard to give them information. You do understand.' Reutenbachen tried to pacify the Englishman.

'Do I look like a bloody pirate?' Harry countered caustically.

'Now you listen to me, Harry,' began Otto, lounging back in the swivel chair with the high padded back. 'I'm the ship's master, out here I'm the law and what I say goes. I'll do my best to get you to your destination as quickly as humanly possible, and if that's not good enough for you, you can depart the ship at Fremantle. Is that understood?'

Harry leant over the chart table, both hands taking his weight, the knuckles of which were nearly as white as his shirt. 'Captain, if I feel the screw of this old tub slow down by one revolution, I'll be down here to find out why. Is that understood?'

The two men glared at each other across the chart table. At least it was out in the open now thought Otto, his attention for the charts, Harry already forgotten.

Chapter 23

The Northern Territory

Travelling generally south, on the sixth day out from Edge Rock, the men reached the first landmark of significance, the largely unexplored Purnululu Range deep in the East Kimberley and from where they turned away towards the east and the feared Tanami desert country. They chanced upon a soak. Its edges not unlike a patchwork quilt, and first to dry, curled to the sky and where only brackish water remained. With their gigantic shadows gliding over the uneven ground like so many ghosts in the silence, they headed the camels east along the crust of the soak. Near sunset they found a suitable lagoon near the eastern most point and the camels drank their fill, removing some 270 gallons of the bore water.

Trekking parallel to unknown ranges seldom they spoke, unless it was to draw attention to some feature such as a pillar of rock or a butte formation, which should be logged for future reference. The drone of flies continually about them did nothing to improve their humour or mood towards the otherwise eerie silence.

For some time, they had been moving through thick mulga scrub interspersed with huge sand dunes which extended in a north-south direction, fiery red in colour. Crabbing their way up the dunes, they would slide down the other side into the mulga where the camels carved a swathe across the flats before repeating the manoeuvre.

With the still heat numbing their senses, the mulga catching at their bodies, the men were in a foul frame of mind. They emerged from the mulga to face yet another steep incline of sand. It was noticeable, its surface was moving and the men, perched on their camels, could feel a breeze at their backs. By the time they reached the crest of the dune, sand was moving at an alarming rate; the wind was howling. Behind them an afternoon sun disappeared and a huge black shadow swept over the land.

It came on a front, a massive reddish-brown mountainous cloud of moving soil with a mushroom crest which spread across the earth's surface for miles; its stem spiralling from the surface of the sand dunes, rose several hundred feet. Cavernous and pockmarked like the surface of the moon, but with none of the moon's majesty, because it rolled on its surface like tumbleweed, exposing a new front of changing shape and energy ever more menacing as it lunged across the intervening space of the gully country towards the three adventurers. They were right in its path as it travelled from west to east carrying more than 25,000 tonnes of dust, the results of two separate depressions, which had combined to form a swathe of destruction across the wilderness.

Less than three hundred yards away, down the moving slope of red sand in the mulga scrub was possible salvation. Mike released the lead rope to the cows. The camels were down, squatting in the sand like nine large boulders, facing away from the front of the storm. Barney, unable to make himself heard above the wind gestured towards the scrub below and together the three struggled with the lead animal trying in vain to make the camel move. The roar of sound increased with every second that passed; the wind now so strong the men were thankful to be holding on to the halter ropes of the animals.

Visibility diminished by the minute. In desperation, they hauled against the camel knowing if they could get the bull to move, the others would follow. Mike drew his revolver and crawled to the rump of the animal indicating his intention to the others. At point blank range he pulled the trigger while Jack and Barney strained on the halter rope. The beast sprang to its feet emitting a cry of changing pitch. The camel charged ahead pulling the men with it down the slope into the mulga, the other's following, with Mike being blown along by the wind, sand, soil and grit that were cutting through his clothing like a thousand needle pricks.

At the base of the dune the light was slightly better. Looking up Jack observed the dust crossing above them driven by the gale force wind. They had stopped the camel's progress and soon the animals were squatting in customary manner facing away from the storm, their heads nuzzling the warm red soil. Frantically, Barney released spades and water drums from the pack animals. Barney jabbed a spade into the soil indicating for Jack to dig for his life.

Jack didn't know why and he didn't waste time asking for an explanation. The deeper he dug, the cooler it became. Finally he was standing in a shallow trench with sweat rolling off his body to form a stain on his trousers. He had exposed hollow tubes beneath the soil where tree roots had withered and died. Beside him, Mike and Barney were also digging.

'Dust storm boss little time him come,' said Barney indicating the darkness rippling across the red dune behind them, a shadow travelling at tremendous speed. Already grit as hot and fine as ash was falling over them, their breathing, laboured, with the sharp rise in temperature.

Barney poured the contents of three water drums over them when visibility reached zero and the first real gust of cyclonic wind reached out to pluck them from the surface of the earth.

'Into hole, breathe through tube till this fella gone maybe,' shouted Barney, not waiting to see if the others followed his example as he disappeared into his hollow, pulling the loose soil over his exposed body.

They were the last words Carter heard. When he had been blown off his feet by the magazine blast in Belgium, he had lost consciousness, he never experienced pain until much later. He was numb with cold by the time the medic and patrol found him. He had no time to experience fear. But now he was terrified. Fear of the unknown, the terrible fury and destructiveness the storm held. He had felt the surface wind striving to carry him away with its intensity, the increased heat, the dryness in his throat and sudden trepidation as he spied the awesome monster following the wind.

Jack pulled the sand over himself and lay helplessly in the cool, wet, shallow, hollow. Face down with both hands over his ears. He was trying not to listen to the deafening roar. He breathed hoarsely into the sand pipe. The stench of stale air did not bother him, the air was cool it was the feeling of being closed in, surrounded by the earth that he couldn't bear. In no time at all, the heat at the soil's surface increased dramatically drying out his clothing. He felt a force trying to pluck him from the hollow. His body heat exploded and beads of perspiration broke out all over his torso. Shortly a sudden increased weight on his back pressed him flatter into the earth and he choked a cry of alarm that wanted to issue from his lips, while his brain tried to reason what was happening. Still the noise heard so clearly, like a thousand head of cattle pounding at the surface of the sand, continued.

His senses were reeling, the heat was becoming unbearable while additional weight hopelessly pinned him in the shallow grave. Jack wondered at his endurance to stand the pressure much longer, his body ached with tension, every muscle, every fibre of his being cried for release. He wanted to claw for the surface and even moved his hands from his ears to begin when sanity prevailed. However the thought persisted—*get out now while you still have time.* He could no longer feel his tongue, the cavity that was his mouth was unbelievably dry and his nose was clogged with sand. Then it happened, the pipe collapsed. Air and sand rushed at his face from the collapsed tube, his air supply was gone. Frantically, his hands searched for the other pipe he knew to be slightly deeper, near his right shoulder. He tried in vain to move onto his hip so that he could wriggle into a position to search with his fingers for the elusive pipe. Like a man making love, instinct guided his hands, then panic took over as he discovered he could not move his body. In desperation he pawed at the sand, a sound like a cry emitting from his throat. Something warm trickled down his chin. His coordinated movements were slower, his mind was clouding, he wanted to shout, no words would come, he felt he was exploding… the heat… and still his brain refused to let him drift away.

Barney, his body taut, every fibre straining, listening for the changing sound which told him the storm had passed. Finally, with every muscle of his body straining to remove the soil, he emerged from the grave, the sand collapsing into the pit. The heat was intense; the sun's glare there once again as was the flies, which appeared as if by magic now the storm had passed over. He looked around him noticing with sudden anguish the fallen tree, one of many, this particular tree had fallen across where boss Carter lay buried below the sand. Unceremoniously, he dragged Mike from his hollow and together they frantically dug for the American. The heat being oppressive, they were shortly fatigued. It was only their will power and concern that kept them at the task. They were shovelling sand and soil when they dared and pawing with their fingers when they were close. Blood was running freely from bleeding stubs. They were near. The sand was running away to reveal boots then trousers. Quickly, they moved along his body until they had cleared his torso. Together they pulled him back from eternity to lay prostrate on the ground beside him, their heavy breathing as harsh as their surroundings.

Mike brushed a hand savagely at the collection of flies driven into frenzy by the smell of blood. Nudging Barney and realising just how hot the surface of the soil was out in the open, they carried Jack into the shade. His face was drained of colour. The eyes were closed, an expression of horror and fear frozen on his features. Blood clotted his nose, it coloured the loamy soil covering his skin and blotted his mouth and whiskers, dribbling down the stubble on his chin where it congealed giving him a ghastly appearance. Barney left them to stumble to where only the heads and humps of the bulls and cows were visible above the hot soil. Shortly he returned dragging another drum of water, removing the screw-down-cap he sluiced the very warm fluid over Jack's face while Mike dabbed at his nose, clearing his nostrils with his fingers, removing dried blood from his ashen face. Barney pointed and Mike noticed Jack's clenched fingers. They resembled the talons of a bird of prey, bared and hooked to pluck its quarry from the surface of the land. It wasn't a comical sight and Mike tried to imagine what was going through Jack's mind as his brain, starved for oxygen, slumped his body into unconsciousness.

<>

In 1913 Jack Bryson Carter was a young man of station and the war clouds of Europe were far from his mind as he stood folding the morning paper and peering into the glass covering of a water painting to straighten his tie. The stiff celluloid collar irritated him. He would be glad when the interview was over. Shyly he followed the receptionist through the waiting room across the plush green carpet pile and into the office of his future employer.

Like his father before him, Jack spent the next four years learning the professional business of mineral research, when in 1917 he did take seriously the war in Europe. Try as hard as he might he did not belong behind a desk. He missed Gramps, the outdoors, the adventure of everyday life, seeing new places, marvelling at nature, until, finally he took his leave and joined the engineers, gained a commission and sailed with the initial American Forces for France.

After the war it would have been easier to remain in America. Drill some core samples to see if there was oil on the property. With that and his speculating on the stock market he would have made his mark in a very short space of time, of this he was certain. However, it was not enough, he had been hurt, jilted by the only woman he could ever love, ridiculed by a man of opulence, who had power and wealth beyond Jack's wildest imaginings. A senselessness for war, the sublime power of aristocratic war mongers, all had incensed him with a loathing which until now he had not fully understood. Motivated by his European experiences he had something to prove. He craved wealth and power. Power to crush anyone who may try to hurt him. Power to dictate policy to governments, power to challenge Lord Anthony. Power to threaten, to achieve his own goals. He was driven by hate, the strongest emotion known to man. When he had this power, only then would he feel he had achieved his goal and some recompense for the humiliation he was made to feel. He was determined and nothing was going to stand in his way.

Consciousness returned, dazed he lay supine for some time before he let his mind register the closeness of death. Suddenly, it dawned on him as he lay watching Mike clean the revolver that where he lay a short time ago Mike could possibly lay somewhere in the future, all because of his disregard for anyone or anything which stood in his way. He did not want that to happen to Mike he realised. He must explain to the only real friend he had in the world the driving force behind their mad dash across the wilderness. He must ask for his understanding, his forgiveness, for the Australian had little ambition. He did not live on hate; his needs were simple. He was here because Jack was his cobber, his friend and the bond of friendship was as strong in Mike as Jack's driving ambition for wealth and power. It was a bond where only death would separate them and deny their friendship.

Mike placed the revolver aside to build up the fire. Barney had just finished their evening meal in the glowing coals when Jack's voice startled him.

'Barney, how did you know we would find the tubes below the surface of the soil?'

To Mike, Jack's voice sounded croaky, as though he had a head cold. 'You all right? Hell you had us worried mate.' Jack managed a grin for their genuine concern, as they commenced to fuss over him like two mother hens.

'A tree fell across you in the height of the storm, probably caused the pipe to collapse,' Mike guessed correctly, handing Jack a pannikin of tea.

'Is that what happened, pressed me tighter than a set of blankets to a mattress? Now Barney, are you going to tell me or not?'

'Just know boss,' grinned Barney, as well as he might. He was taught these things. Survival in the bush was his subject of study from early childhood.

Squatting beside Jack, Mike put his arm on his friend's shoulder, 'Jack, I feel it may be in our best interests to turn back while we still have time, before it is too late. Another week and we will reach the point of no return... ' He added seeing his companion about to interrupt.

'I know,' sighed Jack. 'I've been laying here thinking.' He turned to face Mike, 'But I don't want to quit Mike.'

'The hole we pulled you out of may well have been your grave! You do understand that don't you?'

'Yes,' Jack brooded.

'Look mate, when Harrison realises there is no gold on Tempi, I feel sure he could be approached... '

'Mike. It's red gold. It amounts to the same thing. He would be sitting on a gold mine. With this country crying out to be developed, he could name his own price in a few years. Anyway, I'm more concerned about the Anthony Thornton Consortium than I am Harrison,' Jack cut across his friend's reasoning. 'Mike, I'm for pressing on, but my motives for doing so are different from yours, I realise that now,' Jack sighed, holding out the empty pannikin for a refill.

Mike took the metal cup and filled it from the billy handing the pannikin back to his friend. 'Katrina?' He asked. 'I'm sorry, I had no right... '

'Yes you did. I owe you an explanation.' Jack took the cup holding it between both hands pondering where to start.

He retold Mike of his meeting with Katrina's parents, of the opulence, of her reason for being in France, of her letter. He lent forward easing his trouser belt buckle and exposing a money belt under his shirt. He opened one of the pouches and removed from it a wrinkled discoloured folded envelope. Without a word he handed the envelope to Mike. Mike noted the expensive stationary, the crest; he felt guilty and tried to hand it back, but Jack insisted he read it.

Mike moved closer to the flames of the fire holding the letter to the light. It read like Katrina had used the cooling period in their relationship, when she sailed back to England and Jack was still in France, to examine her position. She had never spoken of Chester Thornton while the three of them had been together in France. But Thornton was iron and steel, and Mike was reading between the lines, a merger of interests, a fairy-tale wedding where both sets of parents stood to gain.

'The uncertainty of giving up everything to live in Australia?' Mike voiced her words. Jack nodded, waving him to read on.

'So you had no station, but you were a man of means, you owned a property,' Mike defended his friend.

'I had never seen the property Mike; I had no idea of its value.'

'When I mentioned Australia, the old biddy really got upset; he supported her stand. I never stood a chance.'

He went on to tell Mike about Harrison's claim that certain letters may have been written by another to discourage their relationship.

'One thing is for sure Jack, they got to her, and they did a bloody good job apparently,' Mike didn't know what else to say.

'I had never made love to a woman before. It isn't something you do lightly. We swore our love for each other,' Jack shook his head, tears ran down his cheeks with a sudden memory followed by racks of hurt which issued from his diaphragm.

'I will never love another woman like I loved Katrina, Mike; it hurts. It bloody well crushes me every time I think of her. Then I get angry; I feel hatred for Sedgwick Anthony and his lady, it was a set-up. Australia... next thing I'm standing there being introduced to this pompous ass Thornton, and instead of belting the shit out of him, I'm shaking his weak sweaty hand. Oh Gawd how I hated myself after I got outside for not belting him one.'

'We'll press on mate, don't worry; nor Harrison or bloody Lord Muck will stand in our way.' Mike now had his reason, they would go on; he would support Jack in any way possible.

They talked for hours, about the mountain, Jack's plans for the future; he only hinted at the important role he wanted Mike to play in this power struggle. Jack intended Mike should enter politics, with his war record it would be an easy matter to gain preselection in the new Territory. Not that he mentioned it, this was not the time; however, he realised Mike would be lost at the plant. He was not an industrialist. This was not his dream. He could do more good in the political arena getting the necessary legislation approved to have development roads, dams and railways built, and to encourage a labour market so necessary for their industry to flourish. It would not be easy luring men to leave the cities for work. And there was no reason why Tempi could not be built up as a ranch. Mike would enjoy that challenge. Sitting there staring into the dying embers of their fire, Jack made himself a promise: as soon as he secured the property, he would write to Katrina. It wasn't until sometime later that the fire smouldered and all was quiet in the hollow between the sand hills where death's touch had come and gone not three hours previously.

Chapter 24

Fremantle, Western Australia

No sooner had the ship berthed at Fremantle, the busy port which served international shipping on the west Australian coast, than Harry Street began an impatient scrutiny for his travelling companion on the dock below. Jonathon Fischer could not survive without the action afforded by cities. It was the only reason he had not accompanied Harry to Edge Rock; he needed to be surrounded by people; he lived for the challenge, the chance to pit his skills against the vulnerable suckers that abounded in cities throughout the world. Harry hoped to make use of those skills once again. It was for that reason he had cabled ahead before departing Edge Rock, for Jonathon to meet him with some ready cash at his disposal. Harry never gave it a second thought that Jonathon would misinterpret his meaning; theirs was a long association.

Harry had missed him; of that he was sure as standing with several people on the terminus, he'd watched the restless pacing of the big man. Jonathon was pleased; a master of the masquerade he had assured himself that if Harry had been deceived then the parties representing Mister Wilcox would not penetrate his disguise. After watching Harry leave the ship's railing, Jonathon collected his luggage and mounted the gangplank taking the first steps towards a new adventure with his former associate. At the top of the landing he paused to scrutinise the terminus below for any sign that he had been followed.

'May I take those for you sir?' The steward asked. Then quick to apologise when he saw the man visibly jump like a startled rabbit.

'I'm terribly sorry sir, I didn't mean to startle you.'

'Quite all right old boy,' Jonathon quickly recovered from the shock, letting his monocle drop from his eye to dangle on the gold chain. 'I was miles away as the saying goes. Would you be so kind as to direct me to Mister Street's cabin?'

'Certainly sir, please follow me.' The steward relieved Jonathon of the suitcase and hurried off before the Englishman could protest.

The steward knocked, and Harry opened the cabin door to be greeted by Jonathon. Soon the two men were in earnest discussion. They had lived well off their wits, but Harry was always looking for that one chance at wealth.

'Eighteen-thousand pounds you say,' mimicked Harry.

'Will we need such a vast sum Harry?' Jonathon was well pleased with himself for having acquired the necessary capital.

'No, I imagine there should be plenty of change Jonathon… ' Harry's deadpan expression was mellowing with satisfaction at the little man's contribution. With what he had their funds came to thirty-seven thousand pounds, more than enough thought Harry.

'Excellent!' Beamed Jonathon. 'I fancy one of those motor cars.'

Harry's lips twitched in what passed as a smile. 'If this works out the way it should, you can own a fleet of automobiles. How did you get your hands on such an amount Jonathon?'

'Well among other cons, I arranged a meeting so to speak, a Mister Wilcox purchased some cattle along with breeding bulls, to which I had a bona-fide deed of ownership.' Harry allowed himself a chortle. 'He bought, I sold, and guided the police to the bush hideout of four cattle duffers. The police arrested them and took them to a rock crushing quarry owned by Wilcox to work off their debt as I was given to understand.' Smiled Jonathon.

'Jonathon, you never cease to amaze me.'

'What is the scam Harry?' Jonathon rubbed his hands together in expectation.

Harry was savouring the moment, slowly, almost deliberately, he rose to his feet removing the leather poke from his vest pocket. He shook the leather poke and lovingly cartwheeled the nuggets onto the small coachwood table. Like dice the nuggets tumbled to lie on the table's surface, their jagged edges so many cats' eyes glittering in the uncertain light of the cabin.

'Good Lord, I say Harry! What have you done... robbed a bleedin' gold mine?' Remarked Jonathon, an expression of glee etched his features.

Fischer knew Harry well, he didn't reach to pick up the gold but rather waited anxiously until Harry beckoned his approval, whereupon he lovingly cupped the largest nugget in his hands, surprised by its weight, and stared fascinated at the small fortune for several seconds not saying anything. 'Jonathon, we are going into the gold business.'

'Has this something to do with the property you wish to acquire?'

'It has everything to do with the property,' replied Harry. He examined his gold fob watch and there was an impatience in his manner as he closed the case, returning the timepiece to its pocket.

'You look worried Harry, is something wrong?'

'Jonathon others are interested in purchasing the property. The consortium and my family for one, although how Father knows with certainness there are iron-ore deposits near Edge Rock I can only guess... damn! That is what Carter must have meant... ' Anguished Harry. *I made the mistake of telling your father of my intentions once I reached Australia.* Harry's brow broke out in a cold sweat; he was shaking. It all came flooding back, his conversation with Carter.

'Something is wrong, isn't it Harry?'

Harry ignored him pacing the cabin. Finally, 'If father was aware of the property's mineral wealth, then it had to be Carter who gave him the information. Carter must believe the mountain is an iron-ore deposit,' Harry surmised, one hand stroking his chin. 'Logical deduction! Therefore, he is not aware of the gold. However, if he beats me, it won't matter; once he gets his hands on the property, he will soon discover the gold, it amounts to the same thing! But how could he raise the necessary capital to purchase the property let alone form a company to extract the iron ore? No it must be the Asian beef market. It has to be!'

Jonathon nodded vaguely following Harry's train of thought. 'Do we have a head start Harry?'

Harry turned to face Jonathon. 'That is my dilemma Jonathon; this American chap is going overland. I have no idea if his journey would be shorter than ours, probably perish in the bleeding desert. Father, well I imagine he will employ someone to do his dirty work; again, alas I do not know,' Harry shook his head. 'I must win Jonathon. This is my chance to gain wealth, power, respectability, my last chance to revenge myself. We must beat them at any cost!' His huge fist slammed into the surface of the table spewing nuggets across the room.

< >

Harry lifted his clenched fist letting his knuckles make contact with the door's timbers. He was in flagging spirits and eager to be under way now that Jonathon was on board and his finances were in order. A nod from Otto saw Willie, *Scagways'* first engineer, open the door to admit the well-groomed Englishman.

'Ah, Mister Street, come in. Well, I understand your associate is on board. I trust he likes the accommodation; it's the best we can offer under the circumstances. I hope you will both join me for dinner this evening.'

Harry was immediately on his guard. 'I beg your pardon. When are we sailing?' Harry had observed Reutenbachen never took time to relax, let alone enjoy an evening meal in the company of others.

'There will be a slight delay, Willie,' began Otto, indicating the white haired little Welshman who was biting his nails and trying to hide his mirth at the sudden change of expression on Harry's countenance, 'has informed me there is not enough coal in our bunkers to reach Port Adelaide. Two ships are ahead of us for refuelling. Just a slight delay, nothing to be concerned about.'

'A slight delay! How long is a slight delay captain?' Harry was brusque.

'Four days Harry, as I said nothing… '

'Four days! Are you trying to ruin me Reutenbachen?' Harry's normally deadpan expression flared with anger.

'I'll not be departing this port without fuel for you or any man!' Stated Otto, although his voice was surprisingly calm, he was seething with anger.

'Well said!' Willie did not bother looking up from his nail biting. Harry, cast upon him a contemptuous glare, before turning his attention back to Otto. He was about to tell the trade's person to be seen and not heard when Otto cut across his thoughts.

'The time we lose here will be made up crossing the bight, so why don't you return to your cabin or go ashore for a while?'

'Explain yourself.'

Otto let out a long sigh. 'We steam south until we pick up the roaring forties, it's a wind-stream which blows from west to east in gale proportions. We will more than double our speed. Was there something else Harry?'

Harry had one hand on the door handle; he said nothing, turning to leave after fixing them both with a glare, the brown opaque eyes like those of a lion, this conversation already locked away in the back of his mind.

With Reutenbachen's suggestion to go ashore, surfaced another dilemma for Harry. *What if parties representing Mister Wilcox or the police for that matter, were at this very moment on the docks and contemplating a search of the ship?* The urgency of this thought and the possible threat it posed took precedence over Reutenbachen's words. He needed Jonathon and the man's exceptional skills. With trepidation Harry closed the door and hurried off astern to their cabin.

Chapter 25

Fremantle, Western Australia

Further along the Fremantle Dock another ship was disgorging its cargo in the form of two large wooden crates from a forward hold. The derrick crane's movements were being supervised by two well-dressed gentlemen. One used a walking cane to support a stiffened leg. He was pointing it towards where the slings were straining against the weight of their cargo. Once the observation was made, the other leaned across and was heard to remark that he didn't think the Biplane was so heavy, whereupon the man with the gold-knobbed cane grinned and explained that it was probably the crate of ammunition, the air cooled machine gun and the several pieces of equipment so necessary to reassemble the Fokker.

'A machine gun Clayton?'

'Yes old boy, to be used by you, the observer.'

'Steady on, I didn't come along to fire machine guns, I'm the photographer.' Merrick was distraught at the thought of laying eyes on a machine gun let alone firing the beastly thing.

'You read Lord Anthony's cable. We are to secure the property at all cost. And crush any opposition. Which means we are not the only group interested in the Hopkins range.'

'Yes but surely you do not intend I should shoot somebody.'

'You may have to Merrick. I'm the pilot.' Grinned Clayton, beckoning for Freddy and Reginald to join them on the dock.

'Have no fear little brother, if there is any trouble, I feel certain Reginald can handle it.' Clayton patted Merrick on the back both men looking at the large frame of the ex-training sergeant, towering over the little English mechanic.

'We need some transport Freddy,' Clayton addressed the dour middle-aged Englishman when he was close enough to be heard over the din of the cranes. 'Afraid we cannot assemble the Fokker here, need a garage, or something on the edge of this beastly little town, see to it please Freddy, take Reggy with you.'

'Yes wing commander sir, won't be long,' Freddy doffed his peaked cap. It was always wing commander; even if Clayton had explained several times that he no longer held his commission. The man does everything but salute, Clayton told Merrick after they had left.

'He gives me the creeps, never talks unless spoken to, ugh,' Merrick shuddered.

'He knows his place and he knows engines like the back of his hand. He may have to tune the Mercedes to suit this damn oppressive heat. I hope they have fuel in this blessed place.'

'Oh I don't know, it's not such a bad part of the world, plenty of young ladies,' Merrick turned as he spoke to gaze admiringly at a young woman who caught his eye, slowly twirling her shade parasol as she watched the cargo being unloaded from the high seat of a sulky. The man beside her was older, obviously her father Merrick made the summation, and possibly they were waiting on an order of machinery to be unloaded so they could take delivery. Merrick liked to think he could interpret the intended actions of others.

'You get control of yourself Merrick; we have an important task to complete. See if you cannot find someone to bring our luggage to the... ' Clayton paused to look at the name of the recommended accommodation. 'Carlton Hotel,' he read from the card.

A bullock team pulling a bung cart was used to remove the crates one at a time from the dock to a warehouse near the edge of town. The assembly of the biplane would take longer than expected. One of the wings, which were constructed of timber, covered with fabric had split at a join. The join would have to be repaired using animal glue and several layers of suitable fabric, which would of necessity be purchased from an emporium. As well it was decided because of the hatred so many bore the Germans, even if the war was over, to remove all evidence in the form of black crosses from the side and tail of the former fighter plane, to be replaced with the British insignia. This white washing and painting would take time. Another subsequent delay for Freddy to tune the fuel-mix until the Mercedes 160 horse-power engine ran smoothly. Then it would be time to tow the assembled Fokker further out of the township so that flying trials could begin. Clayton insisted Freddy would accompany him initially as observer, so he could hear for himself the sound of the aircraft performing in the sky. Merrick was disappointed not to be co-pilot. He had hoped to see the rich-red colour of the hinterland from the air and to take some photographs. Clayton was adamant, insisting Merrick and Reginald should gather as much information about the coastal town of Edge Rock as was humanly possible and in particular Hopkins Mountain and Tempi Station from the locals.

Five days later, the drone of the aircraft could be heard well into the afternoon before Clayton declared the Fokker ready. After taxing the aircraft back to their temporary hanger, he composed a cable for head office.

Sir James Loxton,
   C/o Anthony Thornton Consortium 214-218 Fleet Street, London.
   Arrived Fremantle. Have plane assembled awaiting instructions.... Stop.
   Were you aware? The Northern territory is administered by the Federal Government...? Stop.
   Do you wish us to proceed to Edge Rock and locate Hopkins Mountain...? Stop.
Kindest regards your faithful servants,
Clayton and Merrick Thornton... End.

<>

Sir James had his tailor with him when the cablegram from Australia arrived. The short be-speckled man ran the chalk line down one side of the trouser leg to reduce excess material from the calf of the leg. Sir James stood silently reading the cablegram while Gilstone repined the pieces of material along the new chalk line. Finally, Gilstone stood back satisfied. He would have to take the suit back to his premises on Saville Row to complete the alterations after which, an appointment could be made for Sir James to fit the suit once again. Their arrangements being agreed upon, Sir James left the tailor with his secretary to make these stated arrangements, as suddenly he was preoccupied. Finally, the significance of the second sentence of the cable became clear.

A short time later, in Sedgwick's office, and after he had made the comment, 'what does this mean James?' Sedgwick looked up from his desk cluttered with correspondence, waving aloft the cable.

'The land rights are held not in the Territory but by the Federal government, currently in Melbourne until the American architect Walter Burley Griffin finishes designing their new capital building at Canberra.' He ruminated. 'The Territory is just that, a territory, which was, until recently, administered by the South Australian government. Therefore, no Territorian can legally sell his land or its mineral rights without contacting the proper authority.' Smiled Sir James from opposite Lord Anthony's cherry wood desk.

'So if I contacted someone over there in government...' pondered Sedgwick, leaving his desk to stand before the large window overlooking the Thames and London bridge.

'Lincoln Barnswald?' Prompted James.

'Barnswald, that's the chap James,' Sedgwick turned from his cursory observation of a small fishing vessel motoring up the River Thames to one of the many moorings in the distance.

'They're in power at the moment?'

'The National Party? I should think so Sedgwick, little opposition really.'

'And that is the way it should be, suppress the Worker's Party they wouldn't know how to govern the colony anyway, bunch of shearers as I'm given to understand.'

James didn't bother explaining the Queensland shearing strike of 1891 led to the formation of the Labour Party but did not necessarily mean its members were shearers. 'Shall I cable Lincoln Barnswald to be our representative in this matter?'

'Presently. I would still like to know if the American knew what he was talking about. Have Clayton press on to this town,' Sedgwick could not make himself mention Edge Rock; even the name was distasteful. 'And there make inquiries like I assumed he would have done in the first instance. No initiative James, that's the problem with young people today.'

Sir James nodded. 'How is Libby, Sedgwick?'

'She is still getting terrible headaches but then, she has her good days James; Katrina has been most thoughtful spending much of her time with her.'

'And pressure is causing the headaches?'

'Most certainly, according to Symonds. The fellow is the best there is James,' sighed Sedgwick. 'We can only pray she will recover.'

James nodded his understanding, promising himself he would drive over at the weekend and visit his sister maybe for the last time.

Chapter 26

The Northern Territory

Gradually the valley floor narrowed, meandering into the distance to disappear between two high walls of rock. The camels sedately picked their way down a boulder strewn dried-out watercourse. The slopes changed and by mid-morning the men were shaded by vertical cliffs forming a chasm.

The storm had followed the men across the east, its menace threatening, only to abate. But with every passing day it grew in intensity until finally its watershed burst. The storm was preceded by the wind. However, all this occurred approximately twenty-miles to the north of the men's present position. It struck the earth with such force that it did not penetrate the hard crust of the bleached-soil but ran in sheets forming rivulets of water, which flowed from the highland down the pans between the slopes and the valley floor. Its deluge lasted just over an hour and in that time, six inches of water had fallen in an area spanning three square miles. It was in the chasm, having followed the dried up watercourse. The sound in the chasm was deafening.

Mike unfastened the halter rope to the pack animals at the same time casting a glance to the debris that clung to the chasm walls. Its significance struck him like a thunderbolt, a flash flood; their only chance was to out run the water. Mike pointed to the debris for Jack's benefit, before striking his camel to a gallop.

Jack's look of alarm changed to one of grim determination as his camel bounded forward in pursuit of the lead animal. He gripped the plaited leather with such intensity that blood drained from his knuckles exposing bluish veins to protrude above normally smooth skin. The bull was going at full pace, continually changing direction to follow the floor before it, railing around curves like a racehorse, ignoring everything in its path, sensing the urgency of the moment. Ahead a shadow cut across the chasm floor and up the southern wall. Here, the chasm divided and the camels chose their direction. The chasm was like a straight river channel, carved out by a new river racing onwards through softened material, picking and percolating all in its path to scour its bed and banks.

Sound of the pack animals grew fainter and the ominous rumble of rushing water grew increasingly louder until Mike, releasing his grip on his camel, turned to catch his first glimpse of its snake's head in the distance. The spray washed the walls of the gorge in beads of water. In the sunlight the floods dancing head of spume appeared as a gigantic disarranged rainbow, changing as he stared to a mountainous green wall travelling up the walls of the gorge, steam hissing from the hot rock faces.

As he watched, Mike saw the pack animals beaten in their race for life. One by one, the flood waters swallowed them up. He passed the fork in the chasm without seeing it, his mind a blank, numb, after watching the burdened animals struck down by the towering torrent. His camel rounded a bend in the chasm, swerving once on the rock platform to avoid the drop into the deep pool of water directly ahead. Smith plummeted from the animal, bouncing on his shoulder; the blow driving the wind from his lungs, his momentum carrying him over the lip of rock into the depth of the pool below.

Jack wrenched on the halter forcing his camel's mouth open as the nose peg pulled taut. The big brute skidded on the rock surface, the soft pads of its feet torn to shreds with the heavy punishment as the pressure by its rider urged it to stop. Jack witnessed Mike thrown by the sudden change in direction, bounce like a ball over the ledge. Quickly but without panic, he tied off the rope thrown him by Barney who also witnessed Mike's misfortune. One end of the rope he tied around his middle, the other around the girth strap of the camel.

'Feed the line out Barney!' He shouted. Not waiting to test the strain or to see if Barney was following his instruction, he plunged over the lip.

Barney reached the edge of the steep drop in time to observe ripples from Jack's dive already splashing against the broiled rock-face. He fed out the line then saw it foul at about the same time as he heard a loud sound and a rumble like thunder, only louder in the confines of the chasm. He knew the wall of water had reached the curve where the chasm divided. It was only seconds away in time from where he stood terrified, gazing down at the rope caught fast below the water's surface.

The tracker stood looking down into the green depths, frozen, beads of water dancing on his brow in the sunlight, and the smell of his fear strong in his broad flat nose. Then it came, first a cry, choked, followed by a soul-searching scream from the depth of his guts and he plunged off the ledge into the pool to free the rope as the flood-water hit the rock platform.

Jack reached Mike just as the line went taut around his middle. Then it was free again and they were being hurled downwards, cartwheeling as they went. Suddenly, the surge thrust them forward before the rope snapped tight.

Jack released a grunt as air hissed from his lungs, the sudden stop bringing a sharp cry of pain to his lips as the rope bit into his sternum, threatening to cut him in two. He was conscious of a deafening roar and the force of volumes of water trying to press his skull flat. It took him a short while to come to terms with what had transpired. Swept through the narrow opening, they were dangling by rope under a waterfall. Somewhere below them was the valley floor.

Bruised ribs brought an involuntary gasp as Jack sucked slowly at the air. He was supporting Mike's full weight. They were inside the flow of water, their bodies cannoning off the rock-face. Blood gashed from a wound on Mike's face, he had not stirred. The rope was cutting into the big man, burning his skin just above the money belt strapped to his waist. He searched and found a footing; at first his legs would not support their combined weight. Grimly he clawed at the face with his left hand and noticed for the first time the missing joint. Slowly it registered and all else was forgotten as he made to examine the bloodied stump with the protruding bone. If Mike had not stirred in his grasp at that moment, he would have been dead. The movement was enough to bring Carter back to the present and as quickly his mind was thinking rationally again. Gripping the face and ignoring the stab of pain, he anchored his body fearing to look down. Under the lip, the face of the rock was smooth, being weathered by the interim action of water it did not afford much in the way of support. To his right was a ledge, wide enough for them to sit comfortably, he commenced to yell and shake Mike.

The sound came from far off. Mike became conscious of a grip like a vice about his waist. The scream came once more right at his elbow. He craned his head towards the sound. He was sure now it was not a dull roar in his brain. He beheld a face, contorted with pain, the cords of throat and neck muscles stood out from smooth skin like rain forest twine. Jack! It was Jack. Mike tried again to speak but no sound came, although he could hear himself say the big man's name over and over in his mind.

It came flooding back, their wild race down the chasm trying to beat the flood waters and his falling... He reached out tentatively with his right hand across his body and shook Jack by the shirt front, to no avail. Mike twisted his fingers around the matt of curled hair and pulled as hard as he could. It was a stony look of annoyance, which softened and mellowed after what seemed an age. Mike watched the transformation as contorted muscles relaxed and stretched skin returned to normal, a broad grin followed, then crocodile tears of relief ran down his cheeks, followed by a shudder which passed itself on and through Mike.

Silently he marvelled at the man's endurance, for God knows how long he had been supporting his limp weight. Mike searched and found slight irregularities in the cap-rock wall of the truncated valley which allowed him to take his weight from Jack's arm which was numb and hung limp like the branch of a dead tree.

The ledge was wide enough to enable them to sit and dangle their legs over the rim. Jack untied the rope from around his middle, as it was not long enough to span the distance. They sat side by side on the ledge, Jack holding onto the rope, which he placed under his leg once they were settled. He emptied his pockets and removed the money belt to examine its contents. All he had in the world was contained within the folds of the soft leather pouches. Satisfied and more relaxed, he began to experience the first real spasms of pain from the stub. He sat patiently while Mike made a makeshift bandage from his pocket-handkerchief.

'When did that happen?' Mike wanted to know.

'I've no idea, the first I knew of it was when we were dangling over the drop,' moaned Jack, wincing as Mike tied off the bandage, pulling it tight to prevent it slipping up over the wrist.

'What happened to Barney?'

With a shake of his head Jack replied, 'I honestly don't know.'

Both men fell silent; they knew instinctively Barney had drowned. They wanted to believe his dark face would register his pleasure when they climbed to the lip of the cirque.

Chapter 27

Port Fremantle

Their third morning at port and Harry, irritated by the delay got some exercise by walking about the ship. He was standing in the bow at the time, watching aboriginal children diving into the harbour for silver coins, when he spied them. There were three of them. All well dressed in three-piece town suits. They sauntered up the gangplank and were in close conversation with the bosun. Police! He was certain of it. Surreptitiously Harry made his way aft to their cabin using the starboard side of the ship to hide his movements from the sight of the trio. He was passing the lifeboat, which was covered by tarpaulin when an idea came to him. Harry entered the side door and followed the passageway through mid-ships towards the stern of the cargo vessel. The stewards were cleaning the mess. Harry could hear them washing up after the tars and complaining bitterly because all hands would be required to stay aboard. No shore leave, as soon as the bunkers were full of burning coal, they would be under way, regardless of the time. Their mutterings were of no concern to Harry; he was convinced the policemen intended to search the ship. Boldly, he entered the kitchen. The cook was setting out his preparations for lunch at a stainless steel servery while nearby, two stewards were in the act of washing dishes. Cook spotted the immaculately dressed Englishman.

'May I be of service Mister Street?' For all the ships company knew of, or about Pommy Harry by now.

'Yes, could you parcel me some lunch? I rather think I may go ashore for a while?'

'That'd be right,' one of the stewards uttered to his mate. 'Certainly Mister Street, I will see to it personally.'

'Splendid, could you have one of these fellows bring it along to my quarters. Oh, I am in rather a hurry, please be sure to tell them not to loiter.' Harry glared at the backs of the stewards, willing them to turn and face him, to no avail.

Harry hurried aft to their cabin, looking right and left before using his pass-key. Jonathon Fischer was applying his daily make-up, he would have to continue this disguise until they reached their destination. Seldom did he leave the cabin for fear he may be spotted from the docks below. He turned as Harry entered and immediately read the concern on the big man's features.

'Is something wrong Harry?' He observed Harry peering along the passageway before closing the door.

'Three policemen just boarded the ship Jonathon. I'm certain of it. You must hide at once. I had the steward fix you some lunch. I will bring it to you.'

'Where am I going to hide Harry?' There was a sudden trepidation in Jonathon's voice.

'In the lifeboat, they won't think to look there. You will have to take your attaché case with your several disguises Jonathon, just in case they want to do a thorough search of the cabin.'

'But Harry, the lifeboat, you know how I hate to be closed in, claustrophobia?'

'Jonathon, if they catch you, you will be closed in for a very long time, need I say more?' Jonathon shook his head in submission.

Stealthily, Harry led the way along the passageway keeping ten paces in front of Jonathon and acting as a cockatoo. Harry reached the life raft and unsecured the canvas at the bow. He beckoned for Jonathon and the smaller man ran from his concealment behind a jib to join him. Harry heaved and Jonathon disappeared into the darkness. He resecured the rope, careful to imitate the knot and before striding away, informed Jonathon he would return shortly with his lunch and some liquid refreshment promising to release him once the coast was clear.

The steward brought the prepared lunch to the cabin, Harry barely acknowledging him. As soon as the man was out of sight, he advanced on the lifeboat, undoing the knot and passing the food and drink to Jonathon. Already the heat was radiating from the canvas covering and Harry could imagine Jonathon sweating profusely under his make-up; unfortunately there was nothing he could do and with a word of encouragement, he fastened the line before striding leisurely forward to knock upon the door of the captain's day cabin. Otto opened the door. He seemed very excited about something.

'Do come in Harry.'

Harry looked about the cabin however, it was empty apart from Reutenbachen and his Number One, Oliver Black. 'I was telling Oliver about a visit I just had from a syndicate of wool buyers Harry.' He beamed.

'Buyers? I don't understand?' Harry breathed a sigh of relief.

'They represent a pastoral group. They want me to ship their wool bales to Sydney. The men are moving the jibs in line with the holds as I speak to take the bales on board.'

'Does this mean another delay?' Harry frowned.

'No we will be on our way inside the time I told you Harry... ' Otto was in high spirits. 'Oh by the way Harry, you and your companion may like to go and look at the aeroplane. I understand it is the first of its type ever seen in Australia.'

'An aeroplane?' Harry's brow furrowed with concentration.

'Yes, apparently it will be used for aerial survey work by the Anthony Thornton Consortium, or so the ship's captain divulged to me.'

'The ship's captain?' Harry let the door handle to Otto's cabin support his weight as he strained to hear every word.

'The 'North Star' is one of the Anthony Shipping Lines. I was fortunate enough to be shown over her yesterday by her captain. All the modern technology at his beck and call.'

Harry controlled his anxiety forcing a smile, 'well, we may just take your advice and look over this aeroplane.'

'Don't get lost Harry, we sail first thing in the morning.'

'Then I will not hinder you any longer,' he backed out of the cabin, closing the door. Harry's knees were trembling with trepidation for his conversation with Reutenbachen.

About him as he made his way aft, was a hive of activity. The crew positioned large jib cranes and slings to haul the wool aboard. Other tars were busily removing the hatch covers. Harry was oblivious to their presence as he went about the business of releasing Jonathon.

'A bloody aeroplane!' Harry swore, venting his agitation for his talk with Reutenbachen once they were back in their cabin and halfway through a tumbler of Scotch whisky.

'What are you so upset about Harry?' Jonathon sipped again on the scotch until his tumbler was empty.

'They brought out an aeroplane to search for the mountain!' Harry stumbled about the cabin, and Jonathon couldn't help but observe the Englishman's frustration.

116

Chapter 28

The Northern Territory

They used the last of the visible light to gather firewood, making their camp in silence; each numb with shock and the realisation that Barney was gone, swept away by the flash flood. Too tired and emotionally drained to talk about the day's happenings, they spent a very uncomfortable night, the only sound apart from the waterfall was the crackle of burning timbers from their miserable fire.

On top of the cliff overlooking the pool, they built a cairn of stones to commemorate Barney's final resting place, promising to return one day. It took the best part of the morning. From the bluff they could see the bloated bodies of their camels and equipment scattered for some distance down the valley. The rest of the day was spent sorting their retrieved equipment and pondering their position. They recovered the rope, which was still attached to the bloated carcase of the camel wedged between two partially submerged boulders. Both thanked their lucky stars the cinch strap had held firm. Using his pouch knife, Mike cut strips of meat from the camel to dry in the sun. At least they would have jerked meat to see them through. They had lost their sextant, the compasses, Mike's revolver, both the rifles, most of their clothes and provisions.

'Have you any idea where we are?' asked Jack.

'If we continually head south east, we will cut the Overland Telegraph Line, once there we head south,' Mike answered at length.

'Christ! We could be anywhere,' Jack lamented.

Mike nodded his agreement; both men left the direction finding to Barney who never seemed undecided. Now they were on their own without a compass and the continual uncertainty of not being able to see the sun to take early bearings because of the ranges. The trees, bent and bowed, were not much help as in places the wind eddied in the hollows between the ranges making it impossible to confidently guess its prevailing direction.

'If we head generally east down the valley, we will pick up the desert country.'

'The Tanami Desert?'

'Yeah, one hundred and fifty bloody miles of it.' Mike's voice carried his concern. He was no longer optimistic about their future. In a fitful sleep, Jack saw a ship steaming across the bottom of Australia.

Chapter 29

Edge Rock, Western Australia

A cross wind of little consequence Clayton decided, circling the machine once again over the rutty surface that sufficed as a road while Reginald looked for any obvious danger which would hinder a landing. At a little over stalling speed, Clayton straightened his approach; finally deciding to land the aircraft on the dusty desert road just beyond the ferry which was presently making its way against the strong flow of the river. From his seat in the cockpit, he could see the heavy metal cable drawing the ferry closer to the shore. The line was snaking away in a loop straining to hold the little punt with its singular vehicle, a red truck, in line with the approaching ramp. Then they were past and flying along the road which disappeared with frightening speed for Reginald who had never flown before. Lower and lower the biplane flew. Dust was rising due to the action of the propeller and filtering back into the tinted glasses of Clayton as he steadied the rudders. The ground came up to meet them and with a bump made contact. The plane motored along the road jarring the innards out of the observer in the confines of his less that adequately padded seat while stirring a cloud of dust like a thick blanket to envelope them. Shortly the Englishman turned the machine and veered from the road some fifty paces before switching down.

Bill Myre was suitably impressed. He had run out into the street like the rest to observe the flying machine. Shortly he was confronted by the two airmen in overalls, with flying caps and goggles hanging loosely around their necks, the encrusted dust tracing where the goggles had formerly been positioned protecting their eyes. In a way, he was reminded of Doc Andrews when he drove his tourer around the district. Out on the veranda school kids were peering through the windows to get a glimpse of the two airmen whom they had followed down the street from the schoolyard to Myre's emporium. Bill excused himself and striding purposefully to the front of the shop scooted them, not satisfied until they had rounded the corner opposite Stoddart's pub.

'Well! G'day gentlemen, and what can I do for youse?' Bill smiled at them from across the counter.

'One of the children told us this was the place to get some information mister... ?' Clayton leaned forward expectantly.

'Oh, hell. Call me Bill. Everyone else does.'

'Bill,' Clayton nodded sardonically, 'yes of course. Well Bill my companion and I were told you knew everything that went on in town so naturally we came to you.'

'Oh?' Bill was a little wary.

'Yes, you see I'm rather anxious to locate a friend of mine, from the war you know.'

'And who might that be?' Bill wiped a cheesecloth along the counter.

'Carter. An American. Have you heard of him?'

'Carter.' Bill paused with his wiping as if pondering on the name.

'Yes I thought he had a property, he mentioned something about the Hopkins range...' Clayton paused. Bill nodded looking at and through the two airmen. His conversation with Mike and Jack not forgotten, in particular their mention of being on the lookout for strangers.

'No, I'm sorry fellas, the name doesn't ring a bell,' he replied after some considerable time.

The shorter of the two looked at the larger man and nodded before limping away a pace or two towards the door leaving Bill pondering what was on his mind. He didn't have long to wait; suddenly a closed fist hit him flush on the nose and a spurt of blood quickly followed. Bill was knocked senseless, his hands catching at the counter's edge to prevent crashing to the floor. Before he could realise what was happening, the big man had dragged him across the counter and hefted him to his feet as if lifting a rag doll. The big man turned looking at the other man resting on his walking stick who was standing by the front door. Through a haze, Bill saw him nod and again felt the sting of a cowardly blow to the side of the head, then another, which smashed into his ribcage. Bill's mind went blank; he was floating in a cloud of weightlessness until the cold contents of a bucket of suds kept to mop the floor brought him back to the present. It was the one with the cane who did all the talking. He was leaning over him.

'Are you going to tell me the truth, or does my companion have to hit you again… Bill?'

'He's gone to South Australia overland… ' Bill blurted, spitting out a broken tooth and a blob of blood to the floorboards.

'Oh and why has he gone to South Australia?'

'To buy a property.' Bill found a handkerchief in the pocket of his bib overalls and gently dabbed at his broken mouth.

'The Hopkins Range?'

Bill nodded.

The Englishman knelt beside him; Bill pulled himself to a sitting position against the front of the counter. 'It's the iron-ore isn't it?'

'Don't know nuthin' 'bout any iron-ore,' Bill tried to look the man in the eye.

The man in the flying uniform with the British pilot's insignia on the sleeve of his flying suit turned his head towards his companion once again. Bill watched as he limped towards the front of the emporium, before the bigger man grabbed for him once more.

'No! Please don't hit me again,' Bill cowered back against the counter.

'Tell me what I want to know then William. I do not take any pleasure in having Reginald punish you. Yet punish you he will in a minute if you don't start answering my questions.'

'Gold.' Bill hung his head resignedly.

'Gold! Gold?'

'The bleedin' property is a bloody great reef of gold… ' Bill was resigned to telling all.

'Who else knows about the gold Bill?' Clayton could barely hide his excitement.

'Only Carter and Harry Street.'

'Harry Street?'

'Pommy Harry. He owns that fancy pub up the road,' Bill tried to shake his head in the general direction; the movement brought a cloud of pain causing him to grimace.

'How does Harry know about the gold?'

'He found the nuggets first I heard, he's racing the American to South Australia to purchase the mineral rights.'

'Is that so,' leered Clayton.

'Yeah, whole town knows… ' Bill, missed the sarcasm in the Englishman's voice.

'I see… One last thing Bill old sport, how do I get to Hopkins Mountain?'

Bill looked up at the softly spoken Englishman deciding his position to be hopeless; the big man behind him was hovering in the background waiting further instructions. 'Just follow the river till it forks, Hopkins Mountains' straight ahead, 'bout three or four days by boat dependin' on the tide.'

'Boat indeed, then there is a river and it is navigable? Lord Anthony will be pleased with this news.' Bill nodded wiping his mouth again and examining the blood smeared handkerchief.

Clayton looked up at Reginald, unable to hide his surprise and pleasure. 'There, that wasn't so bad was it Bill.' Clayton stood. He reached inside his flying suit, producing a wallet and from it extracted a folded ten-pound note dropping it beside Bill's legs before moving towards the door and the plane, closely followed by Reginald.

When he was able, Bill sent a cablegram to a friend in Alice Springs advising him to look out for two strangers, one, an American, Jack Carter by name and to warn him of two British airmen and their interest in the Hopkins place and to mention a name, Lord Anthony.

<>

Clayton Thornton had decided to fly north-east inland, to the boom town of Kununurra. It would be his headquarters for operations. He could not very well ask Bill to send further cablegrams, not after the way Reggy had fisticuffed him. Anyway, according to the maps he found in old Bill's store, Kununurra was closer to Tempi than Edge Rock, with the added advantage of being larger with probable roads on which to land the aircraft, and fuel to refill the biplanes tanks.

Tomorrow, he wanted to inspect the mountain from the air. So it was gold, Lord Anthony never said anything about gold, nor would he be aware a third party was interested in purchasing the property. *Who the hell was Harry Street?* Clayton had no idea. However, he realised Street knew about the gold otherwise why would he be vying to purchase the property? Thoughts came and went as Clayton made his preparations, maybe he would have to eliminate Street as well and an omniscient smile played across his cold calculating features.

Chapter 30

St. Paul's Cathedral, London

A wedding and now a funeral reflected Katrina morosely as the cortege of prestigious black Rolls-Royces motored decorously up Ludgate Hill towards St. Pauls Cathedral. Her father beside her shared her grief. However morose better described her frame of mind as the Christopher Wren designed cathedral came into sight and a sudden memory of her wedding to Chester filled her thoughts. She had cried when the news of her mother's death reached her shortly after her return from Warburn Abbey in Bedfordshire where Libby had gone to spend her last days looking out over rolling hills, green hedges, and forests of spruce for as far as the eye could see. Now she only felt bitterness and anger as her mind wandered to her mother's subterfuge ways, which culminated in her being denied love and happiness.

The cortege stopped outside the massive arches today bathed in pleasant sunshine and Katrina alighted the vehicle followed closely by her father and Chester. Chester insisted David should accompany them so the lad could say goodbye to his grandmother; Katrina was adamant the child would not be in attendance, it sparked off a bitter slinging match between the pair but finally Katrina had her way. Libby had tolerated David, nursing him for family portraits, showing affection in front of others, condescendingly imparting information to her circle of friends who inquired as to his welfare, but rarely did she ask about the child and Katrina reciprocated in kind by not making much ado to David about grandmother Anthony. Constance Thornton, Katrina's mother-in-law, on the other hand did not see him as often as she would like and always showered David with affection and gifts. Katrina found her to be a very sincere and likeable person.

Katrina stood letting the sunlight catch on her cheeks through the mesh black veil. She was seeing without noticing the throng of mourners filing into the cathedral, many dignitaries and associates from around the world who had come to pay their last respects to Lady Elizabeth Anthony. Gently her father put his arm through hers and with Chester a step behind, they entered the cathedral to join the phalanx of mourners. When this was over and time commenced to heal her mentally, Katrina vowed she would write to Jack explaining what had transpired to have their engagement quashed.

< >

Three days after Libby's funeral, before James Loxton approached Sedgwick with a request, it was the moguls second day at the offices of Anthony Thornton Consortium. After Libby's death, Sedgwick was detached, his loss so great he found it hard to concentrate on business and he frequented his club. Drinking with friends and associates gave him a direction to focus his attention.

'What purpose would it serve?' He muttered moving aimlessly to the window drawing the heavy velvet drapes, which bathed the room with sunshine. Lord Anthony made a mental note to inform his private secretary his period of mourning was over and his office showered in flowers and letters of sympathy, previously unoccupied during the last five days, should be returned to its former state, business as usual.

'I feel Harrison has a right to know his mother is dead.' James told him.

Sedgwick beckoned James to a chair. 'Forty-five years finished just like that,' he clicked his fingers together looking directly at his brother-in-law.

'Harrison?' James asked at length.

'What about Harrison?' Sedgwick's voice carried his chagrin for a long lost memory of a young man in his elegantly tailored uniform prior to leaving for South Africa.

'A brief letter to make him aware of Libby's demise... '

'Has Katrina sent replies to the many letters of sympathy?' Sedgwick's demeanour was inexorable where Harrison was concerned.

'Katrina is working on it, among other things,' was the reply.

'Good! Was there anything else James?'

'Apparently not Sedgwick,' James sighed knowingly, shaking his head in resignation and rising to leave the office.

'James!' The brusque tone verged on anger. James turned immediately, the cadence in Sedgwick's voice stifling any argument. Self-consciously his hands clasped the back of the chair.

'Where was Harrison when Libby and I needed him most? Why am I still running the business instead of relaxing, well satisfied in the knowledge my son has taken charge? Where is he now when we need him? I'll tell you, he ran away from his duty as fast as he could! He is dead James and will remain so.'

'I don't understand Sedgwick. He did what?' James pried.

Sedgwick was blunt, he didn't wish to discuss Harrison, 'no letter, is that understood?'

James nodded submissively.

Chapter 31

The Southern Ocean, Australia

Wind whipped the livid green ocean into a frenzy, it howled past the bridge sending spray to cascade down upon the wheelhouse. Straight from the ice of Antarctica, it tore at the masts and stays, and whistled through the bulkheads. It was the type of wind that chilled a man's blood and turned marrow to ice. The water's icy tentacles speared into *Scagway*, chipping at her paintwork and glass panels to spatter like molten metal, running down the smooth surfaces of steel and racing back to the welcoming arms of the sea. The once even swells were broken up by the storm's fury to form white-backs fifty feet high. A mountainous sea was running against their beam, bent on tearing the ship apart. The game little hull was bobbing like a buoy anchored to its chain in the wake of a passing boat. Huge walls of water with creamy white foam tinting their crests lifted the bow towards the heavens, running aft to the keel, plunging the bow into the trough with a wicked sideways roll. At times the next wave, towering in turn, would break as they lay sluggishly in the trough and beat down on her, a green wall which would still her progress on impact bringing a shudder of protest that could be felt in every part of her superstructure.

Harry Street was thrown from his bunk to the floor by the sudden change of the ship's motion. Fischer would surely have fallen on him, only he caught the corner post of the bunk saving himself. The hull seesawed with the new motion not letting Harry gain his feet and Johnny watched, hopeless to help him as he was thrown about the cabin. It seemed to the little Englishman that the ship was breaking up. He could hear the pitch of the screw vibrating through the hull and the screaming agony of steel; anxiously he looked at the rivets holding together the heavy boiler plate. There was a new sound, terrifying to the occupants of the cabin that of the joggle and slop in the troughs as the ocean sent green walls of water riding up the side of the hull, passed the portholes where it deposited salt which would later form a crusty scum, and to the railing as *Scagway* listed and rolled. The lamp, one of two left burning, broke in its bracket pitching the cabin into eerie darkness, stuffy with its stale air and the rank smell of coal oil spillage. Chains rattled and clanged as anchored furniture moved in harmony about the room with the roll of the ship, until the links took up the slack.

Chain, steel, condensation, the closeness of the metal cabin, all had an unnerving effect on Jonathon. It reminded him of his days at Highgate Prison. The clang of the steel barred doors, of bunks with chain supports, a single candle and the smell of occupants closeness, the damp smell of kapok, horse hair, urine, and the screams for violent scenes.

'Harry! I have to get out. I can't stand it in here. Please. Help me Harry. Harry!'

'Steady on Jonathon, nothing to be alarmed about,' Harry reassured him with a confidence he did not feel. However, he read the fear in his friend's voice and the last thing Harry needed was for Jonathon to go up the wall.

'I hate being closed in Harry! The noise. We're going to die Harry, I know it; listen to the steel, it's crying. It's an omen. I just know it—Harry! Are you there Harry?'

'Listen to me!' Harry shouted from the floor, his voice rising in pitch to capture the man's attention. When Jonathon regained his self-control, he continued. 'Reutenbachen said we could run into foul weather. Listen to the wind lashing the sea. We could not go out in that! It will not last long old boy. I promise you.'

'Harry, I feel ill, so terribly ill Harry!'

Their cabin was above the stern and the changed rolling motion of the ship had a most undesirable effect. Jonathon was sweating inside the turtleneck jumper even though it was bitterly cold in the cabin. His face was pale and beads of water danced on his forehead. He belched, then dry retched. Trying to hold back the feeling of sickness, he swallowed the water continually forming in his mouth. But the roll and sway would have its way and Jonathon vomited over the side of the bunk, directly over the ungainly shape of Harry who had managed to grab the edge of his bunk.

Street cursed Jonathon in silence as the warm stinking bile ran down his nightshirt. He clung to the bunk's support with one hand, using the other to fend off the sick, conscious of the discomfort yet numbed by his own fear. Harry cast his mind back to another incident over which he had no control, he was only five at the time, but he remembered it as though it were yesterday.

Pony, saddle and bridle were gifts from his uncle, the Duke of Gloucester, and his pater was adamant young Harrison would ride the animal. Tall as the sky it appeared to the small boy, puffing wisps of hot air from its nostrils and stamping its feet on the cobblestone walk, a beautiful black animal with a white blaze between its eyes. The boy glanced at his father then at the groom holding steady his birthday gift and fear smote his little heart. He turned away from the outstretched arms of his father adorned in his crimson riding habit and fled towards his mother and governess. Kindly at first, his father beckoned him back, then crossly adding emphasis to his command with a stroke of his riding crop against the highly polished leather boots. The boy cringed behind his mother's skirts, running from her to his governess at the stern approach of his father and his mother's unwillingness to interfere. Harrison's arms were outstretched towards the one person who gave him overwhelming affection when they were alone, for Mary above all others saw he was starved for love. However she dare not touch him, although her heart went out to him. Beneath her breastbone was a pounding of despair for her loyalty to her employer and her love for the child. Harrison kicked and struggled, crying until his face was blotched, but his father would have his way.

Harrison looked from his high perch in front of his father to the grass below; through his little boy's eyes it seemed a frightfully long way to fall. He turned appealing to Mary his governess. She stood speechless, tears running down her cheeks, feeling for him but having made her decision not to interfere she turned away. A little boy learnt a cruel lesson that day.

Pony and horseman followed King, the stallion, being led by the groomsman, down the side of the forty bedroom mansion past the kitchen where odours of food in various stages of preparation issued forth and on along the cobblestone walk to the green vastness beyond the stables.

Once on the veld, the rider kicked the animal's flanks and the spirited pony streaked away, the drone of pounding hooves at first jarring the boy, unaccustomed to the gait of the animal. By contrast his father sat straight backed, as one with the horse. The soft turf sprayed from behind thundering hooves, gutting the grass at regular intervals. At breakneck speed they headed towards the pond where Harrison would gather hazel nuts from the nearby trees. On and on they raced, his father's laughter drowning the boy's feeble whimpers of anguish, on towards the hedges and the forest of spruce and oak...

Harry was saddened by the memory and for a moment it filled his being. At first he thought it strange that after all this time it should come flooding back to haunt him. On reflection, perhaps it was the motion of the ship and another situation not to his liking but over which he had no dominance. It was a sense of helplessness, of feeling so inadequate he reasoned, more than fear of the unknown. Harry was always in control, never leaving himself knowingly poised in a situation where he felt a disadvantage, always confident in his own ability, to the point of almost being vain. At times life's experiences were cruel and they taught Harry lessons which over many years changed him inwardly, his thinking, his philosophy, and the code of ethics by which he lived. Hardened by his experiences, rarely did he display emotion, it was there, bottled up inside him, like lava inside a volcano, never reaching the surface for others to see, and it would take more than a storm at sea to trigger a reaction hidden behind the deadpan expression. There was only one person who had seen the lava flow, who knew the real Harry Street and Harry suddenly felt angry and ashamed that it was a stranger, the tall American, to whom he had opened his heart, and now the same man along with his father was trying to ruin his claim to untold wealth.

The door burst in with such ferocity it crashed into the timber panelling at the completion of its swing. Closely following its movement, a figure barely recognisable as human draped in a dripping mackintosh was thrown into the cabin by the lurch of the ship. It was Reutenbachen. Not releasing the handle, he thrust the door closed, striving to keep his footing, while straining with every ounce of his strength against the howling wind and the vacuum from within. In the short space of time the hatch was open, cold Antarctic air swirled around the walls of the cabin touching bare skin with chilling suddenness in its eddying charge before the door was resealed.

A stench of seasickness returned, stifling Reutenbachen, just as the smell of salt spray and sea water was evident to the cabin's occupants.

'Are you all right Mister Street?' Otto shouted to be heard above the terrifying din.

It was Street's companion who answered in a fear-riddled voice with a question of his own, 'is the ship going to sink captain?'

'Not if I can help it, Mister Fischer. Bad weather I'm afraid, a southerly buster, they frequent this latitude.' He explained.

In the murky darkness they sought each other out, guided by the voices, even if they were thrown about the room to echo hollowly from the walls of the cabin. Otto left the door and aided by the roll of the ship involuntarily stumbled towards where a lamp should be attached to its wall bracket. He felt and found the mantle was missing, the wick burnt down to the spout of the container. Deftly his fingers found the adjustment turn screw and fed more wick until there was enough to light the lamp. Standing with legs braced and elbows locked about the bracket for support, he lit the wick, satisfied there was enough coal oil to last until daylight only a short time away. The room burst into a glow, enough for the occupants to see each other.

'Shouldn't you be up in the wheelhouse? Who is steering this ship?' Harry wanted to know.

The animosity wasn't lost on Reutenbachen. *That's the thanks I get,* he thought to himself, remembering the treacherous jaunt from the wheelhouse to the stern of the ship. Twice he had lost his footing on the icy metal decking. The rubber soles of his sea boots gave little traction in these conditions. In silence he remembered pulling himself up the pitching deck and holding on grimly as the wash swept along the gangway and over the sides. At times he was up to his thighs in water, its current so strong he was forced to let his feet go with the momentum, clinging to the railing with all his might. Icy tentacles tried to pluck his fingers from their hold while the salt and spray speared into his exposed eyes and face, blinding him. It took all his resolve to hang on until he could steal forward again.

125

Gripped with an ill humour for Street's cutting remark, he retorted, 'Don't come out of your cabin until the storm blows itself out. In the lockers under the bunk you will find life preservers, I want you to put them on and keep them on. One of the crew will come for you if we have to abandon the ship. Above all do not leave your cabin under any circumstances,' he finished, backing to the door and letting himself out of the cabin. The creak of protesting steel reinforcing his words and increasing his passengers fears; if that were possible.

Outside, leaning against the door with icy salt spray hitting him in the face like shards of glass, Otto had misgivings for his statement. He imagined the torment his words would have on the pair. Fischer seemed a decent type, not like Street, and momentarily he pondered their relationship until a green wall of water saturated him from head to toe and he was forced to give all his concentration to the arduous task of returning to the wheelhouse.

< >

For two days and nights the Indian Ocean defied them, the storm ran unchecked, never once relenting on its mission of destruction. Then during the night, their twenty-seventh at sea, the fury of the storm abated. By morning, several nautical miles off course, the only evidence of its passing was a thick creamy scum atop the blue green swells where two ocean currents merged.

Harry and Jonathon drank all the scotch they could lay to hand. They occupied the bottom bunk, both wearing their life jackets. It took Harry a long time to convince Jonathon that Reutenbachen was having a piece of him and that the damn ship was not going to sink. With daylight, the little man felt more comfortable and was able to hold down his share of whisky. He even left the bunk to look through the porthole on one occasion until a wall of water covered the glass, and, horrified, he scampered back to the bunk, his sea legs wobbling about all over the place. Harry produced a pack of cards and they played poker for a while until Harry got bored with it all and threw the cards across the room. It had nothing to do with the fact he was losing, he chided Jonathon. It took some time before they accustomed to the sound, the pitch and sway. Often could be felt the vibrations of the propeller thrashing about half out of the water. They tried to sleep and indeed catnapped for a few hours, the scotch languishing in their systems, their senses dulled by the alcohol. Harry removed his life jacket, advising Jonathon to do likewise; he refused and slept with it on his person.

Finally, after some time, they realised the southerly buster had blown itself out. Convinced this was the case, both men donned some clothes and ventured on deck. It was raining, a storm, and both could see where the rainbow disappeared into the ocean, their pot of gold.

Chapter 32

Anthony Thornton Building, London

Sir James read the latest cablegram from Clayton addressed from Kununurra with a look of foreboding on his features. Hopkins range was rich in iron-ore and… gold! The cable told of Messrs Carter and Street racing each other to South Australia to purchase the property.

Sitting alone in his office, James Loxton pondered over the significance of the cablegram. Now Harrison was caught up in their stupid scheme. But was it gold? Or, was it just a hoax and if so by whom and against whom? Of one thing he was certain, he could not reveal to Sedgwick that Harrison was vying to purchase the property.

Sir James met Sedgwick for lunch at his club. Over their meal the topic of conversation was his report that the range was indeed a rich field of iron-ore. Further, James was able to inform Sedgwick the Margaret River was navigable and therefore suitable for shallow barges. He made no mention of the gold.

'Very good James, now we can contact Barnswald with a lucrative incentive if he can stall any sale of the property until Clayton arrives.'

'Yes it may take weeks before Clayton can reach Adelaide. He will need fuel stops for the plane every five hundred miles,' James agreed.

'I'll leave you to cable Barnswald, and I would like to be rid of Carter once and for all.' He added the timbre of his voice indicating his abomination for the American.

'What are you suggesting Sedgwick?' James paused, a spoonful of turtle soup before his mouth looking suddenly vexed as his mind raced to decipher the implication of Sedgwick's words.

'I want Carter, removed James.' Sedgwick leaned across the table, his voice barely a whisper above muted conversation from around the dining room.

'Do I understand you to say you would like Carter… dead, Sedgwick?' James's voice quaked with the enormity of the idea.

Sedgwick nodded. 'He is a thorn in our side James, he knows about Harrison.'

'That is no reason to kill him for God's sake. You cannot take it upon yourself to take another man's life on a whim.'

'A whim!' Sedgwick looked at James, shaking his head deciding it was time to tell his brother-in-law a secret. 'Carter can ruin me. I believe I discovered how he identified Harrison.' Sedgwick looked wildly about the dining room to observe if their conversation were attracting more than a minute interest.

'Well?' Now James was curious. He had pondered over the same question. He believed he knew Harrison, knew the man would not want to reveal he was exiled never to return to England.

'The ring we had made for Harrison before he went away to the Boer War. It was a replica of our family crest. The letter, Libby gave Carter a letter on our stationary, upon which our crest is embossed.' James nodded slowly at Sedgwick's logic.

'Still, that is no reason to have the man killed Sedgwick.' James did not try and hide his repugnance.

'You never got squeamish when I approved Captain Wilson shooting those pirates?'

'Piracy on the high seas is a crime. They were trying to steal your ship. They would probably have killed the crew if Wilson had not acted when and like he did. Besides, I wasn't a member of this company at that time. For God's sake Sedgwick!' Appealed James. 'I want no part of this,' he finished, folding his napkin and abruptly pushing his chair back.

Angrily Sedgwick pointed to the chair. 'Sit down James! I'm not finished!'

'How can Carter possibly hurt you now?' James lowered himself into the chair, leaning forward across the table, his face sombre to match his mood. Sedgwick looked up in time to see their table waiter push the chair forward.

'That will be all Matthew!' Sedgwick glared at the waiter until he bowed and moved well away.

'Because he would know who told the consortium where to find the lode of iron-ore. It was his ambition to work the range, to produce steel to develop an Australian industry,' sighed Sedgwick.

'You stole his dream?' James eased back slightly but with expectancy, waiting the admission of guilt.

'I had my reasons. And I don't want him using Harrison as leverage for revenge.'

'You are a very powerful man. Did you not tell Clayton to crush any opposition? Good lord Sedgwick he is only one man?'

Sedgwick nodded, 'A man of vision; he wants Australia to become a republic, displace the Commonwealth, very dangerous politics, his cause may be taken up by others.'

'Harrison?' James could not appreciate Sedgwick's concern. Before Australia could become a republic, they would financially have to be able to stand on their own. Removed from Great Britain, its cultural bonding, investment and market outlets, he believed both him and Sedgwick would be long dead and gone before that would happen.

'If he has met Harrison, he could get at the truth. Harrison is a weakling; he ran from a fight, he is not a brave man James.'

'You do not know your own son or you would not be talking this way Sedgwick.'

'Oh, I know him well enough; he deserted a mixed company to save his own skin. I have the official transcript of his trial.' Sedgwick lowered his head with shame; he had just enough alcohol in his system to make him melancholy.

'Not Harrison, never!' James stammered, his jaw dropped. His ashen features told Sedgwick his brother-in-law was indeed shocked by the revelation.

'Yes Harrison, and he may just be willing to tell Carter all about it. Wouldn't that cause a stir?'

'A stir? No! Never! Harrison would be too ashamed to reveal a secret like you have just spoken of to anyone.' James shook his head violently, deliberately, his face downcast to hide the sudden hurt he felt for the boy.

Sedgwick shook his head in resignation. 'Sometimes James I wonder… If Carter were in possession of Harrison's story what is to stop him selling it to the newspapers? Suddenly we are confronted with a mud-raking narrative, which would destroy the family name. I would be made to resign my seat on the House of Lords, sell my many business interests. Too, the royal family would be embarrassed by the scandal. The Prime Minister would be forced to appoint a Royal Commission, a full inquiry! Their investigation would reveal the truth,' Sedgwick was nearly beside himself as the reasons became more transparent.

'The truth?' James prodded, easing forward to catch Sedgwick's every word.

'The murder of some poor soul who died wearing Harrison's uniform in a covert agreement at the highest level.'

'Not the royal family, you cannot be serious.' James gaped in awe as Sedgwick nodded in the affirmative.

'The reputation of Kitchener and Buller would be ruined. The stigma would attach itself to their families. Yes.' He nodded his head slowly. 'It would tarnish the highest level of officialdom. I would most definitely be ruined.' Sedgwick reiterated, his countenance sombre; his eyes blazing into those of James. 'Now do you understand why, if Carter were to have an accident, I would not be disappointed.' Sedgwick held the glare looking him square in the eye.

'I was unaware Sedgwick,' James uttered, barely able to look at his brother-in-law. The ring was the proof; there could be no disputing their family crest. His thoughts were racing to keep abreast of Sedgwick's disclosure.

'No one knew, with the exception of the royal family, and they intervened to have Harrison spared.'

'That's terrible.'

'That's not all; I was confronted by Katrina. How she got hold of... certain information I'll never know,' Sedgwick shook his head not looking at James.

'What information was that?'

'Letters Libby conspired to have written to quell any thought of marriage between her and Carter.'

James nodded knowingly doing his best to hide a smile, 'I see.'

'You don't see at all, she is planning to go to him if he will have her. Apparently she has written to him.'

A cable, James mused. 'And David?' This all came as such a shock.

Sedgwick gave him a perspicacious look, 'What about David?' Did James know something he didn't know?

'Katrina won't go until David is older surely... ' James rushed his reply, assuming Katrina had not told Sedgwick that Chester wasn't his father.

'Certainly not! Neither of them are going anywhere; I have plans for David. This will be his empire, after he attends Sandhurst Military Academy that is. And until he is old enough to take control of the company, I want you to see Katrina exercises greater interest in its affairs.'

'And just how should I go about that?' James was pleased, if unsure how he could achieve the request.

'I intend to make her company vice-chairman,' beamed Sedgwick.

'Will we get the board to approve such a move?'

'I believe we can. With Clayton and Merrick in Australia, and you to support her nomination. I'm reasonably confident. Besides, I hold a majority of company stock.'

'So you feel once endorsed, Katrina will not refuse the position.'

'Something like that James,' Sedgwick seemed well pleased with himself. He intended to tell his daughter if she did not comply with his wishes, his grandson would not receive one penny of his rightful inheritance.

'Now do you understand why I want Carter eliminated? And I want the Hopkins range secured!'

'I understand.' James ruminated when a sudden thought struck him. *Oh my God, what have I done!* He could convince Katrina her going to Australia was presently not a wise move. But not telling Sedgwick about the gold and Harrison's attempt to secure Tempi Station made him part of a conspiracy which could see the paths of Carter, the consortium and Harrison cross again. Maybe it was already too late.

Chapter 33

Adelaide, South Australia

Senator Lincoln Barnswald sat at his inlaid mahogany desk. He watched the nondescript figure of his secretary leave his office, quietly closing the door behind her, before tearing open the cablegram with his letter opener. To his surprise it was from Sir James Loxton, a good friend and former colleague. They had gone to school at Eton and were close chums seeing a lot of each other right up until the time he had been introduced to Elizabeth Loxton. He fell hopelessly in love with Libby and thought she felt the same way about him, until his proposal of marriage was rebuked. Not for his charming Libby a solicitor, Libby had her sights on the aristocracy. Nothing less would appease her ambition. Lincoln's social tree and circle of friends, evenly tolerated. It was a chance meeting with Lord Sedgwick Anthony at one of the many fundraising committees Libby attended that led to a whirlwind romance, mostly behind the back of her other suitor, Lincoln, before it was announced she would marry Lord Anthony.

A dejected Lincoln Barnswald decided to move away; even Scotland or Wales did not appear far enough to quell his loss. So it was, Barnswald sold up his business interests and sailed for Australia.

After Libby came on the scene they had not seen much of one other and Lincoln couldn't even remember saying goodbye to his former colleague and friend, so the cablegram was a complete surprise, and he counted mentally that it must be all of thirteen years since they had last seen each other. Lincoln married Elizabeth Hopkins, Lloyd's sister, after whom Mount Hopkins was named. Elizabeth was attending The South Australian University at the time studying law when the pair met. Lincoln was an associate professor of law and her tutor. Elizabeth was instantly attracted to the young tall well-groomed handsome scholar and teacher. Their honeymoon was spent abroad and Lincoln caught up with his old friend James Loxton to show off his new bride, the daughter of a wealthy grazier he'd told James, sure Libby would get to hear this piece of news; just as Lincoln intended, for he still carried a torch for the voracious Libby Anthony.

Eagerly he scanned the cable once, then read it thoroughly, reading between the lines and realising instantly James was but a mouthpiece for Lord Anthony and his business interests. The irony of the message, his brother-in-law was involved if indirectly at this stage. So the consortium headed by his lordship wanted to purchase Tempi holding, a large cattle station in the Territory and administered by his government? Did Lloyd know of their intention? He read with interest the reference to a party electoral donation. Barnswald was a man of principle; James knew he would not be intimidated by a bribe. Not that he believed for an instant James would stoop to such a low ploy to gain a favour, but Sedgwick Anthony was another kettle of fish and Lincoln wouldn't put it past him to offer a bribe to gain his ends.

On the one hand, he could try and do his old friend a favour or he could let his brother-in-law make his decision for him. He pondered his direction most of the morning before arriving at a decision. He would arrange to have lunch with Senator Gerald Perry, a friend and colleague in the present government whose portfolio was to administer land and mineral rights in the Northern Territory, after which he composed a cablegram for his brother-in-law advising Lloyd of the consortium's interest in Tempi. If Lloyd wanted to sell his land to the Anthony Thornton Consortium, Perry could move any barriers and if Sedgwick Anthony wanted to reward the national party with a donation that was his business.

<>

Clayton Thornton read with interest the return cable from Sedgwick Anthony. He was required to proceed to Adelaide as swiftly as possible and make his appearance known to one, Senator Lincoln Barnswald. Also, to gather without notice to his presence, as much information as he could to the whereabouts of the American, Jack Carter. The double meaning of the last sentence amused him:

Carter, to be eliminated.... Stop.

Clayton took this to mean killed. He had no doubts. Killing wasn't something new to him; he had seen his share of death over Flanders Fields, experienced the adrenalin surge, the pumping of his heart as he sought and shot the enemy from the air, the excitement of the pursuit and that unforgettable moment when he pulled on the firing mechanism watching the trajectories spitting from the Vickers machine gun, strafing the enemy aircraft, the look of astonishment plastered over the features of the pilot, the finality when spiralling, the plane plummeted out of control towards the killing fields below. He looked with relish to meeting and killing this American for no other reason than the adrenalin surge.

The grin of anticipation Clayton allowed himself for the instructions from Lord Anthony was replaced with a calm serenity as he strode across to where Reginald oversaw some of the locals turning the plane into the wind, ready for a take-off down the dusty rutted road. He filled two Jerry cans, besides the plane's single petrol tank, in a bid to reach the city of Perth on the River Swan in three stages. From there he would fly south to Fremantle, pick up his brother and instruct the others to arrange their transport for Adelaide.

The heat was oppressive and Clayton decided to wait until the cool of the evening before attempting the first leg, a flight of more than six-hundred miles. The locals told him the sun rose at five. If he left around midnight, he should be able to land safely in daylight. Clayton estimated with a slight tail wind and flying in a south-easterly direction, he should be able to complete the first leg to Broome in around six hours. Then he could follow the coastline all the way.

The makeshift runway was lined with kerosene lamps purchased from one of the town's hardware stores. If the lucky sales person wanted, he could collect the lanterns and resell them once the plane was airborne Clayton explained, when asked what he was doing with so many lanterns. This appeased the storekeeper's curiosity.

That night at five minutes after midnight and the slight delay lighting the several lanterns, the Biplane took to the air. The cosmopolitan population of Kununurra turned out in their droves to watch the daring pilot and his petrified observer leave the ground.

Chapter 34

Tanami Desert

Soft desert sand crunched beneath their feet, the crust breaking like brittle glass, the particles compressing on the moving sand below. It was quick to sap their energy, making walking difficult and the distance attained of little consequence. They had recovered some useful articles after leaving the truncated chasm upon reaching the valley below. Of most importance was a container of bulk tea, which they emptied and filled with precious water.

Their fifth day on the desert, the thirtieth of their trek, and more than four hundred miles still remained. As each day passed, they pushed themselves harder becoming more and more apprehensive about the progress of the other parties. They moved by instinct waiting for one or the other to drop and spell a rest period. Mike, by now too tired in body and soul to care, ready to accept they had surely been beaten, even if Jack moved steadily onwards with a grim determination.

During the fifth night, a dense blanket of fog spread over the desert. Somewhere behind the men it had rained recently and the prevailing winds had blown the heavier air mass towards the east. The men roped themselves together like climbers on a mountain. Carter took the lead with Mike several paces behind, so dense was the fog they could not see one another, a tug on the rope indicating a stop was required.

Eerie was the desert now; the silence not broken by the drone of heat they imagined came from its surface. The only sound was that of moving soil grating over itself at each footfall and their laboured breathing ringing in their ears while white vapour wisps from tortured lungs mingled with the surrounding air. The going was relatively slow and very tiring at first and as the hours of forced march continued, it was noticeable that small gibbers and fine gravel replaced the sandy soil. Twice Mike stumbled, pulling the line taut, the sudden drag bringing Jack to a stop. He would wait until Mike hauled in the rope and they were standing together. The second time it was noticeable to Jack that Mike had been walking in a half circle, he came in from his right so he decided to stay put and wait for him. When he told Mike that he was flanking him and not walking behind him, Mike became agitated.

'Do you want to shorten the rope Mike?'

'You're the one going in circles, not me,' was the belligerent reply.

'I have not moved since you tugged on the rope, you came in on my right. Another twenty minutes or so and you would have been in front of me.'

'You are the one straying from our course! Anyhow this is madness; we don't know where we are. How do you know you are not taking us in a bloody great circle?'

'I'm feeling the clumps of scrub, there is no range here to distort wind direction; the clumps are following a pattern, leaning towards the east.' Came the sang-froid reply.

Begrudgingly Mike indicated for Jack to lead out with a slight raise of his arm, he was too tired mentally to argue further. He marvelled that he was able to still think rationally. Like Jack, his face was blotched, his eyes sore with the constant glare and wind-blown sand. Thorny scrub cut at exposed flesh resulting in welts and sores, some of which were weeping and inflamed. Their clothes were in tatters and their boots worn and of little protection now against the thornlike needles of the stunted spinifex they encountered.

They were no sooner on the march again when Mike stumbled, or at least he thought he had. Desperately he tried to regain his balance but the sudden drag on the rope gave him no chance. Besides, he was too tired to fight against the rope. He was ready to admit that the wilderness had conquered him unless they could find water, more than would be present on the shrub after the fog lifted. Unfortunately it was true, they were Bushmen but not men of the bush, and there was a vast difference when it came to survival. Five hours had passed since they finished the last of the water. Their throats were parched and uselessly swollen tongues licked dryly at empty cavities. Jack was driven by bitterness, a determination to succeed, goaded on by the image of a thin face, straight silvery hair and a military moustache. The young Australian did not possess the same motivation. And now he was being pulled across the ground like a sack of potatoes, the rope tight under his armpits, the gravelly surface like so many ball bearings overcame friction while plucking away and abrading his chest. Needle pricks of shock and pain saw blood run freely down his chest to mingle with his body hair.

Jack stepped out and there was nothing; he tried desperately to fling his body backwards, too late. Suddenly he was plunging through blackness the rope taut around his middle controlling his speed. His mind was numbly trying to place together what was happening when he felt his body collide with something which yielded under his weight, falling with him, amidst shouts, curses and abuse.

<>

Their day started before sunrise and ended when the heat became unbearable. Even in the fog they found the claim and commenced to remove the overburden from the shaft. Scotty McGregor was making his way up the ladder fashioned from timbers purchased in Alice Springs. Across his shoulders was a pole supporting two large baskets full of broken rock from the workface. Below in the dim shadows, Tiny O'Leary, a mountain of a man, and Jamie McPhee with his mop of red hair, was filling a second set of baskets by the light of the Tilly lamp in readiness for his return. Normally they used a mechanical hoist. However, dust had found its way into the generator causing the machinery to seize. Angus, Jamie's elder brother by seven hours, drew the short straw, and after several hours stripping the machinery had motored to Alice Springs to place an order for new parts if they could not be procured locally.

The four young men worked the Granites, as they named the area, after a large granite outcrop, which stood like a monolith above the desert floor. They had set up permanent residence, bringing all building materials and supplies from Alice Springs. The stone building with its tin roof surrounded on one side by two large water tanks was home and would remain so until 1926 when they abandoned their attempt, the mother lode eluding them. The reef gold scratched from the diggings barely paying wages for their painstaking efforts and time spent at the field.

The war was over, young men could not settle down, the war did this and more, many went crazy, unable to adjust to civilian life after the trenches, death and misfortunes of battle. Their memories could not be shared with those at home, they could not understand, they shared nothing in common anymore and could not take up where they left off on their return from Europe. A time of unsettlement, a time when men craved adventure, when they thought nothing of trekking across the continent or setting up residence in the middle of nowhere to search for that elusive wealth which could change their lives forever.

Jack hit Scotty, bouncing from the rungs of the ladder to land squarely in his arms. The rung of the ladder fractured under the combined weight and together between screams and shouts, the two men fell on the hunched figures below. During the confusion, the lantern burst into a thousand shards, plunging the workings into darkness.

'Tis a brumby!' Screamed Scotty, pushing and kicking himself clear.

'What the hell is ye talk'en about mon. Ye tripped on yon ladder and near come ta kill'en us all.' Tiny was caustic with his partner.

'Ye're a great bloody twit Scotty?' Added Jamie.

'I told ya the load was too heavy for ye, but no, ye would'na listen,' Tiny bellowed in the darkness, rubbing his shoulder vigorously where he was struck in the melee.

'Don't you be so daft! I tell ye, 'twas one of them wild ponies?'

'Bullshit!'

Dust hung thick in the air of the shaft, the smell of sweating bodies, the rank aroma of freshly worked rock and that of the coal oil filled Mike's nostrils as he was pulled halfway over the lip of the hole. The warm, salty, coppery taste of blood filled his mouth and he choked on the words he would have addressed to Jack. Turning his head away from the pit he spat the blob at the rock-face of the shaft.

'Jack!' He got out at last. 'Are you all right? What the hell's happening?' He repeated the call until a muffled reply reached him from the depths of the cavity.

'I think I have fallen into a loony bin… '

This was followed by a poignant silence, which could only have lasted seconds. Suddenly three babbling voices, their brogue just intelligible to Jack, covering himself from swinging fists and thrashing limbs, broke the silence.

Resourcefully, Mike lit one of their remaining wax matches cupping his hands around the flame and leaning out over the hole. To the men sprawled on the workface below, the light took on the appearance of a glow-worm in an otherwise dark grotto. There came stirrings and oaths, but that was all Mike could make out.

'Who the hell are ye mister?'

'Where did ye come from?'

'Ye could've killed us ye stupid git!'

'Well I'm not a horse, that's for sure,' replied Jack, amused once it was realised what had happened. 'Sorry to drop in on you like this, couldn't be helped.'

The dust was settling and three pairs of eyes glistened at him in the darkness. 'How did ye get here mister? We bein' in the middle of bloody nowhere.' Tiny would have an answer.

'My partner and I are on our way to Marree, down South Australia,' he elaborated for their ignorance. 'It wouldn't have happened but for the fog!'

'Ye must be daft laddie!'

'That's the pot calling the kettle black, bloody horses.'

'We be knowing where we are!' Big Tiny stated, rubbing at a trickle of blood running down his chin.

Above them, Mike was edging out further over the opening to ease himself out of the rope. In the process he was causing loose conglomerate to tumble down the workings. 'Would that be ye mate up yonder?' Jamie's voice was charged with anxiety.

'Yeah,' replied Jack, spying the dim figure above.

'Move away laddie. Otherwise, you'll be to burying us alive!' Jamie shouted, his voice chagrined with apprehension for a sudden cave-in.

Chapter 35

Port Augusta, South Australia

Click. Harry Street closed the chrome clasp on the black leather suitcase. He was wearing a light charcoal pin stripe three-piece suit, the cloth the finest money could buy. Harry spent a lot of money on clothing priding himself on his appearance, it gave the impression to those around him of opulence, which is precisely as Harry intended. As usual the white silk shirt was fastened at the collar, stiff with starch, the dark blue tie sitting sweetly under the suit's matching vest. Harry straightened at the knock upon the cabin door.

'Come!' He called, while slanting the dark blue felt hat over wavy hair.

'Mister Street, Mister Fischer, captain Reutenbachen's compliments to you both. The captain would like to see you before you go ashore,' the steward delivered the message.

'Oh he would, would he lad? Well you can tell Reutenbachen he can go hopping to hell. He has undoubtedly cost me a fortune with his bungling.'

'Captain Reutenbachen thought you might be so disposed sir. He asked me to accompany you personally. He is waiting in his day cabin,' he added.

Behind Harry, Jonathon grinned to himself, he knew the big Englishman well, and at any second now fully expected him to grab this cove by the shirt-front and spread his nose all over his face. As he watched, he saw the right fist clench, then as he envisaged the left-hand shot out and grabbed the poor unfortunate steward pulling him forward.

'I wouldn't do that if I were you Mister Street,' said a second voice from the doorway, as Harry was about to flatten the steward. Willie appeared from nowhere brandishing the single action colt, the barrel steady, unwavering.

'Thanks chief,' squawked a relieved steward, fully expecting to be released, instead Harry held him firmly in one hand his feet barely touching the ground.

'Bloody hell!' Whispered Jonathon. He was, peering past Harry at the hollow muzzle of the firearm. 'I say, no need for that Mister Nelson, come on old boy let's go and see the captain. It is not as though we cannot afford the money,' he insisted.

'That is not the point Jonathon; it is the principle of the matter to which I object. Reutenbachen could not captain a dory. He lost two valuable days by allowing himself to be blown so far from his chartered course.'

'You can't blame the captain for that,' said Willie angrily.

'You be quiet! I was not addressing my remarks to you.' Harry was caustic with the engineer.

'Harry, he's holding a blooming gun.'

'Yes and he had better put it away. If he thinks I am going to see the captain with that toy pointing at my ribcage, then he has another think coming.'

'Please yourself,' said Willie, 'I'd as soon shoot the pair of ya and throw ya carcases to the sharks.'

'Harry please, let us go and talk to the captain; there's a good chap.'

'Yeah, then you can tell him face to face what you think of his seamanship,' put in Willie. 'And you can let Henry go, he was only following orders,' Willie waved the colt in the steward's direction.

'I say, please put the gun away Mister Nelson. I'm sure if Harry gives his word to see the captain he will, because he's a gentleman.'

'What about it Street?'

'I'll go first,' offered Jonathon, picking up his luggage and moving past Nelson to stand just outside the cabin.

Harry gave the matter some thought before releasing the steward with a thrust. 'Bring our luggage,' he commanded of the frightened man, moving to follow Jonathon and indicating for him to drop his luggage for the steward to manage.

Sprightly, Nelson moved to one side to allow them through, the gun shielded by his trouser leg. Four figures waited patiently outside Reutenbachen's cabin for Willie to announce their presence. He tapped on the door with the barrel of the revolver.

'Come in,' came the voice of Otto from within.

'Ah, Harry! You weren't leaving the ship without first stopping off to settle your account and say goodbye were you?' Reutenbachen glared at the Englishman from the chart table.

'You are a bungler Reutenbachen,' scowled Harry.

'How much do we owe you captain?' Jonathon cut in before either man could add fuel to the kindling.

'Not a shilling as far as I am concerned Jonathon, he should be paying us for risking our lives on this heap of scrap metal.'

'Why you ungrateful… if it hadn't been for Otto 'ere, you would never 'ave made port,' interjected Willie angrily.

'Rubbish, the man is a bungler; he cost me valuable time I could ill afford,' smirked Harry, looking directly at the smouldering features of the old timer.

'Let me shoot them Otto, please, we can feed their bodies to the sharks.'

'I say, that won't be necessary, I'm quite prepared to pay,' signified Jonathon, gazing fearfully from one to the other.

'How much is our account Mister Reutenbachen?'

'Let me see. Three hundred pounds were the figure bandied about. To be paid on arrival.'

'Three hundred pounds. Isn't that a bit much… ?'

'Shall I shoot him Otto?' Persisted Willie brandishing the pistol at the little Englishman.

'Oh my God Mister Nelson! Please, I spoke in jest,' quickly he finished counting the money and handed it to the captain, much to Harry's disgust.

'Jonathon you are being had, he would not dare to pull the trigger.' Harry told him.

'That's all very well Harry; you know how I detest violence. I don't mind paying, really I don't. There's still plenty to purchase the property.'

'Jonathon!' Exploded Harry, silencing him with a frosty look.

'I don't know why you are so worried Harry. The bones of Smith and his mate will be bleaching the landscape by now. There is no way short of a miracle they could reach Marree in less than forty days, minimum,' Reutenbachen stated.

Both men looked long and hard at each other. Harry wanted to believe him. Finally he broke the poignant silence, which settled over the room's occupants, 'you have your money Reutenbachen.' He pushed Willie aside and left the cabin without another word.

Jonathon was left staring at the captain. 'You must forgive Harry, he'll be up tight until he closes this deal, captain Reutenbachen.' He turned to follow Harry with their laughter following him down the gangplank.

Chapter 36

The Granites

Jack lifted the bottle once more to his lips, emptying the contents with great relish, the beer being cool and refreshing. All their moods changed in the hour or so that followed the incident. Introductions were exchanged and stories sorted out. It was an excuse for a few beers, talk, a smoke and some jibes at the others expense, shared by the laughter of all. Not much damage had been done, although Scotty felt his bleedin' arms were torn from their sockets and Mike's chest resembled a gravel pit.

After a few bottles of beer, Mike allowed Tiny to remove the gravel from his flesh and cleanse the abrasions. For such a big man he was surprisingly gentle, so Jack waited his turn to let him take a look at the stub of his little finger. Tiny cut away the dead skin tissue, satisfied, he bathed the finger, dabbing the stub gently into a cup of beer, the alcohol meant to kill any infection. He bandaged the stub and the drinking began in earnest.

Shortly the talk turned to why the Territorians should want to trek to Marree, the miners listened intently. 'Christ but you can be unlucky,' began Scotty when Jack finished his account.

'Aye, if ye had dropped by yesterday, ye could 'ave got a free ride with Angus,' Jamie informed them, not quite sure why this broke the others into pearls of laughter.

Tiny got their attention. 'Seriously though, Angus left yesterday for Alice Springs to order a part for the generator, you could 'ave gone with 'im.'

The three nodded in unison, 'aye, would 'ave saved ye all of seven days,' put in Jamie.

'I would have thought we were closer to Alice Springs than that... ' Mike was shocked.

'Nah. At least another ten days on foot through the Truer Ranges laddie,' Jamie replied solemnly as he realised the traumatic effect their words had on the pair.

For a moment, there was a solemn silence. Jack looked from the neck of his bottle at Mike. Although no words passed between them, he read in Mike's eyes something he never expected to see, his acceptance of defeat. Including the calculated ten days left to them, they both shared a gut feeling they were too late. It was the reason Jack pushed them to the brink and the single reason they marched in the fog against his better judgement. Through his haze of alcohol, Jack saw a thin face with silvery hair, the face was laughing at him. Mike saw another man disembarking *Scagway* and heading towards Marree on a fine horse, nothing they could do would stop him.

From the other side of the room Mike saw the serious expression of his mate. He lifted his glass of whisky towards Jack in silent salute and a shrug. Absently Jack responded, for he couldn't look at Mike. He believed he was an achiever, a winner, never had he saw himself as a loser once he set his mind to a task. Shortly he got unsteadily to his feet, the alcohol creating a state of melancholy, he hurt, he hurt really badly and he wanted to spare the others his grief, remorse, and frustration. It was a bitter pill to swallow. With uncertain tread, he weaved his way between the drinkers and crossed to the door quietly closing it behind him. He seethed with anger, enough to wrench the door from its hinges. On the veranda he stood clenching his fists as tightly as he could while gazing at the shimmering desert from under the shade of the awning. The fog had lifted, a red haze greeted him, mirrors of sweltering heat, skeletons in the image of Lord Anthony danced across its luminous surface, defying him, taunting. Their victory dance like a chant in his mind. And just then if he could have got his hands on his lordship, he would have torn him apart. He stumbled from the veranda to the water tanks his eyes misting, tears of frustration ran down his cheeks. Blood dripped through his closed fists as the long unkempt nails bit into the soft flesh.

Looking around to be sure the others would not hear him, his closed fists beat at the solid timber supports of the water tank until they were a bloody pulp. The frustration, disappointment, and bone shaking sobs had been spent. Sure it was out of his system, he sluiced his face and washed his hands with a cake of plain soap he found on top of the tank supports. The running tank water stirring inner feelings, he undid his fly with fumbling fingers, skinned and puffed, to urinate against the base of the tank, watching steam hiss from the hot sand and stepping away from the issuing smell. He promised to go back inside and drink himself into a coma. He understood why his thoughts turned to Katrina, more importantly her father, the memory of the man and their fiery meeting. Was his lordship goading him? Even if defeated, he shouldn't have to hear that demoralising introduction…

Lord Chester, let me introduce you to Mister Jack Bryson Carter.

Chapter 37

Alice Springs

A wooden bench served as their table, long stools formed seats, sets of bunks attached to the walls made up their sleeping arrangements, a pot-bellied stove, a cupboard, meat locker, and a picture of King George in a tartan kilt completed the furnishings of their dwelling.

Nature called and Jamie was the first to stir. He stood on the veranda relieving himself when unexpectedly two twin beams floodlit the dwelling. Then the whirr of the motor was resonant on the wind. It was unusually loud in the surrounding quiet of the bush. The little Scotsman pricked his ears, staring at the approaching beams bobbing up and down over the rutted track. Then the silhouette of the lorry was reflected against the Granites and Jamie's mouth fell open in surprise. The utility pulled into the yard with a screech of brakes and a swirl of dust.

It was unbelievable really; if Angus had not forgotten the serial numbers to order the generator part… reflected Mike from the makeshift back seat of the lorry. Four men, in the middle of nowhere, a bloody lorry, a house, and a damn goldmine to boot. Mike didn't believe in miracles, a man made his own luck, took his chances, and if he were a man, accepted the hand fate dealt him. Mike had not missed the look of disbelief on Jack's face, nor did he comment when the big man came back to the drinking with both hands bleeding and puffy. He realised winning meant everything to Jack, but being a realist he could see the hopelessness of their continuing when quite plainly he believed they had run out of time. However fate had been kind, they were in it again with a strong chance if they could reach Alice in two or three days.

'Pass me the jack please Mike,' said Jack, standing by the red lorry's rear fender.

'What!' Came the startled reply.

'The jack! We're blown a bloody tyre,' was the impatient rejoinder.

Miles away with his thoughts, Mike was unaware the vehicle had stopped. Frantically he searched the floor of the truck finally handing the cumbersome looking thing with its rack and pinion raising and lowering device to Jack.

'Alice Springs?' Asked Jack, wanting to know the story, as he worked beside Angus to replace the tyre.

Angus smiled; he knew the story off by heart. 'Build a telegraph line bisecting Australia from Adelaide to Darwin; Charlie Todd was instructed. Work began in 1870 and the OT Line was completed two years later when they linked in August at Frew's Pond.'

'Linked?' Jack was amused by the Scotsman's choice of words.

'To be sure they were comin' from up north and from south towards the north,' Angus explained. 'But the real hero was the Scottish explorer John McDouall Stuart, he made it all possible.' Grinned Angus.

Alice Springs was set in a hollow-bowl, surrounded by undulating hills with acacia trees, salt brush and red loamy soil. The setting was very easy on the eye of the weary traveller, particularly at sunset, as it was when the bone weary trio motored into their destination.

The last dash through Oodnadatta to Marree would be accomplished on horseback. Jack had grown such a fond attachment for the camel that he argued in their favour. Mike would not be moved. In the morning, standing outside their cheap accommodation he voiced his argument yet again while taking their leave of Angus.

'The chief advantage of the horse is his speed and mobility,' said Mike, to which Angus nodded his agreement, the pompom of his chequered hat bouncing about atop his head.

'If we select a string, we can change and rest them in turn.'

'Aye, they will tackle the gibber country you will strike south of 'ere better than any camel,' Angus advised. 'You should be able to cover fifty miles in a day.'

This more than anything convinced Jack and he turned to bid Angus farewell. 'Good luck laddies,' grinned Angus taking Jack's proffered hand in a firm shake.

'Thanks for everything Angus,' Jack was visibly moved by their parting. Mike took the strong work-hardened hand in his, smiling at the Scotsman in turn. Together they sauntered over to the livery stables where a smithy was shoeing a horse, leaving the miner standing on the steps of the sandstock building.

'Is your name Jack Carter?' A shadow filled the doorway of the livery stable.

Jack turned from tightening the cinch strap; he looked cautiously at Mike before replying. 'Yes that's my name.'

'I have a message for you from old Bill Myre.' The man came forward on recognising the American drawl.

'Old Bill?' Mike couldn't hide his surprise.

'Got a cablegram some time ago. Bill said ya might show up. He said to tell ya two British airmen know about the Hopkins place and are on their way to Marree and to take care 'cause they're dangerous.' He blurted, taking a long breath.

'British Airmen?' Jack didn't know what the fellow was talking about.

'He said one of the men mentioned *Lord Anthony would be pleased.* Whatever that is supposed to mean.'

Mike nodded his thanks to the stranger.

Jack tensed, visibly shaken by this piece of news. 'They have an airplane!' Jack almost whispered. 'Come on, we haven't a moment to waste.'

They proposed to follow the Overland Telegraph Line because it afforded a surveyed route direct to Marree, and because it crossed several waters, ponds, and bores speared by the engineers during the construction to water the livestock.

From Alice to Oodnadatta, the country was sparsely settled. It was flat, the soils were paltry and scrub meagrely, gibbers, for miles in stretches, made the going treacherous for man and beast. There was little shade, plenty of wind and dust, lots of red dust.

At Oodnadatta, they encountered their first surprise. A narrow gauge line of tarnished steel, built up above the countryside, which they imagined would turn into a quagmire when the rains came. Here in the middle of the outback was a railway line linking the town to the coast. In the street they stopped a local.

A feller by the name of Baker gave the line the name The Afghan Line because many of the Afghan camel handlers would wait beside the line for the train, kneeled on grubby mats praying to Mecca. Afterwards the name was shortened to the Ghan. The region supports many camel trains bringing supplies to the outlying towns and stations. They were told by the local. They thanked the man and sought out the stationmaster.

Jack elected to stay with the string while Mike found the stationmaster to inquire the frequency of the train. Mike was to send a cable to Mister Hopkins advising of their arrival. Apart from the hotels everything was closed. There was a note pinned to the stationmaster's door indicating he could be found over at Davy's pub if anyone was looking for him. So the procession of eight horses and the single rider turned and followed Mike's progress across the street where they waited patiently his return. He wasn't long. His downcast look said it all. They had missed the Ghan on its return trip to Port Augusta by two days.

Chapter 38

Port Augusta, South Australia

Harry Street was surprisingly calm. As calm as anyone could be when told he had missed the *Ghan* and it would be nearly four weeks before the steel monster took to the north again. He did however manage to find out that Lloyd Hopkins had a copper mine near the small township of Marree. It was further pointed out to Harry by the stationmaster that a camel train could convey him and his assistant to their destination. Harry would have none of it. The thought of riding one of those beasts was repugnant; the trip aboard *Scagway* being bad enough as far as Harry was concerned. Within the confines of their hotel room, Harry cursed Reutenbachen in a new outburst.

'That worthless bounder cost me dearly Jonathon, mark my words!'

'How can you be sure Harry, as Mister Reutenbachen explained it is more than likely the bones of the overlanders are bleaching the landscape of the outback?' Jonathon shrugged, turning the newspaper he was reading to a new page. However the paper, one of many Jonathon poured through every day since their arrival at Port Augusta, made no mention of a confidence trickster operating along the coast nor any report by a Mister Wilcox or the police. Maybe Wilcox was too embarrassed to reveal that he had been swindled by a confidence trickster? Nor was there mention of Adelaide or the Port being employed as a base by Anthony Thornton Consortium to conduct an aerial survey.

Jonathon's eyes lifted from the newspaper to look at Harry. Uncertainly he asked, 'What should we do now Harry?'

'We must find out the bank, or broker, or solicitor Hopkins uses to conduct his affairs. This may give us some idea where he transacts his business. Here, in Adelaide, or at Marree. Then if he is on the train with Carter and his associate, we can assume they are travelling to Adelaide to finalise the transaction.'

'In which case you can approach him with a counter offer,' Jonathon finished for him.

Harry glared at his companion; he didn't like being interrupted when he was speaking, or in this case thinking out loud. Jonathon however did have the right idea he confided to himself. 'Yes, something like that, along with a cablegram explaining that we have arrived and will match any offer.'

'But we don't know what he looks like Harry,' lamented Jonathon, now disinterested in the news copy and placing it on the arm of the chair.

'There was no mention of a British aeroplane landing here or at Adelaide Jonathon?'

'None Harry.' Jonathon shook his head. 'It seems unlikely they could get here ahead of us if, as you said, they would check out the property first.'

'You are right of course. Father is not a fool; he would want confirmation,' Harry contemplated, one hand absently smoothing out his moustache.

'First thing in the morning we are going to the library Jonathon.' He announced finally.

'The library? What the devil for Harry?' Jonathon was bemused.

'Yes, I imagine a wealthy businessman like Hopkins would have his picture on more than one newspaper copy,' whispered Harry, still mystifying Jonathon.

'Library, newspaper copy, what are you talking about Harry?'

'It is very simple Jonathon, in major cities and towns the library keeps a copy of the daily newspapers for reference.'

'You mean, if I wanted, I could go to the library and read about something that made news twenty years ago?'

'That is correct.'

'Struth!'

'So we should be able to obtain a picture of Hopkins, assuming he has had his picture taken,' Harry added, however his voice carried a tone of optimism to his companion.

'How can we be sure he will be on the train?' Jonathon wasn't nearly as confident.

'We cannot. However, it would be stupid of us to travel to Marree on the next train if he were expected in Port Augusta. Besides, we may be able to check that out in the morning as well.'

'How?' Jonathon asked in all innocence.

'By cabling ahead to Marree to see if persons representing Mister Lloyd Hopkins purchased tickets for the return journey aboard the train.' Harry gave Jonathon a look, which indicated he should have been able to figure that out for himself.

'Yes of course, forgive me Harry.'

'Very well then, first thing in the morning I will send Hopkins another cable before going to the railway station and making enquires while you attend the library.' The matter was resolved.

'Today's news is tomorrow's history,' muttered Jonathon, picking up the paper again and accepting a tumbler of Scotch whisky from Harry.

'Yes something like that,' Harry was only half listening. He was asking himself why Hopkins had not replied to his cable. He was certain Reutenbachen would not have tried to intercept any cables. Harry was positive in his own mind. Carter had already arrived at Marree. If that were the case and Hopkins did not afford him the opportunity to bid for the property, he swore the man would pay dearly for his inconvenience.

He left Jonathon with his paper and tumbler of scotch, placing the decanter close by and stole away to his own room bidding his friend goodnight. The thought of Hopkins selling to the others without giving him a hearing followed him down the hall to his room. He settled the key in the lock and let himself into the room, pausing long enough to relock the door behind him. His fixed purpose took him to his briefcase, which was under the bed, away from prying eyes. Selecting the key from several on a gold chain hidden in his fob pocket, he unlocked the case and from under some papers removed the revolver with the polished timber handle. Lovingly he cupped the service revolver in his hands, but the cold feel of buffed steel was unnoticed, for Harry was already contemplating revenge. If the plan he were formulating failed, if he were cheated, then he would extract his revenge on Hopkins. He would not be denied what was rightfully his twice in one lifetime; that would be more than Harry could bear. He sat shaking with anger and anticipation, planning, the revolver the catalyst, power, wealth and position, his motive. Then there was his father; it was the opportunity he had been waiting for, retaliation for the humiliation when told he was to be exiled.

Chapter 39

Marree, South Australia

Eight days from Alice Springs, the overlanders reached their final destination. Jack viewed Marree with some detachment. The small town shimmered in the heat. It was tucked away between a spur of the Flinders Ranges to the southwest and the central range to the east. The main street paralleled the railway line, with the business district facing the line. Between the line and wide dusty road was an assortment of tents and tin shacks; he assumed correctly that they formed residence for most of the single men and for the wives and children of the railway workers. The majority of the shop fronts were crying out for a coat of paint and although the windows showed signs of regular cleaning, it was a losing battle against the dust; and soot from the *Ghan*. Outside the shops, a broad walk extended six to eight feet, covered by galvanised iron awning which was supported by uprights that in turn supported hitching rails for teams of camels, some, attached to drays or *bung carts*. He counted five hotels, a bakery, a butcher shop, a hardware store with a petrol bowser for the town's automobiles, one of which he was to learn belonged to James McTaggart, as well as an emporium with the name Alex Mac Kenzie blazoned across a timber placard attached to the roof front. Further down the street but hidden from where the pair were stopped surveying the scene, there could be heard the sound of a Smithy, hard at work, ringing blows on his anvil. Apart from the hammer blows, the street was quiet, before a woman emerged over near the tracks from one of the canvas tents and pitched a bucket of suds over a dog barking at their string from his chained compound, a hollow log. The drone of flies settling on the salt encrusted flanks of the horses, cacophonous to the riders above. With aching muscles protesting, they dismounted, tethering the animals to one of the vacant rails near a water trough. The men paused long enough to ease the girth straps of the animals before entering the nearest hotel. Unlike Oodnadatta, Jack observed the doors to the hotels were closed. Where there hadn't been a soul on the street, men clustered around the bar, in places three deep, herders, miners, and railway employees for the most part.

Behind the bar, in the absence of mirrors, were paintings of nude women, portraits of bare knuckle fighters, framed pictures of racehorses and a graphic illustration in crayon of a dust storm forming above the town, in the bottom right-hand corner the artist had placed his mark, an X. There was one large ceiling fan to circulate the air thick with tobacco smoke, the reek of beer and spirits and the man smell of men who had not bathed for some time. Bottles lined plank shelves. Behind the bar were packets of tobacco; matches and papers were also displayed for sale. Patiently they waited their turn to be served, the barman eyeing their ragged gaunt appearance, their dirty tattered clothing, unkempt hair and beards over dirty sunburnt skin which reeked with the smell of dust, horse smell, and wood smoke. He watched unmoved as they quickly disposed of thirteen fluid ounces of the dark amber fluid in what seemed a continuous swallow. While waiting for them to finish their bottles, he took the caps off two more and pushed them forward.

'Two shillings each that'll be,' he announced, dragging his cloth across the ring of water where the bottles marked the timber surface.

'Would you know where we could find Lloyd Hopkins?' Mike asked the man.

'Aren't any jobs going if that's what you're about,' he replied sullenly.

They shook their heads in unison, 'No we just want to talk to him,' offered Jack, in a jovial voice.

The barman was suspicious, frowning he continued to wipe the worn planks while looking at them anew. 'You'll not be bringing Mister Hopkins trouble would ya?'

'No, nothing like that, it's strictly business,' replied Mike, resting his bottle back on the plank surface which served as a bar top.

'Then youse should 'ave a talk with Jimmy McTaggart, that bloke over there,' he nodded.

'What be the trouble Ned?' A big rangy bloke came forward to address the barkeep.

'No trouble. These blokes are lookin' for Mister Hopkins, Jimmy.'

Behind him, the group he had been drinking with eyed the pair up and down for some time before Jimmy was want to remark. 'I'm Hopkins Foreman. Can I help you blokes?' The man smiled causing a thin scar, which ran from his left ear to his chin to become a white welt on the otherwise dark tanned features.

Jack turned to face the man. 'Can we talk?'

'Yeah let's go across the road to my place.'

A short time later McTaggart, oblivious to the men following him, opened the door of the shanty and disappeared inside. 'Give us a minute.'

From where Jack and Mike stood they could hear the sound of bottles being kicked out of the way. Shortly McTaggart returned, a grin crossing his features. He bid them to enter. The only furnishings apart from the old stove set into a fireplace were chairs, a table and a dresser which served as somewhere for McTaggart to throw his clothes over. Otherwise, the earthen-floored room was bare.

'Must 'ave a bloody clean up one of these days.' He said by way of making conversation.

'You're James McTaggart, old Lloyd's adopted son?'

'That's right, do I know you?' He indicated the chairs.

Mike let himself ease into a chair, Jack preferred to stand. 'You may know of me through your father. My dad and old Lloyd are good mates. Mike Smith from Margaret River Downs.'

McTaggart said, 'I know your family although I don't think we ever met.' Mike nodded.

'So what do you blokes want with the old man?'

'Tempi station,' Mike beamed.

This brought a look of consternation from Jack. He would rather keep their business private for the time being. 'Has anyone else made contact with Mister Hopkins about the property?' Jack asked seeing a frown cross the features of McTaggart.

McTaggart drew himself upright in his chair, trying to hide his emotions at the revelation. 'Not that I am aware.' He revealed, hiding his eyes from the tall American's scrutiny while taking the caps off three long necks, no glasses and the beer weren't cold.

The revelation brought a gleam to Mike's features. He looked at Jack and saw that amicable grin. It was over. Yet somehow he didn't feel like celebrating or shouting to the four winds, there was nothing left in him for that, he was physically and mentally exhausted, and he noted, a little melancholy, flicking a finger at a tear running down his cheek. Now when he should be elated his thoughts turned the clock back, back further than he cared to remember. He suddenly realised what Doc Andrews meant. He was a man without ambition, being swept along in the dreams of another. A partner yes, but unable to visualise or fully comprehend what it was they were doing here so far from Margaret River Downs, in the middle of nowhere.

<>

That night Jimmy McTaggart visited the old man at his accommodation in the Federal Hotel, where they argued heatedly.

'You told me you took the property off the market? You promised my mother Tempi would be my home.' Jimmy ignored the offered seat opposite his step-father.

Lloyd sighed, a deep tired sigh for the same argument. 'So it was James, until you were full grown.'

'I never wanted to leave. You ran the place down. You were never sober long enough to work the place!' Jimmy accused, hands forming fists by his sides. 'You are going back on your word!'

'What are you talking about?' Hopkins removed his spectacles placing the 'Chronicle' newspaper aside with a show of irritation to look at James anew.

'There are two blokes in town, from the Territory, they want to purchase Tempi Station, that's what I'm talking about.'

'Sit down James.'

'I don't want to sit down. I want answers.' came the raucous reply.

Lloyd gave a gut-wrenching sigh before easing himself out of the chair and moving to find his soiled coat on the hallstand near the door. From inside his tweed jacket he removed a bundle of correspondence held together by a rubber band. Without a word he handed it to Jimmy and resumed his seat.

'You knew they were coming,' Jimmy accused, looking up from his scrutiny of the cablegrams, in particular the one attaining to the restraining order signed by Senator Perry which prevented the sale or lease of mineral rights until an investigation had been conducted by him or a person representing his office.

'I was expecting to meet with Senator Perry the next time I am in Adelaide.' Lloyd replied.

'Oh I understand well enough. You don't want me to have the bloody place but you will turn around and sell it for a price. Well I'll get the money from somewhere, sell it to me.' Jimmy gestured, hitting himself in the chest with a closed fist.

'James, Australia doesn't need any more cattle stations. The beef market is saturated boy. Besides, the Myalls would steal down and spear every last one of them, that or the cattle would become scrubbers again. Or have you forgotten?'

'How would you know? You spent most of your time prospecting and taking a drink. If it wasn't for me and the Scully's, the place would have been run down long before you reneged on your promise to my mother.'

Lloyd shook his head in resignation; he knew it was true; he pined for Cassy and to be fossicking for gold. The property, after he had explored every inch of it for the precious metal, held no interest. 'Answer me this. Are you a miner James?'

'You know I'm not a bloody miner. I hate this bloody place. But I've worked my arse off helping you get established here. That should count for something,' he fumed.

Lloyd didn't want to get into another argument with James over money. He had a more than generous account opened several years ago for the young man; the accumulated interest a small fortune. 'And you are paid well for your efforts but you fritter it away on those prostitutes up the road. When are you going to take responsibility for your life and amount to something?'

'I could amount to something if I had that property. I could make a go of it!' Jimmy stood before Lloyd, barely keeping his temper in check.

'The blacks hate your guts James. You murdered them in cold blood. You rode them down on your stock pony and senselessly killed them where they stood.'

Jimmy stared at the old man in shock. They had never mentioned the dispersal in which he had personally killed seven Myalls. 'They were stealing our stock.' He got out at last.

'They only wanted a couple of cattle to appease their hunger. You started a war which resulted in innocent people getting speared, including old Charlie.'

Lloyd had never spoken about the 1910 massacre or the reprisal, which saw two policemen and their tracker killed. It was his property, he had to take responsibility for what had happened, but before he died old Charlie told him the young bloke went berserk, shooting anything that moved. It was the single reason Lloyd walked away from the property. A property he established in 1883 when he, accompanied by Harry Clifford, pushed a mob of cattle from New South Wales up through Queensland and across the Territory to the Margaret River. Lloyd developed the property for a consortium before purchasing it outright just before the turn of the century. Old Charlie who brought James into the world, the Scully brothers, and others remained to work the place after Clifford secured pastoral rights and a market for their beef. Lloyd, accompanied by Charlie had ridden back to Tennant Creek Relay Station to bring Cassy and baby James, then five years of age back to *Tempi,* where they married and Lloyd raised the boy as his own to honour a promise he made to Cassy on her deathbed, four years later.

'You knew and you never mentioned it until now. After all these years,' Jimmy shook his head. 'I'll take my chances with the bloody abos.'

Lloyd was waiting for him to show some maturity; locally he was aptly known as a barroom brawler, a reputation he seemed to enjoy. Inflicting pain on others. Every spare moment he could be found up at the pub with his mates or over the road at Ivy's, the local whorehouse. Lloyd believed James was a bad seed. It was plain he took after his father who murdered a Dogger, took his identity, raped Cassy and who was subsequently shot by Harry Clifford.

'Well these cables represent the future, the needs of a young nation if we are ever to gain our independence from Great Britain, not bloody cattlemen or pastoralists. Iron and steel are the way forward, secondary industry, and according to those cables Tempi can supply the necessary ingredient for that to happen. Mineral wealth will shape our nation!' Lloyd nearly shouted, the plains of exasperation lining the creases of his countenance.

Jimmy glared at him for some time. 'I warn you,' He pointed a finger directly at Lloyd as if its extension were the barrel of a revolver, his harsh breathing coming in rasps as emotion took over from logic, 'If you sell Tempi from under me, you will live to regret it.' He threw the cablegrams at the older man's feet before storming from the room.

Chapter 40

Marree, South Australia

The sound of machinery was everywhere in the surrounding bush. The tourer crossed yet another stream, its wheels sliding off moss-covered boulders. Jack scratched the back of his neck where the new town clothes chafed his skin. Jimmy had insisted they make good use of the old cast iron bath. He stoked the copper boiler with wood chips and the three men went up the street where McTaggart introduced them to Alex MacKenzie who opened his business so the men could purchase some new clothing. So that now, the uncomfortable prickle irritated both of them.

Mike Smith sat back in the tourer with the hat resting on his lap and holding on for grim life as McTaggart, lead-footed, took them to the mine. He felt much better after shaving, having his hair trimmed and bathing in the first hot water his skin had felt for longer than he cared to remember. Unlike Carter who sported a moustache, Mike was clean shaven, the itch and prickle of growing hair on his face were more than he could bear, yet self-consciously his fingers stroked for the bristles that were no longer there.

While expertly guiding the car along the track, McTaggart maintained a sullen silence only speaking when Jack asked about the copper mine, whereupon sullenly, he explained to the men that Hopkins had bought up several holdings around the district as miners lost fortunes on unproductive mines. *The old man had assessed the claims finding copper, which was a poor substitute to the gold crazy prospectors. However, the old man realised the potential value of the copper ore, he told them. He developed the mines setting up smelting plants and shipping the refined ore overseas where it was transformed into finished products. Presently, Australia doesn't have the technology to transform the refined ore,* he further explained.

The car burst through a canopy of trees into a clearing at the base of a bluff, Jimmy turned the wheel sharply to the right following a dried out water course for about a quarter of a mile until they reached the mine and Hopkin's office. Typical of the man, his office was in the field.

Lloyd Hopkins was by anyone's standards a very rich but unassuming man. He was untidy by nature and disorderly where paperwork was concerned. The drawers of the metal filing cabinet were open, exposing ledgers and files in no apparent systemised order. The single window, which let a shaft of light into the office, was covered with cobwebs and dust and looked as though it had never been opened. Grit and grime from the men's boots covered the floor and a millet broom lay in a corner impounded by cobwebs.

Hopkins was a solid be-speckled man with snow-white hair and nothing like Jack imagined. More like a clerk, he told himself than the man who supposedly opened the Territory with Harry Clifford, until he offered his hand as McTaggart made the introductions. They both noticed the gammy leg as Hopkins moved around the desk to face them. There was a strength in the man's large callused hand that belied his appearance.

'This is indeed a surprise,' began Hopkins, his grin hiding the embarrassment he felt because there were no chairs for his guests. 'How are you young Smith?'

'Fine sir. You weren't expecting us? The cables we sent you from Edge Rock and Oodnadatta, Mister Hopkins?' Mike proliferated.

'Oh I was expecting you, and Senator Perry's representation from the Commonwealth Government on the behalf of a British Consortium and last but not least a Mister Harry Street esquire. Suddenly I am very popular, or rather, Tempi Station has an allure beyond my apprehension, although what that could be I can scarcely imagine.' Hopkins reached for a burnished timber case, which contained cigars and holding the case aloft invited them to partake. They declined.

Lloyd rubbed his hands together vigorously before addressing Smith. 'So, how are Clem and Elizabeth?'

'They're fine, thank you sir.' Grinned Mike.

'Well I'll be damned. You were only a nipper when I lived on Tempi. Knew your brothers better. One of them died of tetanus as I recall. Old Clem still got that jersey milker I gave him?'

'No. The cow died some time ago.'

Mike took the remark about his brother on the chin, he knew the old man did not mean what he had said in a derogatory sense and the fact that he remembered Colin made any reference by Mike unnecessary.

Jack felt uncomfortable. He sensed the animosity between Lloyd and Jimmy. Was it their sudden presence? Or was it because Jimmy brought them out to the mine? He couldn't be sure. The old man's greeting was genuine enough. Jack brushed aside the feeling; he had to know about the property 'Sir, will you sell Tempi Station?'

'I thought we agreed the property wasn't for sale!' McTaggart cast the older man with a knowing look.

Hopkins ignored James, veiling his anger, his eyes riveted to the tall American for a sign; only his thoughts admonished his stepson. Protocol and manners were so important when conducting business or entertaining clients, Lloyd felt the American lacked both, and James should have known better than to disclose his qualms in front of them. For some time Lloyd stared before replying and then surprisingly, addressed himself to Smith although his eyes never left the countenance of Carter.

'You would be aware, young Smith, any Northern Territory property sale must go through the Commonwealth Government?' It was there, the brashness gone, the sudden slump of the shoulders, the American lacked manners; he needed to be taught a lesson in etiquette. Hopkins decided he had put him in his place, without being rude. He felt and found the drawer puller in his desk, he opened the drawer, and rummaged momentarily before holding aloft several cablegrams, the same cablegrams he had placed there this morning. Silently he thrust them at James, indicating for him to pass them on. Sullenly the man grabbed at the cables quickly perusing them, convinced they were the same cables he had read last night, he handed them across the table to Mike Smith, well satisfied with the restraining order, while observing Carter was trying hard to control his impatience.

Mike barely scanned the material before passing them to the tall American. One, the restraining order, was signed by Senator Perry. At length and with shaking hand, Jack placed them on the desk.

'Can they do that sir?' Jack his heart pounding felt the blood rush to his head.

'Yes, I'm afraid so, they administer the Territory.' Hopkins smiled at him. 'Generally there are no problems where the sale of land for the grazing of stock is concerned, it is just a matter of the seller making representation.' He informed Jack.

'Supposing you tell me what this is all about?' He looked from one to the other. His mind was calculating the role of the American in all this. He was after all, still a foreigner.

'I imagine the Lands Council will ask the same question.' He added, rounding his desk, settling himself in the swivel chair and drawing on his cigar.

Mike was unable to hide the rancour he felt for the hopelessness of their situation. He shook his lowered head repeatedly, looking at the grimy floor without really seeing it. 'I feel Jack should answer your inquiry sir.'

Jack took a moment to gather his thoughts, his mind thousands of miles away. His lordship was the only person he had told about the property, about the mountain and his ambitions to mine the ore. Lord Anthony had bought himself a federal senator; it was no mere threat, he was bent on crushing him, just as he had stated in his cablegram.

Hopkins shrugged but sat unmoving.

Reluctantly at first and then with some enthusiasm, as Jack could see the sudden interest shown by Hopkins, he told their tale. At his finishing, Hopkins rose to his feet, resting the cigar in a polished marble ashtray, evidently cleaned every so often because there was no dirt or tobacco stain. He limped away from the table, one hand absently stroking through his thinning silver hair, coming to rest on his chin deep in thought and oblivious to their presence. *So that's it.* He told himself barely able to hide a smirk. After a lengthy deliberation, he turned to face them.

'There is no gold on Tempi, of that I am certain,' he commenced with a wave of his hand, returning to the desk and the torn leather padded chair. 'Those nuggets did not come from the Margaret River, nor any of the streams that feed it, so we can discount Mister Street's interest in the selection. Which brings us to your interest Mister Carter, and that of the British Company? Iron ore, so necessary for the industrial development of this nation.' he glared at Jimmy knowingly. 'You could be right.' He pointed an index finger at Jack. 'I don't know, never gave the mountain much thought, mainly worked the streams and ran a few cattle until the blasted blacks put paid to that.'

McTaggart let out a quiet grunt before turning away to hide his disgust.

Lloyd's voice trailed off, he focused his attention on his stepson's person with a grimace before returning his gaze to where the American was removing a money belt from around his waist. Jack was certain there was bad blood between the pair and if he were any judge, it was over Tempi Station.

'James I want you to cable Mister Street advising that the property along with mineral rights cannot be sold without government approval. Inform Mister Street there is no gold on Tempi.' Hopkins voice carried belligerence. He handed Jimmy the cablegram from Street with that man's forwarding address.

'Anything else?'

Lloyd shook his head resignedly, he turned to study James but already he was striding away towards the tourer and town.

Jack opened one of the leather pouches, producing an ore specimen handing it to the man.

'Haematite! This was found on Tempi?' Hopkins raised his eyebrows, James already forgotten as a new respect was born for the tall American.

'Yes sir, the Red Mountain on Hopkins Range,' Jack answered truthfully.

'I see,' said Hopkins, and he deliberated for several seconds before continuing. 'The Commonwealth took over the running of the Northern Territory because South Australia could not administer nor encourage the population of such a vast expanse of land.' Hopkins paused, retrieving his cigar and drawing deeply on the tobacco. 'People want to settle in cities Mister Carter. Now, if as you say there is iron ore which in turn could produce steel, the Commonwealth Government would sit up and listen.' Both men nodded their understanding for the circumstances Hopkins was painting.

Unperturbed by the sudden silence, like settling dust particles after a sudden draught, Hopkins dragged on his cigar. Slowly, almost deliberately, he rose from his chair and recommenced shuffling about the office.

'I hold several coal leases on the east coast, near a place called Wollongong and up in the Hunter Valley north of Newcastle. Now a fella by the name of Hoskins has reclaimed some swampland. He is part of a syndicate whose members discovered silver, lead and zinc at a place called Broken Hill; they have formed a public company. They are having a bad trot at the moment as the government is allowing British steel into the country to satisfy our growing demands. The war you understand. I have been approached to join their venture, The Broken Hill Company want my coal for smelting.'

'How much has Anthony Thornton offered for the property sir?' Jack needed to know. He felt it was time Hopkins was told who influenced Senator Perry.

'So you are familiar with the British Company? Shipping and steel as I am given to understand.'

'Yes sir,' sighed Jack, trying to hide his loathing.

'Yes, well you would know who is supplying Australia with steel and why they would be interested in an Australian venture.'

'Sir, I could not compete with the Anthony Thornton Syndicate; they have money and influence,' Jack shrugged resignedly.

'Clem Smith is my friend. We go back a long way. I do not need money Mister Carter. The overall picture is one of greed on the part of a British conglomerate. They would bleed the country dry, while the profits would continue to go overseas. My interest is this fine country of ours. OK mister?' Hopkins removed his cigar to stare at Jack and Mike, who exchanged a look.

'Mister Carter, I'm a nationalist.' Jack nodded, at least they had politics in common. 'That is not to say I want to see our industry owned by the state. It simply means I desire our independence from Great Britain.' Hopkins paused to look anew at the American. 'Nor would I approve the sale of Tempi to foreign investment, you included.' The American turned to look at Smith, his jaw dropped. He could not hide his bitter disappointment, this was all too much. 'Any sale I have anything to do with would have to be made out in Michael's name. Or, you denounce your American citizenship,' he revealed.

This revelation struck Jack like a blow to the chest. With a fathomless look for Mike, he finally shook his head. 'I will apply for Australian citizenship.' He challenged. If Hopkins intended to sell and he could meet his price, he wanted their business interests in his name, Lord Anthony would know who was behind the coup to deny him Tempi.

'Good! Then we may be able to do business. Of course I would consider it a privilege if you would allow me to speak with my brother-in-law, regarding your citizenship.' His words flowed like a mighty river in flood; nothing could stop them.

'Now what I would propose is this, assuming the government goes along with the granting of a lease, I sell you my several coal leases, you as part of the agreement would have to supply the company with coal, on the understanding of course that they, we,' he added, 'take your ore. Broken Hill Company are in a bad way at the moment, rising costs, over capacity and increasing prices of coal, and a labour shortage have seen the plant at Newcastle temporarily closed… '

'So you were approached?'

'Yes, an influx of money into a floundering company and a decrease in the price of coal, but it's an Australian company,' smiled Lloyd, shuffling his hands through the air to emphasise his point.

'But surely, even a floundering company's assets would be worth thousands of pounds,' Mike got out.

'Since the shutdown, shareholders have been unloading their shares in Broken Hill for next to nothing... '

Jack chortled. 'And you have been buying stock.'

'You betcha, as much as I could afford. I own half the stock.' He revealed with a grin.

'And you are willing to sell Mike and me a fourth share in the company?'

Hopkins nodded, 'If we can agree on a price. Now you must understand,' he paused to puff on his cigar, 'if you only wanted the grazing rights, it would only cost a song; the mineral rights are worth a lot of money,' he thought about it for a while before continuing. 'To you and Michael, I'd guess about thirty-thousand pounds.'

'I can handle that sir.' Jack was thinking the smelter would have to be put on hold initially until, financially, he could see his way clear to build it at a later time.

'Splendid,' Hopkins rubbed his hands together gleefully, the cigar clamped between his teeth.

Jack smiled for the first time that morning before grasping Hopkins by the hand in a warm shake.

Mike sat silently digesting their conversation. He felt uncomfortable with Jack's reference to 'my plans'; surely they were a team even if he didn't have the foggiest idea of what was expected of him. They ignored him not out of disrespect, here were two men with the same love, drive and initiative, and Mike understood even if with a trace of envy for their passion.

<>

Jimmy McTaggart wanted Tempi. It was home. The old man wasn't a cattleman, he was meant to be a prospector. Minerals and mineral wealth were in his heart, his blood, his imagination; it was all he ever talked about. Until last night, Jimmy had not even suspected old Lloyd knew what part he played in the 1910 Myall massacre. Jimmy had blamed the old man for paying the hands off, for letting the property fall apart. But now he realised why the old man walked away. Old Lloyd would bend over backwards for the Myall tribe. He turned a blind eye to their slaughtering a few cattle. He gave them handouts of tobacco, flour, tea and sugar. Jimmy gave them nothing but a bullet. He hated the dirty bastards.

Jimmy believed the sale of the property was imminent and if that were the case, he would make certain Senator Perry was advised of the old man's intentions so the information would be relayed to the representatives of Anthony Thornton. If he couldn't have the property, then it would be sold to the highest bidder and the hell with the old man's politics and the ambitions of Smith and Carter.

The first cablegram he addressed to Harry Street C/o Port Augusta Post Office, just as he'd been instructed, only he deliberately forgot to mention there was no gold on the property. Maybe Street would be disposed to seek retribution. Jimmy nurtured the thought. The second cablegram, he composed during the drive along the rutted track back to Marree, was addressed to:

Senator Gerald Perry
C/o Parliament House
Melbourne.
Dear Senator,

Please be advised I propose to sell the property known as 'Tempi Station' situated on the Margaret River in the Northern Territory to one Jack Carter, an American investor who plans to develop the property for mineral deposits........ Stop.

I will contact my brother-in-law Senator Barnswald as soon as I arrive in the Capital..........Stop.

Appreciate your earliest attendance with Senator Barnswald, Mister Carter and myself to consider all details........Stop.

It would be appreciated if you would inform your clients' Messrs Anthony Thornton Esq. of my intention...........Stop.
Your servant
Lloyd Hopkins.... End.

If, as Senator Perry stated in his cablegram, the government would not sell to anyone but British investors, James believed the Senator would quash any sale to an American firm or company. It didn't really matter how Carter described himself, he would be seen as a foreign investor and as such denied government sanction. Jimmy was also aware the old man's brother-in-law wasn't partial to Lloyd's political beliefs, which he expressed at every opportunity when the two were together. Also he felt certain Perry would do as the cable suggested, contact the British investors—Jimmy felt certain they would make a more favourable counter offer.

Satisfied, McTaggart crooked a finger at the dispatch clerk handing the man the cablegrams while gripping a thin bony hand and looking the man in the eye.

'Send them and forget their contents,' he instructed passing a crisp five-pound note and telling the thin balding clerk to keep the change.

Chapter 41

Adelaide, South Australia

Clayton Thornton explained to Merrick the events which had come to pass since their parting nearly two weeks ago. He told of finding the property, and the added value because of gold being unearthed by one, Harry Street. He relayed Street's quest to purchase the property and Carter's race across the outback to beat both of them. He further explained their objective was to get to Adelaide as quickly as possible and contact one, Senator Barnswald. When questioned why they needed a senator, Clayton grinned revealing that the Northern Territory was administered by the Commonwealth and that Barnswald had been contacted by the Consortium to look after their interests.

Before leaving Fremantle, he had Freddy mount the machine-gun in the forward turret believing Merrick when he said he could not fire the heavy cumbersome weapon. Clayton was aware the Fokker was designed to use the Maxim from the cockpit where the bursts found space because of the synchronising mechanism between gun and revolving propeller or, mounted to the rear to be used by the observer. Leaving the others to follow by ship with the bulk of their luggage, the brothers set off for Adelaide flying directly east across the Great Australian Bight, their course generally following the coast although several miles inland. Merrick was keen to get some aerial photographs and his camera occupied all his spare time prior to their departure and during flight. Even so, he could not help but notice the heavy calibre gun mounted to give the Fokker the appearance of a war-plane. Security was the fathomless reply by his brother when questioned.

Their crossing of the Bight was uneventful and they arrived amidst a warm welcome in Adelaide, the city of churches. Merrick was given the task of hiring hanger space from several barnstormers who had built the aerodrome. Clayton took it upon himself to contact the office of Senator Barnswald whereupon a meeting was set up for later in the day. They secured accommodation at the Creighton Hotel, which overlooked the harbour. While Merrick was only interested in the development of four rolls of film in their metal canisters, Clayton showered, changing his flying suit for a pair of fawn slacks and a clean white shirt.

At precisely two pm Clayton presented himself at the senator's offices. He was conducted into an anti-room by Barnswald's receptionist. The room was beset by an assortment of chairs, magazines, wall maps, and pictures of the Australian interior. He was informed the senator would see him presently. Clayton took a seat nearest the window which overlooked the busy street and commenced to browse through a magazine.

Clayton Thornton's first impression of the now, heavy set man with the white-wavy-hair and a protrusion of bone at the jaw-line, when he was conducted into his lavishly furnished office, was of a person who was laconic by nature as evidenced by the no nonsense request to be seated, and the brief wave of dismissal for his secretary. His handshake was firm but his demeanour implied he wasn't interested in meeting or conducting a jovial conversation with the young Englishman. And so the room was statically charged from the opening minutes of their conversation, which digested the Great War and the leading role of Great Britain, to London and finally James Loxton.

'Sir James!' Clayton corrected the senator, while displaying a grim smile.

Shortly the conversation came to the reason for Clayton's appointment and the Senator's brevity showed Clayton's summation to be correct. His succinct opening remark put the young Englishman on the defensive.

'We administer the region, known as the Territory Mister Thornton, not my brother-in-law. I am given to understand from correspondence sent to this office by James Loxton, that your people are interested in developing an iron and steel industry?' Lincoln deliberately dropped the 'Sir'.

Clayton nodded, 'that is correct sir.' Was the young whipper-snapper being sarcastic? Barnswald couldn't be sure.

'My brother and I have been commissioned to report on and establish such an industry. The property abounds in vast mineral deposits which indicate a feasible enterprise.'

'So it has met all your expectations?' Barnswald scrutinised the young man sitting opposite him like he was a butterfly under a microscope.

'I have been instructed to acquisition the property.' stated Clayton.

'Is that so?' Barnswald bristled for the cocksure attitude of the Englishman.

'I was given to understand there would be no problems, my dropping in on you a courtesy gesture to the importance of your station. After all, you were forwarded a very reasonable retainer for your cooperation.' Clayton was irritated by Barnswald's indifference to the importance the consortium placed on this venture. Also he didn't like being kept waiting by anyone, least of all a public servant.

'Are you suggesting I am but a minion, to be subjected to the whims of conglomerates intent on global expansion?' Piqued Barnswald.

'Come now senator, let's stop playing games. We are both reasonable men; if the gift was not to your expectations then I'm authorised to increase it substantially.' Clayton realised he may have misjudged his man.

'Are you trying to proselytise me, Mr Thornton? For if that is your intention forget it.' Barnswald's voice rose in pitch with his feelings for the audacity displayed by this young whipper-snapper.

'Apparently I was misinformed by Lord Anthony.'

'That pompous old tyrant.' piqued Barnswald.

'I gather you are not receptive to his lordship's request then,' was the irritated reply for Barnswald's stubborn cocksure attitude.

'Listen to me!' Barnswald's voice carried a twinge of belligerence, although he continued sorting his mail not looking up. 'I contacted the minister for Minerals and Energy as soon as I received the cablegram from your head office Mister Thornton.' He grabbed the chrome letter holder from the desk in front of him, briefly making eye contact with the Englishman, sitting hands clasped together in front of him supporting his torso on the cane, a smug bemused expression on his features.

Intentionally succinct with the Englishman, Barnswald continued, 'I also forwarded him the cheque, attached to which, was a cover note stating the so called... gift... was to be given to the nationalist party to support our next election campaign. Now sir if you have no further business, I would ask you to leave; I find you to be distasteful in your supposition of my person and position,' Barnswald rose to stand at full height eyeballing Clayton, the letter opener subconsciously held in his right hand like a knife ready to thrust. 'As soon as I can make the necessary appointment between yourself and Senator Perry, hopefully tomorrow, you will be notified by my office. Please leave your present address with my secretary on your way out. Good day to you sir.' Barnswald lowered his frame back into the swivel chair, busying himself with the correspondence on his desk, Clayton Thornton already forgotten.

'Now you listen to me you... you pompous old goat. We intend to purchase the property with or without your cooperation. If you oppose the sale, you will live to regret it. Hopkins? Where can I find him?' Clayton's aphoristic caused Barnswald to look up in surprise at his antagonist who stood leaning over the desk. Gone was all pretence of fraternal behaviour, the eyes were hooded the jaw set in a firm line.

Clearly Thornton was serious. Barnswald became uneasy. He dropped his gaze in the hope it would be seen that he was indifferent to the young man's intimidation and informed him that Hopkins and an American party of interested purchasers were at that moment aboard the *Ghan,* making their way to the State Capital.

The young flier pushed himself upright moving the heavy desk in the process, his actions meant to intimidate the senator. Barnswald looked up from the correspondence held loosely in his hands, he squirmed in the chair. Clayton raised his cane and brought it down in a display of anger to thump heavily against the desk. He watched satisfied as Barnswald literally jumped out of his chair with fright.

'If I have to come back here, it won't be to exchange pleasantries.' He backed away to the door.

In the sunlight once more and after some deliberation, Clayton decided to cable the home office of Barnswald's lack of cooperation in the hope that his father or Lord Anthony could cut through the red tape which was frustrating his progress. Meanwhile, he determined to follow his instructions. It was time to find and 'eliminate' the American; he smiled as he remembered Lord Anthony's choice of words.

Chapter 42

Aboard the Ghan, North of Leigh Creek

Jarred to a sudden stop, the engine sent a shudder followed shortly by a vibration, which shook every carriage and occupant therein. Hopkins blew soot from the sill before lowering the window and sticking his head through the aperture, resting his elbow on the sill.

'A sand drift,' he told Jack and Mike a few seconds later. 'It happens from time to time, normally old Henry pulls us up without jarring our gizzards out, bugger must have been near asleep. Thank Christ old Ned was along this trip or we may have derailed.'

Hopkins further explained that Ned Jamerson lived at Leigh Creek, he was the line's inspector and was returning aboard the train after inspecting for damage a section of track which had been inundated by flash water during recent rains.

Lloyd Hopkins removed his coat, just as Jimmy entered the carriage to inform them of the delay. Jimmy occupied another carriage with some mates who were steadily getting drunk. With Jimmy following, Lloyd left the compartment. Jack nudged Mike. 'Come on, sand drift, I expect they could use a hand.'

Together they walked the length of the three carriages separating them with the tender and engine. The breeze, blowing particles of sand from the exertions of the men back in their faces. The glare and heat were oppressive outside the carriage. Mike offered to give one old timer a breather but was politely told... *Go and teach your mother to suck eggs!* However, an Arab close by was more than willing to trade and so Mike shovelled for half an hour beside Snowy Patterson and could not believe his eyes when finished, that the old timer had not raised a sweat.

The drone of sound was familiar to Jack and Mike and both looked up, even if surprised to spy an aircraft here so far away from civilisation. The gaze of the other train occupants followed with awe the Biplane as it seemingly fell out of the sky and commenced to bear down on them. The roar of its approach and black shadow as it soared above them saw all fifteen occupants dive to the ground. Then the plane rolled away in a spiral, gaining height, and Mike could make out the stick like figures of two fliers and the insignia of the British plane.

'Fokker! Recognise it anywhere.'

'I thought that was a German plane,' Jack remonstrated.

'Are you saying I don't know my aeroplanes? I spent hours at headquarters, after I made sergeant, studying the buggers.'

'Why would you do that?' Jack followed the progress of the biplane until it disappeared into the sun.

'They were used for reconnaissance, and dropping hand bombs on our blokes. No it's a Fokker all right; the poms had the Sopwith Pup or Camel as some called them. Buggers are only showing off.' Mike would comment, his eyes squinting against the glare of the sun's rays, he was trying to understand why an aeroplane was out here so far from anywhere.

'The war's over. Why the machine gun?' Jack was disturbed.

Beside him Mike shrugged, 'It's circling, it's coming back'. And already the train's occupants with regained courage were cheering and waving for the thrill of sighting what was for many their first aeroplane.

Suddenly it dawned on Jack. 'That's got to be the syndicate representing Anthony Thornton. The message from old Bill,' He expanded.

They watched as the plane circled towards them once again. 'My God the bastard's going to strafe us,' Mike shouted to make himself heard above the roar of the approaching plane.

'Christ! Get down, get down,' Jack shouted to the train's occupants.

'Mister Hopkins, get them under the train,' Mike yelled, pushing the Arab and old Snow to the ground. Still others mesmerised by the transcendental sighting of an aircraft, remained transfixed until roused from their fantasies by the ominous sound of gunfire and bullets spraying the train.

<>

Shimmering under the harsh outback sky, the Biplane followed the snaking train line until they came upon the *Ghan*. They had been airborne for some three hours when Merrick spotted the spiralling smoke of the train below through the shims of broken cloud cover. Ant-like figures milled about, probably stretching their legs Merrick conjured the thought, and guessed correctly the locomotive had stopped. Merrick touched his brother on the shoulder and indicated with a pointed finger whereupon Clayton moved the joystick manoeuvring the biplane until he could see for himself the focus of Merrick's attention. The rails snaked below him and he observed the sand drift, which stopped the progress of the train. He turned, grinning to his brother from behind the mask while pushing forward on the stick to bring the machine into a steep dive passing over the train then up, spiralling towards the sun and watching with fascination the train's occupants, some waving, others diving for cover.

Clayton Thornton partially turned in the seat and Merrick could see him grinning behind the flying goggles. He adjusted the rudders and sent the Fokker into another steep dive until Merrick was screaming as his stomach tried to catch up with the plane. One hundred feet from the ground, Clayton pulled the machine out of the dive and set a course for the train and its occupants not four hundred yards away. His right hand gripped the cold steel of the Maxim machine gun. He tensed feeling the adrenalin surge hit the pit of his stomach and swell over him as a warm current. He fingered the trigger, feeling the tension spring give under his pressure until the gun jumped against its mountings sending a burst of bullets to strafe the train and laughing as the tiny figures on the ground sought cover under the carriages between the tracks. The reverberations of thunderous sound dimmed the shouts of Merrick as the Maxim continued to spray the terrain beyond the train long after Clayton released the trigger.

Colour rose in Merrick's cheeks, anger replaced fear when he realised what his brother was doing. He raised himself in the seat, shouting and grabbing his brother angrily by the shoulders, shaking him until they were well past the train and climbing once again.

'Only scaring them, old boy. Sit down before you fall overboard,' Clayton laughed, the action brought back sweet memories.

'You could have killed them. You bloody idiot!' Merrick shouted his hostility for the senseless action.

'No!' Clayton shouted. 'Just letting that American bastard know we've arrived.' He turned the machine once more towards the train.

'What are you doing?' Merrick screamed in his ear.

159

'Just one more pass,' Clayton partially turned and pushed his brother back into his seat, his cold calculating features under the goggles told Merrick not to say another word.

< >

Amidst screams and shrieks of damnation and curses, Jack shouted for the train's occupants to stay between the tracks.

'The bastards are trying to kill us, Mike.' Jack lay beside young Smith in between the tracks. The resonating sounds of bullets hitting the steel frame of the locomotive and piercing the timber carriages caused increasing trepidation for the passengers.

'And nobody will ever know what happened out here in the middle of nowhere.' Mike concluded.

Jack cursed, 'I'll bet anything, you like the pilot, has been told to stop us reaching the capital and finalising the sale of the property.'

'They wouldn't know we are travelling with old Lloyd.' said Mike, his arm shielding his head as he squirmed further back from the rail.

'It doesn't make sense, kill him and they lose the property.' Jack expanded.

'Stay under the train,' Mike shouted. 'He's coming in again.'

< >

Clayton pushed the stick away, manoeuvring the plane to a new direction after his second pass, and a brief spurt of machine gun fire to further add to the discomfort of the people on the ground. His features under the goggles smirked; this would make the American think twice about going up against the Anthony Thornton consortium.

The black rippling shadow of the Fokker rushed across the surface of the terrain towards a soak of dirty terracotta coloured water where it fell over a flock of galahs like that of a large bird of prey. Their screech of alarm resonated itself away from the soak towards the surrounding scrub before the beat of thousands of wings took to the air.

Merrick Thornton lent forward in the cumbersome seat to warn Clayton of the flock of birds. He shook his brother by the shoulder. Clayton grabbed the man's hand and squeezed it until Merrick cried out in pain. It was useless, Clayton was captivated with the battle, nothing else mattered Merrick realised. A look of terror crossed his features as the lead birds, sucked into the Fokker's slipstream, smashed into the turning bi-plane before Clayton who was laughing, while gazing back at the train, could take evasive action. The wooden struts broke like matchsticks with the weight of their numbers. Several birds were struck by the propeller, others, screeching in fright flew into the face of the pilot. The force tearing the goggles from his face as he tried in vain to control the hopelessly spinning plane before a number of blows knocked him unconscious. Behind him, Merrick was screaming as the spiralling plane plummeted towards the ground. Shortly it hit the earth with tremendous force forming a crater and soon was an inferno of fire and billowing smoke.

< >

From under the carriage, Jack and Mike saw the burst of flame a split second before the sound of the crash echoed to where they lay. Both men were on their feet in an instant and running towards the crash site, the hot sand particles shaken from their clothing.

Try as they may, it was impossible to get near the inferno. The searing heat engulfed the aircraft and surrounding soil where aviation fuel spewed from the fuselage. The rancid

160

smell of burning flesh came to them where they stood helplessly. Their arms raised protecting their faces from scorching pieces of debris.

Slowly the fire reduced every evidence of the plane to ash and the train's occupants in shock, had to wait another hour before they could wander, dazed, in the still simmering wreckage.

< >

The train shunted into Leigh Creek carrying its shocked passengers, its whistle blowing alerting the residents to its late arrival. No sooner had old Henry brought the steel monster to a stop before Ned Jamerson was running towards the sandstock building at the far end of the wide rutted road to report the catastrophe to the local constable and there to send a cable to the authorities in Adelaide. Mike wasn't surprised to see the passengers hurrying from their seats, each wanting to relive their adventure with the residents of the town with its three pubs, a butcher shop, an emporium, and an assortment of other shops.

'Come on,' called Jimmy from the doorway of their carriage, 'the train won't go without Henry and Ned; it always stops here anyway.' Reluctantly, Jack and Mike joined the mad dash directly across the road to the long fronted sandstone block dwelling with its frosted glass windows and spangled galvanised roof overhanging the veranda. Most of the train's occupants were still shaken by the earlier incident and a few quick beers wouldn't go astray. All conversation was for the mysterious aeroplane and the two lunatics that machine-gunned them before falling out of the sky. Soon the pubs were empty of locals who rushed outside to see for themselves the damage done to the train by the many tears in the timber carriages gouged by bullets.

Along with the other train occupants, Mike and Jack breasted the bar. However, their expressions were sombre.

'I've been thinking. What if they were trying to kill old Lloyd?' Jack broached before swilling at his beer.

'Why would they kill Lloyd?' Mike was mystified by Jack's reasoning.

'Because with him dead, the lease on the mineral rights to the property would revert to the government. Senators Barnswald and Perry know of the consortium's interest. Lord Anthony would have the influence and capital. He would stop at nothing to get Tempi's mineral rights.'

'And destroy you in the process.' Added Mike.

'My God! The restraining orders! Perry must have told the flyers.' Jack's brow creased in a perturbed frown.

Chapter 43

Port Augusta, South Australia

An excited Jonathon Fischer burst through the door of their lodgings with the news that he had obtained a recent photograph of Lloyd Hopkins. Jonathon thrust the clipping with the photograph into Harry's hands.

'You were right Harry,' Jonathon sunk onto the sofa.

'A mine shaft accident, he broke his leg apparently... ' Harry scanned the article.

Jonathon looked carefully at the solid figure of Hopkins, sleeves rolled up, his coat draped over one arm, the stern countenance under the shadow of the felt hat. He decided he could recognise him anywhere.

The train's arrival, the following day, a day late, did not deter the vigilance of Harry Street nor Jonathon Fischer. They watched from the kiosk its arrival with some anxiety for the number of uniformed policemen that were on hand, not having heard the news flash of a plane crash. Already, plain clothed police were waiting unobtrusively in the wings to commence their inquiry, photographers from the various papers had their tripods positioned for quick photographs of the carnage before the *Ghan* could be shunted away, and newsmen were moving among the passengers for a story, sketchy details of which had broken as soon as the cable reached Adelaide.

<>

Inspector Theodore Carson left his sergeant, Jim Bellamy, to watch for the arrival of the *Ghan* at Port Augusta and conduct that side of the investigation. Already Theo was on his way to the crash site. As soon as the cable passed across his superior's desk, he was summoned and given charge of the investigation.

Theo had wanted to be a policeman ever since he could remember. His father had been a policeman, speared to death during a savage attack by wild blacks in Camooweal Gorge back in 1882. Theodore, named after his father never got to meet the man who sired him, being born prematurely shortly after word was received back in Melbourne of the massacre. Tall, handsome, strongly willed, and curt when he wanted, Theo entered the police service as soon as he was of age. Advancement through the ranks was realised when he brought to justice three aboriginal men wanted for the rape and murder of Miss Elsie Moir the schoolmistress at Lyndhurst, the jump off point for the old Aboriginal trading route known as the Strzelecki Track and used since white settlement by cattlemen as a stock route. Alone after his tracker ran off, fearing retribution for aiding the policeman in his apprehension of the aboriginals responsible, and after many attacks on his person by the black's brothers, lack of sleep, having his horse string stolen, he stumbled into Hawker some weeks later more dead than alive and with him still on the chain were his captives.

After his inspection of the *Ghan* and satisfying himself the train had indeed been strafed, Sergeant Bellamy sent a cable of confirmation to Leigh Creek as instructed by his superior. At Leigh Creek, reliable witnesses including Ned Jamerson whom Theo had known for a considerable time told him there was nothing to find. While over near the soak, only parts of the aeroplane's Mercedes engine, and a wheel. Nonetheless, Theodore was determined to do his duty. Accompanied by Jamerson and a tracker, Billy Jack, he pushed on to the site of the tragedy.

His inspection completed, Theo was about to mount his horse when a glint of metal stilled his progress. Handing the reins to Billy Jack, he soon discovered it was a camera lying almost concealed below the red sand. Theo held the instrument at a distance, carefully shaking the powdery soil away then gently blowing the remainder from the metal casing. A smile creased his features.

Chapter 44

Adelaide, South Australia

From a safe distance, Harry and Jonathon shadowed the Hopkins party. They watched mystified by the attention given the train although they could discern broken windows as luggage was disgorged to a trolley and pushed to another platform by the porter where it would be loaded aboard the flier bound for Adelaide. Harry waved Jonathon towards the newsstand for something to read as they were transported towards Adelaide. On his return, shortly they left the kiosk and boarded the Adelaide bound train. Their second-class carriage, while comfortable, not affording the luxury to which Harry was accustomed. Harry unfolded the newspaper and the reason for so much activity back at Port Augusta soon became apparent.

Plane crashes in outback. A sketchy headline reported. *Train strafed. Two reported dead, unconfirmed, police to investigate.*

Harry let his lips part, his cheeks filled and a brief smile broadened his features, the headline could only be referring to those representing the Anthony Thornton Consortium. Too, Harry had recognised the old man immediately from the picture, also Carter and his mate. After they boarded, he took the opportunity to brief Jonathon of his plans in quiet undertones while the train trundled on the last legs of its journey from Port Augusta to the State capital.

'When we reach Adelaide, you will register at the same hotel as our friends, and I will find suitable accommodation in a less conspicuous boarding house within close proximity. You are to gather as much information as possible. In particular I want to know if the transaction has been completed.' Although he didn't take Jonathon into his confidence, he was pleased there would no longer be any opposition from his father. The matter was clearly between Carter and himself now. Those larrikins in the aeroplane got what they deserved as far as Harry was concerned.

'The cablegram indicated there would be no transaction Harry,' Jonathon reminded, his voice full of respect and reluctant to say anything further to upset his friend. Harry had gone off his brain when the cable was received, Jonathon thought he was going to cause a riot in the post office.

He saw Harry's frosty glare, 'I'm sorry Harry,' he profusely apologised.

'Then explain to me Jonathon why Messrs Carter and Smith are accompanying Hopkins to the state capital? No, they got under my guard. However, until the contracts are actually exchanged there is still a chance. All I need is five minutes of Hopkins time, alone,' he added.

'It would be nice to have some insurance, just in case. First thing in the morning, Jonathon, I want you to purchase two rail tickets for Melbourne, first class and book some respectable accommodation.' Harry's mind was racing ahead. He intended to establish an alibi, just in case he had to put his plan into operation and afterwards they were questioned by the police about their movements.

'We have worked Melbourne, do you think your friend Mister Jackson would be interested in making some easy money?'

'Fingers Jackson? He'd jump at the chance Harry.'

'Good! Mister Jackson and a friend of his choosing, male, are to use our accommodation and impersonate us, are you with me Jonathon?'

'The Regent Harry?'

'Yes, the Regent should be fine.'

'The rail tickets will have to be punched to indicate we were inspected by the collector Jonathon. And Mister Jackson and his associate will have to take up residence on the sixth. You had best book them in for three weeks.' Harry was trying to cover all possibilities.

'Leave it to me Harry, all expenses?'

'Yes, why not, we can always cancel and have them thrown out into the street if need be.' Harry was bizarre in his dealings, Jonathon reflected.

Harry brought the conversation back to Hopkins. 'Mind you, I do not feel that contracts could have been drawn up; there has not been enough time. As I said, all I want is five minutes and I will convince Hopkins there is gold on his property. We may have to take him on as a partner Jonathon. However, there is enough gold for all, we will still be filthy rich my friend, yes filthy rich,' he repeated to himself.

Jonathon knew full well what that meant, Harry could be very persuasive when he wanted to be. Some may call it threatening.

'I want a specimen of their handwriting. I want to know of their movements. In short Jonathon, I want to know all there is to know concerning all of them. Do I make myself clear?'

'Perfectly Harry.' And there was no mistaking the smugness in Jonathon's voice.

'Good! We will arrange to meet for supper each evening. Above all, under no circumstances are you to draw attention to yourself that will come later.'

'What do you mean Harry?'

'You will find out if and when the time is right Jonathon, meanwhile see if you can get me some refreshment, something cold, with ice, the heat in this filthy carriage is unbearable. Look at those windows, covered in soot and black deposit, disgraceful!'

<>

By nature James (Jimmy) McTaggart was a suspicious person. He had read Senator Perry's cablegram advising the property could not be sold and initially he believed it to be genuine. It was only after they boarded the *Ghan* that he began to have doubts. Jimmy knew how old Lloyd thought but he was adamant now, the property would not be sold, he would return to Tempi; it was his home!

On spying the two strangers boarding the Flier from Port Augusta and the surreptitious attention they gave his party, Jimmy became more suspicious. When the occasion permitted, he summoned the steward and on the pretext of not being able to gain entry to the men's lavatory and out of hearing of the others, gave that man a ten-pound note to find out the identity of the two strangers.

The steward was a careful and artful eavesdropper, by the time the train pulled into the platform in the city of Adelaide he was able to report that the two were Englishmen, Harry and Jonathon, who were extremely interested in a Mister Hopkins and his party.

At the hotel shortly after they registered, Jimmy witnessed the shorter of the two Englishmen enter the hotel and book a room on the same floor as Lloyd, himself, Carter and Smith. Arrangements had been made for old Lloyd to meet with his brother-in-law Senator Barnswald and Senator Perry in the hotel's dining room for dinner that evening,

165

Jimmy wasn't asked to be present nor were Carter and Smith. He made his excuses and shadowed the small Englishman's movements, observed his rendezvous with the taller and heavier man, whom he believed to be Street and who sported a trimmed thin handlebar moustache. He followed them back to their lodgings. Eavesdropping when he could, he waited patiently for them to leave. A plan was forming.

Jimmy was certain now he was shadowing Harry Street and an accomplice. He watched them leave the boarding house before making his move. It was easy. The flyscreen came off the partially opened window at a touch with the blade of his pouch knife. He raised the timber window and in no time at all stood inside the room letting his eyes adjust to the dark. He found the suitcase under the bed to be locked and spent some time using his penknife to pick the lock. In the case, to his surprise, he discovered a revolver, not daring to touch it or disturb any clothing. But he studied the weapon all the same from its long shiny barrel to the wooden grip, deciding that it may be a difficult weapon to procure being a revolver used by the Irish Constabulary and of .455 calibres, rare indeed.

When he opened the single wardrobe, he spied the hounds-tooth sports jacket; it was the same as that purchased by Carter at Marree. He tried it on. The fit across the shoulders was loose, he being slimmer than the Englishman. The length however was fine. Jimmy removed the coat looking at the label and deciding he could purchase a similar coat here in Adelaide. After a final appraisal of the room, he moved to the window and let himself out to stand against the wall deep in shadow. Seconds later, he was making his way back to the hotel and a good meal well satisfied with the day's results and contemplating his movements for tomorrow.

Chapter 45

Adelaide, South Australia

Immediately he returned to Adelaide, Inspector Theodore Carson took the battered camera downstairs to where a select group of policemen known as the forensic squad resided on the ground floor. Frederick Knowles, department chief, took the camera and placing it on a workbench went to work cautiously opening the partially damaged case not before winding the handle which spooled the film to feel for any resistance. He explained to Carson that the lack of resistance when he gyrated the mechanism in either direction made him believe the film had been rewound and therefore should reside within its canister removed from the sudden light when he opened the back of the case. But on opening the case, the technician was seen to visibly shake his head in resignation.

'Not so good I'm afraid, the film has been exposed to the light, had to be, sand everywhere in here,' referring to the ruptured metal case. Freddy gently brushed away the red sand removing the metal container with a pair of forceps.

Carson nodded gravely, 'As soon as you have anything definite give me a call Fred.'

'Sure thing Theo, no guarantees though.'

'Do your best Fred.' Carson patted him on the shoulder before heading for his office on the second floor and a meeting with Sergeant Bellamy.

The story of the plane, which strafed the *Ghan,* was losing momentum and interest with the Australian public and the media until a photograph appeared in the daily papers, which showed two young fliers standing on either side of the Fokker biplane. The police requested every newspaper to display the photograph in the hope the two could be identified as their investigation had struck a dead end.

<>

It was shortly after he spied the latest news copy, saw the biplane flanked by the two fliers, that Miles Olstrom knew the person who left four canisters of film to be developed would never come forward to collect them. Immediately he informed the police and was asked to present himself along with the material at police headquarters on Jordan Street where Inspector Carson and Sergeant Bellamy were waiting for him.

Olstrom identified Merrick Thornton and then sat passively on the other side of the mahogany desk stroking his beard as the two policemen sorted through the photographs.

Rifling through the stack of photographs, Bellamy suddenly became excited, 'look, the plane, they are loading it into a crate, you can see the marking its... its German!' Bellamy looked up at his Inspector, the photograph clutched between his fingers.

'A Fokker, German indeed,' Olstrom informed them having already perused all the photographs before contacting the police after the photographer had failed to collect them.

'Merrick Thornton, was he German?' Carson sat with knitted brow waiting expectantly Olstrom's reply.

'No,' Olstrom shook his head, 'decidedly British.'

'And so the only photo we have of him was the one sent to the newspapers,' sighed a resigned Bellamy.

'Unfortunately,' nodded Olstrom.

'Yes most unfortunate,' murmured Carson.

'We were lucky Fred saved enough film for us to have that one shot published,' Bellamy explained.

'He was a photographer of great talent,' Olstrom expanded, shuffling through the photographs pausing now and again to admire the work captured so vividly by Merrick.

'I have his Adelaide address if that helps,' Olstrom looked from one to the other holding aloft the receipt signed by Merrick Thornton.

'Thank you. Every little bit of information helps Mister Olstrom,' Carson assured him.

'Thank you very much for coming forward.' The policeman stood, shaking Olstrom's hand before Bellamy conducted him to the door.

A subsequent search of Thornton's hotel room did not reveal much apart from a very interesting cablegram from one, Lord Anthony, addressed to Clayton Thornton. One sentence in particular which read *Carter to be eliminated* stuck in Carson's mind.

Back in his office, Theo wrote out a full and concise report on the horrific accident which took the lives of the two fliers. *Death by misadventure*. Although there remained suspicion in his own mind that the two Englishmen were trying to kill one, Mister Lloyd Hopkins, and an American, Jack Carter. Their motive as far as the policeman could ascertain, to secure the property known as Tempi and owned by Mister Lloyd Hopkins for an overseas consortium.

Chapter 46

Offices of the Anthony Thornton Consortium

The only person who appeared unaffected by the tragic events which took place twelve thousand miles away was Lord Anthony. He was savouring the moment he would confront Sir Bruce to have Katrina endorsed as vice-chairperson. He also used this time to personally contact Senator Gerald Perry. Sedgwick realised Perry was the man they should be doing business with, this after Clayton's last cable advising he found Senator Barnswald to be most uncooperative. Sedgwick asked Perry to be their sole representative in the acquisition of Tempi Station, he indicated the man would be handsomely reimbursed for his trouble signing the cablegram personally.

<>

In her newly decorated office with a full time nurse, play pen and cot for David, Lady Katrina Thornton found time to read the details of the aeroplane crash which made mention of the strafing of a train in the desert. *A foolhardy and mischievous adventure of larrikin proportions, which cost two British fliers their lives,* reported the paper.

First her mother, now not two months later, her brother-in-laws Clayton and Merrick were dead. She contacted Chester who was in Scotland at the time and shared with him her grief over the telephone, unable to believe the apocryphal account. Chester likewise, was returning to London immediately to be with his father.

After much soul searching, Katrina had accepted her father's proposal to join the firm as Sir James's secretary and shortly after the death of her mother, a percentage of Libby's shares were transferred into her name. Katrina's reason for doing so was to gather information, which she could use to keep her father from purchasing the range of iron ore in Australia which would surely ruin Jack. Also, she believed she was securing David's future. She had talked at length with her uncle about Jack, Chester, David and the future before making her decision. James advised her that she could do more to help the man she loved this way than writing or sailing for Australia at a time when he was trying to secure his future. He had further advised that she was needed to strengthen her father's position on the board as Thornton senior was grooming Clayton to become managing director of the company. Having sent the cable some months ago C/o Doctor Clayton Andrews, she fully expected Jack would have replied, even a short letter or note just to let her know he got the cable, however there had been no response.

Katrina put the paper aside, issued some instructions for Milly, David's nurse, and after embracing her son, excused herself to find Sir James.

Her uncle was in his office studying the latest cablegram from Australia, which indicated the firm's bid to secure Mount Hopkins had failed. Katrina knocked and entered beckoning him to remain seated. He passed the cablegram to her without a word his thoughts for Harrison. Had he been the successful purchaser? It would be poetic justice if

Harrison had out-manoeuvred his father and acquired rights to the property, particularly if gold abounded in such an amount as to make him a wealthy man as his birthright decreed.

Katrina smiled; her father had failed in his bid to purchase Tempi Station. She handed the cable back to her uncle.

'There was a third party vying for the property, apparently,' he chided, the death of the two young fliers now foremost in his thinking as he saw her smile.

'I'm sorry… I didn't mean to appear callous. As a matter of fact Clayton and Merrick are the reason I am here.' James nodded beckoning her to a seat.

'Uncle James do we know why Clayton and Merrick were so far from Adelaide in their aeroplane?'

James shrugged, 'apparently they were seeking out Lloyd Hopkins who was reported to be aboard the train,' James spared her the knowledge that Jack Carter and Michael Smith were also aboard the *Ghan*, it would serve no purpose.

'Lloyd Hopkins?'

'The owner of the property the company wished to purchase.'

Katrina nodded, 'then why did they do what the newspapers said?'

'Strafed the train? I've no idea my dear. The bloody idiots could have killed all the passengers with their moronic behaviour.'

'Did Daddy have anything to do with it? Please, I must know?'

James shook his head although it was noticeable to Katrina that he did not lock his eyes to hers nor orally answer her question. Katrina sat silently for some time head bowed, fingers clasped together. She knew her uncle wasn't given to profanity. He was visibly upset by the ordeal. Finally, she looked up, 'the funeral?'

'A service will be conducted at a later time.' He informed her.

'The bodies, have they been recovered? Will they be brought home?'

'Katrina, they were incinerated, cremated,' his voice full of contrition for Bruce Thornton's sons.

'Oh my God.' Katrina placed a hand to her mouth, 'how horrible.' James did not reply.

'Lord Bruce and Lady Constance?' She broke the poignant silence between them.

'Devastated!' James forced the reply, his thoughts harking back to Sedgwick's demand that Clayton eliminate the American and the little white lie of a moment ago to his niece pricked at his conscience.

'Katrina… your father is losing control. His handling of certain… delicate matters recently have placed the company in a rather precarious position.' James revealed.

'I don't understand Uncle James,' Katrina leaned forward, frightened she may miss a word, frightened by what he may reveal.

James sat unmoving for several seconds weighing up what was proper for him to reveal. 'I remain certain there must be mineral exploration companies in Australia who, for a fee, would have explored and found several iron ore deposits if approached, contracted,' he simplified, with a wave of his hands rising from his chair to face the window.

Katrina nodded her agreement. 'Please go on.'

'Your father tried to take the easy way out and at the same time destroy Jack Carter. He failed, we know that now and at what price, two men are dead!'

'Are you saying this tragedy could have been avoided?' Katrina clutched at her throat in trepidation.

'Yes I suppose I am, and I blame myself for not intervening in his scheming which cost Clayton and Merrick their lives. Oh I'm not suggesting he arranged for the young blighters to strafe the train in an attempt to prevent Hopkins closing a sale with Carter,' James explained seeing the look of shock register with her. 'I imagine they did that of their own accord. However, their actions are ultimately the responsibility of your father and Sir

170

Bruce who sanctioned the boys looking to purchase Mount Hopkins or Tempi Station.' He turned to face her.

'Very irresponsible if you ask me,' Katrina affirmed.

'It comes down to this. Essentially, I am very concerned for the welfare of the company. There is a need for positive level headed thinking from someone who would consider alternatives before going off half-cocked and causing a furore throughout the company, indeed the industry, not to mention the harm done by apocryphal media. Do you understand my dear?'

'I think so, positive leadership, somebody to steer the ship as it were.'

'Precisely!'

'Why does Father want to crush Jack? They conspired successfully and got rid of him, weren't that enough?' Katrina was more interested in Jack than solving her uncle's dilemma where the company was concerned.

Sir James was reticent, Katrina must not find out about Harrison. He chose his words carefully, 'your father believes you intend to join Jack in Australia, take his grandson from him, like the war took Harrison from him and, a tumour Libby. He is frightened Katrina.'

'I thought about nothing else for a time after you revealed mother's contriving, however, I came to realise I am a married woman and none of this is Chester's fault, he was the scapegoat, poor ignorant Chester; he does love me so, even if he now acknowledges I do not love him.'

'Is that the only reason?'

'What else could there be?'

'Maybe Carter doesn't want you now. He would still have to be convinced of your love.' James was ashamed of himself for the remark. 'Forgive me my dear, I had no right to even suggest... ' Katrina waved him to silence.

'You are correct in surmising his feelings; then there is David. How was I going to convince Jack that David was his son, after all we only made love that one time?'

'Katrina, your father proposed that you should become company vice chairperson, which would be an unprecedented appointment,' Sir James almost blurted wanting to get back to the point he was making about a company which needed to gain back respectability.

'Because I'm a woman.' Katrina nodded knowingly.

'Yes! Would you accept the position?' He asked, not missing her cheeks colour with humiliation.

'Chester? After all he felt he was in line for the position.'

Sir James shook his head. 'Impossible, Chester could not manage the company, it is too vast and complex for Chester's intellect or ability.'

'Having said that, you are offering the position to me,' Katrina pointed a gloved finger at herself in surprise.

James nodded, a slight smile curving his mouth. 'I'll be there to tutor you at every step until you are fully conversant with our several enterprises and can make the right decisions.'

'I'm flattered, Uncle. I don't know what to say.'

'Accept the position. Since your father lost Libby, his interest in business has diminished and I fear this terrible tragedy will have the same effect on Sir Bruce. I would remind you he was grooming Clayton to take over in his capacity as Managing Director.'

'It's so sad. Two young lives, frittered away like that.' Katrina shook her lovely head from side to side. An expression of sorrow etched her features.

'Well?' Sir James's eyebrows arched waiting her reply.

'I will have to give serious thought to Fathers' proposal.'

Chapter 47

Adelaide, South Australia

It had been easy, they had to register and with a deftness and guile developed over many years of living by his wits, Fischer removed the page from the thick leather bound ledger. Presently, the reception clerk returned holding aloft a master key, required by law, in the event it should it be necessary to evacuate the premises.

'Here you are sir, this pass key will get you into your room.'

'Thank you my good man; I must have left my key in my other jacket when I changed for dinner, frightfully sorry.' Jonathon grasped the key.

'That's quite all-right Mister Ableson, it happens all the time. I'll send the bellboy up in a short while, if that is convenient.' Jonathon knew a moment of panic as the reception clerk straightened the ledger, not happy until the book was positioned exactly where he wanted it.

'By all means, however that won't be necessary; I was on my way out when I realised I could not get back into my room. I shan't be a tick.' Jonathon watched until the clerk's hands moved away from the ledger, he breathed a sigh of relief.

'Just as you wish sir,' said the desk clerk, always willing to oblige.

'Incidentally, who are the party in the suite next to mine? They were jolly noisy last night, people seemed to be coming and going into the wee hours of the morning.'

'That would be Mister Lloyd Hopkins and his party. I'm sorry if they disturbed you Mister Ableson.'

'Could you have a quiet word with the manager young man? After all, this is supposed to be a first class hotel,' Jonathon complained.

'If you insist Mister Ableson, however it won't do any good.'

'Oh, and why is that?' Jonathon's voice mocked belligerence.

'Mister Hopkins owns the hotel sir. That is his personal suite. If you like, I will speak with him, he is a very obliging fellow. However, I am reasonably certain it won't happen again, Mister Hopkins was entertaining Senator Barnswald and Senator Perry, I think they had a big day,' the clerk smiled as he saw the glint of respect creep across Ableson's features for this piece of information.

'Oh, I see, he must be a man of importance and substance to be entertaining such dignitaries. If that is the case I don't think we should bother him. Thank you my good man,' smiled Jonathon, moving away towards the lift and his suite on the third floor.

Some minutes later, after a cautious look along the corridor, Jonathon pushed the master key into the lock to Hopkins Suite. A grimace turned to a smile when the door opened. Jonathon locked the door and hurried to his room. Once inside, he pressed both sides of the key into a piece of plasticine he carried in his makeup case, making a cast before leaving the room once more and returning the key. With a sly smile playing on his features, he made his way through the main entrance into the South Australian twilight, eager to rendezvous with Harry and pass on this latest information. Tomorrow, he would seek out a locksmith who, for a price, would cut him a key.

When Lloyd Hopkins next met with Jack and Mike, it was to inform them the sale could proceed. He had reminded his brother-in-law and Senator Perry of the importance the government placed on the independence of the region known as the Territory and the subsequent development so necessary if this independence was to eventuate. Perry pleaded the cause of the Consortium. Hopkins was adamant. He would not sell to the large British Company explaining the profits would end up in Great Britain. Barnswald agreed with his summation and Perry reluctantly relented; in his mind he was already composing a cable to Lord Sedgwick Anthony.

Their company would be granted a 99-year mineral exploitation lease in the Name of *Tempi Iron Smelter Works* with Mike Smith as principal, pending Jack's citizenship after which, his name could substitute or be added to the legal documentation. Barnswald further explained that such documentation may take several weeks to draw up, after which it was merely a formality. Consequently, a further contract would be drafted between Hoskins and themselves, that man having agreed to the terms put to him by Lloyd Hopkins' solicitors. Both Jack and Mike shook his hand vigorously too overcome with emotion initially to speak, the price, thirty thousand pounds to be deposited into his bank account. Hopkins further explained he would not be able to wait the final signing and exchange of contracts. He assured them his presence wasn't necessary, his solicitors being charged to carry out his express wishes, the documentation having already been signed. Pressing business required he leave on the twenty-fourth for Marree. He also informed them of his interview with inspector Carson, who asked questions about the strafing of the *Ghan* by the two Englishmen. Jack became interested when the inspector had asked Lloyd did he believe the two men were acting of their own accord or whether a third party was responsible. They were both in complete agreement with Lloyd when he told them he had informed the inspector it was the work of two lunatics who got their just deserts, an eye for an eye, no mention being made of the Consortium's involvement.

From then until the contracts could be exchanged, they had time on their hands. It was time well spent, Jack took pen to paper and after several drafts, finally composed a letter to Katrina being sure to send it to her residential address.

Chapter 48

London

Lady Constance Thornton held a deathlike grip on her husband's arm as the solemn service commemorating her sons continued with tributes from several dignitaries. Dabbing at red-rimmed eyes under her veil, she looked grimly to her right where Chester sat quietly listening to every word from Bishop Deakin. It was one of the few times she could ever remember Katrina squeezing his hand as tears of grief ran down his plump sallow jowls into the handlebar moustache. Like the rest, she knew there was trouble with the marriage and, like the rest, she had heard the rumour concerning itself with the company appointing a vice chairman. And she hoped upon hope Chester would gain the position. What she didn't know was that her daughter-in-law was being mooted as the person most likely to be given the station.

For much of his life, Chester lived in the shadow of his younger siblings, he wasn't a scholar like Merrick, nor a competent sportsman and leader like Clayton. But then nor did he have Claytons vindictive streaks. Now he was all she had left, Chester, Katrina, and of course her grandson little David whom she adored. She felt her husband rise beside her, he squeezed her hand gently before excusing himself as he made his way to the pulpit to deliver the family eulogy for his sons.

Lord Bruce took the news of the air tragedy, the official version from Inspector Theodore Carson, with composure, as though Clayton and Merrick had given their young lives for Great Britain in war. He praised his sons in glowing terms harking back to their school days and bringing his captive audience to the present. No mention was made of them strafing the *Ghan,* only that they were on a mission of the utmost importance, to establish a steelworks in the young colony Australia. Constance looked intently at him as he read from the parchment he had spent hours preparing. She saw the sorrow and something else, his defeat, something she never expected to see in the eyes of her husband of forty years as his eyes sought her out from the throng.

'They were being groomed to take my place.' He looked at his wife over his reading glasses, both hands clenching the wooden sides of the pulpit. 'Now that can never happen,' he dropped his head to look at the carefully prepared document but couldn't read on. Emotions racked his large frame and he cried openly and unashamedly while the concourse of family, business leaders and friends sat quietly. Only one moved, Chester gained his feet and shuffled forward to stand beside his father. His hand shook and tears stained his eyes. Nonetheless, Chester's voice was clear and his Oxford accentuated words filled the cathedral as he finished reading from the transcript his father had begun. For the first time in his life, Chester realised he was the centre of attention; he felt a sudden power and liked the feeling. His father clutched his hand below the pulpit's timbers squeezing it with affection, an affection Chester had not known since his brothers entered the world.

Lord Anthony nudged Sir James Loxton, who sat on his left-hand side, his muted words barely heard by James. 'Did you see that? I only ever thought of Chester as a lazy womanising pompous oath.'

'I'm sure you were right,' whispered James, slightly taken aback by Sedgwick's revelation as, until now he only ever spoke of Chester in defensive terms.

'He's displaying grit. I didn't know he had in him.' Sedgwick replied.

'He may pose a threat to your plan's Sedgwick!'

'Most decidedly! We will call a special meeting of the board as soon as possible. Draw up the agenda James. I will speak with Bruce after the service.'

'I received a cablegram from the two support staffers who sailed with Clayton, they have no funds and wish to return home.' James removed his pocket-handkerchief, placing it over his lips to disguise the conversation.

'Where are they?'

'Adelaide.'

'Send them funds. For the moment they are to stay put. We may need their services.'

'I don't follow you Sedgwick.' James coughed into the handkerchief.

'A coal lease,' Sedgwick explained. 'Carter would need coal to smelt the ore.'

'Go on.'

'He may have arranged a contract. He may have formed a company, taken on a partner.' Sedgwick explained unnecessarily.

'How do you know all this?'

'We have been rewarding the wrong senator,' was the curt reply.

With his arm around his father's waist, Chester guided him back to his seat leaving the St. Pauls choristers to sing a final hymn as the phalanx of mourners filed from the cathedral to stand in brittle sunshine, there to offer their condolences to the Thornton family.

Chapter 49

Adelaide, South Australia

Not gracefully, calmly best described how Harry Street accepted defeat. He believed the cable advising the property could not be sold because the Federal Government had intervened was a scurrilous lie to fob him off, just as he knew what he was going to do now. The plan was instilled indelibly in his mind. One thing he could not understand was how the transaction could be completed in such a short space of time, twenty-five days to be exact. It mattered little, after a hurried meal, they walked to Harry's lodgings where Harry revealed to his companion a plan so daring the bristles on the nape of the little man's neck were suspended with anticipation.

'You still haven't told me what you intend to do with Hopkins, Harry?'

'Leave me to worry about Mister Hopkins Jonathon, you concentrate on your part, I do not want any slip-ups.'

'But the others will still be at the hotel, they are not due to leave until the 28th of April.'

'You have already told me that Jonathon and they had better have water tight alibis,' was all Harry would say on the matter.

'Well, I can make you look enough like Carter to pass distant scrutiny. The main thing will be to conduct your business at the bank with a teller, not this Mister Rankin-Park as he may penetrate your disguise.' Jonathon had his back to Harry, he was fixing them a stiff drink. He needed it.

'Simply done; I will have Hopkins telephone the bank and speak personally with Mister Godfrey Rankin-Park and request that man meet him at another venue at the same time as we are at the bank.'

Jonathon wanted to know all; he passed Harry his scotch. 'But how do you intend to make Mister Hopkins accompany you to the depositary.'

Harry contemplated momentarily, the corners of his mouth creasing in what passed for a smile. 'You are going to write a letter in Hopkins handwriting which indicates there is gold on Tempi. Can you imagine the trouble a man can get into for falsifying a document, which if published, would start a gold rush? I will emphasise this to Hopkins. Do not worry my little friend, I have spent every moment since seeing the party arrive from Marree planning my revenge.'

'But Harry there is gold on Tempi, we have the nuggets to prove it,' blustered Jonathon, not fully appreciating Harry's logic.

'Yes, however Lloyd Hopkins does not share our knowledge, otherwise he would not have accepted Carter's story.'

'How can you be certain Harry?'

Harry shook his head. 'I cannot be certain of anything. However, I am reasonably confident he does not know about the gold. He couldn't possibly know.' Harry reasoned, more for his own peace of mind than anything else.

'I will need more than his signature if I am to copy his hand,' deplored Fischer.

'You shall have it Jonathon, never fear, and three days to practice.' Harry sipped on his scotch savouring the spirit and the moment, letting his mind pick over his plot for flaws.

<>

Everything went according to plan. At dusk on the twenty-third of April, Harry presented himself at the hotel duly disguised as a porter. Using the side entrance reserved for employees he waited his opportunity to cross the foyer when reception was attending to a visitor and unobserved, with a silver tray, upon which he positioned a letter and a newspaper, he rode the elevator to the third floor. Using the copied passkey, he let himself into Hopkin's suite.

In the time allotted him, he packed the man's suitcase, ready for when they left later that evening. Then with a patience inborn, Harry commenced his vigil. It was almost midnight before the inebriated Hopkins, Barnswald, Carter and Smith shook hands all round and said their farewells outside Hopkins Suite. That was all Lloyd Hopkins would remember until Harry ushered him into the boarding house, a street away, explaining away his drunken behaviour to the cab driver while Jonathon struggled with his suitcase. There followed an interrogation. Hopkins, an uncooperative Hopkins, swore the nuggets Harry showed him did not come from Tempi. He explained the geology of the terrain to Harry in laymen's terms. It did not have the desired impact. When informed Carter and his companion Smith were after the mineral rights to establish and iron smelter works, Harry went berserk threatening to kill Hopkins then and there. If Jonathon hadn't caught his arm in both hands and shouted long and hard to get his attention, Hopkins surely would have felt the venom of Harry's spleen. Finally he was rebound, gagged and left sitting bolt upright in a high-back chair for the remainder of the night, much to his chagrin while Harry paced the floor for most of the night ignoring both of them.

During the following days, they convinced Hopkins that he would not be harmed if he cooperated. Harry explained he was entitled to compensation for not being given the opportunity to put his proposition prior to the sale. Hopkins argued there was no gold on the property. Harry promptly showed him the cable; there was no mention of gold he bellowed.

Hopkins read the message, shaking his head in anger for James's connivance, 'I never sent this cable, my instructions were clear. James was told to inform you that any sale had to first be approved by Senator Perry or his office and that the range contained no trace of gold.'

'Well you read the cable and that wasn't what it said!' Harry glared at the man, his finger stabbing the piece of paper.

'All I wanted was an audience, five minutes of your time, was that too much to ask?' It was noticeable to Hopkins that Harry was genuinely shattered.

'I would have been prepared to offer you a partnership,' Harry spread his arms turning away from the man so he would not see his chagrin.

Harry turned to face Hopkins, his serious demeanour told Lloyd this was not a man to trifle with. 'If you have any feelings for your sister and Senator Barnswald, you will comply with my demands otherwise my man will send a copy of your letter to every newspaper in the city. The ramifications of which will start a gold rush and after which, if as you claim there is no gold on Tempi Station, you will be arrested, sentenced, and gaoled, not to mention your brother-in-law. His brilliant career will be ruined!'

'What letter? I haven't written any letter. This is just so much nonsense!'

'Jonathon, be so kind as to let Mister Hopkins read his account.'

177

Still bound, all Lloyd could do was stare at the fabrication. He noted it was addressed to: *Senator Gerald Perry Minister for Minerals and Energy administering the Northern Territory.* In principle, it lay claim to the fact that Lloyd had stumbled upon what may be the biggest gold strike in Australia's history and that he, Lloyd Hopkins was presently engaged putting together a syndicate to include his brother-in-law, to mine and extract the ore and if he, Senator Perry, could extend the mining lease from fifteen to ninety-nine years a lucrative bonus would result.

Hopkins shook his head in disbelief. 'You'll never get away with it!'

'Well I intend to try old sport!' Harry advanced on the table, removing the forged document and handing it to Jonathon. 'I intend to try, compensation for your lack of integrity.'

At precisely 10 am on the morning of the twenty-eight of April under the threat of being shot dead and the release of the fabricated letter, a reluctant Hopkins accompanied a surly Harry from his lodgings and together they walked briskly to the main street opposite the hotel where Hopkins had been staying and from there to the bank.

<>

So it had come to this. Jimmy sighed. He let himself look down at the revolver in his lap once more. A collector's item he was told when he questioned the small fortune the arms dealer was asking. Absently he spun the cylinder, the smell of gun oil cut the air, before he closed the weapon and placed it in the band of his pants. He pulled his jumper over the bulge. He would kill the old man for selling what he considered to be his inheritance. Just as he felt cheated, he could imagine how poorly Harry Street must be feeling. He had spied on Harry this past three weeks, eaves dropping, following Jonathon when he went to rendezvous with Harry. He had overheard their plans to kidnap old Lloyd on the twenty-third and hold him hostage until the twenty-eight, and made his own surreptitious plans accordingly. Now it was time to put those plans into action. Jimmy stuffed the kid leather gloves into the coat he was carrying over his arm. He closed the door of his suite behind him and walked the three flights of stairs letting himself out through the side entrance of the hotel and into the street. He knew Lloyd was supposed to have left for Marree. The police had finished their investigation into the air disaster, and Senator Perry, his investigation into the mineral lease for Tempi Station, Jimmy believed he may as well have saved himself the time and energy sending Perry the cable and a fiver to boot for the postie's silence. His failure to prevent the sale of the property was the catalyst for revenge. However, Lloyd and the others must remain oblivious to his plans. While he kept to himself during their stay in Adelaide, his demeanour was cordial on the occasions they were in one another's company. To this end, he accepted Lloyd's charge to accompany Smith and Carter to the railway station when they left for Port Augusta.

<>

Neither Street nor Lloyd Hopkins was aware they were being shadowed. Jimmy McTaggart scurried along on the opposite side of the wide busy street, peering into the many shop-fronts and almost two hundred yards behind the pair. When they entered the bank, he turned in his tracks and started back towards the hotel and his room, which was opposite Lloyds, there to maintain his vigilance. His animal cunning, and overheard conversations between the tall Englishman and his companion, decided Jimmy, the Englishman would bring Lloyd back to the hotel rather than their lodgings before releasing him. Not that it mattered. He was ready for any change of plan. It never occurred to him that Harry was intent on killing the old man, the gun but a ploy to control the situation, nothing more.

<>

Hopkins threw Harry's timing out by almost five minutes due to his limp and walking with the aid of a walking stick. It was time Harry could ill afford and he was sweating under the hounds-tooth coat with apprehension by the time they entered the bank. Impatiently, the night before, Harry had explained the importance of timing to Jonathon.

Timing is important Jonathon. Firstly because Rankin-Park would have left the bank to make his rendezvous on the other side of the city with Hopkins. Secondly, and equally as important, the train to Port Augusta with Carter and Smith on board was not due to leave until 10.55am. Also, Harry reminded Jonathon, his surveillance of the hotel revealed the cleaning staff did not clean the third floor rooms until eleven thirty every morning.

This was important, because if he had to truss Hopkins, it would be at the hotel, not back at the rooming house, otherwise, there would not be sufficient time to perpetrate the crime and escape the scene, not that he revealed this part of the carefully constructed plan to Jonathon. If Harry got the money and if, as Jonathon said, the suite was Hopkins personal room, then it should have been cleaned on the twenty-fourth and empty. Harry would bind Hopkins hand and foot and leave him to his fate. Also, if he left Hopkins at the boarding house, it would remove suspicion from Carter and Smith whom Harry was setting up to take the blame for the robbery and, he might just die before he was discovered. Meanwhile, Jonathon, with the aid of a little coal oil, some empty packing cases and general rubbish in the alley at the back of the hotel, would prepare and start a fire.

The walk from the bank back to the hotel was the longest of Harry's life; it took four minutes more than he had calculated due to Hopkin's gammy leg. Harry clung to the attaché case as though his life depended on it while, with his other hand, he prompted Hopkins to a greater stride.

Around the hotel entry and down the side lane, a crowd was milling. In the distance but approaching rapidly, were heard the clanging bells of a fire engine.

Harry pushed the reluctant man through the entry, passed reception, which was unattended to the elevator. On the third floor he used the duplicate master key Jonathon had copied and they entered Lloyd Hopkins former room. It was then Hopkins put up a struggle when he realised no one would come to his rescue and Harry was forced to strike him across the temple with the butt of his revolver rendering him unconscious. Harry half rolled, half carried the dead weight to the bathroom. He grabbed a towel from its holder, folded it several times and placed it over the man's head to stop the bleeding. He paused above the still form of Hopkins strengthening his resolve to complete his plans, suddenly realising it might be days before Hopkins was freed, when he was struck from behind and knocked senseless.

The single shot echoed about the room. It was done. Jimmy removed the expended shell from the revolver and let it drop to the floor beside the body. Moving Harry's slumped form inside the room proved to be exhausting. He pried the revolver from the Englishman's grasp before closing the bathroom door behind him to lean against the jam fighting to catch his breath. He was shaking and beads of perspiration shone on his brow. It seemed like minutes but could only have been seconds before trepidation forced him to act. Carefully placing the similar revolvers on the dresser near the four-poster bed, he stood examining his countenance in the mirror. Painstakingly, not wanting to leave a single hair

179

to lodge on the dresser, he removed the sandy coloured wig and moustache before sliding it into the back pocket of his trousers. Then, holding Harry's weapon, he placed it in the pocket of his coat. Removing his gloves, he put them in the pocket of the jacket as well, before removing the jacket. He folded and placed the bundle into the linen chute when the noise of someone talking in the corridor outside the room saw him freeze, until a voice further away arrested the attention of whoever was in the hallway and that person moved away. White and clammy with fear, anxiously, Jimmy clawed at the wall, waiting, counting silently to himself. To be discovered now would mean the hangman's noose. Hastily, he stowed his revolver inside the band of his pants pulling the jumper down over the protrusion before advancing on the door to listen for movement outside. His heart pounding, Jimmy let himself out of the room and down the stairwell. Cautiously, he advanced on the main desk, as he hoped, it was unattended. Jimmy placed his room key on top of the register certain it would be found. He moved quickly to the side entrance letting himself out to mingle with the crowd which was being dispersed because it was spooking the fire brigade's horses. It only remained for Harry Street to regain consciousness, thus putting the second part of his plan into action, for Jimmy to have a watertight alibi.

Part 3

Chapter 50

London

The fire had gone from the old man's belly; he was only a shadow of the man who formerly directed policy. The patriarch, who, for more than three decades had guided Thornton Steel to become the largest steel producing industry in the British Commonwealth. Sir James appraised him now as he passed out the agenda for this morning's meeting. He looked drawn, and somehow smaller, as well, his eyes resided deep within their sockets. Beside him sat Chester; a new found confidence radiated itself from his podgy features. Dressed in a smart char-grey Saville Row suit, Chester was quietly confident in his knowledge and the importance his father placed on the outcome of the board meeting. He was under no false illusions that his would be the only name put forward for the highly sought after senior vice chairman's position. What had surprised him was the late night phone call from his father indicating he would like Chester to make himself available to accept the position when nominated and that he would second the nomination. When Chester asked who would nominate him, he was told Lady Bellamy-Jones would put forward his name. Before saying goodnight his father had warned him against saying anything to Katrina. When asked why, Lord Bruce indicated secrecy.

Lord Bruce took the handle of the wooden gavel and brought it down crisply onto the garnished surface of the hardwood block to indicate the meeting was now in session. Thoughtfully, he looked along the table at Sedgwick, any complacency disappeared; Bruce knew instinctively he was fighting to hold the company together. A split could see him lose everything, particularly now the shares held by Libby were gifted to his daughter-in-law. Sedgwick still held 26 percent of all stock. Under an agreement clause written in to the merger, members of the executive were to be given first preference to purchase shares, which came available due to any member of the executive for whatever reason, wishing to sell. And Bruce simmered because he had not been given the opportunity to bid for Libby's shares upon her death. Sedgwick, smug Sedgwick was behind that connivance. Strangely, Sedgwick did not try to purchase the shares held by his sons upon their death. Twenty-five percent of the company was still under his control, the remaining 40 percent of shares apart from 5 percent respectively held by Lady Edith Bellamy-Jones and Lady Veronica Parker Brown-Stope, were distributed among their shareholders with a maximum of one-thousand shares representing 5 percent of company stock. This arrangement was agreed upon by the principals when their company was chartered by Sir James Loxton.

'Do read the minutes of the last meeting, please James.' Bruce requested once the room was quiet.

'Just before you read the minutes James, on our behalf, and I speak for all of us,' Sedgwick turned to where Richard Claymore and Henry Norse, the two executives who had been appointed to the board to replace the vacant positions left by Clayton and Merrick, nodded their compliance, 'we wish to offer our sincere sympathy to you Bruce, your good wife Constance and Lord Chester.'

A thump on the table by the others followed by 'ere-ere' to a man followed Sedgwick's words. Thornton senior looked about the table, which seemed bare in the absence of the secretaries who scribed the minutes of the meetings. 'Thank you, thank you all.'

James cleared his throat, 'return cables from Australia indicate we were not successful in our bid to purchase the Mount Hopkins range. However, I have had correspondence with a mineral consultancy firm based in Adelaide who for a fee will explore the north-west country for iron ore deposits if we so desire.' James, tabled the documentation for board scrutiny.

'As well there is correspondence from the two chaps who accompanied our board members to Australia. Presently, they will remain in Adelaide pending further instructions. Further correspondence from our manufacturing plants in Ireland, Scotland, and an invitation for the board to be present at the inaugural opening of the southern railway to Brighton.' James dropped the correspondence on the desk in front of him. 'And two possible contracts for steel plate, one from Sweden and our own Royal Navy.' He looked about at the room's occupants after reading the last of the correspondence.

'Thank you James. Is there any business arising from the correspondence? Good, I declare they are accepted. We can proceed.'

''Yes,' began Sedgwick. 'Is it necessary for an exploration company to conduct a search for mineral resources when we already know Mount Hopkins to be a very rich field?'

'With due respect Sedgwick, we don't own Mount Hopkins,' Bruce chastised his counterpart.

'The company was bought in partnership with a fellow by the name of Blake Hoskins, we simply make this chap an offer he won't refuse and save ourselves money in the bargain.'

'You are certain of this?' Bruce glared at him down the oval table.

'I have my sources, a senator,' added Sedgwick, seeing their uncertainty.

'The ninety-nine year lease for the mountain and coal lease cost the American thirty thousand English pounds. Hoskins bought into the deal because he has holdings on the east coast and is presently smelting ore, but of poor quality; Carter intends to supply their Wollongong operation with ore and coal.'

'You really hold a dislike for Jack Carter, Sedgwick? Don't you?'

'On the contrary Bruce, I don't like the man's politics, he wants to create a Republic!' This brought a murmuring of disapproval from around the table. The young colony Australia was after all, a member of the British Empire and as such expected to follow Great Britain's lead.

'The bounder,' Chester was heard to say.

'With wealth comes power, power to dictate policy. We can prevent this happening,' Sedgwick told them, 'we can control his activities.'

Katrina sat frostily saying nothing, her eyes cast downwards to her lap. It was then she decided she wouldn't oppose her father-in-law; he seemed to be the only decent man apart from Uncle James in the room.

'Very well are you going to put forward a motion to that effect Sedgwick?'

'I am, based on my knowledge that Hoskins is willing to sell if the price is right. As part of the package, Hoskins is to be retained as manager.'

'James,' Bruce indicated for the company secretary to write the wording of the motion.

'I will read the motion,' James coughed to clear his throat.

'The motion reads, *Anthony Thornton purchase Blake Hoskins one quarter share in the Company known as The Broken Hill Company and that he, Hoskins be retained as manager.*'

After the motion was read to the board members, Sedgwick spoke for the motion, while Sir Bruce spoke against it. He had lost two sons vying for this particular property; it wasn't worth it. Bruce was in favour of allowing a mineral research company finding them a new field, which could then be purchased. Surprisingly with a nod and not looking at his brother-in-law, Sir James supported his stand after which, the motion was read again and put to a secret ballot.

'Two for the motion, five against and one abstention,' James declared.

'The motion, as put, is lost.' Sir Bruce looked at his fellow directors above his reading glasses. Sedgwick shook his head in disgust.

'I would like to propose another motion, *that the consortium employ the South Australian Mineral Research Company which James has spoken of to find an iron ore field.*' Sir Bruce addressed them.

'I second the motion!' Chester was quick to respond.

'James be so kind as to word the motion.' Bruce looked at Sedgwick as he spoke.

'The motion read would anyone care to speak against... '

Sedgwick snapped at him, barely containing his acrimony, 'put it to the ballot.' Jack Carter had won this round but the fight wasn't finished yet. Already Sedgwick's scheming brain was forming a new connivance.

The new motion was accepted six to two, and Sedgwick wondered whom his secret supporter was.

'I declare the motion carried! And James, will you look into Jacque Van Holland's Company? He operates out of South Africa, Transvaal.'

'South Africa?' Wailed Sedgwick, leaning forward in his chair belligerently.

'Certainly. Closer to home old boy!' Sir Bruce gave him a bland stare. 'Now then to the business which brought us here this morning.' Bruce looked around the table compelling them one at a time to meet his gaze.

'As you would be aware, Sedgwick and I are nearing retirement and therefore we feel it is time to appoint a senior vice chairman who would be responsible for the decision making and every day running of the company. Are there any questions? No! Good! I will now accept nominations from this board to fill the position.'

'Yes James.' Lord Bruce saw the man shuffle in his seat.

'I would like to nominate Katrina for the position.'

He had barely finished when Sedgwick seconded the nomination. Chester looked at his wife anew. It would be an intolerable situation, his wife the senior director; he could never face his friends again, the humiliation... It was bad enough having to sit and listen to her defend Carter.

Sir Bruce smiled to himself, *so that is their ploy.* His eyes sought out Edith Bellamy-Jones who coughed into a lace handkerchief sure she had all their attention, however before she could utter a syllable, Katrina broke her silence.

'I am flattered to be nominated for such a position of responsibility. However, I must decline the nomination. My father is not concerned with Jack Carter's politics. He wants to crush the man for his personal reasons. Mister Carter opposed his will and as you all know my father is used to getting his own way.' It was out and suddenly Katrina felt light headed, she had broken her long silence. As well, she realised she could not stand against Chester, for all his faults he was still her husband.

'You are out of order young lady!' From the end of the table her father's sombre features stared at her, willing her to face him so she could see his seething looks sure in the knowledge that she would realise she had betrayed him. Beside him, James smiled to himself, *good on you Katrina,* he mused; she had the balls to stand up to him. But that wasn't all that concerned James; he knew Lady Bellamy-Jones was about to nominate

Chester. He saw her looks. And Chester's new-found confidence wasn't the ingredient needed to take the company into the next decade.

'Are there any further nominations?' Bruce smiled for the outburst, looking about the room in a cursory way.

'Lord Chester Thornton,' blurted Lady Bellamy-Jones before she could be interrupted again.

'I'll second that nomination!' Bruce almost casually endorsed his son.

'Any further nominations? Anyone?' Lord Bruce smiled ruefully.

'Yes.' Sedgwick glared at Katrina sitting back in his seat and hooking his thumbs into his waistcoat pockets, 'Sir James Loxton.'

Bruce glared at Sedgwick before entering James's name on the pad in front of him.

'Seconded by,' he paused expectantly.

'I'll second the nomination!' Katrina raised her hand hesitantly.

'Do we have further nominations? None. Do both gentlemen accept their nomination?' Dutiful downcast nods by the nominees followed, a sudden tension spread itself around the table. 'Good! Then we will go to a secret ballot as both candidates are willing to accept their nominations.' Bruce declared, his voice rich with sarcasm.

With two votes to be counted, the candidates were locked at three votes apiece before Sir James emerged the victor. He didn't want the added responsibility; however he realised Chester could not do the job and if the company were to command the respect it formerly did, then he would have to take control. More importantly, he would have to curtail Sedgwick's ambitions where Jack Carter was concerned. It was now obvious to all board members after Katrina's revelations that Sedgwick was still set on destroying Carter and, in the process, could destroy the consortium. With this in mind, he knew he would have to convince Katrina to take over his role as company secretary.

Chapter 51

Adelaide, South Australia

When Harry awoke, it was to find he was lying in a pool of blood, Lloyd Hopkin's blood. He had been shot through the head and Harry realised through the dull ache emulating from his skull, he had not pulled the trigger. Harry fought to overcome his sudden panic; his revolver was gone. The money! Thought of the satchel saw him groggily rise from the floor and stagger from the room closing the door behind him. The attaché case was where he left it near the bed. Harry breathed a sigh of relief even if he did not understand what had happened. Unsteadily, but rationally, he opened the closet removing the hounds-tooth coat he was wearing and shrugged into the navy blue jacket. The coat had been left there earlier by Jonathon when he came to ascertain the duplicate key would open Hopkin's suite. Harry placed the hounds-tooth coat, a replica of the one worn by Jack Carter back on the hanger. Grabbing the leather bag, he quickly checked its contents. Satisfied, he donned his hat gingerly over his bloodied scalp before letting himself out of the suite and down the stairs through reception, which was still deserted. The diversionary fire had attracted the staff as well as many onlookers just as Harry had planned. Walking briskly away from the hotel, Harry knew a moment of trepidation when he looked down and discovered the dark stain of blood on his fawn trousers. Quickly, he lowered his head increasing his stride. But no one bothered with him, they were more interested in the fire. Two blocks away he rendezvoused with Jonathon.

Briefly Harry explained what had transpired once he entered the hotel room with Hopkins. His head was throbbing and with every stride threatened to explode. He wasn't feeling at all well and Jonathon's persistent badgering wasn't making his discomfort go away.

'I was not seen Jonathon, and further I do not know who or what hit me. Now stop your incessant questioning,' snarled Harry, removing his hat and raising a hand to the side of his head to feel where the skin and hair revealed a large lump emerging. 'Here, carry this for a while.' Harry handed Jonathon the attaché case.

'What do we do now Harry?' Jonathon was plainly scared and relentless in his fear. Periodically he commenced looking over his shoulder as if expecting a police wagon to appear at any moment.

'Please Jonathon, I told you not to draw attention to yourself. Besides, it is time to use Hopkin's letter. Now I need you most. You are going soft on me.'

'Not me Harry, you know you can depend on me. I just didn't think of murder that's all.' Jonathon picked up his stride to match that of the bigger man.

'I never murdered Hopkins Jonathon, as God is my witness, now listen carefully.'

'We are going to use the forged letter to commence a gold strike.'

'But the gold!' Wailed Jonathon.

'Jonathon we will be rich beyond your wildest dreams. And we will not have to labour to get our wealth, now enough!'

'I'm sorry Harry.' It was then looking down Johnny spied the blood on Harry's trousers and shoes.

'Oh my God! I say Harry, there is blood on your trousers.' He whispered his voice hoarse with anxiety.

Harry ignored him initially. He looked at his watch. 10:50 AM. He tried to smile, which was rare in itself, and it pained him. They walked in silence for several minutes before Harry heard the shrill whistle of the train.

'Where is the closest town to Tempi Station where gold hungry miners can spend their newfound wealth? Edge Rock!' Harry answered his own question while turning to Jonathon.

'Edge Rock?' Queried Jonathon.

'Edge Rock will become a city overnight and I intend to own that city starting with Bill Myre's emporium,' he quipped.

'A store?'

'Yes, miners need equipment; I'll contact Lennard tomorrow with an offer Myre cannot refuse. He can still run the place, but the profits will be mine.' Harry revealed.

'We find somewhere quiet and stay out of sight for some time Jonathon.'

'Melbourne! The alibi you have had me establish Harry?'

'I don't think that will be necessary, somewhere here in Adelaide so I can keep a finger on the pulse of the investigation when this mess breaks. Besides I have some unfinished business here.'

'But Harry they cleaned out Mister Hopkin's suite, it will remain locked until he returns, which he won't. They may never find his body,' Jonathon whined.

'Decomposition, they will find him. When it is realised he never returned to Marree, people will start asking questions. We must act before they do find him. In the morning, I want you to put the Hopkins letter in an envelope, seal it, address it to the editor, in Hopkin's handwriting you understand,' Harry paused to glare at Jonathon. 'Then you are to take it to the offices of the Chronicle Newspaper, and shortly present yourself at the Tattersall's Club. It happens to be a gentleman's club where all the press reporters and their touts hang out,' he added seeing his friend's bemused reaction.

'And?' Prompted Jonathon, reaching for their room key in his fob pocket.

'As well as showing off the nuggets, you will be in possession of a bona fide deed, or claim if you like; a registered gold claim. I can assure you, Jonathon, this will be your greatest performance. The greatest con ever pulled.'

'Where do I get the claim form?' Jonathon wasn't so sure.

'The lands Registry Office here in Adelaide,' Harry shook his head for Jonathon's ignorance. 'After which, you will titivate the form to suit our purpose.'

'A piece of cake Harry,' Jonathon grinned.

'Yes, give me the key and go and get some headache tablets.'

Chapter 52

Darwin Harbour, Australia, August 1920

No sooner had the gangway made contact with the dock than three burly figures, one in a town suit, the others, dressed in the uniform of the constabulary, made their way up the swaying landing platform to the deck. Around them seamen were already busy, encouraged by the bosun's bellow. Tarpaulins were removed from hatch covers, jib and derricks were being positioned to unload sling loads of cargo, the funnels were being scrubbed to remove salt and soot, polish was being applied to the many portholes, and still other tars were holystoning the decking. Eight bells sound as the policemen presented their credentials to the shipping master who was conducting a running conversation with the bosun. The shipping master was an obliging person and conducted them up and down companionways to the captain's cabin, wherein they made known their business.

Less than ten minutes passed before Sergeant Bellamy and a colleague debarked the ship with two very despondent men, each given the closest attention. On the dock, they entered a horse drawn police vehicle and were whisked away amidst stares from the sailors and dock-workers.

Within the confines of the sandstock building with its galvanised hip roof, the hour hand on the large Roman numeral clock told Smith and Carter they had been kept waiting for two hours. The pair had been finger printed, while their personal effects were confiscated and placed in large brown envelopes. After which, before sealing them, the desk sergeant scrawled their names on the envelopes.

Lazily the four-foot blades of the fan cut the air some three feet below the heavily scrolled plaster ceiling. But the fan may as well have not been there for all the good it did. Beads of perspiration ran down inside of their clothing. Some of it engendered by the mystery surrounding their apprehension.

Shortly, a third constable entered the building carrying their luggage. The sergeant rose from his swivel chair and rounded the large desk; he tagged their luggage before instructing the constable to put it in the interview room.

Sometime later he emerged and conducted them through a glass-panelled door. It was not the dimly lit hole of Calcutta they expected. The room, while smelling of efficiency and intrigue was bathed in sunlight and Jack could see the head of a gardener, smell the smoke from burning twigs and leaves, which filtered through the partially opened window.

Before Jack and Mike was a middle-aged man, round of shoulder, balding, with tinges of grey through what little hair he had, the once heavily muscled body gone to fat. Seating himself, he beckoned them to chairs with a gruff command.

Above him a fan similar to the one in the outer room turned the air, still the man perspired, rivulets of water ran down his fat jowls and over his chin to disappear in the flurry of hair showing at the wedge of the stained white shirt. A water pitcher with ice cubes dominated his desk, taking precedence over the manila file marked 'Confidential', and two neatly wrapped parcels along with a framed photograph standing beside the jade ink and quill holder.

'My name is Peterson, Chief Inspector Peterson, and this is Detective Inspector Carson from Adelaide, his associate Sergeant Bellamy and my constables, Harrington and Jones.' He moved his flabby hand to introduce his colleagues. Mike watched as he filled a briar pipe, apparently the policeman was in no hurry. The officer took the first drag on the pipe, waving the match out and flicking it at the open window.

'Close the damn window.' he ordered Jones. The tall lean figure moved from the small desk where he would take down the account of the interview to comply with his superior's command.

Peterson opened the manila folder and looked up at the pair deciding they were very calm.

'For the purpose of this interview what is your name sir?' He looked at Jack inquiringly.

'Jack Carter.'

Peterson nodded, 'and your date of birth?'

'June fifth 1894.' Jack supplied the information.

'And your current address?' Peterson looked to be sure constable Jones was getting down his replies.

'Edge Rock.' Jack cast a look at Mike.

'Your station?'

'I'm an engineer.'

'Thank you sir.' Then it was Mike's turn to supply his details, his voice engendered the mystery he felt.

Peterson leaned across the desk, locking his hands together in front of him, his elbows supported his weight, the pipe momentarily forgotten. 'You were escorted here this morning to assist with an ongoing investigation in relation to the murder of Lloyd Hopkins at Adelaide on or about the twenty-eighth of April last.' He looked belligerently at the pair.

'What!' Jack could not believe what he had just heard.

'You've got to be joking,' Mike Smith glared.

'Mister Hopkins was murdered?' Jack blurted. His stare for the policeman.

'You don't honestly think Jack or I killed him do you?' Mike rose to face the inspector.

'Be seated,' an irritated Peterson directed, not satisfied until the pair were silent some moments later.

'I want you to understand that you are not obliged to say anything unless you care to do so, as anything you do say may be used in evidence against you. Do you understand?' Peterson glared at them in turn. Both Jack and Mike nodded.

'Good!' Peterson mopped his brow and took another long swig from the tumbler of chilled ice water and it was noticeable to Carson that the man was nervous. Silently, Carson wondered how many such interviews of this nature the inspector had covered. He requested to handle the matter personally but Peterson had rubbed his hands together gleefully at the prospect of conducting a murder inquiry stating while such an inquiry was conducted on his turf he would be in charge.

It was inspector Carson who asked 'do you know anything about this matter?'

'We were in Adelaide to purchase some property from Mister Hopkins; he left Adelaide on the twenty-fourth of April bound for Marree.' Stupefied, dully Mike heard himself supply the information.

'Hopkins never left the hotel, he cancelled his train reservations.'

Jack frowned, 'we never saw him after that Sunday night.'

The inspector looked to Carson. 'You have the bill of sale Mister Carter?' Carson asked.

'The desk sergeant took all our personal possessions.'

Peterson indicated for Harrington, who was nearest the door to fetch their personal effects.

Harrington returned, closing the door behind him and placed the envelopes on the inspector's desk.

Carson moved around the desk and helped himself; he found the documents and examined their contents for some time.

'They're authentic, if that's what's worrying you,' Mike told him.

'We do not doubt the document's authenticity Mister Smith.' Finally he nodded to Peterson and returned the documentation to the envelope.

'It was the sole reason we were in South Australia because, the property could not be sold, as the Territory is administered by the Federal Government.'

'Yes we understand all that Mister Smith.' Carson finished for him.

'Constable Jones remained on board after you were brought here. And before you get upset, we did search your cabin and asked questions of the captain as a matter of procedure.'

'What did you expect to find?' Mike was curious.

'A large sum of money, thirty-thousand pounds to be exact.'

Jack was plainly puzzled. He didn't like the way this was going. 'Why the connection with us and such a large sum of money?'

'Because on the morning in question, Mister Hopkins, in company with a man answering your description Mister Carter and wearing a hounds-tooth jacket, similar if not the same as yours, withdrew that amount from his account and was seen handing it to the man, in a briefcase... ' Bellamy reading from his notes, spoke for the first time.

'Me?' Jack swivelled in the chair to face him, prodding himself in the chest expansively before shaking his head in disbelief.

'...before they left the bank together. Please don't interrupt!' Peterson glared at him from across the desk; he was following Bellamy's response by reading from the file in front of him.

'Simply gentlemen,' resumed Bellamy, 'that was the sum paid for the property and the coal leases. Then Mister Hopkins was forcefully made to accompany this person to the bank to make the withdrawal, while an accomplice created a diversion by lighting a fire at the back of the hotel which allowed his friend time to make good his escape from the scene of the crime.'

'Someone, held a .455 revolver to Hopkin's head and pull the trigger.' Peterson locked his eyes to those of Carter. 'Inspector Carson found the spent brass cartridge and the flattened projectile in a floor joist under the linoleum floor covering.' He was looking for a reaction; it was a deep frown of grief. Peterson looked up at Carson. From where he was standing, Carson could see the pair shaking their heads.

'Among other things in your belongings, we found this.' He reached behind his desk where their belongings were neatly set out in opened suitcases and held up a hound's tooth coat.

'Your coat Mister Carter!'

'I can't see the significance... ' Jack got out.

Bellamy prodded his memory. 'It was the coat you were wearing that morning when you entered the bank, the teller remembered it. He was able to describe it to us quite clearly.'

'I wasn't at any bank!' Jack exploded. Colour flooded his cheek's crimson.

Carson broke what was a long thoughtful silence, yet could have only lasted seconds, as each pondered the grisly events. 'So you would have us believe that the property transaction was not completed at the bank Mister Carter?'

'No!' Jack shook his head in resignation. 'Millionaires can command respect. Godfrey Rankin-Park conducted his business at the hotel as did Mister Hopkin's solicitor,' Jack supplied the information.

Peterson sat swilling the last of the ice around in the tumbler, minutely he shook his head but Carson was relentless.

'Do you normally wear a ring Mister Carter?'

'Not since college, no,' Jack replied.

Peterson gave Carson a look.

'So you don't own a dress ring?' Carson grilled him.

'No.' Jack shook his head.

'Mister Smith?'

Mike shook his head holding out his hands for their perusal. 'Doesn't Street wear a dress ring?' He addressed the remark to Jack.

'The size of a half penny piece, with a red gemstone?' Carson smiled for their look of surprise.

'He had a motive,' deliberated Jack.

'Harry Street believed there was gold on the property,' said Mike.

'We know about Mister Street. Mister McTaggart was most cooperative.' Carson would say no more.

'We will be interviewing Mister Street and his travelling companion for a statement,' said Bellamy, a slight smugness creeping into his voice.

'A travelling companion?' Jack was surprised by this revelation.

'Yes, a Mister Jonathon Fischer,' Bellamy read from his notepad. He did not reveal they had a statement from Captain Reutenbachen master of the vessel *Scagway,* which indicated Fischer joined Street at Fremantle bound for Port Augusta.

'Inspector, if we did this terrible thing, where is the money?' Jack lowered his head. 'You would have checked my cheque account... '

'Besides, where is the revolver?' Smith wanted to know.

'We have the revolver Mister Smith, it was recovered from the cloth's chute at the hotel.'

'Fingerprints?' Asked Jack, stonily.

'Your fingerprints were found in the room. According to Constable Harrington, who examined both sets of prints, they match perfectly the samples we took not two hours ago.'

'But not on the gun. Besides, I don't own a gun,' chided Jack glaring at Peterson.

'Inspector, we would expect you to find our fingerprints in Mister Hopkins suite. We were in his room on more than one occasion... ' Mike supported Jack.

'Excuse me sir can you get 'em to slow down? I can barely keep up,' Jones appealed from behind the desk.

'Do your best man!' Peterson growled, waving him to silence.

'So were Jimmy McTaggart, Senators Barnswald and Perry, the bank manager Mister Rankin-Park, solicitors representing Franklin and Murdock, the bloody drink waiter, the maids and several other people I would imagine!' Jack let out a deep sigh of frustration.

For some moments, silence reigned over the room. Mike sat hunched forward, elbows on knees clutching at his jaw. Jack stared at the window, Peterson fiddled with the manila folder and indicated to Harrington that he would like more ice.

Carson's normally smooth brow was knitted with a frown. Peterson saw the look. 'What?' He asked.

'Nothing.' Carson was toying in his mind with a theory. *Supposing Hopkins went to the bank accompanied by a man we assumed was Carter. As far as the manager would be concerned, it would appear as though the deal had fallen through and Hopkins was there to withdraw and return Mister Carter's funds.*

Carter's question cut across his thoughts 'Inspector Carson can you tell me exactly what time I was supposed to have accompanied Mister Hopkins to… this bank?'

'Sergeant.' Carson nodded.

Together they watched as Bellamy removed his notebook from his pocket again and minutely browsed before answering.

'The bank opened for trading at precisely 9.30 that morning, Mister Hopkins and another entered the bank at 10.17 on the dot,' he supplied the information.

Jack smiled for the first time that morning, 'well it wasn't us! At that time Mister Smith and I were boarding the train for Port Augusta.'

'That's right, and we have a witness!' Mike told them.

'Yes we know,' Carson paused to cough into his hand. 'Mister Jimmy McTaggart conducted you to the train. However, he left shortly afterwards, and the train did not leave for another forty minutes Mister Smith.'

'And we checked the time factor. Our man covered the course over the overhead bridge, down the steps to the street, across the street to the hotel, a brisk walk to the bank, back to the hotel and then on to the railway station. Twenty minutes! You had thirty-five at your disposal after McTaggart left your company, more than enough time.' Bellamy read from his notes.

'We breakfasted at the station kiosk,' Jack suddenly remembered.

'McTaggart knew of our intention.' Mike told them.

'We have Mister McTaggart's sworn statement. Our inquiry is far from finished.' Carson deliberated.

'He was a beneficiary of Lloyd Hopkin's estate. There was bad blood between them. McTaggart didn't want Lloyd to sell the property.' Mike volunteered the information.

Bellamy was still reading his notes, 'his accomplice?' He didn't look up. 'According to McTaggart, he stayed over as a matter of courtesy to see you off. He returned to the hotel because he forgot to return his suite key at the desk.'

Mike nodded, he remembered Jimmy showing them his room key and apologising that he would have to return to the hotel.

It was noticeable to the pair that Peterson looked to Carson before addressing them again. 'Very well Mister Carter, Mister Smith, thank you for assisting us with our inquiry. You are free to go after you sign the record of interview. Your passport will be held until further notice Mister Carter.'

'I have one more question inspector. Did Mister Rankin-Park actually handle the withdrawal when I supposedly went to the bank with Mister Hopkins?' Carson glared at Bellamy who shrugged.

'Anyone could have forced Mister Hopkins to go with him or them to the bank.' Jack turned on Carson and Bellamy.

'True Mister Carter, but if they got what they wanted, why did they murder him? And why was only a certain amount of money taken? Hopkins had considerably more in his account,' Carson revealed.

Jack shook his head letting out a long breath, 'I don't know; I just don't know. He was a good man,' added Jack.

'What about the British consortium?'

'We are investigating all possible leads Mister Smith.' Bellamy got out.

'Constable Jones, will you photograph Messrs Carter and Smith before they depart the station?' Instructed Carson. 'For the bank teller gentlemen.' He added, seeing Carter about to protest.

193

When they had the room to themselves, Peterson was the first to break a poignant silence. 'Well, I thought that went rather well under the circumstances,' he smiled, rubbing his hands together briskly.

Carson gave him a sardonic scowl before firing a scathing broadside at Bellamy. 'You made us look like bloody amateurs, far too many loose ends Jim. The ring, did you look closely at his fingers? Carter hasn't worn a ring for years! Then there's the clerk at the bank, he would not have been able to recognise Carter if the sale transaction took place at the hotel. Did you check to see who managed the bank and if the transaction took place at the hotel? These points should have been checked thoroughly! I can't be expected to do everything sergeant,' Carson pummelled a clenched fist on the desk top in a display of frustration for Bellamy's incompetence, ignoring the frosty glare Peterson gave him.

'He has a hounds-tooth coat,' reminded Bellamy to add to Theo's woes.

'It was all too pat. Three coats all alike, worn by three different people.'

'Three alibis,' Bellamy hastened to add.

'That, or an attempt to incriminate Carter. I believe the coat in the laundry chute with the gloves and the revolver was probably worn by the murderer.'

'The coat found in the closet at the hotel could have been Lloyd Hopkins,' postulated Peterson.

Carson nodded.

A contrite Bellamy tried to appease his senior's wrath, 'if Carter and Smith are telling the truth, we can clear them soon enough by matching fingerprints found on the weapon with the prints we took a couple of hours ago.' Bellamy was unperturbed by Carson's outburst.

'I'm not sure where this is all heading Theo!' Peterson was bemused.

'If as Carter said, Hopkins commands respect, why didn't he summon the manager to the hotel with the withdrawal? Why would he go to the bank?' Carson posed his question while pacing the room. His expression was thoughtful.

'Yes I imagine his gammy leg would have caused him a lot of pain to walk any distance.' Peterson muttered.

'And why make the withdrawal in cash? Wouldn't a cheque be more convenient?' Carson posed the question, which was troubling him. 'I think we felt we had such a strong case against Carter and Smith that we have neglected others who could also have perpetrated the crime.'

'But the evidence?' Bellamy wasn't so sure.

'I now believe a lot of the so-called evidence was circumstantial, so placed to convince us of their guilt. Them fleeing Adelaide, the coat, finding the revolver, the amount of money taken, the overall description of Carter albeit his build, his complexion. Then there is the fire, which made us believe two people were involved. All but the motive. As they themselves stated why would they want to kill Hopkins? He didn't stand in their way. They have the authentic deeds of sale. No!' Carson shook his head.

'Chief inspector, would you post the finger prints and photographs of the suspects as a matter of urgency to Adelaide… ' Carson requested.

'Most certainly. Where are you blokes going?'

'Edge Rock. There is more to this case than meets the eye. This wasn't the first attempt on Lloyd Hopkin's life.' Carson revealed.

'Oh.' Said Peterson in a way which indicated he would like to be privy to their prognosis.

Bellamy smiled, 'Lloyd Hopkins was on board the train which was strafed by two British airmen whom we believe represented a British consortium keen to get their hands on Hopkin's property.'

'The plane crash out in the bush?' With a wave of his hand, Peterson dismissed Harrington who was poised in the doorway.

'Precisely! Someone wanted him dead and they got their wish,' Carson wasn't prepared to elaborate.

Chapter 53

London

Lord Sedgwick Anthony firmly believed Katrina would take the position of company vice chairman, particularly after James had spoken to her and gained some assurance. So it was an angry company director who sought a meeting with his daughter only days afterwards. Katrina was composed even in the absence of Sir James, her mentor, whom was told beforehand by Sedgwick his presence was not required.

Lord Anthony waved her to a seat opposite his desk dismissing Mildred with an irate wave of his hand and the belligerent command. 'Shut the door. I do not wish to be disturbed!'

He stood over his desk fingers drumming against the timber surface before addressing her. 'Why did you oppose me in the boardroom?' His animosity painted a picture. It was a look which Katrina knew only too well.

'Because you are bent on crushing Jack,' was the equally sharp retort.

'You are a married woman, married to a peer of the realm. Get this American out of your mind. Your place and David's are here with me. Your mother would turn in her grave if she knew what you did in that boardroom,' he bristled.

'I cannot forgive you or mother for conspiring to ruin my life,' Katrina flung at him.

'Ruin your life! Be sensible girl! We saved you from a fate worse than death itself. You are very ungrateful.' Lord Anthony shook his head in despair.

Katrina shrilled, 'and you are trying to crush the only man I could ever love.'

'The man is a bounder. He has no station, no means to support you. Be reasonable. Consider David and Chester.'

'David is Jack's son.' She shouted before sobbing brokenly into her lace handkerchief.

'What! You gave yourself to that... that conspirator!' Sedgwick rose to full height his features scarlet. Yet there was always a nagging doubt where the boy was concerned, Sedgwick believed he had none of the Thornton's features. It came as a shock all the same and Sedgwick let himself fall into his leather padded chair, some of the bristling temper he displayed earlier gone, he felt only a helplessness for something over which he had no control. Sedgwick liked to be in control of any situation.

Katrina sat staring at him ready to defend her love for the American, 'Father you were wrong, mother was wrong... '

'Never, I will never accept that you would give yourself to such a man.' Lord Anthony shook his head vigorously.

'Chester and I are getting a divorce,' Katrina hung her head, her hands fiddled with the embroidery of her handkerchief.

'A divorce! Never!' Sedgwick shook his head in vexation.

'You are not taking David away from me young lady. I have his future planned.' Sedgwick raised a finger pointing at her menacingly, 'If you think you will be free to go chasing your lover do not include him in your plans. Bastard or not he has Anthony blood running through his veins.'

Katrina covered her face lowering her head, sobbing brokenly she replied, 'David is my son he will do as I say.'

'I'll cut you off without a penny, without a penny do you hear!' He shouted his damnation for her.

'I don't want your money father, just understanding... please,' she blurted into the handkerchief.

'Never! Never. I'll crush that son of a bitch now if it's the last thing I ever do. Do you understand? Now get out of my sight.'

Katrina stood looking at his forlorn figure sitting crumpled in the chair behind the desk. 'Chester could accept that I didn't love him. However, he cannot forgive me for standing against him for the position of vice chairperson. He was humiliated. You should have thought of that father.' Katrina turned on her heel and rushed through the door slamming it behind her.

<>

Clandestine could be the only way to describe how Lord Anthony acquired a one fourth share in Broken Hill Company. Shortly after their arrival in Adelaide, Freddy Moylan and Reginald Bundy were summonsed to appear before Senator Gerald Perry where that person charged them with their duty. A day later, they boarded the train for Melbourne, and from there to Sydney.

Blake Hoskins eyed with suspicion the offer put to him by the two weary travellers. Their dress indicated their stations to be underlings, messengers, not what or how he felt representatives of a large British Consortium should conduct themselves. The letter introducing them as such was by a highly respected member of the present government however, Senator Gerald Perry who was known to Hoskins.

Hoskins read the correspondence from Perry twice, not believing the written word initially. He was to be retained as manager on a salary of two-thousand pounds per annum plus a bonus once the site was producing steel. A figure beyond his comprehension, that plus thirty-thousand pounds if he would sell his one fourth interest in the Broken Hill Company to Anthony Thornton Consortium. Hoskins wasn't a young man. Active, yes, but believing this to be a deal he couldn't refuse, he made the necessary arrangements to accompany the two Englishmen back to South Australia where Perry was commissioned to honour the contract on the behalf of the consortium. The only clause of concern initially, until Perry gave him adequate reasons, they were buying his silence.

With Hoskins signatures barely dry on the three copies of the contract, one of which he was to retain, and witnessed by Reginald Bundy and signed by Senator Gerald Perry in his legal capacity, Perry composed a cable for Lord Anthony C/Warburn Abby, advising him of his successful bid to gain one quarter share-holding of Broken Hill Company. Further, the senator requested of Hoskins that he find a suitable position on the staff for Reginald and Freddy. They were instructed to keep Perry closely informed of any developments concerning the company. Business concluded, Perry filed away his personal copy of the contract and hastened to have his secretary send the original via the first ship. The correspondence was marked personal and confidential.

Chapter 54

Adelaide, South Australia

Gold! When the story broke of the new strike in the west, Adelaide, that beautiful city of churches was turned into a city of gold crazy activity. Men from all walks of life started out in pursuit of the elusive dream. For many, donning civvies after shedding uniforms was a new adventure. Gold! The word filled the imagination and gave reasoning to their new freedom.

The press had a field day, researching previously known strikes around the country and featuring them in newspapers as fast as they could be edited and type set. They retold the stories of gold barons, of the Chinese and the bushrangers, and for the adventurous it made fascinating reading.

Harry smiled, a cruel smile that twisted his face in harsh lines. He took one last look at the latest editorial before casting the newspaper aside. Restlessly, he ambled to the sideboard and poured himself a generous scotch. In the weeks following Hopkin's death, there wasn't much to do but wait, play cards, read, and drink. Initially, the alcohol dulled the pain and let him get some needed sleep.

Although his surroundings, like the train, were not to his satisfaction, they served their purpose. There were no maids making beds. Jonathon took care of that, no meals, no sticky beaks to observe their comings and goings. It was time.

'Time to be going Jonathon; they bought it.'

'The mechanical rock crusher did the trick Harry.'

'Yes, they believed you were genuine Jonathon, one cannot purchase machinery like that on the West Coast, you were great,' Harry raised his glass in a silent salute.

'Edge Rock Harry?' Jonathon sounded despondent.

'You need not worry Jonathon, by the time we get back, Edge Rock will be a boom city, easy pickings with plenty of people to satisfy your particular talents. Besides, the local constable is in my pocket; Edge Rock will be a very open town.'

'According to the Truth Newspaper, Senators Barnswald and Perry are demanding an official inquiry into the Chronicle publishing a false statement.' Jonathon handed Harry the paper.

'Barnswald claims the paper is using the death of his brother-in-law and the publicity surrounding his murder to incriminate him and Perry in a scandal by publishing a falsified document. Barnswald claims, *it could not have been written by his brother-in-law.*' Harry read aloud.

'Oh… why doesn't the senator believe Mister Hopkins wrote that letter Harry? Do you think they are on to us?' Jonathon could not hide his anxiety.

'I don't think so old boy. He would only be stabbing in the dark. Apparently Hopkins was a geologist, and Barnswald feels he would not have sold the property if he knew about the gold. Anyway, the police have taken their inquiries interstate. According to this press release, they wish to question two men who were in Mister Hopkins company during his visit to Adelaide at about the time he was murdered. One might imagine it is Carter and

Smith the police are seeking.' But under the jovial mask Harry was wondering who had really killed Hopkins and what was the motive? It couldn't have been for the money. Otherwise, the perpetrator would have taken the case. No, Harry believed it was far sinister than money. Also the mention of two men made Harry realise they may still need an alibi. He reminded Jonathon not to lose the train tickets which showed they were purportedly in Melbourne at the time of the murder.

< >

Almost a week before Harry Street arrived back at Edge Rock, Detective Inspector Carson and Sergeant Bellamy were cooling their heels in the thriving coastal town where all talk centred about a gold strike further inland at a place called the Red Mountain on the Margaret River. Their arrival in the boom town was accomplished by catching one of Otto Reutenbachen's ships from the West's major beef exporting town Wyndham, south of Darwin and from where Carson placed a long distance phone call to Adelaide finally getting to speak with Superintendent Gearing. After bringing him up to date with their inquiry, Theo requested to speak with Freddy Knowles in forensic.

Carson commenced their conversation by asking Knowles if forensic had finished examining the murder weapon.

'You're not going to believe this. We found a tightly rolled cylinder of paper down the barrel, expensive stationary at that.'

'What?' Carson looked in stunned silence at the Bakelite handpiece. The cadence in his voice saw Bellamy cast a perspicacity glance at his boss.

'Is something wrong?' Carson waved him to silence, a puzzled look on his face.

'A cylinder of paper? The numbers 835476.' Carson was bemused. 'What does it mean Fred?'

I can only imagine it is a code of some sort. Maybe a telephone number or a safe combination,' Carson heard Fred through the buzzing line.

'Possibly.' Carson turned to Bellamy, 'Jim, get this down.' Bellamy reached for pencil and notepad.

'Repeat the number's Fred. 835476.' Bellamy heard Theo say them again.

'You got that?' Carson turned to him again, holding the Bakelite handpiece away from his ear. Bellamy nodded repeating the numbers back to him.

'Same weapon as that used in your murder inspector, a revolver used until recently by the Irish constabulary and a rare bore size to boot, .445, but I cannot be certain it has been fired recently,' Fred's voice crackled across the airwaves again.

'Thank you Fred'. Carson held his palm over the mouthpiece. 'Where does that leave us?' Carson asked Bellamy who was removing his coat and loosening his tie.

'The finger prints… Carter and Smith,' reminded Bellamy.

'Of course.' Carson turned back to face the mouthpiece on the wall. 'Have you checked the finger prints I sent from Darwin against those found on the revolver Fred?' Carson fumbled with the hand-set.

'No match Theo, I'm sorry.' Fred added when not realising a response.

'Damn! Thanks Fred. Is the superintendent still there? Good! Put him on will you.'

Carson waited irritably while Gearing came on the line. It was one of the traits of his boss Carson detested; Gearing was so slow in everything he did. Finally, 'Superintendent, the photographs of suspects Carter and Smith that I sent you, did they register with any of the staff who work at the railway kiosk?'

'If it helps, the lad in the newspaper stand remembered them being at the station that morning.' Came the slow drawl over the crackling line.

199

'The time factor was very important sir, can you have someone check what time the lad saw them.'

'I'll go around there and check it out myself Theo. Now you had best get off the phone, it's costing the department a small fortune.' Carson stood looking stupidly at the handset. 'The blighter hung up on me,' he exclaimed in disbelief.

'Well?' Bellamy shuffled uneasily in the single chair of their shared accommodation.

'It may not be the murder weapon, and the prints don't match.' An exasperated Carson threw himself onto his single bed.

<>

Harry Street's return to Edge Rock went unnoticed by many. For them he was just another new arrival with gold fever, a fortune seeker. Certainly not a prospector, not dressed as he was in a three-piece town suit with felt hat, cane and gloves, still they were too busy to care. A new shipment of equipment had arrived and Bill Myre, Harry's new sales manager had stayed up most of the night invoicing and pricing to meet the morning's demands. Word spread very quickly and shortly before sunrise, gold hungry miners clamoured and fought for positions in the queue to purchase their wares.

Constable Mountier had noticed him however. He was patrolling the bustling throng outside Harry Street's newly acquired Emporium to see no man jumped the queue, and today he was wearing his service revolver. He squirmed on sighting Harry.

The Margaret River gold rush put Edge Rock on the map once and for all. Coastal vessels were crammed with diggers, some coming from as far away as New Zealand to try their luck. Edge Rock was the nearest point of disembarkation, a place where they could get supplies before heading on up the Margaret on a wild trek to the outback.

Harry was pleased to see the town had changed markedly. His homecoming was timely. The vastness of Australia and the isolation of the little coastal town saw months pass before the miners in their droves commenced to arrive. Everywhere around him Harry observed change. Tents by the hundreds had been pitched and buildings were in various stages of completion. Prices of commodities had soared, and silently Harry hoped Clarence had enough gumption to follow the example set by the town's businessmen. He observed the cattlemen's cooperative had the common sense to establish a meatworks on the edge of town to feed the thousands of new arrivals. He also noticed the new diner and Chinese restaurant. Yes things were changing rapidly, he thought to himself.

Jonathon Fischer rubbed his hands together gleefully, his mind ticking over the easy pickings that surrounded him. Harry guided him to the safety of the veranda from the path of a dray, laden with fresh sawn building timber.

'Is this your establishment Harry?' Jonathon asked as Harry paused outside the large yellow sandstock building with the boarded up window.

'Yes, however I do not recall the window being broken,' he replied, pointing a gloved finger at the unacceptable renovation, the disgust in his voice transferring itself to his friend.

'Nothing a pane of glass won't fix Harry,' said Jonathon cheerfully.

'Come on,' mumbled Harry, shouldering past a group of drinkers lounging in the doorway and not waiting to see if Jonathon was following.

He paused outside the door of his office, then he did something unusual for Harry, thought Jonathon to himself; he knocked on the doors timber panels.

'Enter!' Said an authoritative voice from the other side of the door.

Harry smiled, 'the bastard's copied me to a tee,' he said half to himself yet loud enough for Jonathon to hear.

'Huh?'

'Nothing.' Harry opened the door.

The shock on Clarrie's face had to be seen to be believed. His jaw dropped, his mouth opened to say something, instead the cigar, clasped between clenched teeth, dropped to the carpeted floor. Clarrie's face paled as he jumped from Harry's chair like a startled rabbit. Momentarily he stood staring at Harry until his nostrils smelt singed carpet and he made a dive for the floor. On all fours he swept his hands around the carpet under the desk until he found the cigar.

'Boss. You're back!' He exclaimed from the floor.

'Yes. It would appear you are rather surprised to see me Clarence,' said Harry. His face displayed no trace of emotion.

'I sure am boss, didn't know when to expect you,' replied Clarrie, regaining some of his composure while stubbing the cigar into the marble ashtray.

'I gather you received my cable? Anyway, I am back and I want to see the ledger and accounts for the past months of my absence!'

'Yes sir, all is in order, business has been booming. You won't believe the figures.'

'I dare say. And my new purchase?'

'I have the deed here for you to sign Harry. That will complete the transaction.'

'Good! Now suppose you tell me what has been happening while I was away Clarence?'

Clarrie coughed into a closed fist. 'Where would you like me to start boss?'

'I suggest you start with the boarded up window downstairs.'

Jonathon watched Clarrie squirm, saw him ease uncomfortably from behind Harry's chair. Harry seated himself behind the desk, not before taking his handkerchief and wiping away tobacco strands from the highly polished black leather. At a signal from Harry, Jonathon moved to the velvet-upholstered chair positioned near the door. It seemed to Jonathon that Harry was a very patient man, considering the story Clarrie was telling. Three valuable horses from his private string were missing, due to the carelessness of some nitwit called Mountier, his beer hall had been subjected to extensive damage, and the girls in his employ had left at the insistence of Clarence following an argument over their working hours. It would seem nothing had gone right from the time Harry left for Marree, apart from the purchase of Bill Myre's store, Jonathon surmised.

Harry's fingers drummed on the top of his desk. His features were impassive, but Jonathon read the hatred; he knew where to look. It was his eyes, like storm clouds, they underwent change from brown to a smoky haze. Yet the voice was calm, controlled as Jonathon knew it would be; Harry had learnt to mask his emotions.

'I'm deducting two pounds from your fortnightly wage until such time as this establishment has regained its reputation for feminine company.'

When Jonathon saw Clarence about to offer an objection, Harry quickly told him, 'that or your job, please yourself.' Clarence nodded dutifully.

'Good! Where is Lennard? I would know why he didn't follow my instructions where the miners were concerned.'

'Boss Lennard McPherson is being held over in Roebourne gaol to be hanged for the murder of the prospector Homer Jones. You didn't know?'

Harry was shocked by the news. 'No, I didn't know.' Harry gestured for Clarrie to tell all.

'Smith's tracker returned to Edge Rock with the news he had found a body partly decomposed three days from Kununurra on the old stock route. Smith informed Mountier and he set out to recover the body. As you would be aware boss, Mountier only had a push-bike to patrol the district. Anyway, he came and asked me to loan him a couple of your horses.' Seeing Harry's frosty look again at mention of his horses, Clarrie was quick to add, 'I told him in no uncertain a manner he couldn't 'ave 'em boss, but he swore he was empowered to commandeer 'em anyway,' Clarrie shrugged.

'Go on Clarence,' Harry ignored the feeble excuse.

'Well when he finally got back he arrested Jackey…' Harry cut him short. 'What happened to my horses?'

'Dunno boss,' Clarrie shrugged with a sheepish look for Harry.

'So Constable Mountier arrested the half caste, then what happened?' Harry and Jonathon were hanging on every word.

'Well he marched Jacky off to the lock up. When he questioned him, Jacky spilt his guts. He put Lenny in the frame and showed Sergeant Mitchell who come over from Kununurra to assist with the inquiry where they could find the rifle. Lenny was charged, found guilty of murder and held over at Roebourne gaol to be hung. Jacky got twelve years hard labour.

Harry let out a tired sigh. 'Was there anything else?'

'No!'

'Very well, listen carefully.' Surreptitiously Harry outlined his plans, placing the gold nuggets on the desk to emphasise his strategy.

'Any questions?' Harry looked directly at Clarence when he had finished.

'Oh, the other day… ' Harry stopped Clarrie in mid-sentence as there came a knock upon the door. Hurriedly Harry scooped the nuggets back into the leather pouch and handed it to Clarence with a look.

'Enter!' Clarrie called, stuffing the poke into his trouser pocket. 'Eh sorry boss, habit I guess.'

The door opened to reveal yet another strange face. 'Boss', he addressed Clarrie, 'there's a troupe of sheilas downstairs.'

'They must have arrived on a coastal freighter this morning. With any luck the new pane of glass for the window should be 'ere to.' Clarrie were all smiles.

Suddenly there was a thud as the half-shut door flew open pressing the messenger between wall and door on the completion of its swing. An obese middle-aged matronly figure filled the doorway.

'Who runs this place?' She asked, collaring an astounded Jonathon from the chair he was occupying and straddling it in one easy movement.

'Dear Madam, in answer to your question, this is my establishment,' replied Harry, rising and bending slightly in what he hoped would suffice as a bow.

'Good! You look like a gentleman, now tell the rest of these gawks too clear out while you and I discuss business.'

'Gentlemen, you heard the lady,' Harry used the word loosely.

'Boss,' wailed Clarrie, his hands clenched together.

'It can wait,' Harry told him, and there was gravel in his voice.

'And you are?' Harry turned to face her after shutting the door behind them.

'Daisy, you can call me Miss Daisy,' she flirted.

'Harry Street at your service Miss Daisy.'

It didn't take Harry long to appreciate he was dealing with a professional. Daisy looked out for her girls, took her percentage and guarded their honour with a derringer pistol carried in her handbag, and which she showed Harry, just so he got the message. She informed him she had been attracted by the advertisement.

'Very good! May I show you around Miss Daisy, so that you and the girls can move in? How many of you are there incidentally?' Harry was counting pound notes per half-hour.

'Including myself seven, Harry, I hope you can accommodate us in a fashion to which we are accustomed.'

Harry was doing his arithmetic, a room for her, one for himself, another for Jonathon, ten in all. Yes that should be all right. Clarence would have to board down at Stoddart's pub. 'Certainly my good lady, please follow me.'

The agreement reached, accommodation checked, Harry was invited to inspect Daisy's brood. Harry had himself a mother.

Chapter 55

Edge Rock, Western Australia

Two days after Harry's return and Clarrie were getting ready to open the club for business when he spied the tall man accompanied by another and he was reminded of the urgent conversation he had wanted to have with Harry. Too late now, Harry would have to face the music. Clarrie tried to disappear behind the bar but inspector Carson had seen his reflection in the mirror as the front door gave under his touch.

'Good morning Mister Ferguson.'

Clarrie's head appeared above the bar, a look of mock surprise on his features. 'Oh it's you is it. Ya wastin' ya time. I told ya before Mister Street hasn't returned from Adelaide.'

'Is that so, well you won't mind if I have a look for myself then, will you?' replied Carson. He was eyeing the stairwell.

'Have you got a warrant?'

Carson replied, 'We don't need a warrant to speak with someone.'

Clarrie looked from one to the other, nervously he rubbed his hands down the sides of his trousers, 'He ain't in I'm tellin' ya.'

Carson nodded and beckoned for Bellamy to follow him up the stairs. If the policemen were surprised to find scantily clad women excitedly moving about in the upstairs area of accommodation, then he chose to ignore it, instead heading for Harry Street's office and there to patiently knock on the door.

'Enter,' boomed a voice from within.

Harry looked up, a sullen expression on his features for the interruption. He was studying one of four ledgers of trade for Bill Myre's store. 'Who the hell are you? Clarence!' Harry bellowed.

'Mister Harry Street?' Harry managed a nod before Carson continued. 'Sorry for the interruption. Detective Inspector Carson and Sergeant Bellamy,' Carson waved his wallet which contained his badge of office. Bellamy closed the door.

Carson smiled, looking about the office, which had been refurbished after Harry's altercation with Jack Carter. 'May we?' Carson indicated the comfortable floral chair for himself. Harry waved them to be seated, placing a red marker in the page he was perusing, giving the figures one last glance before closing the ledger with a bang.

'Sergeant Bellamy and I are making inquiries in relation to the murder of Lloyd Hopkins on or about the twenty-fourth of April in Adelaide. You are not obliged to say anything unless you care to make a statement as, anything you do say may be used as evidence against you.' Carson smiled while Harry's features paled. He moved uneasily in his chair before returning Carson's direct gaze.

Seeing Street's discomfort Carson was want to add, 'we can conduct our interview here where it is reasonably comfortable or, down at the gaol.' Still Harry remained silent, giving both men close scrutiny.

'Sergeant Bellamy will record the interview; then you will be required to sign a record of the interview as a matter of course. Do you understand Mister Street?'

Harry nodded, the account ledgers forgotten with this new threat. In the time allotted him, Harry was going over the events of that fatal morning in Hopkin's suite.

'This is your establishment Mister Street?' Bellamy asked to which Harry nodded. 'So you are a publican by occupation. And your full name is Harry Street, is that correct?' Again Harry nodded in the affirmative.

'We don't have your age Mister Street? For the record,' Bellamy added, his pencil poised above the notepad, his gaze fixed on Street.

'I don't see that trivial things like my age or occupation is relevant.' Harry raised himself in the chair.

'Formality Mister Street,' Carson answered, fixing a smile on Harry.

'January 1875. You work it out.' Was the curt reply.

'I am given to understand you own a revolver?' Carson didn't want to give Harry a chance to gather himself. He could see the man's frustration at being interrupted and wanted to take full advantage of the situation. Leaning over the desk, he placed a photograph of a revolver in front of the well-groomed Englishman.

'I owned such a revolver,' muttered Harry.

'And now it is conveniently missing.' The sarcasm wasn't lost on Harry.

'Stolen,' was the brusque reply.

Carson nodded more to himself than as a gesture to Harry while absorbing this piece of information. 'Your ring?' Carson was relentless, his eyes directing those of Harry to the red gemstone on the gold band.

As if mesmerised by Carson's stare, Harry looked stupidly at his left index finger, 'yes,' he replied his brow knit in deliberation.

'Do you know anything about this matter Mister Street?'

Harry shrugged his features deadpan, 'Like most I read about the murder. If memory serves me correctly… ' Harry paused looking intently at the policeman, 'at that time I was in Melbourne, we stayed at the Kensington Hotel.'

'We?'

'A business partner,' Harry reluctantly supplied the information.

'That would be one, Jonathon Fischer,' Bellamy turned back some pages in his notebook to verify his revelation.

Harry looked at him anew, 'Yes.'

'And Mister Fischer's present whereabouts?' Carson inquired sensing Harry squirming, having had to reveal he wasn't alone in Melbourne.

It was hopeless Harry told himself, 'He is in residence here at the club.'

Just then the door opened and a nervous Clarrie filled the doorway. 'Sorry boss, they were what I wanted to talk to ya about the other day.' He nodded at Carson.

'Mister Fischer, is he in the building?' Carson spoke to the bar manager.

'Yeah, down the hall,' Clarrie waved a thumb through the air.

'Ask him to join us would you Jim,' Carson indicated for Bellamy to find Fischer.

'Come in Mister Ferguson and close the door,' Carson indicated Bellamy's recently unoccupied chair.

'Do you have any objection to my continuing with the inquiry until my colleague returns Mister Street?'

Harry sighed, if only he had listened to Clarence the other day. He shook his head submissively.

'Thank you. On or about the twenty-third you and Mister Fischer were in Melbourne, not Adelaide.'

'That is correct,' Harry responded glibly.

'So you weren't interested in purchasing Tempi Station Mister Street.' Carson was busily writing wondering what was keeping Bellamy.

Harry conceded the detective must have done some investigating and there was no reason to withhold the information 'I was very interested in the property; however, I was given to understand it was sold.'

'Oh, I wasn't aware the sale was made public?'

'I cabled Adelaide,' Harry lied.

'I see, so you and your business partner were merely taking a holiday before returning to Edge Rock.'

'Something like that.' Harry glared at the man.

Just then Bellamy returned conducting a curious Jonathon Fischer before him. Harry moved him to silence with a knowing look. Jonathon was pleading for an explanation but Harry maintained his silent stare. Bellamy opened a case he was carrying and placed it on the desk so his superior could see the contents. 'Will you look at what I found in his room? This bloke is a disguise artist.'

'Well-done sergeant. Do you have a safe Mister Street?'

'No. Why?' Harry was loathe to reveal he had a wall safe because of the letter.

'You are a businessman Mister Street, you would have to protect your interests, assets, cash, ledgers… ' Carson nodded towards the books on Harry's desk.

Clarrie blurted. 'Inspector, we are using the safe in Myre's emporium.' Harry gave him a filthy look, drumming his fingers on the desk and not replying.

Carson ignored him, 'Come Mister Street, I would like to know if you have a safe here and if it is opened by using a combination of numbers.' Carson smiled to display his tolerance for the evasive game the two were embroiled in. 'Would you be so kind as to write down the combination of numbers on my notepad, please?'

'Clarence knows the combination,' Harry gave a deep sigh he was resigned to the inevitable now that Clarence had opened his big mouth. He nodded for him to write down the combination of numbers to the safe in Myre's emporium.

'Thank you Mister Ferguson,' Carson took the proffered piece of paper from Clarrie handing it to Bellamy. Bellamy checked the numbers against those given to them by Freddy over the phone; they differed. He looked at Theo and shook his head.

'And the ledgers, like the one you were working on, and any cash is kept where?'

'My desk drawers are my safe, each one locked after I complete my transactions. Now if you will excuse me, I have a lot of work to catch up on.'

'I am given to understand you own several business interests in Edge Rock? Supposing I do get a search warrant? Or, we can do this the easy way.' Harry ignored the policeman; he pulled the ledger he had been working on towards him.

'Very well let's all go down the road to the emporium you purchased from Mister Myre,' Carson eased himself out of the chair.

'I'm frightfully busy as you can see?' Harry was apprehensive; obviously the policemen were looking for the money he took from the bank. One day that was all he had needed, just one more day. Harry was in the process of purchasing Stoddart's pub; tomorrow was settlement day. The money remaining would have differed considerably from that which the policeman was looking for and they wouldn't be able to prove a thing. And who else knew about the sum of money? The murderer? Harry was clearly puzzled. 'Just what is it you expect to find inspector?'

'Would you care to show the way Mister Street?' Carson encouraged, with a wave of his arm towards the door.

'Clarence will escort you inspector.' Harry made a valiant attempt to open the ledger again, choosing to ignore the policemen.

'I'm afraid I will have to insist that you accompany us Mister Street. Now,' he added in a brisk tone.

Shortly with Clarrie Ferguson tagging along the group made their way to what was formerly Bill Myre's Emporium. It was left to Clarrie to introduce the policemen to Bill; Harry completely ignored the poor fellow moving further into the room until he was standing opposite a feed bin full of bulk wheat. His features deadpan, Harry watched as Clarrie and old Bill moved the bin on its casters to reveal a safe, housed into the brick wall behind.

'Thank you Clarence.' Harry glared at him. 'You may return to your duties Mister Myre,' Harry ordered.

Harry stood back and watched apprehensively as Bellamy twirled the dials back and forth until the large chromed handle turned in his grasp. The musty smell of enclosed paper greeted the gathering.

Carson indicated for Bellamy to empty the safe and bring its contents to the front counter of the shop where the light was better. He undid the attaché case they found among many documents, nodding his head without surprise, when it revealed neatly bundled bank notes. A brief count by Bellamy convinced both men they were looking at the money taken from the bank in Adelaide.

Carson smiled to himself. 'Harry Street. I formerly charge you with the murder of Lloyd Hopkins.'

'Jonathon Fischer I am formerly charging you as an accomplice to the murder of Lloyd Hopkins.' Carson indicated for Bellamy to handcuff them.

'What! I don't know anything about any murder!' Jonathon commenced to shake with fear turning to Harry for support.

'Do read them their rights sergeant.'

Bellamy nodded. Carson frowned at Fischer, now convinced of his guilt. He waited, watching the features of both men as his sergeant read them the official proclamation. Finally when the sergeant had finished, 'Mister Fischer, do you know anything about this incident?'

Harry glared at Jonathon, it was enough to silence any further outburst. Soon afterwards, Carson and Bellamy escorted the pair to the goal leaving Clarrie to ponder his uncertain future.

<>

It was two weeks to the day after Harry Street's arrest when all hell broke loose in Edge Rock. Down in the bar of the Ocean View Club, it was pandemonium. The place was packed, men spilled onto the veranda and into the street as word spread of the miner who had struck it rich.

Gold fever! There wasn't a man present in the bar who wasn't doing a jig, as though they had gone crazy. Then all was hushed as each man strove to hear what the lucky miner was saying. As he finished speaking, men began to break away, heading for the exit, while those outside pushed and shoved to gain entry. While the uproar lasted, Clarrie indicated for the miner to hand over Harry's poke, deciding Harry may have no further need of the gold, a smirk crossed his features.

Chapter 56

Roxburgh House, London

Lord Chester Thornton was in his study when his man's servant Harold, a well-groomed man of middle age, delivered the daily mail. Even though it was only mid-morning Chester was half way through his second brandy, his preferred drink. Since the appointment of Sir James to the privy position of senior vice chairman, Chester had taken to consuming several measures of brandy and was often seen in the Anthony Thornton Building inebriated long before the working day had expired. This morning, his first at Roxburgh House for some time because of his failed marriage and business commitments both at home and abroad, there was a mountain of correspondence acquiring his attention. Rifling through the correspondence one letter in particular captured his attention. It was addressed to his wife and postmarked Adelaide, Australia.

Chester hesitated momentarily before using the letter opener and revealing the correspondence. He took another swallow of brandy before settling back in his padded chair and commencing to read.

Dearest Katrina,

I don't know where to begin. I suppose I should congratulate you on your marriage and the subsequent birth of your son. And I must take this opportunity to thank you for your timely cable, warning me of your father's intent. I realise now what I formerly brushed aside as your imaginings, you tried to warn me however I guess I was just so happy to be in your company that I felt your trepidation for your family's position, their opulence and old school tie tradition were figments of a very lively imagination. He was bent on destroying me and in the process people have been killed. Well, hopefully all that is behind me now. Mike and I acquired Tempi Station, we also hold a fourth share in a company on the eastern seaboard of Australia which should see steel being produced shortly, only waiting on the completion of the Blast Furnace, not that you would be interested in such information. I just thought I should tell you how I am getting along.

Katrina when I read the letter your mother handed me that afternoon in the library, I felt my heart was going to break in two; I was shattered. On reflection and after a conversation with an acquaintance, Harry Street, who is from the old country and cast off from a wealthy family, I am given to understand that for a substantial sum, there are scurrilous people who would copy another's hand for a gift. I hope against hope that was the case and sometime in the future all will be revealed. If on the other hand, I did something to change your feelings towards me then I am truly sorry. However, I cannot to this day honestly believe you did not love me. My feelings for you now are as strong as they were the night we made love. I would do anything to have that time over again.

However I'm beginning to realise that was in the past and we must move on even if the love I felt for you then has not diminished with time. I understand you are a married woman with a husband and son to consider and I have no right to feel the way I do. Just remember Katrina, if you ever need a friend I will be there for you.

Yours sincerely
Jack Carter.

Chester gulped the remaining brandy oblivious to the strong fumes and fixed himself another. His hands trembling he lifted the glass and swilled the contents in one long swallow before slumping into the chair letting the glass tumble to the Axminster carpet, his eyes glued to the open letter on the desk in front of him.

When Katrina arrived home some time later, it was to find her husband inebriated. His sardonic and raucous voice drew attention to himself as soon as Katrina opened the study door. He was waving aloft a letter and calling her the most degrading names.

Katrina knew as soon as she spied the Bentley in the driveway Chester was there, she hadn't seen him since his stated intention of filing for a divorce. Katrina was holding David by the hand; she turned ushering him from the room and instructing him to go upstairs. She closed the door none too gently and stood facing Chester her hands clasped the handle, she eased back against the solid timber.

'You've been drinking again Chester.' She admonished him.

'You... ! Don't you presume to tell me what I can and cannot do!' he shouted.

Katrina was immediately defensive; Chester had seemed amiable enough about the divorce, after all it was at his insistence, so Katrina was taken aback by his malevolent behaviour, and the belligerence with which he spoke to her.

'You have no right to speak to me like that Chester. If you are upset about the conditions of the divorce settlement, we can talk about it but I will not tolerate your malicious language in front of David.'

'David is not my son! Our marriage was a sham. You never loved me, you needed a husband...'

'Chester!' Colour rose to Katrina's cheeks.

'Do not... say another word! You, you vixen!' He waved the letter again.

Shocked, but anxious to hold her correspondence, Katrina strode purposely across the room to snatch the letter from his grasp. But before she could do so Chester pulled it away, rose if unsteadily, and slapped her hard across the side of the face with an open palm. The blow shook her, it being unexpected. Chester had not struck her since her Uncle James threatened him some time ago. Chester hit her again, this time his fist was closed and the round arm blow struck her on the nose with considerable force, a fountain of blood sprayed from her nostrils, giddy, Katrina slumped to the floor trying to protect herself. Chester groped his way round the desk and stood over her.

'Get up you bitch,' he roared, encouraging her to move by lashing out with his foot, the solid blow catching Katrina in the ribcage, she winced, gasping for the sudden pain. Sobbing and crying, she lay in her blood, expecting at any minute to feel a repeat of the cowardly blow, the letter fluttering to the carpet of no immediate interest to Katrina as she doubled up to protect herself from further physical abuse.

'Go to him, I'll see to it you never realise a penny from my estate, you nor your bastard son,' Chester aimed another kick at her cringing form before leaving the room and slamming the door after him.

It seemed like hours but could only have been minutes before Katrina heard the dull roar of the engine then the screech of tyres as Chester raced the Bentley down the drive and all was quiet again. She tried to sit up sucking in her breath as the stab of pain from her ribcage told her she may have broken or badly bruised ribs. Wildly, Katrina looked around for something to support her weight trying vainly to rise from her crouched position. Her eyes misted with tears, pain etched her countenance and racked her body. Tentatively she raised a hand and felt her nose pressed against her right cheek, she knew she must get to the telephone and ring for Doctor Symonds. This time it was more than facial bruising. Katrina could not believe Chester had so brutally attacked her. With head down, hands spread before her and knees taking her weight, Katrina summoned her resolve, pausing to rest twice before easing herself up to cling to the desk for support. The telephone on the desk seemed far away and Katrina willed herself to move inch by painful inch around the desk until she could pick up the receiver. Slowly, for it hurt to breathe, Katrina in what must have been a puzzling conversation for the operator relayed a message to be forwarded to Doctor Symonds, their family physician.

Katrina let the handpiece fall from her grasp as her strength waned and she again slumped to the floor, her hand almost within reach of the bloodied pages, but foremost to her thinking was that David should not see her in this state.

She must have lapsed into unconsciousness for when she awoke it was to find she was in her room with Ethel her lady in waiting, Doctor Symonds, and her Uncle James, peering intently at her from the surroundings of the bed. Absently, Katrina lifted a hand to feel the bandaging covering her nose when a restraining hand and a gentle voice bade her relax.

Doctor Symonds smiled. 'We will let the swelling subside and then I will operate to straighten your nose Lady Thornton. You sustained two broken ribs, which I have bound. I will leave these pain relievers on your bedside table. They contain a tincture of laudanum. Take one whenever the pain becomes uncomfortable. I must be getting back to London,' Symonds glanced at his fob watch. 'I will drive out tomorrow.' He placed a hand over Katrina's forehead and shortly, smiling again, 'you must rest and leave everything to Sir James, I'll see you in the morning.'

James ushered Symonds to the door with instructions for Harold to see the good Doctor to his car before returning to Katrina's bedside.

'Who did this Katrina?' Sir James held her hand pressing her fingers between his hands.

Katrina looked at her uncle through red streaked eyes unable to answer initially. Emotion welled up inside her like a volcano to burst and she was unashamedly crying.

'Chester! Did Chester beat you?' James waved for Ethel to leave them; reluctantly the chubby figure in the starched ankle length uniform closed the door behind her. Katrina nodded, the slight movement hurt her nose.

'A letter, he was reading, I don't know, oh God,' Katrina was shaking.

'Relax my dear, I'll go and see if I can find the letter. Just rest. I'll send Ethel in to sit with you. And tomorrow, I'll have a locksmith out here to change all the locks, don't worry he will never hurt you again, I promise,' Sir James squeezed her hand softly between his in reassurance.

James entered the study in time to see Harold had tidied the room and was using a bucket of hot water and suds to remove a blood stain from the carpet. Harold paused uncertainly, looking up at Sir James.

'A bad business sir, a very bad business, him being drunk, an all,' the man shook his balding head before continuing with the chore.

'It certainly is Harold. Letters, Lady Thornton mentioned a particular letter,' James addressed the crouched figure.

'On the table sir, heaps of them.'

James busied himself looking through the correspondence, 'I thought she said this was an opened letter Harold.' James scanned the pile of correspondence neatly placing the letters back on the desk.

'They are the only letters I know about sir,' Harold wrung out the cloth before plunging his hand back into the hot water and repeated scrubbing the carpet.

'Thank you Harold, she must be confused,' Sir James frowned, looking about the room, and under the desk before gently closing the study door behind him. *Maybe Chester took the letter with him.* He mused.

James climbed the stairwell back to Katrina's bedroom. Before he could open the door the handle turned and Ethel's sudden appearance startled him.

'The madam is sleeping Sir James,' she saw him jump back a pace at her sudden appearance. 'Sorry sir, didn't mean to startle you.'

James held up a hand smiling. 'Did your ladyship say anything Ethel, anything at all before she fell asleep?'

'No sir she was asleep before I entered the room.'

'Oh well it will keep. I will be staying over Ethel. Can you arrange to have two of the guest rooms made available? My driver,' he added seeing her puzzled look.

'Certainly sir. And dinner sir?' Ethel would know so she could inform the cook.

'Please, Donald, my driver, will eat with me. I want to be told when Lady Thornton awakens.'

'Certainly Sir James, you just leave it up to me. And don't fret about the mistress, I'll be with her every moment.'

'Thank you Ethel, you're a treasure.' James gently closed the door behind him determined to go back to the study and open any mail involving the consortium as he had noticed some of the letters were post-dated several weeks ago.

Sir James descended the stairs in time to see Harold leaving the study.

'Harold, I don't want Lord Chester admitted to the house. Is that clear?'

'It will be my duty to protect her ladyship sir, he will never do that again while I'm around.' James wondered where Harold was when Katrina was being attacked; he kept his thoughts to himself.

'Good! Go down and see the gamekeeper, borrow one of his shotguns and if Lord Chester so much as puts a foot on the front steps, you are to shoot him! Is that clear Harold?'

'Yes... sir,' Harold wasn't sure he should shoot his Lordship.

'Oh, and Harold please ask Donald to join me in the study.' Not waiting a reply James let himself into the study.

< >

James woke early as was his custom. After a brisk walk down to the village and a sumptuous breakfast he was ready for any development the new day may bring. Ethel found him in the library reading one of Chester's magazines on Astrology entitled *Observations through the Telescope.*

'Her ladyship is awake Sir James. She is asking for you. She was pleased to hear you stayed over.'

'Thank you Ethel,' James placed the magazine back in the cabinet and followed her out of the room and up the stairs to Katrina's bedroom. David was with his mother when he entered and the boy jumped from the large four-poster bed and ran to greet James. James held him in the air, both arms under the boy's armpits. 'Oh how you are growing master David,' he smiled. 'And heavy too,' he grinned at the lad.

David's arms extended so that he grabbed at the lobes of James's ears. 'I got them,' he shouted. 'See,' he held an imaginary pair of ears for James to behold and they both laughed.

211

James put the lad down again with the stern command, 'Give me back my ears!' Although he could not keep a straight face and commenced chasing David around the room, the child laughing at his feeble attempts to catch him.

Katrina, trying to laugh at the pair through her pain, indicated for Susie, David's nanny to take the boy to his playroom.

When they had the room to themselves, Katrina addressed her uncle. 'Did you find the letter Uncle James?'

James slumped into a chair by her bedside. 'No unfortunately, Chester must have taken it with him.'

'No I saw the letter on the floor after he had left, it had blood on it.' Katrina winced with pain as she tried to adjust the pillows behind her so she might sit more upright in the bed.

'Just the one page then.' James moved from the chair supporting her weight and adjusting the pillows.

'Thank you. Two I think. I cannot be sure. He was shaking the letter in front of me and yelling. I have never seen Chester so upset and angry before. He said something about David not being his son.' Katrina suddenly remembered her voice fading away.

'Maybe if the written side was to the carpet then all Harold would have seen were pieces of paper with blood on them. He may have disposed of them.' James was on his feet and heading for the door.

'Oh no!' He heard Katrina cry behind him.

James bounded down the stairs and entered the study; he was looking for the waste paper basket which stood beside Chester's writing desk. There, crushed pieces of paper with dried blood on them greeted him. James extracted the pages from the bin and slowly pulled them back into their original shape, careful not to rip or cause further damage. He placed the letter on the desktop and ran his hands over the pages smoothing them. A smile broke his features as he saw whom it was from. Then, deliberately, James made himself fold the pieces of paper in two. Patiently, he rifled through the envelopes on the desk once again until he found the one he was looking for while chastising himself for overlooking the neat severed edge, which indicated it to be opened.

Back in Katrina's bedroom, James handed her the letter watching her expression change to one of happiness in the twinkling of an eye and then she was sobbing and handing him the letter from Jack Bryson Carter.

'I intend to go to him, uncle,' Katrina sobbed.

'That would be unwise just yet my dear... oh I appreciate your wanting to be with him,' James rushed the words seeing Katrina about to protest. 'All I ask is that you consider David, his future, the company and the thousands of people we employ... '

Katrina's eyes welled with tears as the enormity of his words hit her like a ton of bricks. Would she ever be free to join Jack in Australia?

'Write to him my dear. Let him know you will come to him in a short while. Think, that is all I ask, if not for yourself then David and Jack.'

'Jack? I don't understand?'

'He is trying to build an empire, would it be fair on him for you and David to suddenly appear out of the blue. Oh I've no doubt he would love to see you and his son but... is the time right for him?' James paused clasping her small delicate hands in his. His face etched the genuine concern he felt for his niece.

Katrina believed him; it was in his eyes, the sincerity. A father image, the misty cloud that reveals a man's inner emotions and leaves one beyond doubt as to his character. She burst out crying again and James drew her to him.

Chapter 57

Tempi Smelter Works

The site for the Tempi Smelter base camp was chosen and four days after the arrival of the drilling equipment, the Sullivan jack hammers broke the quiet of the surrounding bush. Employees of the newly formed company spent two days assembling and cleaning the drills ready for use. The large air compressors were dismantled and man hauled to the top of the west face. It was hard work, gruelling under a blazing sun, twelve hours a day hauling the fifteen-hundred pounds of machinery, couplings and hosing up a slope that would test a mountain goat. It was a feat just short of being miraculous. Jack did the work of two men, and when the shift was finished, he had climbed down the path for a canvas cover to protect his precious machinery from the night air.

The drill bits were in sequence, each capable of drilling to a depth of twenty inches and each successive bit slightly smaller, until finally a hole eighteen feet deep had been drilled, large enough to take a plug of gelignite. It took a crew of three men a day to drill six holes. Each shift worked, covered a distance of forty-eight feet and after two weeks the three crews had drilled sufficient holes to blast the first bench which would remove some 200,000 tons of burden.

Jack supervised the plugging of the holes, after which, the number six detonators were placed in position. By using six feet spacing between the holes, Jack was able to link the thin copper cable attached to the detonators from one to the other, forming a series of links along the freshly drilled span.

Calloused work-hardened hands pushed down on the timber handle of the plunger. It was a dull thump, but there was enough energy to explode the face. The ground vibrated beneath their feet and the lip of rock was seen to disappear in a whoosh of deafening sound. After the dust settled, it was up to the gang chosen as barers to rope themselves to the many tree stumps left standing for this purpose, and lower themselves over the newly formed rock-shelf to the slump slope below. The barers shovelled the freshly exploded ore to the valley floor where it was gathered in large drays and pulled by draught horse teams to the rock crushing plant on the banks of the Margaret River.

The rock crushing plant Harry Street had ordered as part of his confidence scheme, the first steam driven patent of its type, lay on the docks at Edge Rock unclaimed. Doc Andrews heard about the crusher and made some inquiries. Two weeks later, a deal was struck with the company to whom Street owed money for the equipment and the owners of Tempi had acquired the plant. The crushed ore was transported by barges down the river. A contract had been finalised with Otto Reutenbachen two weeks to the day before Jack and Mike returned to Tempi from Edge Rock. Reutenbachen agreed to ship their iron ore to Wollongong and return with coking coal. He further organised to have a dumping bay cleared and the building of an ore-loader near the present docking facilities as part of the document of agreement. Thus, Tempi Iron and Smelter Works had its humble beginnings. But the company's first crisis was fast approaching. An armada of boats laden with men was presently negotiating the river. And gold ran through their veins, not iron ore.

Chapter 58

Margaret River

Sometime before dawn James (Jimmy) McTaggart stirred. Eyes blinking in the half darkness of the tent, he watched as Charlie Anderson, sitting on the edge of his bunk, pulled on his boots. It was Charlie's turn to fire the new bench. By firing the blast early the dust settled and the barers could commence their shift directly after breakfast.

After Charlie had gone, Jimmy lay watching the night disappear, listening to the bush creatures welcome the new day and pondering over his return to Tempi.

On his arrival at Tempi Station and the Red Mountain he remembered as a child, he told a concocted story which when explained to Jack saw that man offer him a job. Along with Mike he was charged with mustering the scrubbers and to get the property into working order as a cattle station, Jimmy couldn't have been happier.

Shortly after the killing, the mine at Marree had been shut down and he was out of work. He hoped there might be a job for him working for the boys. He further explained *Probate Officers and Auditors working under instructions from Senator Barnswald were finalising old Lloyd's estate.*

The explanation seemed feasible to Jack who had asked. *Didn't Lloyd adopt you, so to speak?*

Yes, sighed Jimmy, *and yes I stand to gain from his estate if that's what you are implying.*

I'm not trying to be nosy Jimmy, just a little cautious is all. You must realise we are suspected of murdering Mister Hopkins, Jack remonstrated, a slight anger for the man's appearance at this time and wondering if he had an ulterior motive for being here. They welcomed all the manpower they could get. But as Jack reasoned, they knew they were not responsible for the murder, and if the police have interviewed Harry Street and cleared him of any implication, then that left Jimmy, and Jack wasted no words telling him so.

You too had a motive, Jack pointed out.

Jimmy shook his head before replying, *Harry Street has been formerly charged, him and another bloke.*

Street? Jack's expression was one of doubt.

I never killed him as God is my witness, Jimmy appealed. *And if you blokes are innocent then it had to be Street.* Jimmy wanted to be believed. He had convinced himself this past few months that he was innocent. Carter, Smith and Street had forced his hand along with Senator Perry who had the power to prevent the property falling into the hands of foreign investors.

He's in the lockup at Edge Rock awaiting transfer to Adelaide, I was told. Jimmy gave Jack a coy smile. *You didn't know?*

Jack shook his head, his face ashen as he thought of Katrina and what this would do to her once the story broke and if the man's true identity was revealed.

What about Rankin Park, he knew the exact amount of the purchase price? Jack was clutching at straws he didn't want to believe Harry was guilty even if what little he knew of the murder indicated he could be involved.

Jimmy shrugged, *what would be his motive? Embezzlement?*

Too, Jack remembered the interview with Carson. However he would not be drawn into further discussion on the murder of Hopkins, *OK Jimmy, you have a job, one thing, there is no gold on Tempi only iron ore. If you are here to sabotage our enterprise for revenge, then let me warn you I intend to defend this mine with my life.* He was certain Jimmy got the message.

Thanks Jack. Jimmy had offered his hand, his grip firm; he looked Jack in the eye as their hands shook.

Twice he had been escorted to police headquarters in Adelaide where he had been formerly interviewed about the murder. The first time, at the insistence of Senator Barnswald, he was questioned, with that man's attorney representing him and subsequently not detained. But as the story leaked to the newspapers and they conducted their own investigations, based on supposed revelations, and reliable witnesses; the maid finding the body, the room being locked, a big man with fair hair and wearing a hound's tooth coat lurking about the premises of the Federal hotel, being seen near the bank, and so on; he was again questioned. *Anyone can dye their hair.* He had been told by Carson who was not convinced.

Oh, where was his accomplice, the fire, or was that just a separate incident? Jimmy's barrister wanted answers.

They had no proof; his alibi was water tight as long as he kept his wits. He could wait for his inheritance; he believed he was Lloyd's sole heir. He fully expected the relentless grilling by the police. He was made to try the coat on; it fitted, even if a little big. But they were probing in the dark. While they knew he had a motive, was a beneficiary of Hopkin's estate, the contents of Hopkins will were not known, a fact Senator Barnswald's barrister reiterated when he again intervened on James' behalf. They were clutching at straws. Every so often to appease the situation, releasing statements to the effect that an arrest was near, meanwhile, their investigations were moving elsewhere. After considerable pressure from the media, the police had revealed they were looking for two men who were in the company of Mister Hopkins on or about the twenty-third of April. The State Premier and Senator Barnswald never ceased to hound them and Jimmy continued to wait. Meanwhile, reports of the whereabouts of Smith and Carter came in from all over the nation, so did sightings of Harry Street and his companion Jonathon Fischer.

There had been no mention of a revolver being found in any newspaper account, which Jimmy thought to be strange, until Sergeant Bellamy, during his second interview revealed to Stone, McTaggart's barrister, that a weapon had been found in the cloth's chute at the hotel along with gloves and a hounds-tooth jacket. The revelation only came when Carson requested Jimmy be fingerprinted and Stone had refused initially to allow his client to be so subjected. His prints didn't match those found on the weapon they told his brief, after a wait of an hour for forensic to study both sets at length.

Jimmy now knew the satchel he spied near the bed contained the money taken from the bank. He surmised correctly that Harry Street had the money. All he needed now for Street to be found guilty beyond doubt was to plant the real murder weapon in the man's room or office. He would bide his time. When Street was being escorted to Adelaide, the weapon would be conveniently found.

Jimmy had come home. He knew Mike still held hopes the property could become a working cattle station, scrubbers all mustered, branded, the property fenced. He wanted to be part of it. He wanted the land rights and would bide his time. As soon as the old man's estate was settled, he would have more than enough funds to purchase Tempi. The miners would need fresh meat. Jimmy although resentful, shared Mike's vision. Slowly he threw back the covers to make his way to the tank; the same old homestead tank he remembered from his boyhood.

Chapter 59

Tempi Smelter Works

When Charlie returned from igniting the charge he reported to Jack advising him of a flotilla of boats on the river. It could only mean one thing; Jack had ignored the miners panning the streams and tributaries of the Margaret River. They posed no threat and had already been advised that there was no gold on Tempi. Something must have happened in town to stir up this lot he confided to Mike. Together they made arrangements to meet the new arrivals.

The milling phalanx waited patiently on the bank of the river for those camped along the streams to join them. Suddenly, they felt the tremor of a blast. Clarrie cursed, he'd hoped to take the camp by surprise, drawing Smith and Carter out into the open without endangering himself or exposing any of the men.

'All right men, let's move out, and no noise,' he emphasised. For the most part they were unarmed, except for picks, shovels, pans and supplies.

Carter let them approach through the scrub until they reached the edge of the clearing. There was a distance of approximately sixty yards separating the men from the mob, easily three hundred strong. Holding the Winchester rifle loosely in one hand, he fired a round harmlessly into the air. When the sound was lost in the surrounding hills, he hailed them.

'That's far enough, you're trespassing; this is private property,' Jack shouted.

'Come on men, there's only the two of them,' yelled one brave fellow, breaking cover, followed by the leading bunch and urged on by the thought of gold. He was encouraged by voices from within their ranks.

In one fluent movement Jack smoothly raised his rifle. Easing the slack, he fired at the round-shouldered figure darting for them across the open ground. There was a dull thump as the soft nosed projectile struck flesh. Blood spurting from his leg, the man fell to the ground. Shocked by the suddenness of the rifleman's actions, the others stopped in their tracks diving for cover. He levered the action, but men were cowering on the ground trying to pull mother earth over them in their haste and leaving the victim of his marksmanship wreathing in agony on the powdery river terrace.

While they were stunned by his aggression, he determined to talk to them again.

'Men, there is no gold on Tempi, only iron ore and a job for any man among you that want's it.'

'You're a liar. We've seen gold nuggets that came from the mountain,' came a gruff voice from the scrub.

Instantly, several voices shouted their damnation for the pair from the safety of the scrub. Some were shouting to their fallen mate, encouraging him to crawl back to the scrub. He was too shocked to do anything.

'Listen to me. If you believe there is gold on Tempi, you have my permission to prospect the range for a month.' Silence greeted this offer, most wondering whether there was a catch. Jack continued, 'If at the end of that time no gold has been found, you are to leave and never come back. Tell the truth to others about the Red Mountain. For those that want to stay, and earn a stake, I'll give you a job!'

'And if we do find gold?' Asked one fellow to the encouragement of his mates.

'We'll worry about that if and when it happens.' Jack told them. Many having risen to their feet were approaching the man who had been shot.

Clarrie was worried, he could see their uncertainty, even he hadn't expected Carter's offer. 'There are only two men between you and all the gold you ever dreamed of, two men!' He reiterated.

However the men ignored him, fully realising Carter's offer was fair and they had nothing to lose by accepting his terms. Among others, Clarrie retreated to the boats.

Chapter 60

Edge Rock, Western Australia

Jimmy McTaggart needed an excuse. He had no intention of going with Carter and Smith to Edge Rock in the morning. Not now, not until Street, Fischer, inspector Carson and his associate, were on board a ship for Adelaide. Then he would unobtrusively get to the town and plant the revolver in Harry Street's office, the final evidence needed to pin the murder on the Englishman.

There were four of them to board the sleek little vessel, which the company had purchased. It was the same boat that had taken them down the Margaret River many months ago. Their number only settled after Jack suggested Mike should stay on Tempi to supervise the work and oversee the prospectors. Mike was adamant he was going. He had not told Jack it was his intention to visit Molly Barker. Mike had written to Molly from Adelaide advising that he would like to call on her as soon as he returned to Edge Rock and that had been some time ago. This was the excuse Jimmy had sought, he volunteered to act in their interests and stay behind, so that both principals, along with Colin O'Connor, a sturdy man of ruddy complexion with a mop of curly hair, their site manager, and the wounded miner, were aboard.

They could not get over the change in the town. Even in the first light of a new day they could make out new buildings. Everywhere lay piles of building materials, new cottages, canvas tents and shacks, new buildings extended the town limits.

The able-bodied trio supported the miner who needed medical attention. An excited still half asleep Doc Andrews after greeting Jack, Mike and Colin, confirmed Harry Street had been arrested and formally charged with the murder of Lloyd Hopkins.

'Where is he being held?' Jack's voice like his mood was curt.

Doc frowned in surprise for the abrupt question. 'Down at the gaol, an inspector from Adelaide and a colleague are with him twenty-four hours a day until passage can be had for South Australia.'

'Carson!' Said Mike, turning to face Jack.

Jack nodded, 'I have to talk with Carson; I won't be long.'

'You knew? And you didn't say anything.' Mike was astounded by Jack's insensibility. Jack nodded absently his thoughts for the truth and what may be revealed. He wanted to protect Katrina now more than ever. 'Jimmy told me Harrison had been arrested.' He didn't wish to elaborate in the presence of the others; instead, he placed a caring hand on Mike's shoulder. 'We will talk later cobber, over breakfast.' Without a backward glance, Jack let himself out into the new day and quickly made his way to the lock up.

He was confronted by an over-zealous constable. 'Speak your business… ' the tall, thin-faced policeman with long sideburns addressed him through the aperture.

'I must speak with inspector Carson. Jack Carter,' he added seeing the man was about to tell him to bugger off.

A scrape of a chair and a voice, which Jack identified as Carson, saw Mountier open the door to admit him. Jack wasted no time on pleasantries.

'You've arrested Harry Street for the murder of Lloyd Hopkins.'

Carson nodded, masking his curiosity for this sudden visit. He indicated for Jack to be seated. 'Coffee?' Jack declined the offer.

Jack clasped his fingers together leaning forward in the chair, 'Has he confessed?'

Carson appeared glib. 'We don't need a confession Mister Carter we have the evidence to prove a case beyond reasonable doubt,' he added for Jack's benefit, hands wrapped about the hot mug in front of him.

'I don't understand,' Jack frowned.

Carson smiled, 'We found the money. It was in his safe, and he admitted to owning a revolver of the calibre used in the murder,' shrugged Carson. 'The same make and model, a very rare calibre.' Carson hesitated, deciding what he could reveal while remembering that a short time ago this man had been his chief suspect.

'But has he confessed?'

'He has not said a word. We believe we have the murder weapon, the ring, witnesses… ' Carson sipped on his coffee.

Again Jack nodded, believing Carson wasn't going to say anything to compromise his case, 'There was a near riot out at Tempi. A man was wounded when I was forced to fire upon the miners. The mob believes there is gold on the property. Maybe you will want to question Clarrie Ferguson when you get the chance, Street's bar manager,' he added.

'Constable Mountier will handle that investigation Mister Carter.'

'But while you are here,' Jack commenced to protest.

'My job is done, that is a matter for the local constabulary.' Carson saw the look of disdain; he shook his head not looking up at Jack.

'Your so called riot is a direct result of you, the British Consortium and Street vying to purchase Tempi Station, and as a consequence of all your actions, some people have uncompromisingly been killed, indeed murdered!'

'It was not known to me at the time that Street believed there was gold on the property… ' Jack defended his actions. 'Lloyd Hopkins cabled Street advising him there was no gold on Tempi, or at least that's what Jimmy was instructed to… do.' Sudden thoughts went through Jack's mind. The cable, Harry would feel he were cheated, he would want revenge. The gold rush, of course…

'Something you wish to tell me Mister Carter?' Carson noted the frown.

Jack shook his head. 'Has he legal representation? A solicitor?'

'He will need a troop of Queen's Counsel's and he still won't be acquitted.'

'You seem very confident inspector?'

Carson smiled pausing to take another sip from the cup, 'Fischer, Harry's inside man. Our investigations into his activities have revealed one very clever and conniving confidence-man.'

'So he has helped with your investigation.'

Carson nodded, 'As well as murder, Street and Fischer will be charged with kidnapping, connivance, falsifying documentation against the public interest, commencing a gold rush, and standover tactics to purchase flourishing business enterprises here in town,' Carson elaborated seeing the inquisitive look on Carter's features.

'If you knew, why didn't you warn us about the miners and their intentions?' Jack changed his line of inquiry.

'I overheard whispers nothing more, besides, nobody confides in the police; you should know that.' Jack nodded.

'We have our killer and his accomplice.' Mister Carter.

'Fischer?'

Carson smiled grimly, 'Jonathon Fischer you might say is a gentleman's gentleman, friend, confident, master of deception, disguise, and an extraordinary forger.'

'And Hopkins murderer?' Jack looked intently at the man.

'No!' Carson shook his head. 'An accomplice yes but he had nothing to do with the murder of Lloyd Hopkins. He resided at the same hotel as you and the others, overheard the right conversations, and asked the right questions. He made a plasticine casting of the master key which gained Street entry to Hopkin's room, he created the diversion, the fire,' he reminded seeing the puzzled look momentarily cross Jack's countenance. 'He wrote a letter in Hopkins handwriting which started all this gold business,' Carson confided. 'I had to send a cable to Adelaide exonerating Senator Barnswald from any wrong doing,' Carson rubbed his eyes, obviously tired from his long ordeal.

'Well, Street's friends will stay out at the property until they are convinced there is no gold, there, or in the river. Then I will arrange for reporters to take their story and print it so the world will know there is no gold on Tempi. This valley has been worked over years ago, it yielded nothing then, nor will it now. You have no objection?'

Carson shook his head it was evident from his expression that he was not interested in any gold strike and as far as Jack was concerned he had done his duty.

'Mister Carter, Street asked to see you. Why would he do that?'

Jack shrugged, 'I've no idea.'

Carson looked at his watch, 'nearly seven o'clock; they should be finished breakfast. Give me a few minutes.' Carson pulled at the coffee once more before leaving the room.

Shortly he was back again, leading a dishevelled Harry, hands cuffed behind his back. Carson wasn't taking any chances, Jack allowed himself the thought.

Carson helped Harry to a seat. Harry nodded at Jack. 'You wished to speak with Mister Carter. Well here he is.'

'Privately.' Harry looked up at Carson hopefully, watching as that man rounded on Mountier's desk making himself comfortable again. Carson shook his head remaining silent.

Jack broke their silence, 'How are they treating you Harry?'

'Like a bloody convict,' Harry moved his arms indicating the handcuffs.

Jack smiled, then his face hardened as he remembered how Street had tried to frame him for Hopkin's murder. 'You're going to hang Harry. Mister Hopkins sent you a cable advising there was no gold on the property.'

Harry shook his head, 'that wasn't mentioned in the cable Hopkins sent me.'

'I was there Harry when Lloyd gave Jimmy explicit instructions.'

A frown crossed Harry's features; he wanted to believe what Jack was saying, he lowered his countenance slowly shaking his head. Too late, he reflected, water under the bridge, nothing he could do about it now. After what seemed an age to Jack but could only have been seconds, Harry sat up looking directly at Carson before addressing a pressing concern to Jack. 'Remember the moustached gentleman sporting the monocle and solid gold tooth in my office. Look for a letter addressed to James Loxton about... you know what,' Harry paused, a look passed between them. Harry was reticent to elaborate further.

Jack nodded, 'the Boer war.'

'Precisely!' Harry frowned again not wanting to reveal further sensitive information in front of Carson. 'Would you see he gets it please?'

'I'll do that for you Harry.' Jack showered him with a rueful smile.

'All contents of Mister Street's office, including any letter, will have to be vetted before it can be released, evidence.' Carson further explained.

'The letter has nothing to do with your case inspector, I will vouch for that,' now it was Jack who displayed his annoyance for the policeman's unyielding attitude.

Carson gave him a cursory stare, 'That will be for me to decide Mister Carter.'

Jack looked at Harry as if to say I'm sorry. But Harry could not meet his gaze. 'Maybe it is for the best,' he finally got out.

'No! Don't talk like that. The old bastard should be told!'

'You alone understand, and I thank you for your support,' Harry looked briefly at Jack and Carter saw defeat for the first time since he had come to know the Englishman.

'You maintained your silence when you should have spoken out before, don't do it again Harry, this time your life is at stake!'

'What in blazes are you two talking about?' Carson got out.

'This does not concern you Carson!' Jack felt a rash of colour rise to his cheeks for the first stirring of anger for Harry and his reluctance to defend himself.

'I'm making it my concern,' A petulant Carson half rose from his seat.

'This was to have been a private conversation between two… associates.' Harry hastened to inform the policeman.

'I am not permitted to allow you to speak openly with anybody, your legal counsel accepted,' Carson told Harry while addressing his remark to both of them so Jack might appreciate his position.

'I'm sorry inspector it's just that… '

'Don't apologise to him, nothing but an eavesdropper. Thank you for coming Carter. I'm sorry for all the trouble I caused you.' Harry scraped his chair back indicating their conversation was finished.

'I bare you no ill will Harry,' Jack offered his hand before realising Harry could not reciprocate. Harry nodded tearing his gaze away for the simple gesture.

Carson came around the desk, he paused gathering his thoughts. 'Mister Carter, your passport and other belongings will be returned as soon as possible. I am sorry for any inconvenience, it was not my intention to discredit yourself or Mister Smith. I was only doing my duty.' Jack nodded his understanding.

Carson smiled; he had done his duty, now all he wanted was to get back to Adelaide with his prisoners. He bellowed for Mountier who was in Harry's cell mopping the floor indicating for him when he appeared with a mop in hand to show Carter out the door.

By the time Jack made the good Doctor's residence, the sun was already melting the dew in the paddocks. The birds had welcomed the new day, down on the mud flats exposed by the ebb tide, sea gulls were feeding, their squawking loud and clear in the early morning. Jack wanted to be alone to think. He could not accept Harry wanted to end it all on the gallows. Particularly as he had a strange feeling the man was innocent, that pride prevented him from spilling his guts. Maybe he was taking the easy way out, wealth, position and title eluding him once again. He hoped to be found guilty and sentenced to death by hanging in Adelaide's Yatala Gaol.

Jack let himself think about Katrina as he wandered along the sand spit and to the end of the break-wall. With the memory came choked emotions, which racked his big frame, before anger and frustration saw him lash out in fury to kick the mounds of sand, created by sand crabs. He could not reveal to Katrina that her brother was alive, yet by doing just that he could extract revenge on the man and woman who cast him adrift just as they had their own son. His cabled threats to Lord Anthony, just that, a threat. He realised Katrina meant too much to him to destroy her fondest memories of Harrison. But he believed he understood Harry, the man, his actions, his hatred; they shared that in common and in Harry's case defeat and death, to end it all. And his understanding made him determined to honour what would probably be Harry's last request. He would cable Sir James Loxton, if he were to cheat the gallows, Harry needed legal representation; the best money could buy.

Chapter 61

London

Sir James Loxton read this latest cablegram once again. He was beginning to like this young man who went out of his way to support Harrison and who, having Katrina's address could easily have revealed Harrison's true identity in his letter. He believed the young man to have sound morals and integrity, which was more than he could say for Sedgwick or Chester.

Having arranged for a colleague to handle Katrina's annulment, James's first task, after the weekend spent consoling his niece, was to contact Richard Noble of Noble and Hancock Barristers, and request a restraining order against Chester setting feet on Roxburgh Estate after which, to hasten the draft divorce settlement so he, James, could give the document his closest attention before a copy was sent to Lord Chester Thornton. Now it would appear he would have to take Noble into his confidence once again so that surreptitious arrangements could be made to defend Harrison. Even as he sat pondering, he knew he would have to inform Sedgwick and arranged through his secretary to meet for lunch at the Dorchester Hotel.

Since the fight between Sedgwick and Katrina, he had not seen much of Sedgwick, that man no longer confiding in him. James knew Sedgwick hadn't finished firing bullets at the American, this was revealed in a reticent conversation with Mildred. Something to do with a company called Broken Hill she had revealed, shaking her head, when he wanted to know the details. Well Sedgwick hadn't wanted Harrison informed that his mother had passed away, so he didn't think the boy being held on a murder charge was going to cause him any qualms.

They arrived separately; Sedgwick was accompanied by Lady Parker Brown-Stope, which James found surprising and unexpected, as he had indicated to Sedgwick they had something important to discuss. Irritated James joined them at the table Sedgwick had reserved.

What James didn't know was that Sedgwick's supporter, when he lost the secret ballot to purchase the east Australian Company, was Lady Parker Brown-Stope. That lady had been living alone long enough and now Sedgwick was available as far as she was concerned.

No sooner had James sat down than lady Parker Brown-Stope removed her kid leather gloves, slowly, almost teasingly, much to the amusement of Sedgwick, to reveal a sparkling diamond cluster on the second finger of her left hand. James understood, this was all part of a power struggle. Brown-Stope and Sedgwick were engaged, and with another partner, a stock-holder, his position was strengthened again. No longer could he depend on Katrina to support him in the boardroom. They had not spoken since the incident in Sedgwick's office. Katrina had come to James as she always did and he found his own support for Sedgwick waning. Without Katrina's support in the boardroom when he strongly opposed the South African venture claiming Senator Perry could get them a partnership for next to nothing in the failed Broken Hill Company, Sedgwick for the first time experienced what it was like not to get his own way. Also, upon the death of Clayton and Merrick Thornton, Lord Bruce was now in a much stronger position as their shares reverted to him. And Sedgwick was still smarting because the American secured the mineral rights to Hopkins Mountain.

'I had hoped to speak with you, privately Sedgwick,' James pulled the cable from his inner-suit-coat pocket.

Sedgwick smirked, leaning towards Veronica and placing her hand in his. 'There are no secrets here James.'

'You kept your engagement secret.' James showed his chagrin. 'Rather sudden wasn't it?' He ignored her ladyship's presence.

'Veronica and I aren't getting any younger, are we my dear?' She chortled leaning towards him and James thought for one horrible moment they were going to kiss in front of him.

'I wished to discuss this cablegram with you. However, seeing there are no longer any secrets among the three of us,' James passed the piece of paper to his lordship, his acrimony not lost on Sedgwick.

Sedgwick straightened fumbling to find his reading glasses and turning slightly away from Lady Veronica while he read the cable. It was noticeable to both of them his face was ashen when he came to the part which told him that Harrison was presently in gaol, charged with the murder of Lloyd Hopkins.

'There must be some mistake,' croaked Sedgwick. 'A dirty rotten trick, by that scurrilous conniving American bounder!'

James shrugged saying nothing but amused as he observed Veronica trying to read over Sedgwick's shoulder.

'What is it my dear Sedgwick, bad news?' She tittered in her public school girl accent, although it was a long time since she walked the hallowed corridors of her school, James allowed himself the thought. Four years younger than Libby, not nearly as pretty, but sensually sexy, even James could not deny she had sex appeal. Probably kill the old goat if she is as demanding in bed as her appearance suggests, he told himself.

'Legal representation?'

'Certainly not, if he did… you know, then he deserves to serve a penalty.' Sedgwick blustered, removing his reading glasses and returning them to the pocket of his suit. James couldn't help but notice the new suit and tie; he never bothered when Libby was alive…

'Besides, I don't believe one word of it! Scurrilous tripe!' He handed the correspondence to James.

'Then you have no objection if I take it seriously.'

'Do as you like; I wash my hands of the whole affair. I told you that before. Shall we order dear?' Sedgwick turned to Lady Veronica, ignoring James.

'Suddenly I don't feel hungry,' James stood, his behind easing the chair back before their table waiter could move to assist him. 'I have some pressing business, Lady Veronica please forgive me. Sedgwick.' James faced him the single word all he could manage while still maintaining a semblance of control.

Chapter 62

Edge Rock, Western Australia

Inspector Carson waited patiently for the party from Tempi to leave Edge Rock. Not before giving Bellamy instructions to see that nobody entered Harry Street's office without his permission. He delayed their own departure assured after speaking with Otto Reutenbachen the ship *Scagway* would be departing for Sydney in a fortnight's time. This suited Carson admirably.

With a bemused Bellamy following him up Main Street to Harry Street's establishment, Carson sidled up to the bar for a brief conversation with Clarrie Ferguson. Shortly he returned to where Bellamy stood near the stairwell. With key in hand, Carson nodded and they climbed the stairs making their way to Street's office.

Once inside Carson indicated for Bellamy to lock the door.

'What's this all about Theo? What did you tell Ferguson?'

'I explained to Mister Ferguson that if he cooperated, I would overlook his breaching his bail agreement.' Carson shook his head for the blank expression on his colleague's features. 'Working in a licensed premise until after a full inquiry had been conducted.' Carson expanded for Bellamy's naivety.

Bellamy chagrined, 'I thought he explained to Constable Mountier that Harry was responsible for the riot incident.'

'I know that, you know that, but Ferguson doesn't know he won't be charged,' smiled Carson. 'Your notebook,' Carson held out his hand.

Bellamy produced it and handed it to his superior. 'Take that picture down.' He instructed Bellamy, pointing towards the gentleman with the monocle and gold tooth.

Bellamy removed the framed picture. 'A wall safe, just as I thought,' Carson smiled.

'How did you know about a wall safe Theo?'

'An overheard conversation,' Carson revealed, leafing through the notebook until he came to the combination of numbers.

'We don't have a warrant.' Bellamy coloured.

'Just open the bloody safe Jim!' Carson seated himself behind Harry's desk.

'Very well try these numbers in the order I give them to you, 8, 3, 5, 4, 7, 6.' Carson sat passively yet every fibre of his being was taut with expectation, listening to every sound as Bellamy turned the tumblers. Bellamy uttered a surprised oath as the door swung open.

'Yes!' Carson thumped the desk, not trying to hide his joy.

Something Carter had said, or rather didn't say had nagged at him. The cable McTaggart was requested to send to Street, something about gold on Tempi and Street's reply when confronted by Carter. *There was no mention of gold in the cable I received...*

'The combination of numbers taken from the scroll of paper in the barrel of the revolver.' Bellamy exclaimed, a look of surprise enveloped his features.

'That's right and that is why I now believe Harry Street could not have murdered Lloyd Hopkins.' Carson seemed pleased with himself.

'I don't follow you Theo.'

'For Christ's sake Jim!' Carson was ready to explain the logic anyway. 'Remember Freddy said he doubted if the revolver had been fired recently? I should have gelled then. If it had, the bullet would have shredded the scroll of paper containing the combination of numbers, either that or the gun would have misfired,' he expanded as if addressing a child. 'It was so simple, staring us in the face all the time.'

'Well I'll be buggered.'

'You'll find a letter in there Jim, hand it to me please.'

'It's sealed!' Bellamy told him seconds later.

'I don't intend opening it.' Carson took the proffered letter, with the red-wax seal and stamped with Harry's ring, and put in his coat pocket.

'Why didn't Fischer tell us about the combination of numbers to Street's safe being in the barrel of the revolver when we grilled him?'

'Obviously he didn't know. Maybe now Carter will explain why Street is prepared to go to the gallows rather than prove his innocence.'

'Yes,' muttered Bellamy, rekindling in his mind Street's defence of Fischer. 'Maybe it explains why Street went to such pains to clear Jonathon Fischer of any wrong doing.'

Carson was adamant, 'Street may be a crook, but I doubt he's a murderer!'

'So if Street didn't do it Theo, then who did?' Bellamy piqued, realising this case was far from solved.

Carson shook his head deep in thought. He remembered the conversation between Carter and Street, trying to read between the lines.

'The gloves and the jacket,' Bellamy cut across his thoughts.

'Street was there. We can place him at the bank. And Fischer admitted making the plasticine cast of the key to gain entry to Lloyd Hopkin's suite if you remember.' Carson stated the facts.

'Yes and then there's Street's alibi about being in Melbourne. All we have is the word of management that two men using those names stayed at the hotel,' Bellamy reflected. 'But Fischer did produce rail tickets,' he continued, without having to refer to his notes.

Carson thought Bellamy's reasoning to be futile however, he realised no stone should be left unturned. After all, the lives of two men were at stake. 'As soon as we get back to Adelaide, I'll send their photographs to Melbourne, it's just something else to be checked out thoroughly. Meanwhile… '

'Meanwhile?' Bellamy arched his eyebrows.

'Meanwhile we are going to visit Tempi Smelter Works.'

'Carter and Smith?'

'Not this time Jim,' Carson was reluctant to say anything further.

< >

Following their return from Edge Rock, Mike somewhat reluctantly, because Molly Barker had become the focus of his attention during their stay, they had a surprise visit. One of the workers detailed to start construction on docking facilities at the river came back to camp with news there was a boat coming up the river. The partners just beat the boat to its moorings on the jetty where they recognised the tall figures of Detective Inspector Carson and Sergeant Bellamy standing in the bow of the cutter. Somehow Jack feared this was goodbye, he would never see Harry again.

'A pleasant trip, I expect inspector?' Jack hailed, nodding to Bellamy, hiding his apprehension behind a jovial mask.

'Very pleasant Mister Carter, so this is Tempi?' For the partners had registered their subsidiary company before leaving Darwin and shortly afterwards, Jack had received his Australian citizenship papers.

'Not much now I'm afraid, but it will grow,' Jack lent forward offering his hand to heave the policemen onto the jetty.

'Yes, I'm sure it will,' was the honest reply.

'I thought you were in a hurry to reach Adelaide with your prisoners?'

'Next week.' All the while Carson's eyes swept the vastness before him, momentarily letting his glance rest on the sharp outline of the range of ore, cleared of undergrowth on the southern side it stood jagged and red against the clear blue sky. From the mountain a spiral of smoke told of men at work firing one of the many stacks of felled branches, the solid timber being used for several construction purposes. They walked together across the open sandy loam soil towards the hut. Carson thought to tell Jack, that Clarrie Ferguson was bonded to appear at the station once a month after his statement into the riot had been taken. Carson pointed out Clarrie Ferguson had cast all blame on Harry Street, which didn't surprise Jack or Mike. Carson removed his bush hat and brushed a sleeve across his brow. Heat seemed to literally radiate from the scrub surrounding the camp.

'Come in inspector. Can I get you a beer?' Jack held the flap aside for the policemen to enter.

'No thanks, officially we're on duty, maybe afterwards,' Carson smiled.

Mike offered Carson a seat on an upturned crate. 'Sorry about the seating,' Jack apologised to Bellamy who had to sit on a bunk, that or squat on his haunches.

'So you changed your mind, you wish to get my statement into the shooting of the miner. I have witnesses. It was self-defence,' said Jack.

'Nope,' grinned Carson. 'I have a few questions for Jimmy McTaggart.' Bellamy produced a notebook ready to jot down the exchange.

'McTaggart! What makes you think he is here?' Mike asked in all innocence.

'Oh, just a hunch,' Carson smiled. He didn't reveal that, as a suspect, McTaggart's movements were monitored as well as theirs.

Jack nodded, 'I'll go and fetch him; he should be working on the holding pens this morning.'

'Why do you want to talk with Jimmy?' Mike asked at length while they waited Jack's return.

'Police business.' Carson produced a fathomless look.

Mike nodded his head slowly, his eyes never leaving those of the detective. Carson dropped his gaze to look at his surroundings, the earthen floor, upturned crates, timber racks where clothes were hung, the coal oil lamp on what served as a table, these young blokes were doing it tough he surmised. Shortly, Jack returned.

'Come in Jimmy,' Jack spoke to an unseen shadow presently standing outside the hut.

'Ah, Mister McTaggart.' Carson acknowledged the new arrival.

'Inspector, sergeant,' Jimmy addressed them.

'Would you leave us gentlemen?' Carson looked from Jack to Mike.

'Sure, lots to be done around here, you will stay for dinner? Our cook's a fair hand with a skillet.'

'Thank you and a bed for the night if you can manage.'

'Our pleasure.' Jack assured Carson as they left.

Carson got up and followed their dispersal before returning to his seat. 'We recovered the money taken from your step father's bank account... ' He began.

'Where?' Jimmy struggled to ask.

'In Harry Street's safe.' Carson studied Jimmy closely for a reaction.

'Well that is good news inspector. I heard you had arrested Street and some other bloke, his accomplice no doubt.' Jimmy's chest heaved before a grin spread across his features.

'The problem is Street's alibi holds up, we cannot pin it on him.' Carson sighed, the flat of his hand making contact with the rough timber top of the table in a mock gesture of frustration.

'What do you mean?' Carson noted the sudden belligerence and something else in the man's voice, anxiety.

'There was a scroll of paper in the barrel of the revolver and the chamber under the hammer of the firearm was empty. Do you know what that means Mister McTaggart?'

'I haven't a bloody clue.' Jimmy muttered.

'It hadn't been fired, Harry Street's revolver wasn't the murder weapon.'

'Do you know what was on that piece of paper Mister McTaggart?' Carson pressed the matter of his concern.

'I don't know what you are talking about.' Jimmy looked absently around the tent to hide his growing concern, his brain growing dizzy from trying to stay one step in front of the policemen.

'Numbers! The combination to a safe. Isn't that interesting?'

Was Carson playing with him? Did he know something? Jimmy went over again his alibi. The frown registered itself on Carson 'The ring?' Jimmy spoke at last. 'Street wears an unusual ring,' he announced.

'It doesn't place him at the scene of the murder, only at the bank.'

'You're wrong,' Jimmy persisted in a quavering voice and a slight shake of head.

'The revolver, the one we found in the clothes chute, it wasn't the murder weapon.' Carson smiled, goading Jimmy to do or say something which may incriminate him.

'Then your murderer is still at large, inspector.' Jimmy rose unsteadily from the crate. 'If you're nothing further, I'll be getting back to work,' he glared at Carson who smiled as if he alone was akin to a secret. But Jimmy was also plotting, as soon as he could now, he determined to visit Edge Rock and dump the murder weapon in Street's office.

'You were baiting him,' Bellamy accused once they had the hut to themselves.

'That's right.'

'So, you're sowing the seeds of doubt in McTaggart's mind to see what develops.'

'Something like that. Besides, remember Smith told us Lloyd had an argument with Jimmy over the property? He didn't want the old man to sell, apparently he was very bitter about the deal taking place, according to Smith,' he added.

'That's motive and he had opportunity,' agreed Bellamy.

'He returned to the hotel from the rail kiosk to leave his room key, so we can place him at the scene about the time of the murder.' Carson reminded Bellamy.

'Maybe it was Jimmy who cancelled Hopkin's train ticket for Marree?' Postulated Bellamy.

'Yes. Well, let's find Carter and see if he will offer us a cold beer shall we?'

Something was nagging at Jack, had been since his visiting Harry in Gaol. It had to do with Harry's denial about the contents of the cablegram he received from Hopkins, which Jimmy had been requested to send.

As soon as he was certain Jimmy was back at work, Jack headed for Charlie's tent which the man shared with Jimmy. It took him a second look in Jimmy's valise to find the false lining and free the .445 revolver, using his handkerchief to good effect. Stunned by the discovery, he returned the weapon to its secret hiding place and positioned the man's belongings as exactly as he could remember before backing out of the tent.

'Something bothering you Mister Carter,' Bellamy asked when Carter closed on them. His features were ashen, and a deep furrow etched his brow.

'Yes, I just found a .445 Irish constabulary revolver in Jimmy's suitcase.'

'You didn't touch it did you?' Carson was suddenly apprehensive. Carter may have blotted out any fingerprints. He needn't have worried. Jack shook his head a brief smile playing on his features; he knew better than to destroy possible evidence.

'Will you show Sergeant Bellamy, McTaggart's tent Mister Carter?'

Jack nodded. 'You don't seem surprised,' Jack looked from one to the other. 'I should explain, your unexpected visit, wanting to speak with Jimmy. I guess I became curious,' Jack shrugged.

'Bring me the weapon Jim,' Carson looked gravely at his sergeant who nodded.

Jack pointed out the tent, 'do you want me to go with you?'

'That won't be necessary, bring the suitcase, intact,' Carson added.

They watched as Bellamy sauntered across the clearing to where a group of tents were strung out, sleeping quarters for most of the men, under the shade of overhanging ironbark trees.

Carson muttered 'If only I could get Fischer to talk... '

'Fischer?' Jack looked surprised.

Carson decided he could trust to Carter's discretion. 'I am positive Jonathan Fischer is the key to Street's innocence; however, he is very frightened of Harry for whatever reason. I have to persuade Fischer that if he comes clean he will in all probability save an innocent man from swinging on the gallows, him along with him.'

'Harry?'

'Won't say a word in his own defence.' Carson shook his head.

'Can't you isolate them inspector?'

'We have spoken to Fischer, alone,' he added. 'However, in light of new evidence I intend doing just that on our return to Adelaide Mister Carter.'

'Because of your visit here?'

'That, and this.' Carson handed Jack the envelope from his inside pocket.

Jack took the letter examining the seal with the family crest; it was addressed to:

Sir James Loxton.
28 Spruce Lane,
Kettering.
Northamptonshire.
England.

'I haven't opened it if that is what you are thinking Mister Carter.'

'How did you get your hands on this?' Jack waved the letter at Carson.

Carson smiled. He removed his hat, wiping his brow now they were seated under the large canvas marquee which served as a dining room for the men. Jack signalled for big Daniel to bring them three bottles of chilled beer.

'Well are you going to tell me or not?' Jack's curiosity was getting the better of him.

'I have the combination to Harry Street's wall safe,' Carson shrugged, a cheeky grin spreading across his face.

'You what? How?' Jack didn't understand.

Carson lowered his voice, 'The combination of numbers was on a cylinder of paper in the barrel of the revolver we found in the clothes chute.'

'Harry's gun?' Jack was stunned. He saw Carson nod.

'Which brings us to the letter,' said Carson.

Jack looked down at the envelope and then up at Carson, his mind revolving around all that had happened since their setting out for Marree, could he tell Carson Harry's secret, was it necessary?

'Come now Mister Carter we are not school boys, why is a well-educated, well-groomed Englishman living in a remote little town like Edge Rock?'

'You will have to ask Harry,' sighed Jack, avoiding his gaze.

'A secret, I see. I've been privy to a few in my time,' Carson reached for the long neck bottle of ale determined he would have to make Jonathon Fischer spill his guts in order to save an innocent man from the gallows.

Chapter 63

Anthony Thornton Building, London

The embossed wedding invitation lay squarely in the centre of Lord Bruce Thornton's desk. Beside it was his copy of the Financial Times. Bruce placed his dripping umbrella on the stand peering at the invitation while removing his overcoat. He smiled to himself. Sure in the knowledge the rumours were right. Cousin Veronica had seduced Sedgwick. Even though in her early fifties, he knew his cousin to be lascivious, she would have bedded Sedgwick to see he could still perform before agreeing to marriage, even to such a powerful man. Bruce opened the envelope with careless abandon. The wedding was to be held at Warburn Abbey in Bedfordshire Lord Anthony's parish, 26 May 1923. Lord Bruce closed the card and placed it in the inside pocket of his suit coat, his intention to show Constance when he got home and they could both have a good laugh. Too, he had more on his mind than the marital affairs of Sedgwick and Veronica.

After his dressing down of Chester for his abominable behaviour towards Katrina and having finally listened to his son's account, which revealed David was conceived out of wedlock and Chester wasn't the father, Bruce had agonised over his decision to tell Constance. Initially, he believed his son's marriage would unite two families and strengthen a business bond between himself and Sedgwick Anthony one of the most powerful and influential men in England. However, with the passage of time he came to realise this wasn't the case. He was aware Constance knew there was a problem with the marriage, but neither of them was privy to the circumstances. Now it was out in the open and Bruce had had to inform his wife of the failed marriage, of Chester beating Katrina, and how he suspected Lady Elizabeth of a conspiracy, of Sedgwick's deception in the charade, and the fact that David was not their grandson. He knew she loved David.

More than anything else, his revealing their son was not the child's father had broken her heart. Now, he was burdened with his son's disgrace. He was also concerned for the rift between James and Sedgwick. If James submitted his resignation, which was widely rumoured after his return from a recent luncheon with Sedgwick, the consortium, which had taken years to develop, could be ruined.

Lord Bruce was very impressed with the way James had thrown himself into business. Because of his overseas trips before taking his present station of vice chairman, he enjoyed a position of trust among the European Industrial Community. As a result they had two large naval contracts to fill, one for Sweden, and on the home front, the Royal Navy were updating their fleet after the cessation of hostilities. Demand for rolled wire and barbed wire came in from Australia and Canada to fence off vast tracts of grazing country. And demand for their finished steel products also came from Central Europe. Contracts and propositions seemed endless. The Great War did this and more, a revolution for change, new technology, railways, automobiles, trams, bridges, boilerplates, steam engines, farming machinery. It seemed endless and heralded a new prosperity beyond his comprehension. The South African mining venture proved sound and their ships were stock-piling iron ore ready for smelting at their new Birmingham plant where they had just completed manufacturing and positioning two new open hearth furnaces. As well, a puddling furnace was under way to produce special steels for weaponry, from rifle barrels to heavy artillery. The treachery of newly unified Germany would not easily be forgotten and the countries of Central Europe, the theatre for the Great War, would be prepared for any future encounter. However Bruce was tired, emotionally and physically exhausted. At sixty-five he realised his mental astuteness for business and the day-to-day decision-making was becoming beyond his capabilities. He wanted to step aside and leave the arduous task of running such a large enterprise to younger more virile persons. Unfortunately, he realised long ago Chester was not that person. If only Clayton were alive, Clayton could have managed the company with ease well supported by Merrick. And now the infighting between himself and Chester, Katrina and her father and Sedgwick's lack of trust in James since he didn't realise his support in the boardroom. Despondently, he shook his lowered head making a physical effort to sit bolt upright while reaching for the buzzer which would summon his secretary.

'The correspondence please Eva. Has Sir James forwarded the railway contract for my signature?'

'Not as yet sir, shall I remind him?'

'No he is a very busy man. We all are. It would seem the world's gone crazy!' He smiled up at her over his reading glasses.

'Lord Anthony's secretary just contacted me, can you see him this morning?'

'Certainly.' *About time he involved himself in business instead of gallivanting about London with Veronica on his arm,* Bruce mused.

<>

Sedgwick Anthony read again the cable from Senator Perry before leaving his office and heading down the corridor to confer first, with James then Bruce. James Loxton was perusing a contract for British Rail prior to signing the agreement when Sedgwick, unannounced, let himself into the office.

'That bounder Carter gave you a load of garbage James, I told you the man could not be trusted.' He flashed a recent cablegram in front of James's face inviting him to read it while making himself comfortable.

'How's Katrina?' He thought to ask.

James looked up from the contract deciding he wasn't going to get any more work done until Sedgwick left. 'Symonds performed the operation on her nose last week,' he replied, knowing Sedgwick had distanced himself from his daughter and relied on James to keep him informed. Sedgwick was an obstinate man; once he made up his mind about something, he was inexorable. James scanned the cable, which he noted was sent by Senator Perry.

'You were right about that pompous ass, Bruce sent him abroad for a few months.'

'Yes, I know. And if it wasn't for Lord Bruce and Lady Constance, I would have had him charged myself seeing you weren't going to do anything about it.' James could not conceal his rancour for the man.

'I wasn't informed he beat her until it was too late,' Sedgwick protested.

James nodded not looking up. He had given Chester to understand he should get to like the weather in Belgium. 'Robbery, kidnapping, assaults, conspiracy to fraud!' James glared at Sedgwick.

'Yes. But not murder! One James McTaggart, admitted to murdering Lloyd Hopkins.' Came the sardonic rejoinder.

'Sedgwick, that property has caused more trouble than it was worth!'

232

'Do you think so James? An interesting comment. Now you listen to me.' Sedgwick glared, leaning across the desk to intimidate James. 'I intend to break the son of a bitch if it is the last thing I do.' Sedgwick rose from the chair, his index finger pointing directly at the bridge of James's nose before he turned and strode from the office not giving James a chance to utter a reply.

Sedgwick negotiated his way along the corridor to Lord Bruce's office. He regained his self-control by letting his thoughts turn to Veronica and the forgotten pleasures she had rekindled in him. This and anticipation for the news he had to break to Lord Bruce. Rifling through the pocket of his suit, Sedgwick produced the wax-sealed documents, before knocking on Bruce's door and beckoning his secretary back to her seat. Not waiting an invitation to enter, Sedgwick swung the door open and moved to the chair opposite his co-director.

'Good morning Bruce, you got the invitation I assume.'

'Yes rather surprised really. Such short notice, congratulations,' Bruce offered his hand across the table in customary gesture.

'Veronica has taken years off my life old boy.'

'She certainly will. Old Boy!' Bruce let out a sardonic chortle.

'Bruce, I want you to look at this correspondence… ' Sedgwick handed him the parchment, all business now, letting himself relax in the soft leather padding of the chair.

Bruce read in silence the details of the neatly embossed deed then handed it back. 'I thought we agreed to have mineral consultants look to our interests in Australia.'

'Has anyone contacted our office in that regard?' Sedgwick was flippant. He knew the answer already.

'Adelaide Mineral Explorations accepted our contract. It takes time, mineral research. You should know that Sedgwick.'

'We have a quarter share in the Broken Hill Company!' Sedgwick waved the parchment at him. 'And an option to Hopkins fourth share when his estate is settled. He was the fourth shareholder.' Sedgwick felt he should explain.

Lord Bruce sat with his hands clasped in front of him as though in prayer. 'So you didn't win the battle Sedgwick but you may have won your war.'

Sedgwick gave a chuckle then a wry smile. 'The young pup never stood a chance. We let him develop the company for us then make a takeover bid.'

'Just like that!'

'You appear to have a problem with us controlling BHC Bruce?'

'Tell me Sedgwick, why do you want to crush this man, some say you would kill him if you could?'

'Nothing of the sort, business!' Sedgwick pondered, had James confided in Bruce behind my back?

'You instructed Clayton to eliminate any opposition. The word can easily be misinterpreted. Maybe that's what the young fool was doing, carrying out your directions'

'Nothing of the sort,' Sedgwick reiterated, trying to bluff his way through Bruce's reasoning.

'My sons are dead.' Bruce reminded. 'And Chester has been sent to… Coventry… ' Sedgwick was silent, pretending to read again the deed of sale.

'David is not my grandson!'

Sedgwick was caught off guard, 'What?'

'David… '

'So you know. I'm terribly sorry old chap. Carter will pay for the disgrace he has brought to my family, to my reputation.'

'Our reputations.' corrected Sir Bruce with a glare. 'Katrina needed a husband, a scapegoat! I imagine Elizabeth, God rest her soul, had a hand in that sordid business.'

'Katrina wanted to marry the American, as distasteful a person as I ever want to meet. Libby felt she had no choice.'

'So Elizabeth knew Katrina was pregnant before Chester agreed to the marriage?'

'What! Heavens no!' Sedgwick shook his head vigorously, the lie rolled of his tongue. 'As God is my witness Bruce, until very recently I was unaware David was not Chester's son. We were given to understand Katrina was heading back to that horrible hospital in France, Libby wanted to prevent that happening at any cost.' Sedgwick countered Bruce's bland stare.

'I don't believe you Sedgwick. Both you and Elizabeth conspired to have my son marry your daughter just as soon as it was known she was pregnant!' Although Thornton senior did know this part of the conspiracy to be true, as, Chester had made mention Lady Elizabeth was concerned Katrina wanted to return to France.

'And I'm certain Libby didn't know.' Sedgwick banged a closed fist on the desk, his look of acrimony to silence Bruce. 'She would turn over in her grave if she could see how Katrina has conducted herself. I feel for Constance, she adored the little chap.' Sedgwick mellowed channelling the conversation towards Constance. Like Harrison, Katrina was no longer family as far as Sedgwick was concerned.

'The revelation nearly broke both our hearts,' Bruce paused. 'Still, Chester had no right to strike Katrina. Two wrongs do not make a right.' Sedgwick nodded his agreement.

Bruce lent back in his chair a long loud sigh escaped his diaphragm. 'I want this ended Sedgwick.' Bruce levelled his gaze to meet Sedgwick, his sombre countenance told the magnate he was deadly serious.

'The merger, you cannot be serious. We are amassing a fortune!'

Bruce shook his head, 'Your obsession with destroying this American chap has brought us nothing but pain; it has to stop Sedgwick, now!' Bruce lent forward in the chair his arms taking the weight of his torso as he glared at Sedgwick across the table. 'Also,' Sir Bruce waited until sure of Sedgwick's undivided attention, 'there will be no divorce!'

Sedgwick nodded, it made sense, avoiding another scandal, 'Agreed, they live separately if that suits,' Sedgwick looked at Bruce expectantly to which Thornton senior nodded.

'I will ask James to take care of the details,' Bruce smiled, thinking how some good news may help Constance get over the shock where David was concerned.

'Good! Can we get back to this other business?' Sedgwick raised his eyebrows at Bruce to a slight nod. 'We will shortly be in a controlling situation where BHC is concerned.'

'Would you care to elaborate?' Bruce was perturbed by the hint of further trouble.

'Shortly we will own half the stock in the Broken Hill Company, silver, lead, zinc, iron and steel, as well as most of the coal leases on the eastern seaboard. Senator Perry assures me McTaggart will hang for murdering his father.' Sedgwick felt Bruce should be able to put two and two together.

'I don't understand what that has to do with us.'

Irritated by the man's lack of perception Sedgwick explained. 'BHC will need someone to take up the shares which will otherwise automatically go into internal revenue.'

'The Hopkin's estate?'

'Precisely! Now the government cannot afford to financially assist the company. As a matter of course, the shares will have to be sold off to an investor.'

Bruce nodded knowingly, 'And we are the investors!'

Sedgwick smiled, 'not a foreign investor, sovereignty old boy, British,' he added to be sure Bruce understood.

'And this Senator... '

'Perry,' Sedgwick supplied the name of his contact.

'Yes Perry, will, because of his position see we get first option. Do I have it right?' Bruce was now interested, BHC may be a fledgling company now, and temporarily out of commission according to his sources however, he realised from the orders being placed for steel, the world was advancing at a rapid rate and after all, Australia was a developing country they needed an infrastructure based on heavy industry. Steel for railways, shipping, factories, automobiles, cable wire... Thornton senior was aware they were presently supplying Australia with finished steel products and making good profits into the bargain.

'Very well Sedgwick, if it ends the vendetta and we get a controlling interest, I will second the motion at a special board meeting to purchase should you move that way.' Bruce acknowledged.

Sedgwick smiled his understanding. 'Thank you Bruce.' *Yes I should think this would be enough to break Carter once and for all,* he mused. 'Oh, as I stated earlier, we should retain Hoskins as managing director, first class chap according to Perry, and, he knows the steel business inside out.' Sedgwick rose to take his leave, well satisfied. He made no mention that an arrangement had already been agreed upon with Hoskins, nor of the secrecy clause, which forbade him revealing anything to his fellow shareholders of that covert arrangement. Just as he and Bruce along with the two junior executives, whose presence was necessary to form a quorum, would in a clandestine board meeting, approve the purchase of one-fourth share in BHC, without sharing their coup with the rest of the board.

Chapter 64

Edge Rock, Western Australia, 1923

Doctor Clayton Andrews greeted Jack and Mike with handshakes all around. Mike was to be married to Molly Barker after a whirlwind courtship the following day and Doc had graciously put the men up so they could change for the wedding. Also, it was a place they could come back to if able, after the bachelor bash at Stoddart's pub. All talk turned to news just in from Adelaide which told of the McTaggart trial, his plea of guilty and the subsequent sentence, death by hanging. Harry Street and his accomplice Jonathon Fischer were more fortunate. Both plead guilty. They escaped the hangman's noose because they had the best legal minds defending their circumstance; they were given sentences of fifteen and twelve years respectively.

Sir James Loxton had cabled Jack offering legal counsel to represent Harrison. Jack replied indicating he had engaged legal counsel for Harry. To which Sir James agreed to accept all costs. Jack acted quickly to afford Franklin Murdock the opportunity to establish an accord with both Harrison and Jonathon Fischer well before the trial commencement date. Barnswald could attest to the character of Sir James, so Murdock was guaranteed his service fee plus a considerable bonus for his trouble. Initially Harry could not be cajoled to enter a defence according to Barnswald, who agreed to keep Jack posted on developments, and had refused point blank initially to any representation. It was only after testimony by inspector Carson during the McTaggart trial, which proved Street's revolver had not been fired, that Harry had allowed Murdock to represent him.

In a surprise revelation the speculation over Lloyd Hopkin's will had been put to rest. While a considerable cash benefit had been left to James McTaggart in a trust set up for him when still a child, the bulk of Lloyd's estate was left to his sister and all shares in the Broken Hill Company to the senator with the proviso that should Barnswald unload the stock, both Jack Carter and Michael Smith were to be given first option to take them up. His final will was dated only ten days before he was killed. Jack and Mike were not surprised when Jimmy broke down and confessed to murdering Lloyd during cross-examination.

James (Jimmy) McTaggart was hanged in Yatala, Adelaide's gaol 3 June 1923. Senator Barnswald contacted Jack giving them the opportunity to be present at Jimmy's execution, however neither Jack nor Mike had the stomach for such a public display. They wanted to remember Jimmy as he was when he worked for them on Tempi, happy. This is home he had told them. Maybe if they understood his position earlier, they may have been able to avert the double tragedy.

Shortly after the execution, Jack arranged for Jimmy's body to be brought back to Tempi where he would rest in peace overlooking the Margaret River. The marble headstone told anyone who cared to look that here lay: *James (Jimmy) McTaggart aged 41 years.* The other option was to leave his body reposing in an unmarked grave in the prison grounds; this had been unacceptable to both Mike and Jack.

After the men were made comfortable, doc opened each a chilled long neck and they relaxed for the first time in many months. The mother company was prospering. They had an abundant supply of good quality iron ore and access to readily available coal deposits. As well, an additional bank loan. Both Jack and Mike knew they had Lloyd Hopkins to thank for their new-found prosperity. Along with Clem, Mike's dad who wanted to see something done to remember Lloyd, Jack and Mike approached the Town's council with a cheque to cover the cost of a memorial to be erected in the proposed Edge Rock Botanical Gardens.

Chapter 65

London, 1923

With an air of expectancy, Sir James Loxton closed the door to his office and sauntered down the corridor to Sedgwick Anthony's office like a man might take a leisurely stroll through the park. His right hand let the envelope smack against the side of his trouser leg several times before lifting his hand and staring again at the embossed seal. He wondered what this would do for Sedgwick's constitution so shortly after his marriage to the voracious Veronica, yet not really caring. So long as he was allowed to stay and see Sedgwick's expression. James had waited a long time for this moment when the truth would be revealed. He believed with all his heart Harrison was a victim of his circumstances, never could he have imagined what the young man had to endure during the campaign and subsequent trial which saw him found guilty of cowardice in the face of the enemy. James believed Kitchener and Buller should be exposed for the conspirators they were. Their covert action sent an innocent man into exile so they could cover their own backsides.

James didn't bother knocking and Sedgwick looked up at him over his glasses with a look of disdain for this breach of decorum. Plainly Sedgwick was upset. He banged the cable he was reading a second time down on his desk before addressing James.

'Do come in James,' Sedgwick chided, removing his reading glasses and staring frostily at his brother-in-law; the cablegram from Senator Perry, advising the Hopkins shares had gone to Senator Barnswald and not into government coffers as previously envisaged, momentarily forgotten.

James smirked at him across the desk revealing and handing him the envelope with just a hint of panache to the movement.

In the time it took Sedgwick to look at the red wax seal with their family crest, his countenance turned ashen and he could feel his heart rate rise. It didn't matter that the envelope had been opened because, on further examination, he could see it had been addressed to James.

James remained motionless, watching as Sedgwick read each of the eight pages without pausing. Finally it was done and Sedgwick, hands shaking, placed the letter on the desk in front of him staring at and through James for what seemed an eternity before lowering his head into his hands and sinking down in the chair. From where he sat, James clearly heard the sobs become a steady flow and soon Sedgwick's frame was shaking with his pent up emotions. James sat unmoved by the display. He would have been bitterly disappointed if Sedgwick hadn't broken down and wept for his son.

When Sedgwick Anthony addressed him some moments later, his tear streaked face and the look of pleading in his eyes was satisfaction enough for James. 'Please James, bring him home.'

'I cannot do that Sedgwick.' The emotion in James's voice carried itself to the older man.

Sedgwick stared at his brother-in-law. 'Harrison is in gaol,' James reminded.

Sedgwick lowered his head again sobbing. James reached for his handkerchief, handing it across the desk. 'You will have to continue living the lie Sedgwick.'

Suddenly Sedgwick wast bolt upright both hands clutching his chest, his mouth opened to make a wheezing sound as though fighting for breath.

Oh my God, thought James, *he's having a fit of some sort.* He rushed to Sedgwick's aid calling out for Mildred.

The gurgling sound continued as James undid the stiff celluloid-collar removing Sedgwick's tie and encouraging the man to breathe deeply.

'Mildred!' James shouted again before his former secretary showed herself through the doorway.

'Phone doctor Symonds.' He didn't have to utter another word Mildred saw the look on her employer's face. She rushed from the room to do James's bidding.

James pulled Sedgwick's chair away from the desk and somehow eased the man back in the chair to a more comfortable position.

In the time it took for doctor Symonds to reach his patient word had spread like a bushfire throughout the Anthony Thornton Building. Mildred summoned Katrina and Lord Bruce who hurried from their respective offices to be with Sedgwick. Shortly Lady Veronica was given a hasty message via the Anthony Thornton telephonist and was speeding towards the building in her chauffeur driven limousine.

Ashen and shaking uncontrollably, Sedgwick was lowered to the carpet by James and Mildred who found a pillow on the couch to prop under his head.

'A blanket. Mildred,' James encouraged the woman to action once again.

Sedgwick was desperately trying to say something. However, James was unable to understand. Sedgwick moved his bulging eyes towards his desk holding his head away from the pillow, his frantic head movement a signal and James scurried for his desk, grabbing Harrison's letter and the envelope. He approached Sedgwick holding the letter aloft and Sedgwick seemingly relaxed closing his eyes his head sinking into the pillow. James returned the letter to its envelope placing the material inside his suit coat pocket. He had expected a reaction, but never in his wildest dreams could James have imagined Harrison's saga would bring on a heart attack, assuming that's what it was.

<>

Sometime later, in his office, James sent for Katrina. His features were grave. James had just got off the telephone to the hospital. Sedgwick had gone into a coma. He let his mind go over the little white lie he was about to tell his niece deciding he had no option. Katrina must assume control of Anthony Thornton Consortium. Any thought she had of fleeing to Australia to be with Jack Carter would have to be put on hold until David was old enough to manage running the company. That, or lose everything if public confidence in the company's board of directors saw Anthony Thornton shares fall dramatically.

Without a word, James handed her the cablegram sheet which had been on Sedgwick's desk and which he had quickly browsed. Katrina noticed it was addressed to her father.

Hopkins quarter share in BHC reverted to Senator Barnswald...Stop.
Barnswald approached to sell to Anthony Thornton... Stop.
Refused... Stop.
Barnswald retiring, indicated his intention of selling his share interest in company to
Carter and Smith... Stop.
Regards, Senator Gerald Perry.'

Katrina looked at her uncle before placing the cable back on the desk.

'The reason for the stroke I presume. Sedgwick wanted that fourth share in BHC, I guess the shock was too much for him.'

A sigh escaped Katrina's lips. 'At last! Jack is free of Daddy once and for all.'

'Yes my dear that was your father's last chance of destroying him. Now, along with Smith, Carter owns half the company.' He smiled at her.

'Thank God!' Katrina sank into the nearest chair, a sigh of internal gratitude escaping her lips.

An ephemeral silence filled the room broken shortly by James. 'Katrina, your father cannot manage the consortium any longer. I have spoken with Lord Bruce at length and he is in agreement to have you invested as managing director. With both himself and myself to support you,' he added, seeing the intractable look his niece was giving him.

Katrina looked down at her hands, the fingers interlaced. From where he sat facing her, James saw the melancholy look for his disclosure.

'We have no choice, my dear. In a few short years, David will be able to take his rightful place as chairman of the board.'

'Uncle James at the end of those few short years, I will be in my forties. Will Jack want a middle-aged bride?'

'So much depends on your decision, my dear.'

'Chester?' She asked hopefully.

James shook his head, 'Chester will do all in his power to disinherit David from any control in the Company. You know that.'

Katrina shook her head eyes downcast before looking up at James. 'With your support and that of his father, I am confident Chester could manage the company.' She challenged.

James shook his head, 'I don't think you understand—'

'I do not want the position,' shrilled Katrina, clenching her hands to form fists and beating them mercilessly against the arms of the chair in her rising anger. 'I've done everything you asked of me Uncle, the sham marriage continues, my apologising to Daddy, accepting Lady Veronica as a member of the family. I have a life too... we have had this conversation before!' Katrina lent forward tears streaming down her cheeks, her body rocking with her racked emotions.

'Listen to me Katrina. Your son is the rightful heir to take over the Anthony Thornton dynasty. As his birthright decrees, he will become a lord of the realm, a member of the House of Lords. I beg of you do not deny him of his entitlements, his peerage. If Jack wants you, he will wait; meanwhile he is trying to establish his own destiny and at the moment it may not include you!' James went to her consolingly. Placing one hand on her shoulder, with the other he raised her face to look at him his features solemn, sincere, 'I'm sorry, I had no right to say... Katrina your father needs you to do this for him.' he blurted. 'Harrison was to have been his redeemer, but alas, he gave his life fighting for king and country,' he reminded. 'Sometimes we have to make sacrifices Katrina, life wasn't meant to be a bed of roses... ' At that moment James hated himself for the lies, the deceit, realising if he had been man enough he would have stood up to Sedgwick and Libby years ago and revealed their.... nay, he thought to himself, it was his secret too. Damn!

Tearful red-rimmed eyes stared at him for what seemed eternity, before Katrina nodded, lowering her head in defeat. In that instant, James's heart went out to her, he knew she would sacrifice her happiness. He bit down on his lip until a trickle of blood appeared. He wanted to hurt himself just as he knew he was hurting her and full in the knowledge she didn't deserve to be hurt, while believing he had no choice.

Shortly after this conversation with her uncle and in a better frame of mind, Katrina sat down and wrote to Jack a frank open letter telling him of her love and promising to come to him as soon as she could. She made no mention of David. He would remain a surprise, a bonding between three strangers.

Part 4

Chapter 66

Great Britain, July 1929

The approach to Roxburgh House through the corridor of birch and spruce was barely recognisable to the diminutive figure gazing anxiously through the windscreen. The car's electric wipers beat time with the Smith instrument clock mounted into the coachwood panelling of the Rolls Royce as the icy, wind-driven snow bunted the occupants' progress in this last leg of their long drive. The end was near however, and David, perched on a satin cushion to see above the dash, observed the elated driver give a sigh of relief. They shared a close friendship since David first started school nearly five years ago. Silently, he marvelled how the driver with the gammy leg manoeuvred the large car with such grace and poise.

Harris flicked the lights so that the twin beams played against the walls of the stately mansion through the murk. David watched Harris steady the huge machine, guessing at the location of the kerbing, for between the conifers was one white blanket with no evident sign to indicate the driveway's exact position. Harris came to grips with the drive from the road to the house while David was coming to grips with the events of the past two days.

He knew something was wrong when requested by the Dean of his school to attend his office. The circumstances surrounding his sudden summons home were explained in as diplomatic and an understanding way as could be expected from an educationist with little or no parental skills. Without an outward display of emotion in front of the man, David nodded his thanks and asked could he wait for Harris, their family's chauffeur, in his dormitory, while silently he wrestled with his father's death. Not once did David mention his father since getting into the car for their two-hour drive. Although quieter than usual, he talked of the school's first eleven and one Desmond Cartwright, its captain, to whom, he acted as a fag, and of his being chosen in the junior rugby team. He knew Harris was listening attentively by the way he encouraged his conversation, praising his merit and laughing at his pranks.

The absence of tyre tracks in the snow made David ask 'Has grandfather Anthony arrived?'

'Yes lad, he came down yesterday, as did the Thornton's,' Harris added, not missing David's omission of his grandparents on his father's side of the family.

Wisely he said no more, knowing David rarely made reference to them, unless it was with some remorse he found he had to make a visit during vacation to see them with his father who would promptly make some excuse and leave him in their charge while he philandered about London on the pretext of conducting business. David knew, he read the newspapers, he saw references to his father's comings and goings and the occasional photograph in the society column, usually with a strange woman in his company.

David believed Harris would have heard the gossip like the rest, there was no love lost for the boy by the Thornton's. Not since his father had been sent to Europe to manage a plant in Belgium. David was never told why, but from that time onwards he was barely acknowledged by the Thornton's and it hurt deeply as he had a strong liking for

Grandmother Thornton. Their behaviour was very strange, considering he was their only grandson. David had asked his mother but she was evasive telling him Grandmother Thornton wasn't well, mentally unbalanced his mother had expanded, not that David understood. Harris would probably know but David never asked. Harris had been in the employ of the Thornton's since the motor accident which finished his career as a racing car driver, one of the Bentley team. As Bentley had a close relationship with Thornton for steel and was known personally by the car manufacturer, it was but a small favour to ask that the former world champion be considered for a position. David understood for Harris the appointment was God sent, the gammy leg having ended his racing career, he needed to drive, it was in his blood as he often explained to David, even if the pace were more sedate, he had no reason to complain; he drove the best cars money could buy.

<>

Lady Katrina Thornton peered through the glass of her bedroom window for the first evidence of David's arrival. She had excused herself after lunch to come upstairs to her bedroom on the pretext of a headache, which wasn't completely an untruth for she did have a dull pounding behind the eyes from listening to the continual banter of Lady Veronica. The contents of the small phial on her dressing room table prescribed for her by her physician, Doctor Symonds, after being summoned to the mansion when news of her husband's tragic riding accident broke, did little to comfort her. Katrina knew she wouldn't be herself until David was home and this horrible experience was behind her, for although she loathed Chester, she did not wish him dead.

The first thing Katrina did when she assumed the role of chairman of the board was to have Chester moved back to London, this against the advice of Sir James. However, Katrina felt for David's sake, Chester should be returned. Also, Lady Constance was pleased to have her son back and although he would never admit it, so was Lord Bruce. Katrina had a good head for business albeit initially she found herself frustrated at every turn, particularly as her heart was in Australia while her head was sinking into an abyss of fatigue for the immense learning curve. Being Sir James's secretary was one thing, running such a large enterprise, as Anthony Thornton, was another. The first year Katrina wanted to walk away, indeed she wanted to run, to board a ship for Australia with her son and never come back. However like her father, Katrina had a will of iron and she began to see her leadership as a challenging role which strengthened with her involvement and because so many people depended on her for their livelihood. The consortium employed twenty thousand personnel at the end of the 1925 financial year. Not that Katrina understood accountancy, payroll tax, insurance premiums, or corporate law, that was the role of her chartered accountants, corporate lawyers, and taxation specialists; their meticulous reports were intended to keep Katrina informed with the consortium's transactions. Along with Sir James and Lord Bruce, Katrina saw her role as decision-making. Little did she realise what an erroneous mistake that was, until she came to grips with the real situation. One wrong decision could lose the consortium a small fortune and this error in judgement would be immediately shown by a fluctuating market, which could result in Anthony Thornton share price plummeting.

Katrina became very conscious that to remain successful, the Consortium should be continually addressing a program of expansion, to take into account rising cost of raw materials, wage rises, insurance coverage, infrastructure development, modernisation of existing facilities and the general economic environment their business interests generated on the rest of Europe and their eastern trading partners. By 1929, Katrina was considered throughout the business world as an entrepreneur, her astute business views published by

246

The Financial Review. As well, Time Magazine featured her on the front cover of their May edition and most critics agreed, her articles on administration, business protocol, were widely read and accepted throughout the European Business Community which placed more pressure on her because she was invited almost continually to attend and address corporate business gatherings. She was lauded with an honorary degree in Business Principals from Oxford University and asked to accept a title from Cambridge.

Katrina gathered about her professional people whose individual skills were brought to the conference table once every week and along with Sir James Loxton, Lord Bruce Thornton and to a lesser extent her father, whose recovery was considered by the medical fraternity to be a miracle after lapsing into a coma which lasted several weeks and left him partially paralysed down his left side, Katrina would chair corporate meetings which set the framework for the consortium's future. Katrina did not have a life outside the office. There were not enough hours in the day; it was as well David was at boarding school. His homecomings, birthday, and the end of school semesters were set down on a special calendar which graced Katrina's desk top alongside several photos of him to continually remind her she had a son. Katrina hadn't realised it but she was becoming that which she so detested in her mother and father. Rarely did she have time to read newspapers, or the Financial Review. Pages of interest were placed on her desk by her secretary, with particular attention to paragraphs or headings which told of the Consortium's interests, a new ship being launched; export of steel tonnage to China or the like. Katrina was startled when, rifling through the contents of one magazine, she came across a photograph of three men standing before a large furnace. She recognised Jack Bryson Carter almost immediately.

Australian Iron and Steel Industry Comes of Age. Commenced the article, and continued.

Today Australia took the first step towards economic realisation when the first billet of steel rolled from the ultra-modern plant at Port Kembla on the Australian Eastern Seaboard. Presently, the company is looking to expand its interests to incorporate an international market....'

Katrina had read the article twice but the only mention to Jack was a short postscript under the photograph, which she hastily removed from the journal with her fingernail. Placing the photo in her handbag, she had sat trembling in the plush leather padding of the chair before rising to pace restlessly about the room. She was pleased to see Jack was becoming an industrialist in his own right, and wanting to spread the tentacles of BHC to encompass the four corners of the industrial globe. Seeing the article gave substance to an idea she had wanted to broach with Sir James now for some time. She would propose the Consortium concentrate on manufacturing finished steel product and convert most of their steel making plants, purchasing their material requirements from overseas, in particular, from Australia. It was one way their industry could help decrease the smog and pollution they helped generate and which shrouded Great Britain's industrial cities in a blanket, also, BHC could realise international markets for their steel. Albeit, Katrina was very much aware the current government under Ramsay MacDonald was encouraging British industry to clean up its act, Anthony Thornton Consortium would be showing the way.

After reading the article on BHC, the realisation was so natural that shortly she had put her proposal to Sir James, who applauded any new and innovative measures which would advance the Consortium. Unbeknown to Katrina at that time, Lord Bruce would have supported the proposal anyway as he was aware the Anthony Thornton Consortium owned a fourth share of BHC. Unfortunately, the date of Chester's fatal horse riding accident coincided with this very important meeting agenda. The meeting would have to be put on hold and, silently, she thanked Chester for coming between her and her plans for the future. She didn't realise how rundown she was both in body and spirit. She also thanked him because soon she would be reunited with her son.

After what appeared an age, Katrina saw the flicker of lights, her hand spread the drapes wider and she gazed through the leadlight panes at the spot with renewed anxiety. It was hard to tell from the distance because of the light in the room behind her and the driving snow pounding against the windowpane. She wished the window had windscreen wipers like the car bringing her son to her, so that she might have a clear view. Again the light, now she was sure, David was home. Colour rushed to her cheeks as it always did at the thought and sight of him. Impatiently, she pulled the heavy drapes closed and rushed from the window to the side of the bed where she had kicked her shoes off, insisting Ethel leave them where they fell from her tired feet. Sure she was the first to sight the car's headlights, she set off downstairs to inform the others and to convince herself the staff would be ready to greet him.

With Benson guiding his wheelchair, Lord Sedgwick Anthony, a blanket covering his frail lower limbs, followed his daughter out through the foyer. Together, with Benson a respectable distance behind, they braved the elements beyond the marble entry on the top step above the courtyard.

Smoothly Harris pulled the huge black machine to a stop at the foot of the stairs, restraining David with a word while he ambled around the rear of the vehicle as fast as his limping form would let him to open the passenger's door. Even with his back to the dishevelled figures on the foyer, Harris could feel the frown of disapproval for letting David sit up front with him. He doffed his cap and bowed slightly to David as the boy alighted the vehicle to run up the stairs three at a time, his call of *Thank you Harris* not lost on the man as he lent lower to retrieve David's pillow which had slid from the highly polished seat to the snow-covered roadway. As he walked around to the driver's door, he stole a look and was in time to see mother and son sharing a very warm homecoming.

Tears of joy and anguish mingled into one as David felt his mother's arms enfold him. She leaned over him crying quietly into his fair hair, pulling him into the hollow between her breasts, the soft flesh yielding to the contours of his face. Then it was Grandfather Anthony's turn, Benson helping his lordship from the cumbersome chair to stand unsteadily, and David could feel his cheek being pressed against a button of his grandfather's suit coat. He didn't pull away; he loved the old man. He was David's idea of God.

Once inside the house, David was greeted by the staff before retiring to the library to meet with their many house guests gathered for the funeral. Grandfather and Lady Thornton greeted him with the customary handshake, he with hands that felt as rough as the steel he produced, ruffled his hair, and her ladyship ran a glove-covered hand gently down his cheek following it with what could only pass as a smile. Next came Lady Veronica daintily fluttering a scented handkerchief in front of her nose. David stood passively while she went through the motions of hugging and giving him a perfunctory kiss, never once did she look him in the eye while addressing him, not that David minded, he could not stand the overpowering woman smell of her, all that perfume. David looked for and found James, his hair now silvery grey. Sir James stepped forward, lowering his person, waiting for David to grab his ears and laughing. Shyly, in front of the others, David explained that he no longer grabbed people's ears offering to shake James's hand instead at which the older man laughed anew while offering his hand in friendship.

It was quite late that night before the house retired, for most, the coming events of the morrow made the evening a solemn affair. Most, if not all the ladies, retired to the powder room at some stage to freshen up their tear stained make-up as the events surrounding Lord

Chester's death were brought up afresh, even to the putting down of the horse, and to some of the servants attending the guests, an unspoken agreement, they would rather attend the funeral of the horse than that of their late employer. This they were obliged to attend, seated a respectable distance from the guests and mourners from the neighbouring hamlet.

Chapter 67

London, October 1929

In her capacity as a business magnate, Lady Katrina Thornton was a visitor at Number 10 Downing Street, home of the Prime Minister, on more than one occasion. It was late in the day and Katrina had to cancel some important business meetings when she received the urgent summons to attend the Prime Minister at his residence. Katrina was not alone. There were ten business magnates representing the most powerful companies in Great Britain. To say they were surprised on entering the building to find theirs was not a singular invitation was an understatement and soon the historical charm which surrounded them was forgotten to be replaced with a feeling of anticipation and anxiety for their immediate summons without notice.

Ramsay MacDonald, a largely self-educated Scot, made no apology for their being brought together at such short notice. Presently they were to understand why. They were informed of the Wall Street Stock Exchange collapse, which was to throw America into a depression so deep the nation would not fully recover until the 1940's. They were informed it would ultimately affect Great Britain and the Commonwealth of Nations, as well as Central Europe.

Thoughts rushed through Katrina's mind on hearing this devastating news. For the past five months, Anthony Thornton had been refurbishing and tooling up to manufacture finished products, all at considerable cost. The government was encouraging this move towards a cleaner environment through grants and subsidies so that across the nation factories and mills turned towards assembly-lines and the production of finished commodities leaving the specialist heavy bulk steel production to companies like Anthony Thornton and Sheffield Steel.

Not that the Anthony Thornton Consortium sought financial support, their executives were in agreement this was the future direction for their varied industrial interests and was carrying out Katrina's initiative long before the government came to the same conclusion. The subsidy agreement was between the government and the Commonwealth of Nations, particularly Australia whose Nationalist Country Coalition Party were anxious to occupy all Australian Territories and thus avoid conquest by neighbouring countries such as China, Japan or Indonesia. However because of changing technology, Anthony Thornton, along with other heavy industry had over capitalised, which in light of the P.M.'s devastating news could have catastrophic consequences.

The evening newspapers carried the story of the Wall Street Stock Exchange crash and Katrina chaired without prior notice, a special meeting of the board the next morning. Her father was last to arrive, semi-retired the only time he could be found in the building was when the board met. For the rest of his time Lord Anthony lived the life of a recluse, doted on by his second wife at Warburn Abbey in Bedfordshire. Although astute where business was concerned, his personal life revolved around his thoroughbred horses and his lascivious wife. Veronica's fetish for sex amazed him and she would do all in her power to help him achieve the act, which left him drained but quite pleased he could still perform even if going on seventy. Rarely did he read the newspapers anymore, further, he refused to pick up what was once his favourite reading material, *the Financial Review,* he was sick and tired of reading the gloating accounts of Broken Hill Company achievements. That Carter had beaten him, soured his interest for business, and when told shortly after his partial recovery from the stroke, his daughter now ran the Consortium, he stepped down gracefully. Not that they didn't argue, Katrina had her own agenda for the Consortium and there were times their belligerence ran unchecked in the boardroom until one or the other gave ground, usually at the insistence of Sir James, ever the mediator. But they were together again, bonded by business and commitment.

Katrina brought the gavel down and abruptly the room came to order. 'There was no time to formalise an agenda for this special meeting, so please bear with me.' Katrina paused to look about the room. She perceived a slight nod from Dudley Morecombe, the latest executive to join the board of Directors at the insistence of Sir James, who relied more and more on the expertise of the young corporate lawyer. 'You would have read the headline news regarding the Collapsed Wall Street Stock Exchange.' This was followed by a muttering of acknowledgment. 'What we have to take into account is how the collapse will affect us.'

'It may only be a storm in a teacup, my Lady,' Henry Norse reasoned.

'I do not share that assessment,' Lord Bruce lamented with a shake of his head.

'Please continue Lord Bruce,' encouraged Katrina.

'Business revolves in cycles.' Bruce looked along the table seeking and getting Sedgwick's support by way of a slight nod. 'We have a recurring pattern of fluctuation. If I may,' he looked at her to augment his postulation.

'Please continue.'

'We have seen prosperity since the 1893 crash, now a phase of liquidation where we are absorbing most of our capital into refurbishing our business interests,' Lord Bruce was counting on his fingers. 'This is generally followed by depression, and then recovery.'

'I contacted our New York Brokers last night, they are running scared they have never seen the market so... devastated, crushed.' Richard Claymore, supported his lordship.

'Yes the Prime Minister feels it will spread throughout the business world. My immediate concern is our cash flow. I met with Richard and Dudley last evening and put simply ladies and gentlemen, we over capitalised on our venture to specialise in production assembly lines. Because of this latest threat, I propose we look to sell off some of our assets immediately.' Katrina revealed.

'And just what did you have in mind, young Lady?' Quipped Sedgwick.

'Possibly our Irish shipping yard father,' Katrina frowned at him. Until Katrina talked privately with her uncle, knowing he had travelled widely acquiring companies throughout Europe, she was not in a position to say which businesses they should let go.

'Never!' Sedgwick's right fist struck the mahogany surface of the table with sufficient force for their ink quills to teeter.

'We may have no choice Sedgwick.' James supported Katrina.

'Either that or our munitions factory in Belgium,' Lord Bruce countered.

'Our European interests should go first,' Sir James agreed.

'I... we, that is, built this great company by buying not selling,' Sedgwick scowled at Lord Bruce and his brother-in-law in turn.

'Well we could always sell our fourth share in BHC.' Lord Bruce did not try and hide his frustration for Sedgwick's lack of cooperation.

'Hold your tongue sir!' Came the brusque reply.

'BHC? We do not own stock in that company?' Katrina looked wildly from one to the other before locking her eyes to those of her uncle and glimpsing the slightest of nods.

Sir James saw the bewildered look, her shock for the revelation, followed shortly by anger as Katrina regained her composure. 'Well that makes it easy,' she leaned forward placing both hands on the desk top to glare at her father and Lord Bruce in turn, 'We sell our stock in the Broken Hill Company! How much would that realise Uncle James? Ten million pounds?'

'No! Never!' Sedgwick tried to rise out of the wheel chair, his face ashen with anger for the disclosure by Lord Bruce and the audacity of his daughter.

James looked long and hard at Sedgwick, he felt someone should explain why they couldn't sell their interests in the Australian company. It was Bruce who broke the poignant silence.

'The vendetta is finished Sedgwick, I will not stand by and watch this company ruined by your pigheadedness and stupidity!'

James appealed to Lord Bruce. 'Tell them Bruce.'

'No!' Cried Sedgwick.

'Oh do stop behaving like a deprived schoolboy. Sedgwick.' Veronica chastised him.

'You hush your mouth, this has nothing to do with you Veronica.' Sedgwick was gulping for air, his face as white as the shirt he wore under the suit.

'Father, it has everything to do with us!' Piqued Katrina not trying to hide her anxiety.

Bruce was thoughtful, 'We came to an understanding with a chap by the name of Lance Hoskins who owned a fourth share in BHC. He agreed to sell us his shares and we in turn agreed to retain him as managing director of the Newcastle and Port Kembla plants. Presently, the chaps who accompanied Clayton and Merrick to Australia, one of whom is an engineer, are working as overseers looking to our investment interests.'

'And Jack never suspected we were shareholders?' Katrina's voice conveyed her astonishment.

James shook his head looking at Lord Bruce who nodded before he explained further. 'Hoskins was sworn to secrecy.'

'A covert plot when all else failed,' Katrina stared at Lord Bruce for confirmation. Lord Bruce avoided her gaze.

'Damn you, Father!' Katrina picked up the gavel in front of her and hurled it at him. This was followed by an outburst from around the room as the board members watched the projectile take Lord Sedgwick in the chest, the glass of water Lady Veronica was handing him spilt down the front of his suit.

'Uncle James if the tentacles of depression do spread to encompass our interests, it may be necessary to approach BHC to make reasonable offers to purchase subsidiary companies under our control.' Katrina never took her eyes from her father's face; the reaction was like an electric current suddenly passed through his body. Convulsing in his chair, the other board members gathered about him as he gargled and gagged for breath.

'How could you? How dare you?' Shouted Lady Veronica.

'Take Father home please Veronica. Now!' The cadence of Katrina's voice dropped to a mere whisper. However, the venom with which she gave the instruction could not be ignored.

Sir James eased his way around the table until he stood by Katrina who was visibly shaking as her emotions took control of her body.

'How could you Uncle James? I trusted you.' She appealed to his silence.

Minutes later when they had the room to themselves and Katrina was composed, James raised her face to look directly at her. 'You conspired against me!' She managed to say.

'The arrangement was done behind my back and before you took control of the company my dear.'

Katrina sniffed wiping her eyes with her handkerchief.

'Katrina, according to Lord Bruce, your father promised, if the company purchased the quarter share in BHC, the vendetta between himself and the American would be over. His damn pride I imagine. I had no say in the matter and I did feel rather foolish and deceitful when Lord Bruce dropped his bombshell. I'm terribly sorry, my dear. I will compile a list of those subsidiary companies I feel we could sell.'

'Is he all right, I didn't mean to?'

'He'll be fine. Sedgwick has a lot to answer for and now that time has come; he finds it hard to cope, but sell we must if we are to survive this depression,' James agreed.

'This man, Hoskins, is there no way we can warn Jack of his deceitfulness?'

Sir James let out a long sigh to portray his frustration. 'When told of the purchase by Lord Bruce, I warned him that we have broken several sections of the corporate law act. The least numbers of people who know of the arrangement the better.' Katrina nodded her understanding.

<>

The Economic World Conference held in London in 1933 and attended by among others the executive of Anthony Thornton was a failure. The Great Depression, as it became known, spread to encompass world economy. Mass unemployment saw thousands of men and women tramping the country for work. Coupons became the form of currency guaranteeing a handout. And although Great Britain closed ranks, adopted a *Buy British* slogan and introduced import duties and tariffs, it was not enough to avoid the inevitable...

Lady Katrina Anthony, with the support of Lord Bruce, and Sir James Loxton at a specially convened executive meeting unanimously agreed to sell off subsidiary companies to realise cash flow. Among other companies, BHC was approached. And in a twist of fate, an agreement reached, BHC purchased *Allied Steel* from the Consortium.

Chapter 68

Adelaide, South Australia, 1936

Jack Carter stood leaning against the ford V8 sedan, hands folded, his hat pulled down against the glare of the cement walk, which led to the government building. He looked at his timepiece again before resuming his vigil. An unsighted 'clang' some minutes later saw him straighten dropping his arms to his sides with expectancy. Shortly, a tall man with silvery white hair brushed back and carrying a cardboard valse, walked through an archway and accompanied by a man in uniform fronted a set of heavy double wrought iron gates. The tall man stood passively while the man in uniform proceeded to unlock the gates fronting the concrete path.

Jack watched as the man in uniform attempted to shake the hand of the taller man who ignored the gesture walking through the aperture towards where Jack stood on the curb to the 'clang' as the outer gates were closed none too gently for the rebuff. Jack grinned, *same old Harry,* he mused watching as the Englishman broached the footpath looking right and left for a cab and with scant attention for the man leaning against the car.

'Taxi Mister Anthony,' Jack addressed Harrison, a smile plastered across his countenance.

Harry turned sharply and stared at the man in the three-piece suit and matching hat without recognition initially. 'Carter! What the devil are you doing here?'

'Oh a little bird told me you were a free man as from today. Thought I'd pop down and see if you still remembered me.' Jack smiled that amiable smile which broke any mounting tension between them.

Harry gave what passed for a grin extending his hand, 'That was decent of you, and rather unexpected after all I put you through.'

'Forgive and forget, that's my motto,' Jack responded to the warm hand-shake.

'Yours?' Harry indicated the gleaming white sedan.

'Hop in, it's going wherever you want to go,' Jack grabbed Harry's luggage turning to the boot.

'Business must be good,' Harry remarked as Jack eased the car away from the curb.

'Can't complain, what are your plans Harry?'

'Edge Rock to see for myself how Clarence is spending my money.'

Jack grinned, tongue in cheek he said 'You own half the town, the Commonwealth Bank opened a branch just to look after your account.' Surely Harry would realise the government confiscated his business interests.

'Splendid, then I might settle down, maybe do some fishing.'

'You fishing? That'll be the day!'

'I'm getting on, old boy. I had plenty of time to reflect in prison.'

'You must have been a model prisoner, to get two years off for good behaviour?'

Harry shrugged, easing his frame to a more comfortable position.

'Your buddy?'

'Jonathon? He never made it. He went down to the infirmary one morning with a chill, caught pneumonia and died.'

'I'm sorry I didn't know.' Jack muttered.

'Did you know Chester Thornton was killed? Fox hunting I'm given to understand, never did like the bloody sport?'

Jack nodded concentrating on the traffic.

'Well?'

'Well what?' Jack asked.

'Katrina, have you spoken?'

Jack shook his head. 'I'm too busy making a quid to think about women.'

'Not even a letter?' Harry admonished, remembering how the American chastised him for not writing his side of the events leading to his court-martial.

Jack chortled, 'Not that it is any of your business but yes we correspond and as soon as her son is capable of taking control of the Anthony Thornton Consortium, she intends to join me.'

'The telephone?'

Jack shook his head. 'I'm scared Harry, I've changed, no doubt so has your sister. We will need time together again, to get to know each other,' he expanded.

'I see. Well, that's good news. Romance through the pen what?'

'Mightier than the sword as I remember my lessons,' was the gruff reply.

'And your father?' Jack was aware Harry would have received correspondence from James Loxton, via Murdock his barrister.

'Suffered a stroke, something to do with a letter,' he gleamed.

Jack grinned. 'The letter you finally got around to writing?'

'Yes, came as rather a shock. Apparently enough to cause a stroke. The last straw was Katrina selling you Allied Steel. I'm led to believe he has turned his back on them all. It would appear you got the bastard.' Harry's voice was charged with acrimony for the mere mention of his father.

Jack nodded, he didn't want to reflect on the rivalry between himself and Lord Anthony, it was over; he had won. And every time he doubted the reality, he would look through the same magazines as his lordship had read, like they were the bible, and reflect to himself that it was indeed over. Sedgwick Anthony was a broken man. Jack had achieved what he set out to do and within the time frame. He now owned 50 percent of all stock in Australia's biggest company and owned one of the largest steel-producing firms in Great Britain.

'The bloody depression nearly got all of us. The Anthony Thornton Consortium had no choice apparently. Recovery has been slow, particularly in America.'

'Diversification is what saved you and Senator Smith. Property, the gold mine at Tennant Creek, your lead and silver mine at Broken Hill, coal leases. Father always drummed into me, 'never put all your eggs in one basket'.' Harry's voice faded to a near whisper.

'Appears he was right.' Jack made a right hand turn which would take them to the airport. 'It seems you have made quite a study of me, old boy.' Jack remarked with a grin splitting his features.

'I envy you. You are living your ambition, your dream,' sighed Harry.

Jack nodded, his attention for the midmorning traffic, 'Got a proposition for you Harry, a real job with a salary of forty thousand pounds a year, your own car, house, and hired help.'

Harry straightened in the seat. 'So that is what this is all about.' His voice had a pensive ring to it.

'Hoskins tendered his resignation. I want you to manage BHC's Newcastle and Port Kembla Plants, upwards of twelve thousand personnel under your leadership. Do you think you could manage?'

'You are offering me a station on your executive, knowing I tried to destroy you that I have been in gaol, and lack experience. You need to see a psychiatrist old boy,' Harry laughed. It was the first time Jack had heard Harry laugh and immediately he was reminded of Katrina, his ulterior motive for offering Harry the position.

'Do you think you can handle it Harry?' Jack was insistent.

'Oh I'm a born leader, just look at my record old boy,' Harry suddenly went quiet.

'I think you can and I have the men in place to help you through the transition period. I don't expect wonders Harry, each department has its own engineers, manager, foreman, and leading hands, all know their job, you would be responsible for the overall administration of both plants.'

Harry shook his head turning to study Jack. 'I don't know Jack, I just don't know if I am up to such responsibility.'

'You let me worry about that Harry. There is another reason.'

'Do go on.'

'We are selling half our annual tonnage to Great Britain. I don't know if they are stock piling and if they are, why?'

'And you're worried?'

'Yes.'

'You should be delighted old boy. Unless of course they fear the new might of Germany and her arms build-up.'

'How do you know about such things?'

'I am an avid reader old chap, didn't have much else to do this past decade or so.'

'Another war?'

'I hardly think so old boy. Progress, finished commodities, cars like the one you are driving, a world coming of age and demanding new technology.'

Jack laughed, 'you're probably right.'

'Oh of course I am. When do I start?' Harry reached a decision.

'Just as soon as I can get you tailored for some new clothes, order a car and rent you a property over on the coast, about two months.'

'Is Senator Smith in agreement with my being offered this position?'

'Mike? Hell he hasn't been involved in the actual running of the company for years. Mike's role is developing an infrastructure for Tempi, the town and the mine.'

'Do go on old boy.'

'He has been responsible for the development roads, the rail head the electricity sub-station, all of which have encouraged people to settle in the valley. And when he has time away from Canberra, he rides around the cattle property issuing orders,' Jack laughed.

'It would appear your enterprise has done markedly well,' murmured Harry, unable to hide some remorse for his own situation.

'Thank you. Harry, could you have killed old Lloyd?' Jack asked at length.

'It was never my intention, but I was certainly angry enough,' grinned Harry.

'But the gold nuggets didn't come from the Margaret River, nor any of its tributaries,' Jack explained.

'At the time I couldn't bring myself to believe that was the case. It was my last chance. The gold?' Harry asked.

'Alas,' sighed Jack. 'The government confiscated your poke Harry, claimed it was stolen from the body of the prospector by Lennard, they also confiscated all your assets

Harry. They asserted your business interests in Edge Rock were gained through improper means. I guess you could say you're broke old chap.'

'That figures,' sighed Harry wistfully. 'Just my luck, still, my pension is ongoing; Uncle James will always take care of me.'

'Well, it's water under the bridge. I'm giving you a chance Harry. Now it's up to you.'

Chapter 69

Great Britain, January 1939

With the coming of the new-year, David Thornton was twenty years of age, had just graduated from the Sandhurst Military Academy and was ready to embark upon a military career. His position at Sandhurst having been secured for him by Lord Anthony since his birth, as was his seat in the House of Lords when he came of age. His grandfather, aged and in poor health, doted on the boy even if he were Jack Carter's son. His lordship was adamant; David would take up where Harrison left off by restoring the Anthony name and honour.

Katrina protested heatedly when David stated it was his intention to follow in the footsteps of her brother and become an officer in His Majesty's Service. Initially, she had refused to sign his entry documentation for Sandhurst handed her by her father, Katrina believed Great Britain may shortly be drawn into another war with Germany. David sided with his grandfather, believing the old patriarch could do no wrong.

As David was not twenty-one years of age, she would have to give her consent, her signature of approval before the documentation for him to join the service was legal and binding. Katrina briefly visited Warburn Abbey to point this out to her father, whereupon he hastened to inform her that for a few hundred pounds he would soon have her signature appear where it should and not to be so childish. The colour crept up her neck to her cheeks and not trusting herself to say another word, she fled the house. Katrina must find some way to break the dominance her father had over David and her son's adoration for his lordship. She was terrified he must surely be killed if Great Britain was again forced into a war with Germany. She couldn't bear the thought of losing her son.

Katrina arrived at the Anthony Thornton Building at precisely 7.30 a.m. as was her custom. She entered the building and approached the lift, an impatience to speak to Sir James hurrying her stride. Standing holding the lift's wire cage open for her was Mister Downing.

He doffed his cap, 'Morning your Ladyship.' Politely and with a certain flair that at any other time would have Katrina respond, her voice edging on laughter, not this morning however.

'Fourth floor, me Lady. Hey, just a minute,' he addressed the paperboy who had done his rounds of the several offices and was wanting to return to the ground floor. A collision was imminent, Katrina's preoccupation, the boy's eagerness to enter the lift...

'Sorry my Lady,' said the boy, raising his cap then bending to scoop his newspapers from the hallway.

'Quite all right young man; I should have looked where I was going.'

'Clumsy fellow, it was your fault, not her Ladyships,' Downing chastised the lad.

Katrina knelt to help the boy and it was then she saw the headline of the *Times*.

AUSTRALIANS FEAR WAR, SPECIAL ENVOY TO MEET WITH PRIME MINISTER.

A war hero, Senator Michael... the article commenced.

Katrina passed over a shilling, being the smallest change in her handbag.

'Gee, thank you my Lady,' the boy eyed off the coin excitedly. Katrina folded the newspaper, thanked Downing and strode quickly to her office. Katrina bid her secretary to bring her a cup of tea and settled down behind her desk to read the article.

A war hero, Senator Michael Smith, veteran of the Great War, heads the delegation of Ministers representing the Chairman of Foreign Affairs and Defence. Judging by this man's outspoken tirade in the Australian Parliament recently, Number 10 Downing Street could be buzzing with excitement over the next few weeks.

The paper read from cover to cover, Katrina, smiling to herself, folded it and placed it on her desk. Shortly she would rendezvous with Sir James and reveal to him her plan for David's future.

<>

Senator Michael Smith felt inside the pocket of his coat to where his fingers brushed lightly over the embossed crest on the envelope. He was standing outside London's fashionable House of Dunhill, having finished his shopping by purchasing some gifts for Jack. He had planned to use the respite in talks with the British Prime Minister, and his War Cabinet to see the first day's play in the fourth cricket test between Australia and England at Leeds. They would have time to kill now, while Chamberlain met with his full cabinet and had talks with the king. Another George. The delegation had expressed their concern over German rearmament and her close allegiance with the Italians who had openly attacked Abyssinia.

It had been the name more than the letter which decided him to meet with the lady, a lady whom he had not seen for twenty years.

The Silver Ghost Rolls Royce slid smoothly into the curb side on the opposite side of the busy street from where he was standing reading the morning edition of the Clarion. Mike barely took notice, motor vehicles had been coming and going all morning. From the plush red-leathered upholstery of the rear seat, Katrina eyed him unsuspectingly for some time before she bade Harris hasten forth and escort the Australian Minister to her side.

He hadn't changed all that much she thought to herself, still handsome, probably bigger than she remembered, definitely heavier. However, he looked healthier for a few pounds, as she remembered, he was formerly lean, even if big boned. But most of them were, lean, gaunt, they lived on their nerves during those terrible years, seldom receiving adequately to eat and never full nutritional needs such as fresh fruit and vegetables, so that by the end of the war most of them were like walking skeletons, their tattered uniforms hanging to their bodies. She remembered the face. It had been long and gaunt, weighted with responsibility and combat fatigue. Now his face was deeply tanned, filled out, the brown eyes twinkling, full of life she decided as she watched him cross the busy thoroughfare talking to Harris as though they had known each other for years, and she thought how good it would be to hear that slow Australian drawl after all this time. He was very erect, straight of back and square of shoulder, just like her father in his prime. The natural swing of his arms was checked by the cluster of parcels, which he surrendered reluctantly to Harris before entering the saloon.

Mike looked forward to their meeting with some misgiving, even sadness. Sight of her he knew, would conjure up memories of Jack, that forlorn figure slumped against a gum tree pouring his heart out after just cheating death in the sandstorm so long ago, the only time he had ever spoken of her. She was beautiful, just as Mike remembered her and knew she would be. Silently he wished it was Jack sitting where he was sitting now.

Her golden hair was still worn long; fashionably cut to suit the delicately shaped neck not hacked as he remembered it in France. She was dressed in a suit of fashionable cloth and cut, with square padded shoulders and pleats where a gentleman's suit would have pockets. A pale blue silk blouse buttoned to the throat while a single edging of a frill showed above the coat lapel. The suit was a shade lighter than navy blue, the curve hugging skirt ended just below the knee, double pleated for more comfortable movement. Mike also noticed she wore little jewellery and no rings. The smell of her perfume was not overbearing, very pleasant within the confines of the car.

'Oh Michael, I'm delighted to see you again after all this time,' she welcomed him.

'Katie, you're lovelier than ever,' he replied, lightly kissing her on the cheek. Her delicate milky white skin was soft and responsive to his touch.

Mike felt the big car pull away from the kerb, gliding them smoothly through the London traffic and into the countryside beyond.

'Were those for me?' She asked at length to break the awkward silence that had settled between them, indicating the packages on the seat beside them.

'Huh, oh—sorry Katie, I did a bit of shopping for my family and Jack while I was waiting,' he replied, a little embarrassed.

Looking straight ahead to avoid his scrutiny, 'How is Jack?' asked Katrina.

Mike detected the name choked in her throat, he could almost feel her increased heartbeat at the mere mention of the name, and it took but a moment for him to realise Jack was not forgotten.

'Are you still in love with him Katie?' He asked finally.

'Yes, we correspond; however, I cannot wait until we can be together again.'

'So many wasted years! Obviously your parents felt he didn't measure up to their standards and Chester Thornton did.' He saw Katrina shudder at mention of the name. Mike wanted to understand why Katrina married Chester.

'I… it was a marriage of convenience,' there was no mistaking the bitterness in her voice.

'Well, why did you marry him for God's sake?' Mike's voice conveyed bitterness.

'Because,' began Katrina, when the intercom let them hear the deep articulate voice of Harris come between them to advise they were approaching Brighton.

'No, we will continue on to Portsmouth as arranged, thank you Harris,' Katrina answered her chauffeur. She threw the switch so they could not be overheard.

'Because I was pregnant with Jack's child.' She revealed.

'Good Lord! He never knew… '

'No.' Katrina cut him short. 'I had no choice but to enter into a forced marriage arranged by mother. I vowed I would never become pregnant to Chester. But I wanted that first child,' she hissed the words at Mike.

'I have lived for that boy Michael, every time he came home from school I was reminded of Jack, such are the likeness and I dreamed of the surprise, introducing Jack to his son.' She began to weep.

'It's O.K. Katie.' Mike threw his arm around her, drawing her quivering form against him. 'You and the boy can come home with me, the hell with this place. Jack is a rich man, you would have everything,' he finished.

'It is not that simple Michael, oh I wish it were,' she replied clenching her hands into tight fists.

'Why? I don't see the problem? Your son would be with his father and you would be reunited with Jack. You owe it to each other for all those lost years,' he pleaded, not understanding her reservations.

'Please Michael, do not make it harder than it already is. I cannot explain to you... '

'What's to explain?' Mike cut her short. 'I don't understand!'

'Michael, I am the chairperson of Anthony Thornton Enterprises, we are a Multi-National Company,' she hedged. 'I cannot walk away from that responsibility.' Katrina could see Mike's indifference, she added, 'please try and understand Michael. The Consortium is David's rightful inheritance.' Katrina clutched his hand.

'David?' Mike muttered the name.

'My son... our son, Jack's and mine.' A lump rose and fell in her throat.

Static hissed through the intercom again. 'Portsmouth my Lady? Jeffersons?' The voice inquired.

Leaning forward Katrina moved the switch connecting them to the driver. 'Yes, thank you Harris, is our table reserved?'

'All taken care of Lady Thornton.'

'Thank you Harris.' Katrina threw the switch again sitting back beside Mike once more.

Katrina was glad of the interruption to change the subject. 'I feel I should explain about lunch. I have been coming to this quaint little inn since I was a girl, they make a special dish, have done for more than a hundred years, nothing lavish mind you. However, I think it will be to your satisfaction.'

Katrina watched him straighten his tie and adjust the sit of his coat on his shoulders before they alighted the vehicle. The tailored dark brown jacket blended well, and the matching tie sat sweetly against the crisp starched white shirt. A short, bandy-legged man, in a crisp black suit approached the car. Katrina made the introductions before the couple were eagerly led into the tavern by its manager.

'Your speciality, for two, to be followed by the trifle, my Lady?' Said the short squat man introduced to Mike as Duncan, the inn's manager.

'Yes thank you Duncan,' replied Katrina, letting him seat her at the table.

'Oh, and a bottle of Bass and Co. Ale for the senator, also a bottle of your best burgundy to be served chilled with the meal.'

'Very good Lady Thornton,' Duncan bowed and backed away after first placing their napkins at hand.

They didn't linger after their excellent meal. Katrina appeared anxious to reach Southampton.

'Why Southampton?' Mike was curious as he made himself comfortable beside her in the fast-moving car.

'I thought you would enjoy seeing our shipping yard.'

'Business?'

'Very important business.' Katrina's voice encouraged a reply.

However Mike would not be drawn into conversation, being content to look out over the English Channel, towards the Isle of Wight.

'Beautiful isn't it?' He remarked at length.

'Yes it is.'

It seemed no time at all before they reached the large double wrought iron gates, to one side of which stood a pillar-box not unlike a sentry post. Harris slowed the Rolls Royce to a stop and a man rose from his seat inside the box and approached the car. Senator Smith was surprised to see that he wore the uniform of a naval policeman, complete with a side arm. He took Katrina's pass, which she carried inside a small leather wallet and bade them to wait. Mike observed him enter the pillar-box and make a phone call, turning to face them as he did so. Shortly he was back, apologising for the delay. He beckoned a second figure until then unsighted. The second naval policeman opened the gates from inside the yard remotely, closing them immediately, the saloon entered. Mike spied the Tommy gun as they passed the security box.

'What was all that about Katie?' He asked once they were inside and travelling sedately along a concrete strip, which continually crossed railway lines, on towards a large red painted corrugated-iron building in the distance.

'Security,' she replied, her features a fathomless book.

'Security hell! I feel like I'm in prison. Are you sure you are not abducting me?' Mike grinned while looking about him.

She smiled that disarming smile. 'I want you to see something. It may help explain the real reasons for keeping you away from Leeds today.'

'How did you know I intended going to the cricket today?'

Again the smile. They entered a car park where another uniformed policeman conducted them to an external elevator. From within the building was heard, the sound of riveting, overhead cranes moving along their tracks and a various assortment of noise indicating a hive of industrious activity. They entered the lift; the doorman also in uniform and armed, pressed the single button on the panel. Mike stood facing the yard where an assortment of steel was being scraped and colour coded. He felt himself being lifted and then the sound of a door opening behind him. He whirled around in alarm. Katrina followed his movement, smiling at his concern. She beckoned him to follow and together they stepped through the doorway into a soundproof room surrounded on three sides with reinforced glass. They were in a workshop, able to observe all that went on below them. Mike stepped to the window; the building was at least one thousand yards long and easily fifty yards wide.

'Hell's bells!' He exclaimed, with a whistle to cap it off.

The dapper of a man, in the charcoal grey suit with the white hair and hands clasped behind his back, turned to greet them.

'Michael, I would like you to meet my uncle, Sir James Loxton,' Katrina introduced them.

'Delighted my boy,' Sir James responded as their hands locked in a firm but warm hands shake. 'I have heard a lot about you Senator Smith.'

'Likewise.' Mike responded. 'I'm very pleased to make your acquaintance at last.'

'Shall we begin Uncle?' Plainly Katrina was nervous now the moment of truth was near.

'Yes, if you like my dear.'

Mike watched as Sir James pressed a green button on a panel board. The glass cage commenced to glide along an unseen track towards the far end of the building.

'My God! What are you doing, here?' Mike cried in alarm after they had gone but a short distance.

Katrina could not look at the tall Australian, 'I feel you should explain Uncle James.'

'But of course my dear,' was the quiet, authoritative response. 'Senator, you are seeing what no outsider has viewed before, that is outside our Government, the Royal Navy, and the War Department. Oh it's quite all right old boy, they cannot see you, mirrored glass you know.'

'Submarines!' Blurted Mike, barely paying attention to what Sir James was saying.

'That is correct, the silent deep running enemy to all shipping; a real war machine.'

'Why?' Mike was puzzled.

'Because, like your countrymen Senator, we fear the new might of Germany. We feel the world could be on the brink of yet another war. So, under the strictest navel security and using naval labour, we have been commissioned to build the Government eighty 'T' type submarines. '

'Christ!' Mike was unable to take his eyes from the scene below.

'The Prime Minister attended Munich, he had talks with and appealed to Germany to annexe part of Czechoslovakia, to no avail. He fears treachery from Germany and her strong allies, Italy and Russia, this time we will not be caught napping. All over Britain factories are being converted, arms are being manufactured, ships are being refitted and munitions are being piled. We pray it never happens. However, we must be ready,' finished Sir James, sharing Mike's scrutiny of the shop floor and the gleaming metal hulls.

'Oh my God!' Mike smote his head with his palm. 'As if last time wasn't enough. To think we sat there for three bloody days talking our heads off with your Prime Minister, and behind the scenes all… this is taking place,' Mike choked on the words, a dark anger surfacing in his voice. 'It must not be allowed to happen.' Mike struck a clenched fist against the panelling in his anger.

'And you Katie, do you condone this build up? Didn't you see enough death and suffering before?' Mike chastised her.

Katrina was defiant, 'No Michael, however if a war is inevitable, we must be prepared to defend England at all cost!'

'So this is what the future holds. I have come twelve thousand miles to have my gravest fears realised… ' Mike shook his head in resignation.

'If it makes you feel any better, the Prime Minister gave permission for your being here today. Like you Senator, he… '

Mike cut across Sir James's reply. 'You said all major industries in this country are manufacturing arms and munitions?' He was back in Jack's office, reading a steel order for Great Britain, which Jack had thrust triumphantly at him. It was indeed a large order and Jack wondered at their plants capacity to meet the consignment. Now he understood, Allied Steel was producing finished armaments.

'I must get to Birmingham right away. Today! Katie will you drive me?'

Sir James chanced a glance at Katrina, the index finger of his right hand brushing gently up and down the side of his nose, his brow creased in a frown.

Katrina stole a look at her uncle when Mike leaned against the railing again, taking in the scene below. She saw him shrug, pause then nod, resigned to tell all. All this took but part of a second and when Mike turned to get Katrina's answer, her anxiety disappeared to be replaced with a warm smile for him.

'Why certainly Michael. Is something wrong?'

'I've reason to believe it could be,' he began, 'recently BHC received a very large order for steel, mainly boilerplate. At the time, Jack was delighted. Now I'm beginning to understand. We are pawns, producing steel that will be used to manufacture weapons of war. More killing,' he went on, 'as if the stupid imbeciles didn't get enough of it last time. Well! If that's the case, they won't be getting any more steel from Newcastle or Port Kembla. You can bet on that. We will shut Allied Steel down.'

Katrina choked on a reply; she looked from Mike to her uncle, her frown deepened.

'Hmm,' began Sir James thoughtfully. 'Well, let us go down to the boardroom where we can talk, shall we?'

'Yes, some refreshment would be welcome, Uncle James, if I am to drive Michael to Birmingham this afternoon.'

'Splendid,' Sir James rubbed his hands together.

Mike could only nod. He was still digesting the industry below. Shortly they were seated in plush black leather chairs in a fashionably furnished boardroom complete with a cocktail cabinet, sound proofed against the clamour of production out in the factory. The boardroom served as a meeting place for the executive staff who could relax and be waited on just as Mike was now. He accepted his scotch and soda from a short wizened white waist coated man who tilted the soda until Mike indicated his pleasure. As soon as drinks were served, the man left the room without having invited conversation apart from requesting their individual pleasure.

'Senator,' began Sir James, 'there is something you should know.' He paused while removing a set of keys from his vest pocket and unlocking a drawer in the large oak table, which served as a conference table for board meetings. He took from it an envelope, a rather large envelope with a broken red seal and hand outstretched, passed it across the table to where Mike was comfortably seated.

'Would you look at the documents contained therein Senator, particularly the signatures?' He sighed, beaming a tired smile upon their guest before resuming his seat.

The hand which held the glass shook visibly and then steadied. Mike tilted the glass and took a good swallow. He rifled through the document, all ten pages of it.

It was plain enough now. Under Lance Hoskin's signature appeared the signatures of Senator Gerald Perry and Lord Sedgwick Anthony, the Managing Director of Anthony Thornton Enterprises Proprietary Limited. Mike sat dumbfounded, with ashen-face he could only stare at them, speechless.

'The bastard sold us out... .'

'One must admit it was hoped to avoid disclosure. However, upon your insistence to visit Birmingham, we felt it was as well that you should know. Documents such as this are kept at our London Office. I chanced to bring it down with me this morning when I knew you were coming. Let us just say I had a premonition that it may be needed,' Loxton raised his glass and sipped at his scotch.

Mike looked up at the pair. His face a mask while thoughts raced through his brain. They stood facing him.

'Michael, you must never reveal the truth to Jack,' burst out Katrina, apprehensively.

'Your father?' Mike would hear all of it.

It was Sir James who replied, 'When he couldn't secure the Mount Hopkins range he knew defeat for the first time. You don't know Sedgwick, Senator, he wouldn't let go. So he appealed to Perry to make a deal with one of the other two parties involved, Lance Hoskins displayed interest, the other chap, Delprat, was retired and had distributed his shares equally among his children. They would only benefit upon his demise.'

Mike nodded. 'I think I need another drink... ' He exclaimed at last.

'Certainly my boy, and we owe you a full explanation.' James cast a glance at Katrina.

Mike sat glued to his chair for the next few minutes as Sir James meandered his way around the room revealing all and answering Mike's fears and questions without one word of prodding.

Finally, Katrina put his last reservations down the drain. 'So you do see Michael why I cannot go with you, not at this time. I could not tell you before, as much as I would have liked. It was hoped to avoid this revelation. However, now you know I feel a whole lot better,' she finished, her look of concern disarming him.

Mike nodded managing a smile, 'are you interested in selling the shares back?'

'There's a slight problem of protocol. The underhanded way Sedgwick acquired shares in your company... ?'

'I see,' Mike nodded.

'Rest assured. Anthony Thornton had no interest in acquiring your company Senator. Sedgwick Anthony no longer has any influence whatsoever in the Consortium. He is,' sighed Sir James with a look for Katrina, 'a broken man ailing in health.'

'I have had documentation drawn up which suspends Anthony Thornton from any interference in the running of BHC Michael,' Katrina sought Sir James's support with a look.

'However, we do need your steel Michael. Regardless of what you may think, England must be ready to defend herself and her colonies.' Katrina appealed.

Mike shrugged his shoulders; there was nothing he could do. He couldn't reveal Hoskins sabotage, and they needed all the steel orders they could get because Jack was ready to embark on an expansion program, which would require capital. It was Sir James who brought him out of his reverie.

'There is another reason we asked you along here this afternoon Senator, a more personal reason,' Sir James caught Mike's attention.

'Go ahead, nothing you could say would further surprise me.'

'We believe that if war is inevitable, its theatre will again be Europe.'

'Michael, I want you to take my son with you,' Katrina cut her uncle short.

'David!' said Mike, trying to read her expression.

'Yes, you see old chap, his grandfather, Lord Anthony, wants the boy to take up a career; he has arranged for the lad to enter the military. Uphold the family tradition and all that nonsense,' explained Sir James, fingering his moustache.

'And David? What does he want?' Prompted Mike.

'He is strongly influenced by Father, unfortunately,' revealed Katrina.

'He thinks he would jolly-well like war games,' added Sir James.

'Oh he does, does he?' Mike was thinking of Jack and the son he never knew, had never seen. 'I'll take him with me if that's what you want Katie,' he looked at her, wondering how much Sir James knew of their conversation shared that morning in the car and deciding she would have had to confide in the man to get his cooperation.

Sir James next statement helped to clarify the situation. 'We hoped we could count on you. We want you to teach him the steel business, he needs to be groomed if he is to take over the running of the Company.'

A thought crossed Mike's mind. 'How are you going to explain to his grandfather that his only grandson is leaving England for Australia? It seems to me, if memory serves me correctly, Lord Anthony takes a very dim view of Australia?'

'He lost his only son fighting in the Boer War, when he is reminded that it could happen to David, I honestly believe the old boy will see the light,' Sir James kept a straight face.

'I believe you could be right, particularly if he wants David to take his place as chairman of the board when Katrina joins Jack in Australia,' replied Mike, locking his eyes to those of Sir James for some reaction, he was not disappointed, the silver haired statesman nodded his approval.

Just before parting, Mike was reminded his visit to the plant should be regarded as top secret. Still Mike was angered, possibly Chamberlain could not reveal anything to the Australian delegation without first gaining approval from his cabinet and the verbal support of the King, maybe by letting him see the plant he was revealing more than he could while conducting the talks.

There was an urgency now; he wished to return to Australia as quickly as possible. Yet they were not due to meet again with the Prime Minister and his cabinet for another three days. Also, the revelation that Jack was a father weighed heavily upon him, and the more he thought of the son Jack had never seen going off to a war like they had survived, scared the hell out of him. Like himself, he imagined the youngster looked upon war as an adventure, the place for an officer and a gentleman to be, a show of bravado, with no fear for the unknown that only surfaced when you were being bombed and fired upon incessantly.

'Thank you Michael! You have no idea how worried I have been.'

Mike nodded, grim faced, 'Would you mind if David accompanied me to the cricket tomorrow? It would give us a chance to get to know each another,' he added, not expecting a rejection anyway.

'I'm sure he would love to go.'

'Great, shall I send a car for him?'

'I'll have Harris drop him at your hotel first thing in the morning.'

Plainly Mike was troubled about something else, a secret. A secret he must carry to the grave.

< >

Less than a fortnight later David Thornton, tall, handsome, broad of shoulder, and dressed in grey flannels and a dark blue blazer stood beside Senator Michael Smith at the ship's railing. On the terminus below, Katrina was holding tightly to the coloured streamers, her eyes misted behind the tears, which ran unheeded down her cheeks.

For the man beside her, this scenario had been staged before. Solemnly, he had clasped Harrison's hand in his. Sure in the knowledge they would never see each another again. He had turned away to hide his emotions from the boy and shortly had stolen from the terminal, ashamed for his own actions and those of his brother-in-law. Sir James Loxton had read the only letter he would ever receive from Harrison Anthony. It set out to explain his account of the happening at Eland's River in Transvaal. Sir James cried then. Just as Katrina was crying now, instinctively he placed an arm about her and drew her close. Together they waved to the boy and Senator Smith.

Above the harbour in the terminal building behind the plate glass window, a shrivelled old man in a wheelchair, supported by Harris and Benson, took one last look at his grandson before requesting that Benson escort him back to the black limousine. While Benson turned the chair away from the window, Harris lingered momentarily his lips forming the words *God bless you David*! A tear rolled down his cheek and he brushed it away before pushing past Benson and the old man to open the car door.

A fog settled over the harbour of Bristol. Hanging like a blanket, it cut visibility to a minimum. There was a sudden thunderclap of sound as the ship's foghorn blasted the eerie silence of the morning, followed by that of her tug escorts. Like the long silent running submarine, the ship, her massive engines running over, her twin screws barely churning below the water, were hauled away from the terminal. David and Mike stood shoulder-to-shoulder waving. The colour-dyed streamers were losing their splendour with every passing second in the heavy water filled air. Finally, the tri coloured paper ribbons parted, and the men's view of Katrina and Sir James Loxton diminished in the murk. David released his hold on the streamers, and Katrina released hold of her son. Mike witnessed the saddened expression on David's features; gently he placed an understanding arm around the young man and, like Katrina, David drew strength from him.

Chapter 70

Tempi Homestead

Senator Gerald Perry read with interest and a smile, the cablegram from Lord Sedgwick Anthony. It was a request for him to get in touch with Reginald Bundy and Freddy Moylan both working at the Port Kembla Steel Works and instruct them to proceed to Edge Rock as quickly as humanly possible there to await further instructions. If he was curious as to those instructions then the last sentence, which promised a large retainer to be transferred to his bank account, saw his mind at ease as he contemplated the best way to contact the two Englishmen without drawing attention to himself.

<>

The road was tar sealed for the first forty miles and David gazed about him at the ever-changing landscape. The low rolling coastal hills with their splashes of browns and greens tempered by yellowish thickets gave way to sharp jagged rock outcrops. The smell of the sea air disappeared to be replaced by the hot dry inland air and a faint scent of wind-blown dust which filtered through the open window from somewhere up ahead where the tar petered out and the gravel road commenced.

David was amused to watch Mike fondle the floor change gear stick, pushing the Ford sedan to the limit over the rough terrain. The V8 was one of the first of its kind assembled at Ford's Australian plant in Victoria.

'What is he like Mike?' David asked at length.

'Who, Jack?'

'Yes. Mister Carter. Mother speaks very highly of him, quite frankly, he was the subject of most conversation prior to my departure.'

'He's the greatest bloke I ever met,' said Mike smiling, pulling on the steering to avoid a fallen clump of coal dislodged from one of the trucks transporting the material to Tempi.

'Look, there's plenty of room up at the homestead, you don't have to stay at the pub.'

'For the present, I would feel more at home at the tavern,' David indicated, making no mention of the fact that he wanted to telephone his grandfather to let him know of his safe arrival, as well as contacting his mother for the same reason.

'Suit yourself, Molly will be disappointed.'

'I appreciate your hospitality Mike, just a few days.'

Mike brought the vehicle to a stop outside a fashionable two storeyed sandstock building, the Tempi Hotel. There were three doors fronting the main street. He parked the car and leaving the keys in the ignition, headed for the furthest door. They were greeted in the lobby by Sally, who had seen them drive up. Some time ago, Jack realised he needed the presence of women to look to the needs of the miners.

'David, this is Sally. David will be staying here for a while Sal. He can have Jack's old room.'

267

David eyed off the shapely woman in the low cut gown, her smile was friendly, not forced, and he decided he may get to like staying here in the tavern.

'Did you have a good trip Mike?' Sally asked brushing her lips against Mike's cheek, and David was surprised she should have such a deep husky voice.

Mike gave her a friendly hug before they stepped apart, 'Yeah, glad to be back though. Jack been in?' Mike was being courteous. He was anxious to see his wife.

Sally shook her head, 'No, we don't see much of Jack these days.'

Mike got the impression she was going to say more but decided against it. He nodded. 'Well David, I'm off to see Jack. You freshen up and I'll see you this evening, eight o'clock sharp for dinner, O.K.?'

'I'm looking forward to meeting your wife and Jack,' replied David, lifting his suitcase.

'Look after him, Sally,' said Mike with a knowing wink.

'Sure thing Mike,' she replied. 'We'll have to put you in one of the front room's David, one of my girls is occupying Jack's old room,' she told him, ushering him upstairs to take a look at his room.

<>

David closed his room and went down the side stairway, out through the foyer and private entrance reserved for houseguests. Out on the street the motor vehicle was where Mike had left it, keys still in the ignition; a card was balanced in the spokes of the steering wheel. David opened the door and settled behind the wheel. He tore open the envelope with the company seal and removed the card.

Welcome to Australia David
From the Company.

David frowned, he was used to being doted on by his grandfather, this was different, and he felt a new emotion engulfing him for the man he had known but a short time. He knew Mike had accepted him from the moment they first met. He however was more reserved. Now the final reservations were disappearing. It was strange really, he thought, kicking the motor over, it was as though he were one of the family, a long lost son, returning home to a family he could not remember, but who knew and loved him very much.

The drive out to the house was very short, over the bridge; a sharp veer to the left before the gates to the plant and straight on up the hill, the noise of the plant growing fainter with the passing distance. Shortly, he was in sight of the house, a large sandstock dwelling with a green galvanised iron roof, brown shutters and a white picket fence. The sun's bold red ball spread a crimson haze over the coastal hills. Down in the valley dark shadows and spirals of smoke indicated women-folk were getting supper ready for their men after a hard day's work at the plant. David gunned the motor and cattle moved hurriedly away from the noise. He wheeled the Ford parallel to the front fence near the gate. Removing the keys he hastened to the boot and removed Mike's suitcase and briefcase, and with one attached to each hand, closed on the dwelling.

Mike met him at the front door having heard the car and proceeded to take the luggage while introducing Molly, radiant as most pregnant women, with big eyes and lashes. David decided she was a very attractive woman. Her hands were white with flour, and Molly rubbed them on her floral apron while kissing David warmly on the cheek to make him welcome. She soon departed for the kitchen leaving the men in the family room with its large empty fire-place and well-stocked bar. Mike gestured for David to make himself comfortable in the high-back leather lounge chair while he fixed them both a drink. Shortly, could be heard, the sound of an approaching vehicle which heralded Jack's arrival. David stood immediately; he heard the car's door slam. Mike beckoned him back to his chair.

'Relax David. I'm as much the boss around here as Jack. Don't let the big bugger make you nervous,' Mike told him, smiling at David's apparent uneasiness.

Together they turned as the fly screen door closed. David's jaw dropped, it was a giant of a man who filled the doorway to the living room dressed in slacks and a hounds-tooth sports jacket.

'Evening folks, where's Molly? Told her I'd spruce up for this evening, even brought some flowers and a box of candy,' offered Jack, displaying the bright array of blooms to the room's occupants before disappearing towards the kitchen.

David was nervous, and unable to understand why. It was something he felt deep down in his innards, as if this were all part of his destiny, like a dream that had come true. Without Mike noticing, he pinched himself to see if it were real, and from the kitchen there came laughter, light banter and screams of delight followed by sounds of feigned anger.

'Oh, get out of here you philanderer. Go in there with the men and let me get dinner in peace. Jack, leave the roast alone. Mike! Come and get this pest out of my kitchen.'

Mike looked at David grinning. 'How's the scotch?'

'Fine thank you Mike,' replied David and Mike detected the edginess in the young man's voice.

'Ready for another?'

'Yes,' came the quick rejoinder.

'I'll make it three,' said Mike, hearing Jack's heavy tread through the house.

Could he know? Mike asked himself seeing the thoughtful look on the young man's features. *No!* He told himself, *Molly only found out this afternoon, and only then because he was unable to keep the good news to himself any longer.*

'Jack. This young fella has come all the way from England,' commenced Mike, leading David forward by the elbow to where Jack stood just inside the doorway. David had risen at the sound of the man's approach.

David watched the change of expression come over the big man's countenance. The cheery grin replaced by a sombre expression, the eyes became hooded, guarded.

'David Thornton, I would like you to meet Jack Carter,' finished Mike with a wink for David.

David ignored him, he was watching the big man's eyes intently, he saw the chill come over them, watched the chin jut out from the freshly shaven face, saw the pronounced dimple enlarging as the jaw tightened, saw the hair at the nape of the man's neck seemingly bristle. He felt the man break their handgrip and could sense his animosity. Like electricity, the waves of hatred spread to engulf David.

The two men stared at one another for what seemed to David an eternity. Both were oblivious to Mike as he outlined for Jack's benefit that David had been sent to Australia to learn what the founders of BHC could teach him about the iron and steel business. David's mouth was terribly dry, he felt butterflies in his stomach and decidedly intimidated by this man who was standing before him with the hooked nose, the deep tan, the moustache with tinges of grey through it and the golden brown hair slicked back, parted, and tinted with silver flecks at the temples. David was nearly six feet in stockinged feet, and this man towered over him. Poignant was the silence. They stood staring into the other's eyes, with Mike looking from one to the other not quite understanding nor knowing the chemistry, which flowed like an electric current between them.

Jack remembered being introduced to another man, a long time ago, a man he instantly detested, and now as then, he couldn't think of anything to say; that only came later when he had walked through the English night. He was reliving the moment as though it were yesterday, and the man was standing before him again. Another incident flashed before his eyes as it had many times since the Belgian, and he saw again the fight going on within the man before he had finally brought the stock of the shotgun crashing down on his jaw. Now it was his turn to feel anger swelling up through his body, his breathing became raspy; he experienced a sudden pain in the chest, an ache for release, an opportunity to hurt as he had been hurt. David saw it also, saw the struggle in the big man's eyes, but he was powerless to do anything about it. The years of toil, of struggle, hatred and bitterness towards the Anthony's and all they stood for fogged Jack's tired brain and he bunched his fist and hit David square on the jaw with all the power he could muster; a sound like a cry omitting from deep within his diaphragm. David plummeted backwards to the floor, as if poleaxed.

'What the hell did you do that for?' shouted Mike. The anger in Mike's voice bringing Molly running from the kitchen.

Jack couldn't answer; he stood over the slumped figure, his huge frame heaving, his breath coming in gasps as though he had run all the way from the mine to their front door.

'Get him out of here,' he uttered at last. 'I never want to lay eyes on him again,' his raucous voice cut like a whip.

Mike's jaw dropped in amazement; then anger replaced shock. 'You can go to hell! The boy is a guest in my home.'

Jack went for him, pinning him by the throat with his left hand, the stub of the little finger lost so long ago saving Mike's life was raised towards his eye, the other hand clenched to strike a vicious blow.

'Stop it! Stop it,' wailed Molly.

Mike tried to push her to one side as she made a grab for Jack's wrist, while watching Jack intently. Slowly he saw the fight, which was being waged within the man, die. He felt the grip of steel fingers around his larynx loosen. The glaze over the steel blue eyes lifted and like mist shrouding a lake the eyes were suddenly swimming in tears, and from within Jack quiet sobs of pent up emotion choked in his throat. His left hand shook like a jack-hammer. Alligator tears rolled down his cheeks. He pushed Mike away almost gently and let himself out into the moonlight.

Molly and Mike stood listening in the new silence to the sound of the motor when Jack gunned the Chevrolet to life followed by the squeal of protesting rubber as the car flew down the grade and through the cattle grid towards Tempi.

Mike sat on the end of the lounge, sucking fresh air into his bruised larynx, his chest heaved over his heart. He rubbed his throat while Molly looked from him to where David lay unconscious on the carpeted floor. She came to Mike and he waved her away indicating he was all right while his mind turned over the events from the time he had arrived back at Tempi.

Jack had been glad to see him, of that he was sure. They welcomed each other in an embrace and with fondness they reserved for each other. Yet he had sensed rather than felt at the time that Jack was preoccupied and that he had been in the way. His desk was full of correspondence, with papers scattered between the incoming and out- going trays. He had been studying blueprints, and Mike remembered resting against the door jamb on his way out, turning to remind Jack again about dinner and didn't he detect a look of exasperation, or, was it his imagination? Certainly Jack looked tired, and the room reeked with stale air, as though he could not spare the time it took to open the windows.

Molly cut across his thoughts, 'David will need medical attention Mike.'

Mike forced himself from the lounge and crossed the room to where Molly was positioning a cushion under David's head.

'Did you see the look on his face? Like a madman.' Molly rose and hurried to the kitchen for a cloth.

'Phone Doctor Andrews; I think his jaw could be broken.' She shouted from the kitchen.

Mike had seen the look, had witnessed the change and suddenly he to remembered Cornelius Le Brun.

Molly returned a short time later, swathing the young man's jaw in cold packs, from the ice chest, wrapped in cloth. 'Mike, I'm scared, maybe he's heading for a breakdown; he has been working long hours of late. All the men are talking... '

'What are the men saying Molly?' Mike's tone was solemn.

'They have noticed the change.'

'What change?' Mike asked, giving the phone his immediate attention. Mary Regan was on the switch and she connected him through to the hospital at Edge Rock. Arrangements were made to Mike's satisfaction whereupon he hung up and then, picking up the receiver again, made a local call.

'Col...'

'Is that you Mike? I heard you got in this afternoon.'

'Yeah, look, Colin, we need to talk, can you meet me at the runway in ten minutes?'

'Hell Mike, you sure picked a bad time. It's Jack isn't it?'

'Ten minutes!' Mike replaced the receiver yet again. Now he was troubled, Colin O'Connor's tone indicated he knew what Mike wanted to talk about without further conversation taking place between the pair.

'Is he meeting you?' Molly appeared anxious.

'Yes, ten minutes. Sounded like he was with one of the girls.'

'Huh! Well there is no point things going on the way they are, Colin can put you straight better than anyone else I imagine,' she would overlook O'Connor's womanising on this occasion.

'Yeah, I guess I hadn't realised how much of a strain the big fella was under, look after the boy until I get back.'

'Isn't he coming here?'

'We have to light up the runway, Doctor Cole wants to make the flight tonight.'

'Tonight! Isn't that dangerous?' Molly was tucking a blanket around David to keep him warm.

'He can't miss the place, the plant is well lit, easy to spot from the air, and the runway won't present any problems.' Mike tried to allay her fears, while rummaging through the hallway closet for a jacket.

'How is the boy?'

Molly was bathing his brow with a wet flannel.

Molly shook her head. 'Still senseless, his pulse is strong; he is young.'

'Yeah, he'll be all right. That stupid big son of a... he could have killed him.'

'You didn't tell him that David was his son?'

'He never gave me the chance, it all happened too quickly. They were eyeballing each other like you could not believe.'

'Do you think David knew the truth?' Molly looked up at Mike who had opened the screen door.

Mike shrugged. 'I won't be long love. Keep him warm.'

< >

271

Two hours later the Percival Gull, a De Havilland Gipsy Series, landed at Tempi Airport to evacuate David to Edge Rock hospital. Mike contemplated making the return flight with the boy only deciding against the impulse when he remembered he had to fly out to Canberra in the morning. Besides, there wasn't sufficient room once David had been placed on a stretcher for three to make the trip comfortably. Mike stood beside a dishevelled Colin O'Connor on the runway and watched the all-metal monoplane taxing for a take-off. Shortly, the pair was in deep discussion.

It was early in the morning before Tempi's manager finally left the Smith residence. Mike sat back on the lounge exhausted, Molly curled up asleep, her head on his lap. He sat watching the sky dawn on a new day, his fingers absently stroking her long red hair while going over again his conversation with O'Connor, oblivious to the noise of the birds and the generator cutting in out the back.

Smithy, he's going bananas. He has been driving himself flat-out without a break, seven days a week and me along with him.

Mike was partially ignorant to the change and partially protected because Jack always put on a front in his presence. He was aware that to succeed many man-hours of work would be necessary, not just one year, maybe five or six, and he had assessed that Jack had energy to burn. The man was forever enthusiastic when talking about the company, whether by phone, for Mike was away a lot of the time, or whether they were strolling through the plant to look at some new innovation. Mike was wrong, every man has his limit, his threshold, even Jack, he realised that now, but maybe now was too late.

'*The problem Mike,*' *O'Conner had explained,* '*is labour shortage, and more and more orders to fill. Our delivery dates are falling further behind. The big bloke is always on the phone to Harry Street insisting the plants under his control are not producing enough steel. And Harry is bellowing back that Tempi cannot supply enough iron ore for production to be increased. If Jack doesn't slow down soon, he will have a stroke, mark my words.*'

'*I've done my best to have our prime minister, Lyons, reintroduce Bruce's policy of a five-year tenure agreement for incoming migrants. But, his party will have none of it, discrimination they call it. A free country should have in place freedom of settlement, for all citizens, they claim.*' *Mike had clenched his fists in anger.*

'*Well something has to give Mike, we can't go on like this much longer.*' *O'Conner had retorted.*

It may have already happened, thought Mike to himself, reflecting on Jack's behaviour of last night. But the anger was gone and Mike felt nothing but admiration for his friend, not appreciating until now just how much responsibility Jack shouldered on himself. He never once worried Mike with the pitfalls or short-comings of the Company.

Chapter 71

Edge Rock Hospital

The Douglas DC2 stood on the tarmac, both engines idling over. First of its kind, it offered a new dimension to air transportation. The sleek single wing metal monoplane seated fourteen passengers. It was fitted with variable pitch propellers, which contributed significantly to its performance and gave it better single engine characteristics than previously achieved by any twin-engine aeroplane.

Seated and strapped in, Mike waved through the porthole window to Molly standing on the verge of the tarmac, Molly holding the dress down over her bulging belly against the rush of air from the twin propellers as the plane swung around to commence its taxiing run into the wind. Mike got one last glance of her before he felt himself being pushed into his seat as the plane gathered momentum. Slowly, the ground fell away and the DC2 climbed steeply for the clouds and altitude.

Just as Jack had promised to return to the small cairn of stones above the rock chasm where they had paid their last respects to Barney, so to Molly assured him she would visit David during his absence. He realised, due to aviation and the technology of the future, it may be possible to find the chasm from the air. He no longer had time for cattle, his wife or family; he was Jack's right arm he realised, the architect who made gains for their Territory in its quest for statehood and to further Jack's business interests. Yet somehow he believed he was his own man, maybe after the next Term he would resign from politics, to manage Tempi Station and realise the only life he ever really wanted. Jack would understand, he was an empire builder, he was living his dream, even if the circumstances were not quite as he had planned. Things were starting to come together, the boy, and in the near future Katrina; the three of them would be together, with David to take over BHC. He gazed for hours, thoughts coming and going, the past, present, and future all visited before sleep overcame his exhausted body.

Two days later, Mike was in his office at Parliament House Canberra. It was necessary for him to outline his report for the Cabinet on his recent trip to Great Britain. He called the document the *Salmond* report after Smith, Almond and Mondise, the three Australian envoys representing the Australian Government. In the report he outlined the British Governments fears of aggression from Germany and her allies' Italy and Russia. He told of her massive arms build-up. He reiterated the British Prime Minister's belief that in the event of war, Australia could best be defended from the air, and appealed to the Minister of Defence to heed this advice and build up the RAAF immediately. Satisfied, he addressed the document:

Confidential.
Sir Archdale Parkhill
Minister for Defence.

He placed a round blue seal on the back of the envelope, which indicated a code priority and distinguished the letter from many in the attaché case. Sighing, he rose from behind the mahogany desk, begrudging the time he was away from Tempi to attend the special meeting set up by the Prime Minister and the Defence ministry to hear first-hand the report from the delegation.

It would be another fortnight before Mike's commitments in Canberra were completed and he was able to visit David on his way home to Tempi.

<>

The quiet surrounds of Edge Rock Botanical Gardens were shattered early in March 1936 when a grant was approved and work commenced on the single story building that became Edge Rock Hospital. Constructed from brick with timber windows, galvanised roofing and completely surrounded by an overhanging veranda, it was considered a modern building. Equipped to cater for the needs of a growing population, it boasted forty beds. A staff of eighteen including a resident doctor, Doctor Cole, and Doctor Clayton Andrews— its first superintendent.

Now, three years later paving and lawn skirted the building. Trees and shrubs given undivided attention by the ground's curator were angling towards the heavens, while birds chirped in the trees during the day and frogs croaked in the drainpipes during the evenings. It was all pleasant enough but David could feel himself becoming bored with his surroundings. He occupied a room with sweeping views of the Botanical Gardens and from where he sat, propped in the bed, he could see the remembrance statue in the distance. He wondered at the memorial here in the growing coastal town, and not in the grounds of a university or a public school, to which he was accustomed. He promised himself he would dress in due time and abate his curiosity. Meanwhile, Molly had motored down from Tempi on more than one occasion, and on her second visit presented him with a book bound in a leather cover. His love of adventure would not let him put it down until read from cover to cover. He was reading from the text when Nurse Johnston, in stiff starch uniform conducted Senator Michael Smith into the room.

Mike was deeply touched to find the boy wading through his personal copy of *Across the Waste Land*. It had been published as a hard cover text three years ago by the Government Press.

'Hey, you're into very heavy stuff there,' Mike indicated the book while offering his hand in greeting.

'I find it fascinating reading,' was the reply. 'Of course I find it hard to believe... ' David placed the book on his bedside dresser.

'To be honest with you, David, I haven't had time to read the published version, so I'm not sure just how closely the publisher followed our notes. I imagine it wouldn't have varied too much.'

'So it really did happen?'

'It certainly did,' Mike nodded in confirmation.

'What chapter are you reading?'

'The Granites. That's a bit far-fetched isn't it, a motor vehicle in the middle of the desert?'

'No,' began Mike, 'it was there all right, no figment of our imagination.' He smiled as he saw David try to whistle through his wired jaw, saw the wince of pain immediately covered by a brave grin. And Mike was reminded of his father, never a murmur of complaint. Mike was also going over in his mind the reason they undertook the epic journey in the first place. It was to beat this young man's grandfather, to a destination for the chance to prove themselves, or for Jack to prove himself, how ironic it all turned out to be. Mike smiled to himself.

'What is so funny?' David asked in all innocence.

'Nothing David, just thinking of the past; someday I'll tell you a story, a story so entwined you probably won't believe it.'

'Why not now? I have nothing better to do.' David's curiosity was aroused.

'It will keep. How are you feeling David?'

'Good! Doctor Cole says the jaw is mending rapidly. I will be eating solids shortly, so it should not be long before I am out of here.'

'I am sorry I wasn't able to visit you sooner, I've been down to Canberra this past two weeks,' Mike explained his absence.

'I understand Mike; you do not have to apologise. Molly has been to visit me. Do you really think there will be another war?'

Mike said nothing for a while, he wondered what foolish ideas his wife had been putting into the young man's head. But he believed there was nothing to be gained by telling David a fabrication.

'What I have to say is confidential.' David, nodded his understanding.

'It could be another war is imminent.'

'So that explains it,' David half said to himself.

'Explains what?'

'It explains why Mother insisted I accompany you to Australia.'

'You're here to learn how to run a company, Iron and Steel production is the basis upon which shipping and ship building depends. You are here to gain background knowledge… '

'Come off it, Mike, we do produce steel in Great Britain you know. Mother could just as easily have sent me to our Cumberland Plant if that were the only reason. The truth of the matter was she did not want me to enter the armed forces. Grandfather and Sir James staged a dreadful scene one morning and soon after, I was informed that I was to accompany you to Australia.'

'Do you blame your mother for wanting to protect you, is that so wrong?'

David wouldn't look at him. He was looking forward to becoming an officer and going to war. To Mike his face was a mask of hurt, obviously he felt Mike was part of the conspiracy. David reached for the book on the dresser, deciding to ignore his mentor.

Angrily Mike swept the book from his grasp and it careered across the room. 'Damn it David, you listen to me, you wouldn't like war, it isn't a game, men get killed, statistically more than half the fighting force get killed or badly wounded. For Christ's sake, wouldn't you have done what your mother did if the position was reversed? Besides, there was another reason, a more important reason for your being here than the bloody war and the outdated thinking of a bitter old man… '

'You have no right to talk about my grandfather like that, you do not know him,' there was belligerence in the young voice.

'Don't talk to me about your grandfather; he wants you to uphold the stupid family tradition and go off to war and get yourself killed! For what?' Mike raised his voice in anger, he hadn't meant to, but David and his attitude were getting to him.

'He wouldn't give a damn if your life's blood spread itself across some muddy bunker somewhere in Europe. All he would think about was family tradition, wave the flag, do your duty and all that rubbish!' Mike sighed, not looking at the boy.

'It is you who are talking rubbish. My grandfather was a distinguished soldier, he fought in the South African campaigns against the Zulu and lived to talk about it.'

'God almighty! They threw sticks at one another and fired cannon balls from hill to hill; he was a commander, probably never raised his pistol in anger.' Mike gritted his teeth to control himself.

'Mother had no right not to sign the papers; I trained to be an officer. I want to serve my country! And look what has happened? I am in this God forsaken place less than a month and a person, whom, you say, is your best friend, breaks my jaw.'

'Do you want to know the real reason you were sent to Australia or not?'

David shrugged.

'Jack Carter is your father… ' Mike informed him.

'My father is dead, has been dead for several years,' David corrected.

Mike shook his head, deciding to continue, after all, David wasn't going anywhere; he had a captive audience. 'Jack and your mother met during the Great War. They fell in love and decided to get married. However, your grandparents felt Jack was not a suitable suitor for their daughter. They conspired to have some letters written to chill the romance. The short of it all is that your mother informed your grandmother that she was pregnant with Jack's child. So the old biddy arranged a marriage of iron and steel to shipping; she didn't give a rat's arse for Katrina's wishes, all she could think of was the smear on the family name if it were known her daughter was to have a bastard child. So your mother married Lord Chester Thornton because she believed Jack actually wrote the letter, which explained he wanted to get on his feet first then he would send for her. But your grandparents were very pleased, a merger of two of the most powerful and influential families in Great Britain.'

'You are making all this up Mike, there is no way Mother could have fallen in love with that big, over-weight, uncouth, rheumy-eyed American.'

'I don't tell lies David; Jack is the reason you are in Australia, it was the express wish of your mother and Sir James Loxton.'

'I am very tired Mike, I would like time to myself to think on what you have said.'

'Of course you feel hurt; I can understand that, suddenly you don't know who you are anymore. All I ask is that you give Jack a chance to explain, to apologise. David, he deserves that chance, he never married, he still loves your mother, and she loves him, you judge him harshly without reason.'

'Sure Mike that is why my jaw is wired, he loves me like a long lost son, the hell he does!'

'Don't judge him too harshly David. He's been through hell these past few months. You couldn't begin to understand the impact of that moment. Imagine if you can, suddenly you are confronted by the son of the woman you loved more than anything in the world, and you couldn't have her. Yet before you stood her son, sired by another. How would you feel?' Mike didn't wait for an answer; he picked up his hat from the chair near the door, rose and quietly walked out of the room.

To David it all began to make sense, his mother never marrying again, Grandmother Thornton's remoteness, her tolerance of him, seldom could he remember her affection, and also, Grandfather Thornton, who would rustle those rough hands through his hair. Grandfather Anthony was the only one apart from his mother and Uncle James who doted him with affection. Too, there were his father's womanising and socialising, the terrible arguments and his hitting mother. And, lately, his mother's incessant talk of this Jack Carter prior to his departure. He didn't think anything of it then but now… As well there was the unexplainable feeling he held for the Australian, as though Mike were part of his destiny. And finally, the magnetic meeting with the tall American, the unexplainable feeling that they shared a deep relationship. The look of blatant hurt in the big man's eyes just before he struck him, the frustration, humiliation, anger, David read it all, the hate festered over many years, carried like a torch of remembrance. David fought back tears, until a lump formed in his throat and suddenly he was crying into the pillows.

Chapter 72

Tempi Smelter Works

Mercilessly the sun beat down on Mike as he strode across the dusty path towards the maintenance shed. The white shirt clung to his back and his trousers pressed to his legs. He pushed his meeting with David and the anger he felt for the young man's stubbornness to the back of his mind. His concern at this time was for Jack.

Jack would be in the shed supervising the running repairs to one of the large generators, which supplied electrical energy to the plant. Molly thought to tell him of the recent power blackout and that mechanics were trying to fix a generator thought to be responsible. Jack was wiping grease from his hands. Seeing Mike approach, he cupped a couple of salt tablets and turned to the tumbler to wash them down with the ice chilled water. He turned to face Mike but could not bring himself to say anything; or rather he didn't trust himself to say anything. So it was Mike who broke the silence.

'Did you get it fixed?'

'I think so, they are going to give it a hit out now,' was Jack's perturbed reply.

'Can we talk?'

'My office.'

Together they walked across the open space, the breeze at their backs, shoulder to shoulder across the ground where years ago they had stopped the rioting miners, on towards the newly fabricated office block. It was a slightly emotional Jack who stood aside holding the fly screen door and motioning Mike to enter.

'About the other night… ' he began, only to have Mike cut him short.

'It's forgotten.'

'I can't imagine what came over me. All I could think of was that bastard Chester Thornton and Katrina. I must have gone mad; suddenly I wanted to hurt more than I've ever wanted to hurt anything or anyone before in all my life. I'm sorry. Molly must think very poorly of me,' he finished, downcast eyes studying the flower patterned linoleum. His voice caught in his throat, 'I came very close to striking you.'

'I told you to forget it. You have been under tremendous stress for some time. If anything, I should be apologising to you. These days I never seem to be around when you need me,' sighed Mike, clasping his hands together in front of him.

'Nonsense! We both agreed you could do more to help the Territory and this company in your official capacity than twenty businessmen by bringing pressure to bear on the government. I'll not go back on that, already the road is completed between here and the coast and telegraph cables have been laid, power lines are in place, the railway between here and Darwin has been surveyed and pegged, we have an airstrip, and while you were away, Cornellan Airways rented hanger space. Funds have been made available to the stations during drought and famine, two dams have been constructed along tributaries of the Margaret River bringing countless acres under cultivation, Edge Rock has a hospital and a Technical college so necessary to train our technicians; all because of your efforts.' Jack, adumbrated while seating himself at the desk covered in correspondence.

'Which reminds me? Did you get to speak with Chamberlain?' Jack's glance fell on the pile of letters, which needed his attention.

Mike's eyes followed Jack's movement, he winced. Jack had him in a corner. He thought of changing the subject back to David, it would be the easy way out, yet somehow he could not bring himself to avoid answering the question, above all others he owed this man the truth.

'Great Britain is preparing for war!' He dropped the bombshell.

'What?'

'I've been to Southampton, I saw submarines being constructed, and across the country armaments are being manufactured.' Jack's next remark startled him.

'I suppose our mob is doing the same thing. That would account for the large consignment of boilerplate.'

'I thought you would hit the roof... ' Mike was puzzled.

'Years ago I probably would have.' Jack sank into his chair. Mike had his undivided attention now. 'It was thought America got into the Great War to profiteer from the world's misery. When it was suggested, I was angry, not anymore,' Jack shook his head.

'I'm beginning to understand this bloody world, and the name of the game is survival. Now this may sound callous, but reason this, without markets for our steel we no longer have an industry. I think it took the depression to teach me that. The bastards are determined not to break the pattern.'

'Jack, I won't be standing at the next election; I'm through with politics.'

Jack sat in the chair reminiscing, turning the clock back to 1916 when he took the Great War seriously. When at last he did look at Mike he mirrored vagueness. 'I'm sorry Mike, miles away, what were you saying?'

'I said I'm going to resign from politics,' Mike repeated.

'You can't quit, not now. If there is going to be a war, you must make certain Australia is prepared. Have you anything in writing from Chamberlain to substantiate your report?'

'No, he wouldn't go that far, however he advised us that he would clarify the position personally with Lyons if requested.'

'Well that's better than nothing! You would be aware that there are those in the cabinet who will take your report with a grain of salt. The treasurer is one, and without his support you will never pass a bill to finance munitions, ships, planes and conscription. You must fight him tooth and nail Mike!'

'Lyons must be aware of the situation. He approved in principle that the RAAF should be increased markedly,' said Mike.

'Yeah, I received notice while you were overseas that we would be contracted to supply steel and support financially the development of our navy. I agreed in principal, however, I advised that due to a labour shortage, we may not be able to honour our part of the contract.' Jack smiled; obviously he was not revealing everything to Mike.

'And?' Mike's tone indicated he was sceptical.

'The federal government are going to see we get a labour force.'

'Hey that's great!'

Jack laughed, 'Finally.'

Mike nodded sinking further into a chair. 'Anyway, we will soon know, I'm expecting a dispatch from Canberra as soon as Parkhill makes a decision.'

'Jack there is something I must tell you.'

'Go on.' Jack read the sombre look on Mike's features.

'I met with Katie while I was abroad... '

'I'm all ears,' prompted Jack.

'Well, the long and the short of it was that she requested I bring your son to Australia.'

'My son!' Jack jerked a thumb into his chest.

'Yes, that was what was so special about the other evening; David is your son.' Mike smiled at Jack, guessing at the impact this was having on his friend.

'David! My son,' muttered Jack again. His cheeks flushed and Mike could almost hear his heart pounding at the rate of knots from where he was sitting. Suddenly, Jack leaped from the table a shout of joy ringing from his throat as tears rolled down his face. Then they came together, both men laughing, embracing and Mike was lifted bodily from his chair and effortlessly whirled about the room and just as suddenly dropped again...

'Christ! Oh my God! Hell of a way for a father to greet his son?' He added, turning to Mike, a doleful expression on his features. 'I didn't know Mike, I... ' the fingers of his hand absently brushed his moustache, while his mind, raced to keep up with his thoughts for his felling David with the viscous blow.

'You weren't to know,' reasoned Mike, catching his breath.

But Jack wasn't listening, 'I could have killed him. Why now, after all these years?'

'Because Katie and Sir James Loxton want the boy away from the influence of his grandfather,' Mike explained.

'That old bastard!'

Mike only nodded.

There were so many questions Jack wanted to ask that he did not know where to begin, and Mike could see him searching for the question which would unlock the others muddled around in his brain and he was reminded of himself when standing in Lloyd Hopkin's office so long ago. This time he had the answers.

'Katie was holding on to the only thing that really mattered to her; if she couldn't be with you, she was determined to have your son.'

'She never intended to tell me about the boy?' Jack wanted to know. His features a mixture of emotions.

Mike smiled, 'It was to be a surprise.'

'A surprise! I have suffered all these years?' Jack whispered, both hands touching his chest, tears running freely down his jowls.

'Yes, you have suffered Jack; God knows how you have suffered. She realises that now, it was probably her strongest motive for sending the boy to you.'

'The boy, does he know I am his father Mike?'

Mike nodded 'I stopped off at the hospital on my way home.'

'After what I did, I cannot imagine him wanting anything to do with me,' Jack mumbled.

'Oh I think he will be all right, once he gets used to being slugged every time you get together,' Mike kept a straight face.

Suddenly he grinned and Jack's sombre expression softened, a flicker of a smile crossed his features. Somehow David knew, Mike had the strangest feeling as he recalled the evening.

'And Katrina, how is she?' Jack held his breath.

'She is still in love with you, but then she would remember a dashing young officer sweeping her off her feet. She hasn't had the pleasure of meeting an over-weight, untidy, belligerent and ageing Jack Carter.'

Jack displayed that big irresistible grin. 'I'd give anything to see her again. Lord Anthony had no objection to Katrina's plans?'

'Somehow I have a feeling that his lordship got the message. We met with no resistance when Katie told him David was coming to Australia. Well I assume she told him, after we sailed,' Mike grinned.

'Undoubtedly Loxton sorted him out,' Jack was want to add, a smile etched his features.

'Apparently he was so hurt he didn't come to see the boy off. If he was there, I never sighted him.' Mike added.

< >

When Doctor Cole looked in on David, the morning following Mike's visit, it was to find him dressing. An argument ensued after which the good Doctor relented. David would be allowed two hours each day to wander the hospital grounds that was their agreement. However this was an agreement David had no intention of keeping.

David waited until the sun dried the dew on the grass before crossing the lawn towards the gardens, sure that Doctor Cole had told the others of his decision. Hastily, he scampered over the low hedge fence that separated the hospital grounds from the botanical gardens. Once on the other side, he made a beeline for the statues ignoring one, which indicated someone by the name of Lloyd Hopkins, had helped pioneer the country. The plaque, which intrigued him, was commemorated to the bravery of among others:

Sergeant Michael Smith VC
Australian Expeditionary Forces,
Second Division.
1914-1918.
Lieutenant Jack Bryson Carter: Recipient of Legion De Honour.
United States Expeditionary Force
First Engineers.
1914-1918
'LEST WE FORGET'
Commemorated this day of our Lord 25 April 1926
By
Right Honourable Bede Hogan. MP OBE QC

David stared at the plaque in disbelief as their names cannoned at him from the white marble. Shocked, he sat on the ground and could only stare, his mind swimming with thoughts, his reverie interrupted minutes later when he was confronted by two men wearing town suits, their faces partially hidden by matching felt hats.

'David Thornton?' Asked the larger of the two.

David hesitated before answering, his gaze for the larger man who spoke with a cockney accent. 'Yes.'

The man grinned, seeing the discomfort on the lad's features, 'you 'ave nothin' to fear from me or my companion Mister Thornton. My name is Reginald Bundy and this is Freddy Moylan.'

'We are employed by your grandfather,' Freddy Moylan added with a shy smile for David.

'Been keepin' tabs on you for some time now,' Bundy explained.

David nodded cautiously.

'Certain arrangements have been made by your grandfather, should you wish to exercise them, sir. We were told to give you this.' Bundy handed him a package.

David moved to the nearest seat, shadowed from the glare of the sun by a large Kauri tree. He examined the manila envelope carefully recognising almost at once the familiar red wax seal embossed by the Anthony crest. With heart racing furiously, David tore at the

280

opening. He read the brief note from Grandfather Anthony, a smile breaking his countenance.

David, should you decide to honour our family tradition and defend your country above all else, open the drawstring purse and wear the ring therein. Should you decide against the honour that befalls your name and title, then, I will know the bond between us has been broken for all time.
Yours Grandfather Anthony.
Lord Bedford of Bedfordshire.

David opened the small velvet purse letting the contents fall into his palm. Slowly he lifted his eyes and addressed himself to the man named Bundy.

'You said arrangements had been made Mister Bundy?'

'Among several, a ship lies off the coast some ten nautical miles to take you to Canada.' Bundy watched amused as David placed the ring on his finger.

The gauntlet thrown, the challenge accepted by the young pup. Just as his Lordship had anticipated and as explained by Senator Gerald Perry. Momentarily, Bundy let his mind dwell on Jack Carter imagining what this would do to the man who may one day be awarded a knighthood for his service to industry, and a sardonic smile pursed his lips. The old patriarch would have the last laugh yet.

<>

They gave him time. It wasn't until a week after Mike had spoken with David that he and Jack accompanied Molly to Edge Rock. Her baby was due any time now. Jack paced restlessly while she registered and was conducted to her room, bringing up the rear with her suitcase while Mike fussed over her. Once Matron had settled her new charge, the men gathered briefly about her bed before taking their leave to visit David. Walking down the east wing, Jack lingered behind Mike uneasily fidgeting with his tie. Mike noticed his friend's restlessness with a sidelong glance; he knew Jack was as tight as a kettle drum, nerves. Oh well, let him sweat a bit, he thought to himself.

Mike pushed open the door to David's room and stopped in mid-stride, Jack barging into him. David Thornton had gone. His bed was empty, the room obviously unoccupied and a quick check of the bedside dresser showed his clothes were missing. Seconds later, the echo of their running feet could be heard all over the hospital as they sought out Doctor Cole for an explanation. He revealed that David was given two hours a day to wander about the hospital to regain his strength, thus allaying their fears that he had discharged himself.

When it was found he had not returned to the hospital by nightfall, the pair became frantic with worry. The following day Jack had posters printed and immediately contacted his old friend, Superintendent Theodore Carson, who from information supplied by Mike and to a lesser extent Jack, had a police artist draw an identikit which was distributed throughout the land. Nothing was heard of the young Englishman, it was as though he had disappeared from the face of the earth. Jack placed his first person to person overseas phone call to Katrina. Mike felt responsible for what had transpired; he would carry the guilt for many years. However, Jack was adamant the blame was his and that he should be the one to tell the boy's mother.

Her voice had matured, it was at first strange to his ears as he imagined his must be to hers, even allowing for his quaver of dread, and the static created by the distance which separated them. Shortly, Katrina began to cry before Jack could explain the reason for his phone call. Strangely Jack found himself removed from her emotion on hearing her voice, and this was soon conveyed to Katrina, who, took hold of her emotions and soon was in control again, as if this were a boardroom discussion she was conducting. Jack explained as best he could, his meeting with his son, his striking the boy, and his subsequent disappearance. Not believing he could just vanish Katrina felt her son may have been kidnapped. Jack had considered this and told her of his contacting the police who had issued a description across the continent. Their conversation continued in this vein with Katrina probing and Jack reassuring her that everything that could be done was being done. Slowly, their conversation waned and suddenly was spent and to Jack it was as though preoccupied with her thoughts, Katrina placed her receiver down, the click faint but distinct to him. He looked first at the handset, then cast his eyes to the floor, the blips dully pounded his ear before Mary advised the other party had disconnected. Sluggishly he reached out and replaced the handset. His heart was heavy, at that moment he felt he may have lost her forever, her and the boy. Strangely, his thoughts were for his son, at that moment he would have given his life gladly for one more glimpse of the boy and the opportunity to make things right between them.

Chapter 73

Edge Rock / London

A week passed without word of David and Jack realised he must return to Tempi and from there fly to the east coast for his quarterly meeting with Harry. He was paying his room account when he had a surprise visit from old Bill Myre. It was a frightened and cautious old man who sought him out in Stoddart's pub. After an exchanged greeting, old Bill pulled Jack away from the reception counter to the far corner of the barroom, not before ordering two beers, where an unoccupied table arrested his attention.

'He is here Jack, the man who beat me.' Bill began, not touching his beer.

'I'm not sure I follow you Bill.' Jack drew on his beer waiting for the older man to explain.

'The bloke who visited me premises that day, ta find out about the mountain. The fliers sent by that Pommy bastard,' Bill was becoming agitated.

'Reginald, that bloke of Thornton who was killed in that aeroplane called him.'

Suddenly it registered with Jack, 'The bloke who busted you up to find out about Mike and me trekking to South Australia?'

Bill nodded accompanying it with a wry grin. 'That's him!'

'Here, in Edge Rock,' muttered Jack, slowly pondering his supposition.

'Do you know where they are now Bill?'

'Stayin' right upstairs they were, haven't been game ta come into the place this past month for fear of him recognisin' me. Lucky I was across the street when I saw you at reception; I've been keepin' tabs on 'em since I first saw 'em hanging around the gardens.'

'The botanical gardens near the hospital?'

'They're the only gardens I know of,' was the curt reply.

'Thank you Bill; do you want another?' Jack indicated the beer in front of the old man.

'Nah. Is ya gonna get 'em Jack?' But already Jack was heading for the reception counter and information from Dot's granddaughter the receptionist, concerning itself with two Englishmen who may have registered at the pub.

The glee on old Bill's face five minutes later had to be seen to be believed as Jack escorted two badly beaten men from the building towards the gaol for further questioning. Shortly afterwards, Jack telephoned Katrina with good and bad news. David was on his way to Canada aboard an Anthony Thornton vessel. He intended to join a Canadian fighting unit.

<>

Darwin was a refuelling stopover for international flights to Europe and it was here Jack caught a connecting flight to London.

On arrival at Heathrow Airport, Jack asked the driver of the Hansom taxi to be taken to the Anthony Thornton Building in Fleet Street; London. Thirty minutes later he entered the Anthony Thornton Building, placed his single suitcase on the carpet beside him and addressed himself to the lass behind a large counter which stated **RECEPTION** in bold gold caption.

Jack removed his hat, 'good morning, could you direct me to Sir James Loxton's office please.'

Self-consciously, the receptionist patted at her fashionable hairdo struck by the demeanour of the tall middle aged man with the sky blue eyes, tinges of silver through his wavy hair, neatly trimmed moustache, and with a tanned countenance. 'Do you have an appointment sir?'

'No however I feel certain he will see me... ' Jack smiled that congenial grin.

'May I ask?'

'Jack Carter.' He finished for her.

'Please take a seat, I won't be a moment Mister Carter.'

Jack watched as she switched a lever and talked into the intercom, impressed with the technology. Shortly, a dapperly dressed man with thinning silvery white-hair emerged from the lift not before taking the time to thank the lift attendant. He strode directly across the reception area hand extended towards where Jack sat nursing the felt hat, which matched his char-grey suit. The office staff had never seen Sir James Loxton extend this courtesy to anyone before, usually the visitor was asked to take the lift to the fourth floor and make his or her way along the corridor where Sir James's secretary would attend their needs.

Jack stood and offered his hand that genial grin accompanying the action. With introductions completed, Jack collected his suitcase but was immediately told to leave it. Whereupon, Sir James instructed the receptionist to have someone bring Mister Carter's luggage to his office. The pair, in close conversation, made a beeline for the lift. James ushered Carter into his office, indicating a comfortable leather chair, while requesting Mildred bring them morning tea.

'This is indeed a pleasant surprise. I had hoped we could meet one day.' There was no doubting the genuine warmth that radiated itself from Sir James's personage.

'Thank you, I also hoped our paths may cross although I feel I already know you,' smiled Jack.

'Yes,' laughed James, 'all those blessed cables over the years.'

The light banter continued until they were served morning tea. James followed Mildred to the door with instructions he was not to be disturbed under any circumstances. He locked the door behind her.

'Now then Jack, what brings you to England?' James played host positioning the silver tray so Jack could sugar his tea.

'My son, he was kidnapped or influenced by Sedgwick Anthony to sail to Canada where I fear arrangements have been made for him to join some fighting regiment.' was the frank reply.

James vented his frustration, 'Curse the man! Sedgwick will never let go'

'Well he is going to let go this time. The letter Harrison addressed to you explaining his position during the Boer campaign, is it still in your possession?'

'Yes, however Sedgwick has read the letter Jack, I don't quite understand.' James was bemused by the request.

'I have formulated a plan which I would like to put to you. If you feel you cannot support my proposal or if it does not succeed, I would request you give me Harrison's letter. I intend to visit Lord Anthony and demand the ship be diverted here to Bristol. If he refuses, I will explain he has left me with no option but to give the letter to Katrina,' shrugged Jack.

James studied him for some time brow knitted in thought, 'My God you are serious aren't you.'

'I have waited too long. I should have done this years ago after I learnt of Chester's death. James' we have wasted the better part of our lives.'

'Katrina had far greater responsibilities. Rather unfortunate really Jack.' He waved his hands about his office to indicate the Consortium.

'My proposal?'

'I just don't know.' James shook his head in contrition, for he wanted to help his niece. 'She has grown in her commitment for the Consortium. It has become her life. Katrina has the responsibility for thousands of our employees who depend on Anthony Thornton for their welfare, not to mention the importance of our industry in the eyes of the government.' James indicated the scones laced with cream and jam which were getting cold.

'Sir James, this company and all it represents stands for Sedgwick Anthony, a tyrant! Hasn't he hurt her and Harrison enough? Now he has schemed to have David taken away from her. Not to mention what he has tried to do to me over the years!' Jack appealed, leaning forward in his chair to face the elder statesman, the scones ignored.

James's did not try and hide the pang of worry Jack's words held for himself and the Consortium's future. A heart-wrenching sigh escaped his lips, the sigh of a tired man. 'Since the death of Sir Bruce Thornton last year, Katrina and I have held the Consortium together. David would not be able to leave. This is his company, his inheritance.'

'I want us to be together as a family.' Jack lamented, his big frame shaking with his chagrin when he observed Sir James's obstinate shake of his head. Clearly he was tired and Jack understood this, he reflected this man would have walked on water for Katrina but he was visibly aged by years of leadership and resolving disputes. However, Jack hadn't travelled half way around the world to accept defeat.

'I understand your position and your dilemma; all I ask is that you hear my proposal. I believe it has merit and should meet with your approval once explained.' Jack appeased, accepting a scone.

Sir James was sceptical however he indicated for Jack to outline his scheme with a wave of his arm.

Jack's proposal required an audience with the king and a proposition so daring James felt the hair at the nape of his neck prickle against his suit coat. James rose unsteadily to thrust his hand forward to shake Jack's with an eagerness, which conveyed his full sanction for the plan. They deliberated at length, honing the finer details for flaws before Sir James excused himself. Rounding on his desk, he threw the intercom switch.

'Mildred, connect me to Lord Rushworth the King's personal secretary.' He paused while Mildred said something Jack could not pick up on. Sir James smiled his eyes never leaving the panel in front of him. 'Yes you heard me correctly, Lord Rushworth, straight away Mildred. Thank you.' James pushed the switch so they again enjoyed their privacy.

While James waited on his phone-call, they talked at length, about the aeroplane incident, Harrison, Katrina, BHC, and Senator Michael Smith whom James described as a man of substance.

'You know, Sedgwick never forgave Katrina or me when we sold you Allied Steel Jack!'

'Nobody was more surprised than myself when my solicitors advised me of your offer.'

James nodded, 'We needed funds. Unfortunately the depression took its toll on conglomerates like Anthony Thornton.'

'Yes we all felt its tentacles Sir James.'

'You diversified,' smiled James. 'Very shrewd move.'

'I was pleased to take your company.'

'Yes another victory in the power struggle between you and Sedgwick.'

'Now he is retaliating and the stakes can't get any higher.' Jack's voice dropped to a mere whisper. 'The ship? How much time do we have?'

Just then the phone rang and Mildred's voice came clearly to them advising that Lord Rushworth was on the line. James hurriedly picked up the receiver, his eyes not leaving those of Jack as he spoke into the Bakelite handset. Sir James requested an audience with the king as soon as was humanly possible. There was a short delay during which James smiled at Jack before jotting information onto a pad in front of him.

'That is the earliest audience, no... fine... two thirty in the afternoon. Yes I understand Lord Rushworth, very good... yes before the PM arrives good...yes...thank you very much.'

'Thursday 2.30 in the afternoon,' James looked up at Jack after having replaced the receiver. 'We have until 3.30. He has an important meeting with Neville Chamberlain later in the day and wishes to have a nap before crossing wits with the PM.'

'We?' Jack jabbed himself in the chest expansively.

'Why not, dear chap? I gather, he is very much aware; you represent the largest single company in Australia. One imagines he may want to ask your thoughts on some matter of grave concern to the nation.'

Jack nodded, 'The pending bloody war!'

'Possibly,' grinned Sir James.

'And David?' Jack was anxious to have the ship recalled before it entered Canadian waters where David may ask for political asylum.

'Straight away.' James threw the intercom switch, which would summon Mildred. When she banged on the door only then did he remember he had locked it to avoid interruption, hurriedly James rose to her summons. When she appeared, some moments later, he addressed her. 'I want you to send this cable to captain Lindsay aboard our ship *Rushcutter*. The cable is to be marked as important and to be answered immediately by Lindsay indicating his acknowledgement. Is that understood Mildred?'

'Your instruction is very clear Sir James.'

'Thank you Mildred. And Mildred, not a word to anyone.' James turned to beam a smile at Jack as Mildred closed the door behind her retreating figure.

'Now then, isn't there someone else in this building you would like to see?'

'Yes, very much.' Jack smiled.

On their way out of the office, Sir James paused by Mildred's desk to issue an instruction. He waited patiently while Mildred connected him to the party before taking the receiver and speaking patiently with the person, sometimes gesturing and shaking his head before finally returning the set to Mildred. Joining Jack, he informed him he had just spoken with Veronica, the proposed meeting to take place at Warburn Abbey could go ahead on a date to be determined. Jack grinned, beckoning Sir James to show him the way.

Briskly, Sir James walked along the corridor to Katrina's office, if, deep in thought. It would appear his companion was more than a business entrepreneur. Although James wasn't sure how Sedgwick would react to all that was planned, but then he thought, *who gives a damn!*

Finally the moment had arrived. Jack removed his hat and stood patiently and with a certain apprehension while James knocked on her office door. Just the sound of her voice saw goose bumps appear on his skin and James moved aside so he could enter first. Jack would have none of it. He was too nervous and pushed James before him into Katrina's office.

'Uncle James. What is it,' Katrina saw first the smile which threatened to explode her uncles' features before she saw the taller figure partially concealed behind him.

'Well do come in and sit down, and your acquaintance,' she added, seeing James grab for Jack who was cringing behind the frosted glass door.

'Katrina, I would like to introduce you to Jack Bryson Carter,' James moved easily to one side leaving Jack standing there, his hat held firmly between his hands and too shy to look up initially.

'Jack… ' The name caught in her throat. Katrina stood awkwardly, momentarily too stunned to do anything, before kicking her chair back, rounding her desk in a bound and running the few yards that separated them and flinging herself at him. 'Oh Jack! Jack! Darling.' Katrina sobbed, clutching him to her.

Jack's response was immediate he drew her to him hugging her as if there were no tomorrow. He sobbed her name over and over; large alligator tears welling behind emotional eyes fell unashamedly over the pleated shoulder of her suit.

They stood like that, Katrina was on tip-toes, her face pressed into his shoulder for what seemed like an eternity to Sir James who suddenly felt embarrassed. Then Jack released her and they stared at each other, drinking in the difference twenty years had to show, before melting together to share their first kiss in such a long time; Sir James forgotten until several moments later a polite cough reminded them of his presence. Katrina was so emotional that one moment she was crying, the next clutching for Jack again to be kissed. It was several minutes before Sir James felt he could intervene.

'Jack and I have done some scheming, my dear.' he told her. 'Conniving,' he smiled.

'Scheming?' Katrina guided Jack to a chair and sat on his lap drawing his arms around her and indicating for her uncle to use her chair.

'Remember I told you how your father arranged for David to sail for Canada? Well, we proposed to have the ship diverted. That young blighter isn't going to fight a war like you, Mike, and I had to endure Katrina.' Jack's look was solemn. It eased the creases of worry from her features. Everything would be all right now she told herself, feeling the strength of Jack's body pressing against her.

< >

Apart from Jack accompanying Sir James to his audience with King George, the days that followed were spent at Roxburgh House, where he and Katrina made love. Their appetite for one another insatiable. They wandered about the estate hand in hand, often stopping to clutch each other in an embrace and to kiss, assuring themselves this was actually happening while discussing their plans for the future. Jack contemplating having to build a home of grandiose proportions for them at a place of Katrina's choosing, not that it mattered. He could give her the world. While Katrina was imagining the three of them in a little cottage overlooking a hamlet with green grass and a brook running its course.

'Oh Jack, I'm so happy; I wish these days could last forever.'

'I promise we will never be parted again Katie.'

'If only,' smiled Katrina snuggling into him.

'What is he like?'

'Who?'

'My son… David,' the name choked in his throat.

'Oh Jack, he is so much like you. Michael said he was *a chip off the old block.* David asked me what he had meant and I couldn't reveal to him that Michael was comparing him to you,' she laughed.

'Do you think he will accept me as his father? I mean, will he forgive me for striking him?' Lamented Jack.

'I'm sure when I explain what happened he will understand.'

'I just saw red, all I could think about was you and that... ' Jack shook his head.

'Darling do not torture yourself; just love him, be his father, he will accept you.'

Finally, Sir James phoned confirming their expected arrival at Warburn Abbey, home of Lord Sedgwick Anthony, for Wednesday the following week. On receiving this news, Jack placed an international phone-call advising Mike that everything was going according to plan. Mike had some news of his own; he was a father, twin boys. Molly and boys all well. It was great news and Jack couldn't wait to inform Katrina.

Chapter 74

Warburn Abby

Seated in his wheelchair, a feeble Lord Sedgwick Anthony faced the heavy oak, panelled doors. His legs were covered by a chequered rug while a heavy scarf was wrapped around his throat for extra warmth. Beside him stood Lady Veronica dressed in slacks with a woollen top. She indicated for an aging Benson to admit their visitors.

It had been several months since Sedgwick last saw his daughter, they had argued heatedly over David's leaving for Australia. That she would be accompanied by his brother-in-law indicated to Sedgwick they wanted something. When James telephoned, Sedgwick told Veronica he did not want to see them. In particular, he didn't wish to see him, James, because he had sided with Katrina and threatened to show her the letter from Harrison if he did anything to stop David sailing for Australia with Senator Michael Smith. Now, Sedgwick could only imagine word had leaked out that his grandson was abducted and on his way to Canada. His plans were meticulous, his co-conspirators sworn to silence and paid handsomely for their service, so be it. Anyway, he believed it was none of their damn business. David was old enough to make his own decisions. Finally, Lady Veronica persuaded him to relent advising that it may only be a business decision and that they were seeking his advice. And so a meeting time was agreed upon. However, he could never have imagined in his wildest dreams the scene which was to greet him when the door opened to the library.

Sir James entered the room with Katrina beside him, his hand guiding her by the elbow. She made no attempt to greet her father nor did Sir James' offer his hand in friendship. Rather, they turned waiting for the man following behind to materialise.

It was Sir James who broke a poignant silence. 'You would remember Jack Carter, old boy?'

Sedgwick was staring at the man standing before him. Involuntarily, his arms clenched the sides of the wheelchair; his face distorted to take on a startled expression and he tried to rise to meet his adversary. However, his frail body would not respond to his will. He felt Veronica place a trembling hand on his shoulder, trembling with interest for the ruggedly handsome man who stood before Sedgwick not offering his hand.

'It's been a long time. Your lordship.' Jack spoke at last, nearly convulsing into laughter at the expression of shock on Sedgwick's features.

'You! What are you doing in my home?' The voice surprisingly strong was brusque and chagrined with hate.

Jack ignored the acrimony drawing up a chair, the others doing likewise. Only Lady Veronica stood unmoving, staring with trepidation, and something else, for this man who had the audacity to make himself at home uninvited.

'I came for your daughter and my son,' began Jack, when he was comfortable.

'Never!' Jack could see the man's eyes bulge in sunken sockets; the hands that gripped the chair were shaking.

'I thought you would be so disposed,' beamed Jack, reaching for the letter inside his suit coat pocket holding it towards where Katrina sat next to her uncle.

'Harrison's letter... ' Jack managed to suppress a chortle as leathery hands tried in vain to sweep the envelope from his grasp.

'No! You cannot!' One hand rose as if to ward off a silent blow.

'Then you condone the ship's Master returning David to Bristol... ' Jack glared at Sedgwick. Sedgwick glared back shifting his weight awkwardly in the chair indicating for Benson to bring him a pistol, one of a matching brace which graced the nearest wall.

'I say. There will be none of that, old boy.' Sir James rose to prevent any such Tomfoolery. 'Give Katrina the letter Jack; let us clear the ghost from the closet once and for all. Besides, she has the right to know why her father so despises you.'

Just then the door-bell sounded in the background indicating someone to be at the front door. Sir James gestured for the emulating sound and promptly Benson, glad to escape and without a backward glance, left to do his bidding.

'I'm sorry to have to do this Katrina, but it would appear there is no other way. The cantankerous old so and so would see David murdered in the theatre of war.' Jack faced her.

'It's no more than the bastard deserves!' Shouted Lord Anthony, his pallid countenance vividly so, now, with his blasphemous outburst.

'Father!' Katrina rose, fists clenched to face him.

'Get out of my house the lot of you. Ring the police commissioner Veronica.'

'Read the letter Katrina, it is from your brother, Harrison, who has spent most of his life in exile.' Jack placed a steadying hand on her shoulder, his eyes never leaving those of Lord Anthony, triumphant at seeing the final defeat etched in sunken rheumy eyes.

'Harrison is dead, he died... '

'Read the letter my darling,' Jack reiterated.

Just then the door opened and Lord Anthony emitted a shrill shriek before clutching his chest, 'Harrison... '

Jack stood, turning to greet Harry with a warm handshake. 'Glad you could come at such short notice, old boy,' he grinned. 'Katrina... meet your brother, Harrison Anthony,' Jack wanted to smile for her look of astonishment.

'It can't be!' Katrina felt her body trembling, this, was so unexpected. 'Father, you led me to believe Harrison was dead,' Katrina turned from the stranger to face her father, a look of bitter resentment spread to engulf her features.

Sedgwick Anthony couldn't answer; his heart was racing he felt tightening across his chest, as though it were clamped in a vice.

Sir James was on his feet in an instant to embrace Harrison, tears of happiness unashamedly running down his jowls.

'Thank God for showing his mercy,' James finally got out standing back to appraise his nephew before hugging him again.

'Thank your king for granting Harrison a royal pardon,' Jack smiled to see the astounded look on Sedgwick's face when struck with this revelation.

'It's... not... possible...' Sedgwick finally found his voice.

'The king was kind enough to grant us an audience during which he read Harrison's account which neither you nor the tribunal wanted to know about at the time.' James informed him.

Sedgwick slumped further into the chair, his senses not believing what was happening while around him the tight knit group were hugging and crying their joy.

Finally Harrison tore himself away from James's embrace. 'Hello, Father, not feeling well?' Harrison smiled down at the feeble creature in the wheelchair, then ignoring him to embrace Katrina again. 'Do read the letter Katie, it will explain better than I my circumstances.'

Dazed Katrina slumped into the chair. With her tears splashing across the pages, Katrina read Harrison's account of his experiences in the Boer War, subsequent court martial and exile.

'Oh Harrison it is so wonderful that you are alive,' She rose from the chair and they embraced again.

'Katrina, you are embracing the new chairman of Anthony Thornton Consortium,' Sir James laughed.

'I've been grooming him these past four years. And now there is a new king on the throne and Kitchener and Buller are dead. The past is just that and Harrison can take his rightful place as chairman.' Jack explained, turning to Sedgwick Anthony ready to admonish any resistance. There was no response. A decrepit old man could only stare disbelievingly.

<>

David Thornton stood beside the marble headstone of his grandfather's grave before stooping to lay a solitary yellow tulip across the sepulchre. In the shadows of the limousine, his mother and father waited patiently for him. Shortly they would all return to Australia before the tentacles of war prevented their leaving the country. David could never remember seeing his mother so happy. It was this more than anything else which decided him to place the ring, a cartouche of their family crest over the stem of the flower before rising and walking swiftly to join them. A bond was broken and a new one waiting to be forged.